**“DON’ [illegible] BITCH,”**

[illegible] menacing enough to freeze whoever was waiting in ambush.

Because the plain truth was that, taken unaware and thinking about the bed rather than any possible danger, he’d let his night vision be lost to the flare of the match.

At least for the next few treacherously long heartbeats, Longarm was bat-blind and defenseless.

He just hoped to hell he was the only one who realized it.

Off in the direction of Norm’s parlor he heard the scrape of a shoe sole on wood. Longarm’s heart jumped into his throat, and he blinked furiously in a useless attempt to force his eyes to readjust to the darkness.

“Try anything an’ I’ll shoot,” he snarled.

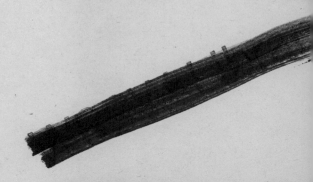

TABOR EVANS

# LONGARM AND THE KANSAS JAILBIRD



JOVE BOOKS, NEW YORK

LONGARM AND THE KANSAS JAILBIRD

A Jove Book / published by arrangement with
the author

PRINTING HISTORY
Jove edition / March 1999


For information address: The Berkley Publishing Group,
a member of Penguin Putnam Inc.,
375 Hudson Street, New York, New York 10014.

The Penguin Putnam Inc. World Wide Web site address is
http://www.penguinputnam.com

ISBN: 0-515-12468-0

A JOVE BOOK®
Jove Books are published by The Berkley Publishing Group,
a member of Penguin Putnam Inc.,
375 Hudson Street, New York, New York 10014.
JOVE and the "J" design
are trademarks belonging to Jove Publications, Inc.

PRINTED IN THE UNITED STATES OF AMERICA

10 9 8 7 6 5 4 3 2 1

# Chapter 1

Longarm was tired. Bone weary. He had been on the road, what, three weeks? A little more? Something like that. And he'd been rushing from hither to yon—wherever the hell Hither and Yon were—the whole damn time.

Still, it was worth it. The Baines boys were securely ensconced behind bars down at the Denver city jail waiting arraignment before a federal magistrate, and the postal officials in northeastern Wyoming were happy as hell to know that the mail had a pretty good chance of getting from one place to another again without the Brothers Baines first browsing through it all to see if there was anything they wanted for themselves.

So, yeah, the effort had been worthwhile. But now Longarm was worn down and ready for some rest. Which he intended to get starting right about . . . right about now, he thought.

After all, the United States marshal for the Denver district was gone for the day, busy doing the bullshit political stuff that seemed to be the bane of every administrative employee of the United States. Politics and paperwork. Between them it was a wonder they didn't drive Billy Vail crazy. For sure Longarm couldn't have put up with it. Good thing he didn't have to.

A little paperwork—as little as possible, actually—and that was more than enough for him.

And right now, dammit, his report on the Baines chase was done, signed, and in two shakes would be delivered. After that, he intended to disappear for the rest of the day. Maybe longer.

He stood, a sharp pain in his lower back from bending over the writing desk and a cramp in his fingers from holding a pen too long, and pushed the six pages of his report into a more or less tidy pile that he carried over to Billy Vail's clerk Henry. Longarm tossed the report onto Henry's desk and announced, "I'm gonna go get myself a haircut, Henry. Then a drink. And then I'm gonna crawl into a nice soft bed an' stay there for a couple, three days or so."

"After which," Henry said dryly, "you may find time to get some sleep, right?"

"This may amaze you, old son," Longarm told him, "but right now I'm so damn tired I intend to sleep first. The ladies will just hafta wait an' suffer along without me." He winked. "For a little while anyhow."

Henry gave Longarm a look of open disbelief, but did not bother to comment. "Drop by tomorrow if you can find the time," Henry said. "The boss may have something for you."

"If you get the chance, pard, try an' talk him out of it. I need some serious rest."

"I'll mention it," Henry promised. "Not that I see anything for you to worry about. We aren't all that busy at the moment. In fact, I don't know of anything on the schedule that you would have to be involved in until the Baines arraignments. That hearing will be next Monday or Tuesday."

"I might stagger in again by that time. If I sleep real fast," Longarm said with a grin.

Henry smiled and told him good-bye, and Longarm headed for the street, grabbing his flat-crowned Stetson hat off the coat rack on his way out.

He paused at the top of the granite steps leading up to the handsomely massive front doors of Denver's Federal Building, cupping a match in his palm and lighting one of the slim, dark cheroots that he favored.

Marshal Billy Vail's best deputy was a tall man, standing in excess of six feet, with wide shoulders and a narrow waist. He had the born horseman's powerful legs and a carriage that conveyed self-assurance but that stopped short of being cocky. Custis Long had no need for displays of bravado, false or otherwise. He knew how good he was and was comfortable with the knowledge.

The one thing that he failed to fully appreciate about himself was why women so often found him of interest. Not that he minded it. Not hardly. But he did not really understand it. When he looked in the mirror to shave each morning, all he saw was an ordinary male countenance, a little too wrinkled and craggy if anything. He had brown hair, brown eyes, and a huge sweep of brown mustache that like his hair was overdue for some trimming.

At the moment he was wearing a tweed coat and calfskin vest, with a slim gold chain connecting the two watch pockets, one of which held the expected pocket watch, but with the other end of the chain attached to a .44-caliber derringer. He had on dark brown corduroy trousers tucked into a pair of tall, stovepipe cavalry boots, and a gunbelt snug at his waist with the butt of a double-action Colt revolver slanted for a cross draw and worn just to the left of his belt buckle.

All in all a rather ordinary appearance in Longarm's opinion, although a fair percentage of the female population tended to take exception to that modest viewpoint.

He drew deep of the pale, refreshing smoke from his cheroot, and exhaled slowly, then ambled down the stairs and turned west on Colfax Avenue toward Lloyd's Tonsorial Emporium, where he sometimes enjoyed stopping in for a haircut and shave. Lloyd charged more than most barbers, but he had a magician's deft touch with a razor, a litany of jokes that would keep a man in fresh material for a month of conversations with friends, and the best-smelling bay rum to be found anywhere in Denver. Maybe anywhere in Colorado, come to think of it. Anyway, this morning Longarm felt like treating himself to Lloyd's and the hell with saving a nickel.

Longarm enjoyed the stroll to the barbershop, feeling relaxed and unhurried now that he was out of the office and free for the rest of the day.

It was just short of noon when he reached Lloyd's. It was no particular surprise for him to see that there were five other customers waiting in line ahead of him. Obviously there were plenty of others who appreciated exceptional service and good company.

And anyway, Longarm was in no hurry for a change. He nodded to Lloyd and received a smile in return, then settled into one of the chairs to begin his wait. He crossed his legs, made sure there was an ashtray within easy reach, and bent forward to pick up the latest edition of the *Rocky Mountain News*. Even if it weren't the latest edition, Longarm wouldn't have cared, having been away from the city for the past several weeks.

He opened the newspaper in his lap, yawned without bothering to try to stifle the impulse, and began to read.

Less than a minute later Longarm was on his feet, sudden alarm creasing his forehead and bringing a frown to his lips.

He whirled and dashed out of the barbershop, the rumpled newspaper still in his hand. Once on the sidewalk he broke into a run, loping back the same way he had just come. His haircut, and his fatigue, were quite forgotten.

## Chapter 2

"You're going *where*?" an incredulous Henry yelped.

"Kansas, dammit. I already told you that."

"But . . ."

"Crow's Point, Kansas, if it matters."

"And just what is it I'm supposed to tell the marshal when he asks where you've flown off to and why you up and went there, Custis?"

"Tell him . . . shit, I dunno . . . tell him I'm gone to see an ailing sister."

"Custis, you don't have a sister. Not in Kansas or any other place. I know that. So does Marshal Vail."

"So tell him anyway. Damn, Henry, I don't care. Tell him anything you like."

"How about if I tell him the truth."

"If you want to, go ahead."

"It would help if I knew what the truth was in this case, Custis," Henry said, belaboring the obvious.

Longarm sighed and rubbed nervously at the back of his neck. He hesitated. But only for a moment. Hell, if he couldn't trust Henry . . . and for that matter Billy Vail too . . . then he was in a lot of trouble. "Look, it's . . . you might say that I'm takin' personal time off. You know?"

"Tell me," Henry prompted.

"It's this newspaper article that put a bee up my ass." He waved the crumpled paper at Henry as if the man could tell from that what the problem was. "You ever hear of a man named Norman Wold, Henry?"

Henry shook his head and removed his glasses to polish them with a handkerchief he extracted from a coat pocket—Henry religiously maintained proper attire, even inside a stifling office at the height of summer—and carefully unfolded the handkerchief before giving every appearance of total concentration on that homely task, as if Longarm's story was of little interest indeed.

"Norm Wold is . . . more'n a friend," Longarm haltingly tried to explain. "He's what you might call a . . . mentor. Yeah, mentor. It fits."

"Yours?" Henry asked.

"Uh-huh. From a long time back. There was a time, see . . . I don't talk about it much . . . there was a time I coulda taken a different road from what I done. A time I coulda wound up in the wrong place with the wrong people doing some wrong things. If you know what I mean."

Henry grunted noncommittally, and continued to pay attention only to the cleanliness of his spectacles. It occurred to Longarm that Henry looked slightly owlish and—it took him a moment to figure it out—sort of incomplete without the familiar glasses in place on his nose.

"What I mean is, I coulda wound up on the wrong side of these law-an'-order chases, Henry. Coulda, that is, but for Norm Wold. He's the one grabbed me by the collar one night an' gave me some straight talk. Didn't just talk to me, though. That wasn't Norm's way. Oh, he said all the usual words, sure. But then he up an' did something about it. Backed up his mouth with his actions. You know?"

"Not, um, actually."

"Yeah, well, that's what he did. Norm didn't just say he had faith in me an' in what I could become. He showed it to me. Hired me for a part-time deputy town marshal. This was after I'd paid off from a trail crew driving a herd of mixed cows an' steers up from Texas, me and a bunch of other wild an' randy young assholes. We paid off an' blew our pay in no time, an' were thinking of ways we could all get rich again without having to go to all the bother of working for it. If you see what I mean."

"Uh-huh." Henry scrubbed at his already gleaming disks of glass some more, not so much as glancing toward Longarm.

"Yeah, well, Mr. Norm, he singled me out from the crowd. God only knows why, what he saw in me that he figured was worth saving. He found me drunk in an alley this one time, an' hauled me back to his jail, but instead of whipping my ass an' taking me before the justice of the peace like he probably ought, he let me sleep off the worst of my drunk, an' then came in with coffee and crullers an' sat me down for a talk, like I already told you. An' then he went out an' talked with the mayor an' the judge an' got them to let him hire me. I kinda suspect my pay come outa Mr. Norm's own pocket 'cause that shitty little brand-new cow town didn't have hardly any money to waste on public works at the time. Anyway, he taught me that bein' a peace officer can be a thing a man can take pride in.

"It wasn't much of a job, mind, an' it didn't last long, just long enough for me to get shut of those boys I'd been running with and get my feet back under me some. Then Norm grinned an' fed me a big dinner an' fired my ass so I'd get on back down the road where I belonged. But God, he taught me an awful lot in that little while, and I'm grateful to him still.

"Which he knows, of course. I've written to him a couple times over the years. No, don't look at me like that, dammit, I have too written to him, real letters an' everything. And I've seen him a couple times when I found myself in his part of the world. I'm still grateful to him, an' some of the lessons Norm taught me then came back an' helped sway me when the chance came to pin a badge on for real, riding for Billy here. So you can see that I'd be partial to Norm. That I'd feel I owe the man for what all he done for me."

"I can see that," Henry agreed.

"Right. Well, this article says that Marshal Norman Wold of Hirt County, Kansas, has been arrested an' charged with arson an' grand larceny along with malfeasance in office an' half a dozen other damn things. Can you imagine it? Norm Wold? Why, he's the most honest man I ever in my whole life met. Can't be any truth to what this article says, but obviously somebody's got it in for Norm. An' Henry, the thing is, I appreciate what Norm did for me those years past. So now I reckon it's my time to go do something back for him. I got to head back to Kansas, Henry. I got to. You tell Billy that. If I can't have the time off, well, he can let me know. I'll head for the nearest post office an' mail my badge back to him. All right?"

Henry set his spectacles carefully onto his nose and one at a time hooked the gilt sidepieces over his ears, then took still more time to fold his handkerchief and return it to an inner pocket before he responded.

"I'll tell him, Longarm. This town in Kansas. What did you say the name is?"

Longarm had to consult the newspaper again to be sure. "Place called Crow's Point, it says here."

"Any idea where that is?"

"Not the faintest. But I'll find it, Henry. Damn me if I don't."

"Try and be back by . . . oh, hell, never mind. We'll make do somehow, ask for a continuance or something if the prosecutor thinks he absolutely has to have your testimony for the arraignment. We'll take care of it."

"Thanks, Henry. You're a friend."

"Don't let that get out, dang it, or every one of you lazy so-and-so's will be wanting favors from me."

Longarm smiled. And hurried back out onto the street. He had to go by the boardinghouse to get his gear, then head to the railroad depot for the next available eastbound.

He could figure out where he was going once he was on his way.

# Chapter 3

It took a train and two stagecoach transfers to get there, but Longarm was able to find Crow's Point, seat of Hirt County, Kansas, with hardly any trouble at all. Unless you wanted to count two and a half days of hot, dusty, bone-jarring travel as trouble. If Longarm had been tired before, he was damn near a state of collapse by the time a taciturn and grumpy coach driver dumped him and his luggage onto the empty main street of the town.

Longarm had no idea what Crow's Point looked like nor how large a place it was, mostly because by the time the stage arrived—hours late thanks to repeated problems with one of the wheel hubs—it was nigh onto midnight and even the saloons, if any, seemed to have shut down for the night.

"You aren't gonna just leave me here, are you?" Longarm protested to the surly jehu on the driving box.

"Mister, if you wanta buy a ticket on to Riceville you can stay with me. Otherwise you get off here."

"But dammit, the stationmaster has closed up an' gone home for the night. You can at least point me to a hotel or a boardinghouse, some damn thing."

The driver let fly with a stream of dark brown juice that narrowly missed splattering Longarm's coat sleeve.

"Take your things off here or buy another ticket, mister, it don't make no never-mind to me." He picked up his driving lines, and Longarm had to hurry to snatch his carpetbag and saddle off the roof before the stage rolled on with them still there on the luggage rack.

"Thanks a helluva lot," Longarm grumbled as the coach clattered off into the darkness, the driver trying to make up for lost time.

Longarm scowled, realized that complaining would not do much to improve his situation no matter how often or how fervently he went back to that same dry well, and decided the only sensible thing here was to set about making things better.

The first order of business was to trim and light a cheroot. The next was to open his carpetbag and find the bottle of finest-quality Maryland rye whiskey he'd packed. A dram of that made the current misery a mite more bearable, and he corked the bottle and returned it to the protective nest of clean drawers he'd wrapped around it for travel purposes.

"Now," he told himself aloud, "whyn't I do something 'bout a place to sleep. Damn place is sure to look better to me after a good night's rest." He picked up his things and set off down the barren main street in search of a place—any would do—where he could spread his blankets.

No, he thought, Crow's Point looked better at night than in the gray light of dawn.

Longarm stood in front of the barn where he'd helped himself to a free night's lodging—a sign beside the wide doors claimed it was a livery and wagon park, but he hadn't been able to find a hostler or anyone else in charge last night—and surveyed what he could see of the burg.

He wasn't impressed.

There were a few dozen sun-weathered storefronts along the street, and scattered pretty much willy-nilly around the business district, perhaps twice that many houses. The homes did not look any tidier or more prosperous than the businesses. Longarm judged there hadn't been a paint salesman come through in a good many years, but the next man in would have a world of opportunity.

It was colorless, Longarm decided after taking a few moments to figure out what was wrong. There was no color here. The buildings were all weathered, unpainted wood. The few scrawny trees and undernourished shrubs were dry and dust-covered. If there were any flower patches to be found, Longarm couldn't see them from where he stood. Hell, even the couple of stray cats he saw slinking out of the barn—no doubt with their bellies full thanks to all the rodents he'd heard during the night—were drab and gray. He got the impression that an ordinary old yellow tomcat would have been cock of the walk in this town, and a calico likely would have made all the lady cats moan.

The nearly flat fields lying outside the town proper ran mostly to farmland, with very little of the ground left in grass. Longarm had had the idea that Hirt County in central Kansas would have been on the edge of cow country, but he could see he'd been wrong about that. Apparently this was country more given to small farms and smaller livestock holdings of milk cows, maybe a few pigs and goats, and like that. For sure this was not the sort of rollicking cow town that Norm Wold used to specialize in taming.

Shit, a dump like this was already so tame, it would take a kick in the ass just to make the residents wake up enough to yawn and roll over.

Well, in that case, Longarm thought, it was time to commence kicking.

He left his things stashed inside the barn together with a note saying he'd be along later to collect them and settle up for use of the straw pile, then headed into town.

Breakfast first—his sense of smell assured him that somewhere up ahead there was bacon frying—then he'd have to find Norm and get filled in on the bullshit charges against his old friend and mentor.

# Chapter 4

"By God there's still one thing I can be sure of," a deep voice boomed from somewhere toward the back of the county jail. "Now I know there's at least one human person in this county that's uglier than I am." Longarm heard a well-remembered laugh fill the sheriff's office. Grinning, Longarm ignored the young deputy seated at a desk near the front door, and hurried on back toward the cells where he could see Norman Wold behind the bars.

Behind the bars. Incredible. Longarm had expected that, of course, but he found that it shook him anyway. Norm was one of the people who put others in jail, not the other way round. Yet here he was.

And he'd changed. Lordy, but he'd changed. It had been five years or so since Longarm last saw him, and back then Norm was still the same tall, lean old fart he'd always been. Now his hair was thinning and his belly was spilling over his belt. Five years, but it looked as if Norm had aged fifteen in that time.

"Damned if you ain't still the same handsome son of a bitch you always been," Longarm declared as he reached out to shake Norm's hand. "You haven't changed a lick since the last time I seen you." It was a lie, sure, but what the hell.

"Just happen to be in the neighborhood?" Norm asked.

"Something like that."

"Sure. I believe you."

There was a slightly oily metallic sound behind Longarm that was all too recognizable. Longarm froze in place.

"Don't move, mister. Don't you move." The young deputy's voice was shaky with fear.

"I wouldn't think of it, son," Longarm assured him without so much as turning his head.

"Dammit, Jeremy, you ought to be ashamed of yourself," Norm scolded. "It isn't polite to come up behind folks with shotguns. Not very sensible either. This here is my old friend Custis Long. United States Deputy Marshal Custis Long. You might've heard of him? Goes by the nickname Longarm?"

"Shit!" the deputy muttered.

"Believe me, Jeremy, if Longarm wanted to do you any harm, he could've shot you ten times by now. Then reloaded and done it all over again. Now be a good boy and put that scattergun back on the rack where it belongs. Then why don't you run down to Dottie's place and bring us up a pot of coffee and three cups."

Longarm decided it was safe enough to take a look. Jeremy's shotgun was no longer aimed in the direction of Longarm's backside—it seemed a pretty safe assumption that it had been a few moments earlier—and the young man looked pleased to hear that he was invited to bring a cup for his own use.

"Yes, sir. D'you, uh, want any doughnuts or like that too, Marshal?"

Norm patted his belly and shook his head. "Just the coffee for right now, Jeremy."

"Yes, sir." The deputy returned the double-barreled shotgun to a wall rack and hurried away. Longarm could hear his footsteps loud and hollow on the stairs leading down to the ground floor. The Hirt County sheriff's office and jail were located on the top floor of a three-story building, above the first-floor county offices and the second-floor courtrooms and judge's chambers. Longarm had noticed that much on his way up to find Norm.

Longarm waited until Jeremy was well out of hearing, then asked, "That kid know who he's supposed to be working for, Norm?"

"Jeremy's a good boy, Longarm. Don't you go confusing him any."

"I'll try an' keep that in mind," Longarm said in a dry tone of voice. "So while we got some privacy here, whyn't you tell me what this crap is all about, Norm."

"It's a long story and kind of stupid."

"That sounds like one of yours, all right."

"If you want to hear it all, friend, drag that chair over and make yourself comfortable. And don't worry about Jeremy. He isn't as dumb as you might think. He knows I'll be wanting some privacy and he won't be back for a spell."

Longarm nodded and hauled out smokes for himself and for Norm, then did as the old man suggested and made himself comfortable in anticipation of a lengthy yarn.

# Chapter 5

"Politics," Norm said with a shrug and a grin, as if that explained everything. And hell, maybe it did at that, Longarm conceded. Politics was responsible for most of what was fine and good about the country. But partisan political bickering was also responsible for one hell of a lot of what was ugly and rotten too. Not all, of course. But certainly an outsized proportion of the bad could be chalked up to politics.

"Tell me," Longarm said, crossing his legs and drawing deep of the clean, rich-tasting smoke from his cheroot. Inside the cell, perched on the edge of a mighty hard and uncomfortable-looking bunk, Norm did the same.

"Like I said," Norm repeated, "politics. In a nutshell."

"That mayhap tell everything, but it sure doesn't tell a man much, old friend."

Norm grinned again. "Relax, Longarm. I got time to tell it all." The grin turned into a laugh. "It isn't like I'm in a hurry to go someplace, y'know."

Longarm leaned back and decided to let Norm tell the story in his own good time.

• • •

Come September there was a referendum election scheduled in Hirt County, Kansas. Crow's Point, which used to be the focal point for cow-country ranching in this part of the state, was the current seat of the county. A nearby farming community called Jasonville wanted that honor. In September the voters would decide where to situate a planned new courthouse along with the sheriff's office, county clerk and records, all of that.

The result of the coming election was a foregone conclusion, Crow's Point Town Marshal Wold admitted. The residents of Jasonville outnumbered those of Crow's Point by a good three to one. More to the point, the population of farmers in the county was at least six times larger than that of the ranchers who'd remained after the cow business had moved north into Nebraska, Wyoming, Dakota, and lately, Montana. Cattlemen were getting kind of thin on the ground these past few years, Norm allowed. Soon after the election the county seat would leave Crow's Point, and a new one would be born at Jasonville.

"And you, you old curmudgeon, you're still thought of as a cow-town peacekeeper, I take it," Longarm said.

"Hell, yes, I am. I was a town tamer, Longarm. The real thing. Dammit, Custis, should I start in to be ashamed of that all of a sudden? I did a fine job for these folks . . . and for the folks in a lot of other towns and railhead cesspools . . . for a lot of years. I'm proud of my record."

"As you damn well oughta be," Longarm agreed.

"Right. But that won't buy me no groceries once the farmers take over everything. Which they will come September." Norm sighed. "I'm getting sidetracked here, aren't I?"

"Are you?"

"I expect so. It's just . . . it gravels me, that's all."

Longarm nodded and took another drag on his cheroot, waiting patiently for the old man—Norm hadn't been old the last time Longarm saw him, but now he sure as hell was—to go on with his story of how he came to be sitting inside a jail cell.

"The county seat moving, that's going to have a lot of consequences, you see. This old courthouse, such as it is, will revert to the town as a town hall. Not that there will be much point to having a town hall, since most of the business will move to Jasonville along with the courts and all those public jobs that go along with a seat of government."

Longarm nodded. He too had seen the same thing happen in a dozen towns or more. Once the source of money left, so did the people who fed off the government, those who held the public jobs and those who depended on them for trade. Crow's Point was sure to wither if not entirely die once this Jasonville became the county seat.

"What it means to me personally," Norm said, "is that I'll soon be out of a job. Hell, I know that. I've been out of work before, you know. They can fire me, but they won't be getting no virgin. Every town tamer I ever knew has had the same. We're heroes as long as we're needed, but an unnecessary expense once that need is gone. That's when we get fired. Hell, I don't mind that. But I expect some folks don't understand it. There's some that think I want to try and hang on here no matter what. Which is where these charges come in, if you see what I mean."

Longarm didn't see. Yet. But he didn't say anything about it, just let Norm run on.

"Somebody . . . I don't have any idea who and can't look into it so long as I'm sitting in here . . . tried to burn down the courthouse. Or at least to burn all the voting records that are stored downstairs. The popular theory is that I did it in an attempt to destroy the voter registration records so the election can't be held. Dammit, Custis, an accusation like that is purely crazy. If every voter record went up in smoke tonight, there'd still be plenty of time for it all to be reassembled before the election. If nothing else, they could re-register everyone, pass a special resolution allowing folks to register at the polls on voting day. Burning those records wouldn't accomplish a damn thing. Which I've tried to point out, but no one is listening."

"So why'd they point the finger at you anyhow?" Longarm asked.

Norm snorted loudly. "Evidence, of course. I have a little place over on the east edge of town. It isn't much, but it's mine. I'd even thought of retiring there. Now I'm not so sure. Anyway, out back of the place I got a shed. Somebody . . . whoever it was that started the fire, I'd expect . . . hid an empty coal-oil tin there along with a couple things that'd been stolen out of the clerk's office."

"Somebody tried to frame you, Norm?"

The tired old town marshal shook his head. "The truth is that I doubt it. I don't own a horse. Haven't bothered to own a mount of my own in years. Don't have any saddle or harness or anything like that either. The fact is that I own that shed but don't hardly ever use it. Hell, I doubt I walk inside the thing twice, three times a year. Anybody that knows me could know that. No, what I think is that the arsonist, whoever the hell he is, just thought my shed was a good spot to hide something. Likely thought it wouldn't be looked at, me being a law officer and everything."

"So how was the stuff found?" Longarm asked.

"Our sheriff . . . he's favored by the sodbusters, Longarm, but he's a good man. Thorough. Him and his deputies looked every damn place. It wouldn't have occurred to any of them, I suppose, to walk past my shed. They were intent on looking for evidence, and so they searched everything they came across."

"Like you said," Longarm agreed. "Thorough."

"Sure. And I got no grief with that."

"Malfeasance in office?" Longarm asked. "I think that was one of the charges the article in the newspaper mentioned."

Wold chuckled. "Longarm, if arson and larceny aren't malfeasance, then I don't know what would be. I mean, if all the others are true, then that would sorta have to be too."

"Do you have any idea what the motive of the arsonist might have been?" Longarm asked.

Norm shrugged. "I've wondered about that. Believe me, I have. But without knowing who, it's hard to figure out why in this case. It could be as simple . . . and as stupid . . . as some cowman not wanting to lose the county seat to Jasonville like they're accusing me of thinking. More likely, I'd think, it could be some idiot thinking to get his tax records done away with or . . . I dunno . . . get rid of some sort of evidence against him.

"Or hell, I suppose it could be nothing more sinister than some kid breaking in to see what he could steal and thinking to sweeten the fun by watching the courthouse burn. After all, it's going to be abandoned by the county soon anyhow, right? And the town won't hardly need anything this big for what little business the town does. Damn fool just might've wanted to watch the flames and see everybody get in an uproar. It could be nothing more than that, Longarm. I wish I knew for sure."

"I expect you won't mind if I poke around some, Norm? Ask a few questions here and there?"

Norm kneaded his chin and jaw with his hands and made a great show as if pondering Longarm's offer. "Oh, I suppose I won't get too awful mad at you if you want to hang around for a few days." The old man's grin returned again. "My trial comes up in a couple weeks. If nothing else, you'll be able to learn what prison I'm sent to so you'll know where to send my card come Christmas."

Norm Wold seemed to be taking the possibility lightly

enough, but Longarm's expression hardened. "You aren't going to any damn prison, Norm. Not you."

"All in all," Norm mused, "I expect I'd rather not. Considering what the other cons are like to do to a former peace officer behind prison walls."

"We can't let that happen, Norm. We just can't."

"Longarm, old son, if you can think of some way to keep the wolf off my doorstep, then I reckon I'd go so far as to thank you." Norm winked at Longarm, then turned to face the doorway and bellowed, "You can bring that coffee up now, Jeremy. But mind that it's hot, you hear?"

"Yes, sir, Marshal, I hear," the young deputy's voice called thinly from the next floor down. "I won't be long, so wait there for me if you don't have more important stuff to do." Longarm could hear a distant clatter of boots on the staircase.

## Chapter 6

Longarm glanced down to check the crude sketch he was carrying in the palm of his hand, decided this pretty much had to be the right spot, and nudged the gate open with the toe of his boot. His hands were full, what with his saddle and carpetbag and other gear, along with a sack of canned goods and such that he'd picked up on the way over.

He carried everything up onto the porch, and unloaded it all onto the pair of aging rocking chairs he found there. That part of the chore done, he fished in his pockets for the ring of keys Norm had given him back at the jail—as a prisoner Norm wasn't allowed metal objects inside the cell, but the young deputy named Jeremy had been helpful about fetching anything Norm wanted from among his personal possessions—and let himself into the house.

There was a musty scent in the place. Likely the windows hadn't been opened since Norm was locked up. Longarm went through the house opening windows and shutters to let in both light and air, and by the time he was done with that, everything looked and smelled considerably better.

There wasn't much to Norm's little house, just a parlor

and small bedroom and overlarge kitchen. Obviously the kitchen was intended to be the main room of the house, but it was not where Norm seemed to spend the bulk of his time, as the kitchen shelves and cabinets were mostly empty. The parlor, on the other hand, looked well used, with a man-sized overstuffed armchair, ottoman, and reading lamp filling most of the space. A pair of spectacles lay atop a recent issue of the *Police Gazette*. Longarm hadn't ever seen Norm wear eyeglasses, but then there appeared to be a good many things that had changed in Norm Wold's life these past few years.

An ashtray handy to the reading chair showed more pipe dottle than ashes, and there was a fancy-looking cut-glass container close by that held an amber liquid. Longarm pulled the glass stopper out and smelled the stuff. Brandy, he guessed, which didn't interest him much. Too syrupy for Longarm's taste. But then, every man to his own vices.

Longarm poked through the rooms for a few minutes, then carried his gear in and distributed the things among the rooms as future use would require.

Norm's wide bed, soft and comfortable, with a deep goose-down mattress and a heavy quilt on top, was as tidy as a virgin's drawers, and the sheets even smelled clean. Longarm took that to be a welcome bonus as he put his carpetbag onto a straight chair beside the wardrobe. He dumped his saddle and Winchester in a corner, and considered himself fully moved in.

Out in the kitchen he had the wherewithal to build himself a lunch, but Longarm wasn't much bigger on cooking than Norm seemed to be.

Besides, a man can keep his belly from going empty if he takes care of his own needs, but he won't learn a whole hell of a lot from talking with himself.

Seeing as it was coming lunchtime anyway, Longarm took a last look around Norm's little house, then went back outside and headed for town and another crack at the cafe where he'd had breakfast earlier.

He didn't bother to lock the door behind him. Marshal Wold's recent experience aside, Longarm kind of doubted that Crow's Point was the sort of place where a man had to worry overmuch about burglars, snatch-purses, or other such miscreants. Excitement in a town like this wasn't apt to consist of anything much more serious than Sister Hattie's mule getting rambunctious and causing a display of stocking.

# Chapter 7

The same young fellow who had served Longarm his breakfast was still on duty. He greeted Longarm at the door with a smile and a nod toward a table in one of the far corners. "Nice to see you again, Marshal," he said. "You're invited to join the gentlemen over there."

Longarm supposed there was no reason to be amazed that he was already known in town. After all, no one had told Jeremy it was to be a secret. Nor would that have done any good, even if Longarm had wanted his identity unknown while he was here. It was too late for that as soon as he walked inside that jail and spoke to Norm, so there was no sense in having second thoughts now.

"Thanks, son. Do you mind telling me whose company I'll be enjoying?"

"The gentleman in the suit coat and tie is Mayor Chesman. The man next to him is Pete Hankins. Mr. Pete is our pharmacist. He's also a county commissioner. And the gentleman on the right is Sheriff Jonas Brown."

"And they were expecting me?"

The young man grinned. "There aren't so many choices you might have made, sir, and I expect the folks over at Dottie's place will have been told to send you over here if you were to show up for lunch there instead.''

``Thanks, son.''

``Will you be wanting the special for lunch today, Marshal?''

Longarm looked at the chalkboard listing the choices, which were headed by mutton stew. If there was any one eatable that he could reasonably be said to detest. . . . He made a face. ``Not damn mutton, I won't. Just bring me a steak and some fried taters. Coffee, biscuits, you know how it should go.''

``Yes, sir.'' The waiter started to turn away, then hesitated. ``In case you're wondering, Marshal, this place is favored mostly by the town folk and farmers. The cowmen generally take their meals over to Dottie's.''

Longarm nodded his thanks, and made a mental note to add a tip to the boy's income from this meal. The waiter was trying to be helpful.

Longarm racked his Stetson by the front door, and ambled over to the corner table where the Crow's Point gentry were expecting him. It wasn't strictly necessary, but he went through the motions of introducing himself, and received the same courtesy in return.

``It's nice you could visit our little community,'' the mayor allowed. ``Are you on official business here?''

``No, sir, I'm not. Come to visit an old friend, you might say. I hope you won't mind that.''

``Not at all, Marshal. Not at all, I . . . would you mind if I called you, uh, Custis, is it?''

``My friends generally just call me Longarm. I'd be pleased if you felt so inclined.''

``Now that is just fine, Longarm. Just the sort of attitude we were hoping you would have.''

``You don't have any objection either, Sheriff?'' Longarm asked.

``Not at all. In fact, I'll be glad to show you everything I have in Norm's case. And I'll instruct my deputies to cooperate with you any way they can. Believe me, Longarm, I like the old fellow too. Having to place Norm Wold under arrest was one of the hardest things my job has ever forced me to do. No, I take that back. It wasn't one of the hardest. It was hands-down *the* most difficult single thing this badge has ever required me to do. If there is something I've missed, in Norm's favor or otherwise, I would be pleased for you to point it out to me. If you want to look into his case—and I have to assume that is why you came here—you won't get any resistance from me. You and your expertise are more than welcome here.''

Longarm was quite frankly surprised. Damn near dumbfounded, in fact. This was not what he would have expected. Dumbfounded, but almighty pleased. He truly appreciated Sheriff Brown's welcome.

Moreover, the welcome seemed to be matched by that of the Crow's Point mayor and County Commissioner Hankins.

''Is there anything I should know? Anything you'd like me to avoid looking at while I'm here?'' Longarm asked in a deceptively mild tone. If there were any reservations lying unstated behind the welcomes, that might be a way to sniff them out.

Each of the three gents in turn shook his head. ''No,'' the sheriff said, ''nothing at all that I can think of. You look into anything or anybody you want. I mean that. Anything. You won't be grating on my nerves any.''

''You know,'' Chesman confided, leaning forward a little and dropping his voice a mite, ''we wouldn't necessarily be this open with just anybody riding into town. But you aren't exactly unknown, Longarm. You have a good reputation. It's said you're honest. So are we, and that is all we would ask of anyone. You, Norm, anybody. Just be honest with us. We won't get our backs up about anything that's true. And that is a promise, sir.''

''I wish I had to deal with gentlemen like you three

everywhere I go,'' Longarm said, meaning it quite sincerely. ''Thanks.''

''If you want to start this afternoon, Longarm,'' the sheriff offered, ''I'll tell our court clerk to open the records to you. I'd go over everything with you myself, except that I have a meeting this afternoon with the county attorney. As soon as I'm done there, though, I will be glad to make myself available to answer any questions you have at that point.''

''And if you need me for anything,'' Chesman said, ''I operate the livery down at the edge of town. You'll find me there most times.''

Longarm was amused. Mayor Chesman was the most carefully dressed of the three. And he was the one running a livery where you would normally expect overalls and grime. ''Gentlemen, I thank you for your welcome,'' Longarm said.

Of course, it remained to be seen if the fine words were genuine. But if only for Norm's sake, Longarm damn sure hoped they were.

The waiter came with their food, and conversation slowed considerably while that was tended to. Afterward, the gents excused themselves one by one, until Longarm was the last man left at the table. When he tried to pay for his meal, he was told it was already covered. A request for the name of the friendly soul who'd paid for his lunch brought only a smile and a shrug.

''Thanks,'' Longarm told the young fellow, and remembered to add an extra-large tip.

With this kind of cooperation, he thought, he should have a shot at clearing Norm's good name in no time at all.

He lit an after-dinner cheroot and wandered outside into the afternoon heat.

# Chapter 8

Since he would be downstairs anyway, Longarm trudged the extra set of stairs to the top-floor jail to look in on Norm before he spoke with the county clerk. Besides, he reasoned, he needed to give the sheriff time to let the man know a stranger would be prowling through the records. Most clerks Longarm was acquainted with would get their hackles up mighty high in the air at the idea of someone—pretty much anyone—coming in and wanting access to their files.

In the sheriff's office and jail, young Jeremy was nowhere to be found. Norm was in his cell enjoying a dish of cherry cobbler that was layered thick with sugar and was swimming in cream so rich it was yellow in color.

"Sure looks good," Longarm said.

"Tastes even better than it looks," Norm assured him. "Dottie, she makes the best."

"I'll have to try her place next time."

"You do that. So what brings you back up here, old friend?"

Longarm explained, then shrugged. "Remains to be seen what happens next, don't it?"

Norm's expression clouded into a scowl. "Don't let those good old boys fool you, Longarm. Somebody . . . I won't claim to know who or how many, maybe all of them, but maybe not . . . somebody has it in for me. And whoever those somebodies are, they want my butt on a platter. Bad. Don't believe quite everything you hear around here. And maybe half of what you see. You know what I'm telling you?''

Longarm gave the old man a smile and advised, ''Go teach your grandmother to suck eggs. I might look easy, but I ain't exactly a virgin when it comes to poking my nose in other folks' affairs.''

Longarm heard Jeremy coming up the stairs. He touched the brim of his Stetson and made his way back down to the clerk's office.

The county clerk turned out to be a fat, balding man who was puffing from climbing the short flight of stairs from ground level, but who did not stint in his welcome.

''The sheriff told me to expect you,'' he announced. ''He said you're federal and that you have a good reputation. His recommendation is enough for me. Can I call you Longarm?''

''I hope you will.''

''Good. I'm John Stein, but my friends generally call me Schooner.''

Longarm raised an eyebrow. ''You a sailing man, are you?''

Stein threw his head back and roared. ''Lord, no. I turn green and puke all over myself if I have to take a ferry across a creek. But I've been known to lift a schooner of beer now and then.''

Longarm grinned. ''A man after my own heart, I'd say. Well, then, Schooner, what can you tell me?''

''Step right this way, Longarm, and I'll tell you everything I know. That should take, oh, six or seven minutes.''

''Lead the way, Schooner. I'm right behind you.''

• • •

Hirt County, Kansas, did not own a fireproof vault to protect its documents. Had the county been prosperous enough, and farsighted enough, to buy one, Longarm thought, Norm probably would not be upstairs in that cell right now. But then hindsight is always perfect, he conceded. The hard part is preparing for odd contingencies ahead of time.

The most important records, such as tax and voting rolls, court documents, and a few pieces of physical evidence relating to criminal cases pending in the county court, were all—or at least had been all—stored in a wooden locker that occupied much of one wall. The locker stood roughly eight feet tall by twelve feet in width, and was—Longarm measured—fifteen inches deep.

The arsonist who'd tried to destroy it had very nearly succeeded. The three sets of double-wide doors had all been left standing open—they'd been locked at the close of business hours, but the locks had been forced open with a pry bar or some similar instrument—and the heavy, canvas-bound ledgers rearranged on the shelves so they were fanned partially open. That had allowed the flames access to the pages. Closed books were not exactly immune to fire, but it took quite a blaze and a very long period of exposure for closed books to burn.

Coal or whale oil had been splashed liberally inside all three sections of the locker and set on fire.

Enough damage had been done that Schooner was having difficulty reconstructing the records.

"I won't ever get all of it down," he admitted. "Not exactly the way it was."

"How serious will that be?" Longarm asked.

"In the long run?" He shook his head. "More like a nuisance than a disaster, really. Nobody will lose his farm because of it, or be disenfranchised from his vote. We don't have so many folks around that we can't know them all. Some better than others, of course, but I don't think you could say there's any strangers in the county. And most of the people here aren't all that contentious. We get along with each other pretty well for the most part. I mean, there won't be anybody suing his neighbor over a fence line because the survey records burned, nothing like that."

"Uh-huh. Was there any other damage?"

"Down in the corner there were the town records. There isn't any city hall, you see, won't be until we move the county seat and ownership of this building goes over to the town. We let the city clerk keep his stuff there. I wouldn't have any idea what he lost, but I know whatever was there is pretty much gone now. It was on the bottom there, and of course the coal oil ran down onto the floor, so it was down at that level that the fire was the worst. We were able to salvage some of the stuff from the higher shelves, but you can see how the whole cabinet was doused with the oil."

Longarm nodded. He could see that plain enough, all right. The wood was charred, and there was still, after all this time a faint, rather unpleasant scent lingering inside the records locker. Longarm supposed Schooner was so used to the smell that he was no longer aware of it, but Longarm would have found it unpleasant to have to work at one of the desks close by.

"None of the desks was bothered?" he asked.

Schooner shook his head. "Not even messed with as far as we can figure out. Not that we lock them at night. Never had any need before, if you see what I mean. But the things in the drawers, stamps and little personal items and like that, nothing was missing, nothing seems to've been disarranged."

Longarm frowned. A vandal—and the truth was that he'd been thinking of this in terms of it being done by some half-grown idiot who liked simple meanness—more than likely would have helped himself to some petty thievery before calling attention to himself with fire.

If the desks were ignored, that made casual vandalism much less likely as a motive.

"Mind if I look through what's left in there?" Longarm asked. "I don't have the vaguest idea what I'm looking for, but I'd kinda like to poke around just in case something catches my eye."

"Help yourself," Schooner invited. "That desk over there isn't being used by anybody. Consider it yours for as long as you're in town if you want. Anything you can find, Longarm, you're welcome to look at. And if there's anything that you want but can't find, just ask me. I'll be glad to lend a hand."

Longarm was pleased. Obviously the town fathers had meant every word at lunch when they'd told him he could count on their cooperation. He couldn't ask for better than this. Longarm removed his coat and Stetson, and hung them on a deer-horn rack, lest he end up smearing them with the soot that coated most of the remaining record books in the big locker. Then he pulled one off a shelf at random, settled in behind the desk Schooner assigned him, and prepared to spend some time in a state of total boredom.

## Chapter 9

At five o'clock Longarm laid a slip of paper into the record book he was browsing through and closed it, marking his place so he could pick it up again come tomorrow. He would have continued reading, except that Schooner Stein had been coughing, shuffling his feet, and otherwise making small sounds for the past fifteen or twenty minutes. Longarm guessed this was not an office where the help liked to work late.

But then, hell, it was not really the sort of place where anyone would generally need to work late either. Very little would happen here that could not be put off for a spell and no harm done.

"If you want to stay longer, I'll keep the place open for you," Schooner said. Longarm would not exactly say the fat man sounded eager to do that. But it was damn sure nice of him to make the offer.

"Thanks, but there's no need for that. Can I buy you a beer?"

Schooner smiled. "That's the sort of thing I do like to hear, but we have a rule at home. Me and the kids all show up on time for dinner. That keeps the old woman from getting her apron in a wad. If we want to socialize afterward, that's fine, but we all line up fresh-washed and hungry when supper goes on the table. Tell you what, though. If I run into you later on of the evening, I'll darn sure take you up on that beer."

"Count on it," Longarm told him. He wondered briefly what it would be like to have the secure and orderly—and undoubtedly dull—life that Schooner Stein had.

Not that Longarm expected he would ever know. But sometimes he couldn't help but think about how things might have been but weren't.

He retrieved his Stetson and tweed coat, and got out of the way so Schooner could lock up. Down at street level, Schooner turned one way while Longarm went the other.

He thought about his own supper. The thought of cooking for himself—and more, of eating by himself in a strange house in a strange town—was not especially attractive. But then neither was the thought of taking his meal in the same cafe he'd already been to twice today. Not that there was anything unpleasant about the place. It was fine really. It was just . . .

It occurred to Longarm, not that he really needed an excuse, that Norm seemed to prefer this Dottie's place to the restaurant favored by the town folk. So in a way it could be considered in the line of duty for Longarm to go there as an alternative eatery.

He asked a gentleman passing on the sidewalk how to find Dottie's, and was promptly turned around, taking the same direction Schooner had moments earlier, although by now there was no sign of the fat court clerk on the main street of Crow's Point.

Dottie's proved to be small, friendly, and favored by a far noisier and more rambunctious crowd than frequented the other cafe.

In the other place Longarm had dined among men wearing suits and sleeve garters, with a few in overalls and clod-stomper shoes who pretty much had to be farmers. In Dottie's, he found mostly boots and spurs and wide-brimmed hats.

He helped himself to a seat at one of the unoccupied tables—there were a good many of those to choose from even though the place wasn't all that big—and was greeted by a woman who he assumed was Dottie herself.

Dottie would have been a fine match for Schooner Stein. Longarm guessed she would tip the scales at well above three hundred pounds. Maybe four hundred. It wasn't an area of speculation that he considered himself expert at. Great sausages of fat dangled, rolled, and rippled when she walked, which she did with a slow and ponderous gait.

When the woman smiled, however, she made the room brighter with the unstinting welcome of it. As she came near, Longarm could see that she was immaculately clean, and her coming was preceded by the delicate aroma of rosewater and scented talcum. Longarm liked her. He doubted he could have helped that had he wanted to. She just plain had an indefinable but likable special something about her.

"You're that marshal, ain't you?" she asked.

Longarm stood and snatched his hat off. He admitted to his identity, and added, "But my friends all call me Longarm."

"Then I'd best learn how to say it, hadn't I?"

Longarm grinned. "I hope you will. And you'd be . . . ?"

"Dorothy Tutwiler. Not that any of these half-witted stump-standers can prob'ly remember that." The volume of her voice increased considerably with that friendly accusation. Then, in a more normal tone, she said, "Everybody hereabouts calls me Dottie, and I reckon you'd best too, else I have to remember to call you Marshal Long from now on."

"It's a pleasure to make your acquaintance, Dottie," Longarm said. And meant it.

Dottie dragged a rumpled and ratty-looking notepad from a pocket of her apron and held it out as if ready to jot down Longarm's food order. Although he couldn't help but notice that she did not seem to possess a pencil to write with. He guessed the pad was part of the routine, never mind that it was neither needed nor used. "What can I do for you . . . no, what do you bet I already know what you want?"

"And what would that be?" he asked.

She squinted at him, looking him up and down, although he suspected that inspection was about as necessary as the notepad. Dottie was simply having some fun. "Steak," she said. "Burned hard and black. And fried spuds and a gallon of coffee followed by my famous dried apple pie."

"Famous?"

"If it ain't, it oughta be." She grinned back at him.

"I admit it. You have me pegged."

"Good. Now let me tell you what I'm gonna bring you instead."

Longarm was confused. And no doubt looked it.

"Steak and pie, Longarm, my new friend, costs twenty-five cents and ain't half as good as my special tonight, which is a pot roast so tender I won't even bother to bring you a knife to cut it with. The pot roast comes with the spuds and pie, just like the steak, and will only cost you fifteen cents. Now thens . . . what is it I should bring you?"

Longarm chuckled. "If it wouldn't be any trouble, I think I'll have some pot roast."

Dottie beamed. "See? I told everybody you'd turn out to be a sensible sort."

Longarm wasn't sure just who might constitute "everybody," but he was pleased to learn that he was hereby certified as sensible. At least he thought that was what she meant.

"Will you have the pie first while you're waiting on the pot roast?" Dottie asked.

"Sure, why not?"

"Then set still, son. It will be right out." The big woman turned and made her way through the tables toward the kitchen at the back of the place.

Longarm thought it no wonder that Norm favored Dottie's cafe.

And there was no doubt whatsoever once the dried apple pie arrived.

Dottie was right. If her pie wasn't already famous, it damn sure should be.

# Chapter 10

After supper Longarm stepped out onto the sidewalk and stopped to pull a cheroot from his pocket. He nipped the end off the cigar, struck a match, and hands cupped around the flame, bent his head to bring fire and tobacco together. Wreaths of white smoke and whispers of bright sound swirled around his ears. The first he could understand readily enough, but it took him a moment or two to figure out where the gay music came from.

It was a piano. Light and lively. And soon after it came the sounds of laughter. It occurred to Longarm that he hadn't yet seen any sign of a saloon or other night life in the town. That did not necessarily mean there was none. Only that he hadn't found it.

Following the faint but enticing sounds of the piano took Longarm off the main street to a small, isolated block of businesses that apparently served Crow's Point as a tenderloin district.

In Denver this little clutch of sin and depravity—at least that was what Longarm hoped he'd come upon—would have gone unnoticed amid bigger and more flamboyant competitors. But here, well, a body had to make do with whatever was at hand, or so Longarm believed.

He stepped through the bat-wing doors of the first of

the tiny businesses he came to. There seemed to be half a dozen of them or so, all jammed together with not even room for alleyways between the side walls of one building and its neighbor in this one small area. Convenient, a man might say. The saloon Longarm found himself in—if it had a name, Longarm did not see it posted anywhere in sight—had a crude bar set against a side wall, a ratty-looking faro table at the rear, and a pair of ugly, over-powdered whores begging for drinks. No piano. Longarm shrugged and tried the next place.

In the third place in the line he found the piano he'd been hearing from afar. And a slightly better-looking back-bar. And a card game that looked in need of another player. Longarm smiled. Hell, he was as good as home.

Longarm yawned. He didn't know what time it was, and did not bother dragging the Ingersoll out of his pocket to find out. Whatever the hour, he was purely tired from a day of travel and disappointment. It was time to make his way back to Norm's house and go to bed.

He swept his pile of loose change into the palm of his hand, and dropped the coins into a pocket without bothering to count them. He knew he was down a little—say, a dollar or a bit more. He didn't mind. It was the price of an evening's entertainment, and he did not begrudge losing a little in an honest game. That was the way the cards ran sometimes, and a man learned to take whatever came his way.

He thanked the gents at the table for the play—farmers, he gathered, although he hadn't come right out and asked—and excused himself.

A thin woman with artificially bright red hair and the smell of sour sweat hanging in the air around her intercepted him at the door with an offer that he had no difficulty refusing. What he did have a little trouble with was remembering how to find his way back to Norm Wold's house in the dark. He had to find the main business district first. Then, with his bearings restored, he had no trouble aiming for Norm's place on the edge of town.

Longarm pulled a match out to have it ready once he stepped inside. He didn't want to stumble over anything in the pitch-black interior and maybe break something valuable. Then, yawning again, he pushed the door open, stepped in, and flicked the sulfur-tipped lucifer afire.

The yellow gleam of light prompted a gasp of surprise and a dimly seen spurt of movement from somewhere to Longarm's left.

Someone was hiding there in the dark in Norm's house, dammit.

Longarm let the burning match fall unheeded from his fingers. He dropped into a crouch and swept the big Colt out of its holster.

"Don't move, you son of a bitch," he warned.

He hoped to hell the sound of his growl was menacing enough to freeze whoever was waiting in ambush.

Because the plain truth was that, taken unaware and thinking about the bed rather than any possible danger, he'd let his night vision be lost to the flare of the match.

At least for the next few treacherously long heartbeats, Longarm was bat-blind and defenseless.

He just hoped to hell that he was the only one who realized that.

Off in the direction of Norm's parlor he heard the scrape of a shoe sole on wood. Longarm's heart jumped into his throat, and he blinked furiously in a useless attempt to force his eyes to readjust to the darkness.

"Try anything an' I'll shoot," he snarled.

# Chapter 11

"My God, don't shoot. Please don't shoot me." It was a woman's voice. Longarm felt at least some of the tension leave his body. Enough that he was no longer riding the razor edge of shooting blind.

Not that a woman couldn't be treacherous. He knew better than that. But most women didn't display their forms of treachery by way of ambushing a man in the dark. The ladies seemed to have a habit of smiling real sweet when they set up to stab a man in the back, figuratively speaking. Or for that matter, literally as well. The point was that since he was being confronted by a woman, it wasn't real likely that he had to worry about a gunshot or the working end of a cudgel coming his way.

"Show yourself, dammit. Who are you?" he demanded, blinking at a furious rate, even though he knew that was not going to make his vision come back any quicker than the natural course of things would allow.

"Just a minute. Here," the soft voice said again. He heard the scrape of a match, and then saw the flare of a match as the lady leaned forward to light Norm's reading lamp.

Longarm scowled and shoved the big Colt back into the holster at his waist.

"I'm sorry," she said in a shaky voice. Well, he couldn't blame her if she was a mite scared. She'd come damn-all close to getting herself shot. "I must have fallen asleep."

With the lamp lighted and the wick turned high for light enough to read by, Longarm had an opportunity to get a proper look at her.

She wasn't half bad.

She was a big woman. Not fat. Not a bit of that, at least so far as he could see. She was just built to a slightly larger scale than most. Big bones, he supposed would be the best way to put it. Big tits too, although a gentleman wasn't supposed to mention that. He couldn't help but notice them, but it wasn't polite to talk about melons like those.

She had light brown hair piled in a mass of curls the size of a beehive, a complexion so pale she looked near to being ghostly in the glare of the lamplight, and delicate hands.

Her face was, well, damn near stunning. High cheekbones. Huge dark eyes, the exact color of which he could not make out. Large, soft-looking lips set around a wide mouth. Bold nose. Sharp chin. Large forehead. Now that he was paying attention, Longarm could see that her whole head was slightly oversized, big enough that it would have looked ungainly on a normal-sized woman, except that on this one it was merely in proportion with the rest of her.

She wore a throat-high dress with big, puffy sleeves, and had a cameo brooch pinned up by her neck. Apart from that, she was wearing no jewelry that he could see. No rings anyway. No wedding band, for instance. Her hands were bare of jewelry, but didn't really need any to set off those long, carefully manicured fingers.

She was . . . shit, she was a stranger found sitting inside a single man's house in pitch dark, that was what she was. Which asked a hell of a lot more questions than it answered.

"Who are you?" Longarm demanded again.

"I'm sorry, I . . . I must have fallen asleep."

"Yeah, but unless I been misinformed, lady, or somehow lost my way, this ain't your house to fall asleep in."

She dropped her eyes and glanced into her lap, managing to look sheepish by doing so. "You embarrass me, sir."

"I'm like to do more than just embarrass you if you don't pretty soon explain yourself, lady." He wasn't sure just what he was apt to do if she refused to say more. Lock her up on trespass charges? He didn't much think so. But hell, the threat sounded good.

The lady sighed. Loudly. Then did it again, probably to make sure he heard it.

Longarm wasn't buying. "Well?"

"My name . . . you don't have to tell anyone about this, do you? Please?"

"Lady, I don't know anything to tell. But I'm fixing to. Now, do you want to come clean your own self? Or should I haul you outside an' commence asking the neighbors to tell me what I got in custody?"

"Custody? Are you an officer of the law, sir?"

"Never mind who I am, dammit. The point is, who are you and what're you doin' here in Norm's house at night?"

She sighed again. This time not so loudly. Longarm thought that this time the exasperation might well be genuine.

"My name is . . . do we really have to go into all this?"

"Yes, ma'am, I expect we do. Else we go out into the street an' do it that way."

"Very well. My name is Eleanor Fitzpatrick. Mrs. John J. Fitzpatrick."

Longarm's eyebrows went up a notch or two.

Mrs. John J. Fitzpatrick gave him a haughty glare. "I am widowed, sir. I am not the sort of lady. . . ." She stopped there. It occurred to Longarm that she was likely realizing she hadn't much room left to travel in that direction, seeing as how he'd just found her sitting in the dark in a single gentleman's house, never mind her protestations about what she was. Or wasn't.

"I am a . . . a very close friend of Marshal Wold."

"Uh-huh. Is that supposed to tell me anything?"

"Damn you."

"Getting testy with me will make you feel a whole lot better maybe, but it won't make me quit wanting to know why you're here like this. You got a gun on you maybe? A knife? Am I gonna have to search you to see if you're dangerous?"

"Please, I . . . all right. But please, *please* don't talk about this to anyone." She paused and gave him a big-eyed pleading look that might have worked under other circumstances, but wasn't going to touch him right here and now.

"You were saying?" he demanded.

She sighed again. This time he thought she sounded more pissed off than anything else. "Damn you," she repeated.

"We covered that territory already, but go ahead if it makes you feel any better."

"All right. All right, you win. I am . . . covertly, you understand, the stiff-necked farmers around here would turn me into a pariah if they ever found out . . . Norman and I are . . . what you might call *very good friends.*" She bore down extra hard on those last three words. Boyfriend-girlfriend to one extent or another. Not that Longarm figured that part of it was any of his business.

"An' that's supposed to tell me why you're camping out in his house in the dark when Norm is over there locked up in the jail, lady?"

"You will refer to me as Mrs. Fitzpatrick if you please. And I happened to overhear someone in my shop this afternoon . . . I operate a millinery establishment, not that it is any of your business, sir . . . I overheard someone mention that there was a man in town to get Norman out of jail. I thought . . . I thought he would be home tonight. I wanted to be here for him when he came back. But I could hardly light the lamps and announce myself, could I? So I sat here in Norman's favorite chair. I slipped in the back door . . . I have my own key, if you must know . . . just after dark so no one would see me. I—it is the usual way for me to come when we meet, do you see. I wanted to be here for him, to surprise him. I . . . guess I just sort of . . . fell asleep. I didn't even hear you at the door. I heard something. I suppose that roused me from my sleep. Then you struck that match. And . . . you know."

Longarm grunted. Yeah, he knew. It was his turn to sigh. He explained himself to Mrs. Fitzpatrick.

"You are the officer they call Longarm?"

"Yes, ma'am."

She smiled for the first time. It was a mighty fetching expression too. Made her look extra handsome when she smiled. "Norman has spoken of you. He is very fond of you."

"Yeah, well, I'm fond of him too. Which is why I'm here. But to try an' help him outa this jam permanently. It's got nothing to do with bail."

"I should have known that, I suppose. The justice of the peace here . . . he's the man who signed whatever stupid paper it was to charge Norm . . . he claims Norm is a risk to jump bail, so he wouldn't set any. He insisted on holding Norm without bail. Isn't that the awfullest thing you ever heard of?"

It wasn't, but under the circumstances Longarm decided not to say so. Actually, it made sense. Hell, everybody knew that one way or another Norm didn't have any kind of permanent ties to Crow's Point or to Hirt County, Kansas. Facing criminal charges and a possible jail term here, never mind the truth or falsehood of the situation, Norm Wold would hardly hesitate to throw his things onto a horse's hind end and slope on out of town. He could go someplace else without raising a sweat, and obviously the town justice of the peace knew that.

"Yes, ma'am," was all Longarm contributed in response to Mrs. Fitzpatrick's rhetorical question.

"I suppose . . . well, I'm sorry if I startled you," the lady said. "Will you be staying here while you're in town? You will stay and help Norman, won't you? Is there anything I can do to help you help him?"

Longarm might have come up with a few suggestions, actually. But they wouldn't have related to helping Norm exactly. Mrs. Fitzpatrick really was a right toothsome-looking female. Big. But mighty tasty-looking. He cleared his throat. And shook his head.

The lady glanced toward the curtains, which were decorously closed. Anyone out in the street would be able to see there was a light burning inside, but could not see in to know who was there or what they might be doing. Longarm understood now why the curtains might be kept that way instead of being open to let light in during the day.

"If you will excuse me, sir?" she said, rising. He could see now how tall she was. This woman was big all over, by damn. She stood there looking him almost eyeball-to-eyeball. And there were not a whole hell of a lot of women who could make such a claim.

It seemed that Norm's woman was a handful and then some. Longarm kind of envied him that.

Mrs. Fitzpatrick smiled again—damn, but she was fine-looking when she did that—and held a hand out to shake. "I do apologize for startling you, sir."

"Longarm," he corrected. "You can call me Longarm."

"Then you must call me Eleanor."

No, he thought. Ellie or El or any of the other possible diminutives just wouldn't have fit. Not for this one. "Yes, ma'am," he said, then smiled and quickly changed that to: "I mean, yes, Eleanor. I hope I'll see you again under, shall we say, more normal circumstances?"

He thought he saw a twinkle of amusement in her eyes—they were sort of a gold color, he could see now—and she answered, "More respectable, you mean."

Longarm grinned. "Whatever."

Eleanor Fitzpatrick turned to gather up a velvet handbag and a small, paper-wrapped bundle—a homecoming present for Norm, probably—and started toward the back of the house. "You needn't see me out," she said over her shoulder. "I know the way."

Yes, he expected that she did at that.

That was confirmed later, after he'd naturally gone to see her out, when he went into Norm's bedroom to turn in for the night. The bed there was turned down. On both sides.

Longarm considered it something of a pity that the preparation wasn't being put to use.

But Eleanor—Mrs. Fitzpatrick, he told himself somewhat sternly—was Norm's woman. She might be a large and lusty chunk of female, but she was Norm's, and that meant she was not up for grabs.

After all, dammit, a man had to draw the line somewhere.

Didn't he?

# Chapter 12

Longarm yawned. He wasn't tired. Hell, he was bored half into a stupor. He dragged the Ingersoll out of his vest pocket. It was 4:48 in the afternoon. Close enough to quitting time for his purposes, thank you. He bit back another attempted yawn, his teeth chattering lightly as he did so, and laid a sheet of paper into the pages of the musty, soot-stained ledger he'd been prowling through. That would mark his place for tomorrow's labors.

Not that he expected to learn anything really. He certainly hadn't found anything of interest to this point. Nothing that would tell him why anyone, Norm Wold or any other human soul, should take any interest whatsoever in the continued existence of the records of Hirt County, Kansas.

It probably would have helped a great deal, Longarm conceded, if he'd had any tiny notion of what it was he hoped to find.

Unfortunately, he did not. Not the least lick of an idea existed at this point.

But surely there had to be *some* reason why a party or parties unknown tried to do away with the damn records.

Longarm could buy Norm's theory that there was no deliberate attempt to frame the town marshal for the crime, that indeed it was only very bad luck that led the arsonist to hide the evidence of his crime in Norm's unused carriage shed. Longarm could accept that. But that did not negate the fact that to prove Norm innocent would likely require proof that someone else was guilty. And the undisputed best way to get that, considering that all the evidence was aimed at Norm Wold, would be for Longarm to collar the genuine miscreant and toss the son of a bitch to the wolves of the court.

And the only problem with that was that now Longarm was obligated to find answers for all the usual questions. Like who, what, why, where, and when.

What, where, and when were no problem. But who remained a mystery. And with nothing else to go on, Longarm figured his best chance right now was to concentrate on why. Hence this mind-numbing stint in the county offices—to say nothing about the butt-numbing abilities of the desk chair Schooner had so generously loaned him.

Longarm yawned again, didn't bother trying to stop it this time, and shoved back away from the desk. "Mind if I leave the book here overnight?" he asked.

"It won't bother me any."

"Thanks. Schooner?"

"Mmm?"

"That invitation to join me for a drink or whatever is still open."

"Thank you, Longarm, but I still better say no." The fat man grinned. "My wife promised pot roast and new potatoes for supper, and she makes the best." He patted his own more than ample belly as evidence of his mate's excellence in the kitchen.

"I expect I'll be playing cards tonight at the place," Longarm said. "I don't know the name of it, but there's a piano player who knows what he's doing and the bartender's name is Jake."

Schooner nodded. "I know where you mean."

"Join me there for a beer if you're of a mind to."

"I just may do that later."

Longarm retrieved his hat, waved good-bye to Schooner, who was busy tidying up and locking things away, and went outside. Supper at Dottie's, he figured, then over to the saloon for a friendly game and a nightcap before heading back to the lonely silence of Norm's little house.

He was halfway to Dottie's cafe when the fellow with the gun stepped out in front of him.

# Chapter 13

"Howdy," Longarm said.

The man—he was more boy than man, actually—responded with a wild-eyed look.

Longarm tried again. "Something I can do for you, son?" Smiling, he reached inside his coat—with his left hand; the right remained unencumbered as a precaution, not that he saw any particular need for worry—and pulled out a cheroot. Keeping his eyes on the boy in front of him, Longarm bit off the twisted tip of the cigar, clamped it between his teeth, and then dipped two fingers of his left hand into a vest pocket for a match. He lowered his chin, but not his eyes, when it came time to light the smoke.

Through all this the boy was standing there so tight and nervous, it was a wonder he didn't vibrate and thrum like a damned violin string.

Longarm guessed his age to be eighteen, nineteen, somewhere in that neighborhood. There were some youngsters who could count themselves grown and responsible at that age, but this one had an air about him that said he still should be in knee pants. He looked, in truth, as if his belfry wasn't quite full, as if somebody had shorted him half a peck when brains were being portioned out. Not that Longarm was in any position to pass judgment on short acquaintance. If that was what this was.

The boy continued to stand there, giving Longarm a vacant, open-mouthed stare.

He was towheaded, with hair like sun-bleached straw that had gotten wet and was commencing to mold. His hair should have been trimmed two, three weeks ago. He had blue eyes that darted nervously, and a twitch or habitual tic that made the left side of his cheek flutter. A few wisps of pale hair dangled from his chin. Longarm guessed this kid hadn't ever had to shave.

The boy wore a tattered bib overall that was near white from age and countless washings, and was worn out at the knees where several patches had been applied long ago and now needed to be done again. Underneath the bib was a pink pullover shirt that might once have been red. It too was ancient and worn thin. He was barefoot, the bottom ends of his pant legs stopping four or five inches short of his grimy ankles and filth-encrusted feet. He was bareheaded.

The oddest thing about him, though, was neither his appearance nor his attire. A body might see that in any young half-wit.

The thing that captured Longarm's attention most was the gun the boy clung to. It was an old Remington revolver, a brass-framed model, so it almost had to be of the old cap-and-ball design from back before Remington received patent rights to offer cartridge guns. There was no loading lever visible on this one, so Longarm assumed it had been converted for cartridge use at some time in the past, most likely to the once-popular .44-rimfire cartridge that worked so nicely in the old Army .44-caliber loose-powder shooters. From the distance, which Longarm judged to be eight or ten yards, he couldn't tell any more than that.

Even from so far away, though, Longarm could see

that the boy clutched his gun with a grip so tight it made his knuckles white.

The boy was breathing hard, and sweat plastered strands of hair across his forehead.

"Is there something you want, son?" Longarm tried again. "Anything I can do for you?"

"I want . . . I want. . . ." The voice was practically a croak. The boy licked his lips and tried again. "I'm supposed . . . in the back . . . can't." He shook his head wildly from side to side and spoke again. "Can't do that, can't."

"Can't what, son?"

"Not right. From the back. Can't."

"Can't do what from the back, son?"

"Can't . . . shoot."

"Shoot someone in the back? No, that wouldn't be right. Look, can you tell me what's wrong? I'm an officer of the law. A peace officer. Maybe I can help you."

"Can't . . ." The boy's face twisted and twitched, and there was a brightness in his eyes that hinted of welling tears that he refused to let fall. "Can't. Not in back."

"No, of course you can't," Longarm agreed calmly, puffing on his cheroot. "Tell me what's troubling you, son. I'll help any way I can. Will you do that for me?"

"You aren't. . . ."

"Aren't what, son?"

"Mean. I mean, not alla time you aren't. Are you?"

Longarm smiled. "I hope not. Let me help you now, will you please?"

"Gotta . . . shoot."

"Who, son? Who's done something so terrible that you think you have to shoot them? Tell me, please. I'll help you. I promise."

The boy started to cry. "Got to . . . got to do it."

"We'll take care of it together, son. Whatever it is, tell me about it. Me and you together, we'll take care of it."

The boy sobbed, his chest rising and falling at a furious rate as he gulped for air and cried the breath back out of him again. His neck was red with strong emotion, and Longarm doubted he could see worth a damn with all those tears pouring out of his eyes.

"Oh, Jesus! Jesus Lord!" the boy gasped in what was obviously a genuine plea from the depths of his heart. "I'm sorry, mister. I got to."

He raised the big Remington—damn thing looked several times larger from the front end than it had from a side view—and shakily aimed it square at Longarm's chest.

"No, let's ta—"

The Remington roared, and a gout of white smoke blossomed at the muzzle.

Longarm felt a ball tick the tweed of his coat somewhere low on his left side. Close. The kid couldn't see worth shit because of all his tears, and maybe because of that, he was shooting without really being able to take solid aim.

Longarm had time to think that this might have allowed the damnfool kid to shoot straighter than he probably could have if given time for serious aim.

But damn it . . .

The boy used both hands to drag the hammer of the Remington back for a second shot.

This time Longarm found himself staring straight into the gaping barrel of the old but still all-too-workable gun.

He hated it. God, he hated what he had to do.

But he couldn't stand there and let himself be gunned down by some poor, simpleminded kid who didn't know what the hell he was doing.

It was lousy. But Longarm didn't have a whole hell of a lot of choices. Not when the boy had another four or five rounds left in the cylinder and there was no cover around close by for Longarm to duck behind.

The boy, chest heaving from the effects of his crying, steadied himself to shoot again.

Dammit . . .

Longarm raised his Colt—he didn't so much as recall drawing the thing, but it was already in his hand—and shot deliberately low, hoping to take the kid in the hip and knock him off his feet.

All Longarm wanted to do was disable him, dammit. Make him quit shooting long enough that he could be disarmed. Then, well, then Longarm would try again to help him. He meant that. He had no ill will toward this frightened child who seemed bent on Longarm's demise. But first Longarm had to do something to keep the boy from killing him before that help could be given.

Longarm's slug hit exactly where he wanted it. It struck the kid on his right hip and spun him half around.

The Remington flew out of his grip to clatter harmlessly to the ground.

Longarm jumped forward, kicked the gun out of the boy's reach, and turned back to see what he could do now to straighten out this stupidity.

Somewhere down the street Longarm could hear the buzz of excited conversation and the approach of townspeople. Good, he thought. Among them, dammit, they should be able to help this boy. And find out what had gone wrong inside the poor kid's addled brain to bring this about.

# Chapter 14

"Damn," somebody whispered. "I never seen so much blood."

Longarm glanced up from where he was kneeling beside the boy. He recognized the man who had spoken as another saloon customer from last night, but Longarm did not know him. He did, however, agree with the fellow. He supposed that, technically speaking, he probably had seen more blood than this in the past. But there was an awful lot of the stuff pumping out of the kid right now. The street was puddled thick with it, the blood mixing into the dirt to make a particularly unpleasant sort of dark red mud that had a cloying, coppery stench about it and a look of ugly menace. The bullet from Longarm's gun must have severed a major artery somewhere in the vicinity of the youngster's pelvis.

And because of the placement of the wound there was nowhere to tie off a tourniquet, no way that Longarm knew of to stanch the all-too-vigorous flow of blood.

"Is there a doctor?" Longarm asked. "Does anybody know how to make this bleeding quit?"

No one spoke up. Not that he'd expected any help. Longarm himself had seen more than his fair share of gunshot wounds. This was one he doubted the finest surgeon in the land could repair in time to save the boy's life.

"Anyone?" he repeated. But there was no one.

He looked down at the blond boy. The kid was actually smiling. His lips were moving. Longarm leaned lower and put his ear next to the boy's mouth, so close he could feel the warmth of the kid's breath on his skin.

". . . bedtime already, Mama? Now I lay me down to sleep, I pray the . . ."

The sounds became too faint to hear, although the lips continued to move for several moments. Then they stopped too. The kid just sort of drifted away from life. He was still smiling at the time.

Longarm felt a relief of sorts. At least the boy hadn't been in pain there at the end.

But the kid's death was so damned . . . useless. So stupid. There hadn't been any reason for it. None.

And although he'd had to do it more often than he'd ever wanted to, Longarm still did not like killing. He especially hated the need for a damned stupid death like this one. A kid, for crying out loud. Hardly more than a boy.

Longarm shook his head and gently pulled the boy's eyes shut before he stood and, shaking his head sadly again, brushed off the knees of his trousers from where he'd been kneeling in the dirt at the dying boy's side.

"What was this all about, Longarm?"

Longarm glanced at the man who'd spoken. It was Sheriff Brown. "God, Jonas, I wish I knew." Longarm explained what had happened, why he'd had to shoot. "I shot low deliberately, Jonas. Tried to keep from killing him. It was just lousy luck the big vein was cut so he bled to death. I wish. . . ." He shrugged.

The Hirt County sheriff gave him a sympathetic look. "I think I know what you mean. I've never had to kill anyone myself. Can't say that I want to."

"You're fortunate," Longarm told him.

"I agree. But you say you have no idea why Dinky came at you?"

"Dinky? That was his name?"

"It's what we all called him. Dinklemann was his real name. John Dinklemann? I think John was his real first name. Like I say, everybody called him Dinky. Right from when he was little. You didn't know him?"

"Jonas, I never laid eyes on this boy until a few minutes ago. I don't know of any reason in the world why he came at me like he did. None."

Brown fingered his chin and shook his head. "Longarm, I've never known poor Dinky there to so much as have a harsh word for anybody. Never known him to get mad, even when he was teased. He was kinda soft in the head, you understand. Not the least bit bright. But he was a good kid. Never any trouble." Brown raised his voice so those close around could hear. "Does anybody know any reason why Dinky would have tried to kill the marshal here?"

No one answered. The looks on all their faces showed the same depth of incomprehension that Sheriff Brown displayed.

"Sheriff," one man said, "I never seen Dinky with a gun. Never seen him with money enough to buy one neither. And you know he wouldn't have stole anything. That boy was honest as the day is long. I never heard of him ever taking anything that wasn't give to him fair and square."

Brown sighed and agreed. He explained to Longarm, "You could say that Dinky was raised by this town. Everybody liked him, and he sure liked everybody else. Like Harry just said, he was sweet and honest and a good boy. Not smart, but decent despite his blood. His mama was a whore. This was in the early days, back when the cow herds were trailing through. No one knows who his papa might have been. Some Texas cowboy with a loaded gun between his legs, likely. Cloretta Dinklemann had the boy and was taking care of him proper. She died when Dinky was, oh, nine or ten, I'd guess. Since then he's just kind of lived all over. Slept in sheds or on cold nights someone was sure to take him in. He'd do odd jobs, whatever was needed, and the folks here made sure he had a mite to eat and hand-down clothes to wear. We all of us raised him, you might say. Everybody knew him. He was a good boy, Longarm. A good boy."

"Not so good that he wouldn't try and kill me today," Longarm insisted.

"I can't explain that," Brown said. "I surely can't." He motioned for his young deputy Jeremy to come closer. "Son, I want you to take this gun around town. Talk to everybody here first, then carry it around and show it to everybody you can find. I've never seen Dinky with a gun and I doubt anyone else has either, but I want you to ask them. And if they recognize this gun as belonging to anyone else. There aren't so many of these old models kicking around, especially ones that were converted to take cartridges."

The sheriff examined the Remington himself before turning it over to Jeremy. He showed Longarm the cylinder. Only four of the six chambers had been loaded. All were rusted, and there were cobwebs in the empty chambers. Brown handed the revolver to his deputy, then pointed to another man standing in the crowd and motioned him over.

"Cy, this is U.S. Deputy Marshal Custis Long. I know of him, and he's all right."

"Pleasure t' meet you, Marshal. I'm Cyrus Cantwell." He extended a hand to shake.

"Cy, you know what's happened here. Do you recognize the gun?"

"No, I don't, Jonas. I'd remember it if I'd ever seen it before."

Brown told Longarm, "Cy is our gunsmith in town. Also our saddle and harness maker, watch and clock repairer, pretty much anything that can be done with small tools in good hands. Cy also does what little buying or selling of guns that takes place in this end of the county."

"The conversion is to .44 rimfire," Longarm said. "Do you stock ammunition for that?"

"Of course," Cantwell said. "That cartridge fits the old Henry rifles. There are a few of those still around. I have a brand-new one still on my rack, in fact, and two used Henrys that I've taken in trade over the past couple years. I still carry the ammunition."

"Cy, I'd like you to think this over, then write down a list of everybody you've sold .44-rimfire ammunition to in the past—oh, hell, let's just say you should try and remember everybody that's bought from you in that caliber. You can give the list to Jeremy when he comes around to talk to you later."

Longarm was impressed. Sheriff Jonas Brown was a small-county lawman who admitted he'd never had to fire a gun in anger at any human soul. But he was a lawman and not a slacker. He seemed to know how to jump into the guts of an investigation and do it right. Longarm was glad to have him in on this. And wished Brown was as keen on learning the truth about Norm Wold as he was about finding out who it was who put the boy called Dinky up to attempted murder.

Brown asked several of the bystanders to take Dinky's body to the town barber, who apparently also served as the local undertaker. Once the body was gone, the crowd drifted apart as well. The sheriff sent Jeremy off to begin questioning folks about the gun.

"If there is anything else you can think of . . . ," Brown said.

"Well, yeah, I guess there is," Longarm replied.

"Name it."

"You tell me that Dinky was a good boy, honest and decent?"

"That's right. Every day of his life. I would have

sworn to that. For that matter, Longarm, I still think so. I'm not doubting what you said, mind. But I still think Dinky was a good boy."

"And apparently he was," Longarm agreed. "Which makes me think it would have taken an awful powerful influence, along with a pack of lies, I'd think, to get him to try and gun me down. Now that I think back on the few things he said, I'd guess he was told to shoot me in the back, like from ambush. But he couldn't bring himself to do a low thing like that. If he had to kill me, then he'd do it, but he'd do it fair and stand there facing me."

"That sounds like something Dinky might've done," the sheriff allowed.

"Which makes me wonder, Jonas, just who in town was so close to him, who had that kind of strong influence, that they could've convinced him to commit murder."

Jonas Brown grunted and shook his head. "Dinky liked everybody, Longarm. Everybody."

"He had to like someone mighty strong for it to come to this, though."

"I can't think of anybody special," Brown said. "He worked for pretty much everybody, one time or another. Slept in a couple dozen different places now and then. Would show up just about anywhere, with just about anyone." The sheriff shook his head again. "I surely can't think of anyone closer to him than any other. Not that I ever noticed."

"You might ask around and see if everyone else has that same view," Longarm suggested.

"I will. I surely will."

Longarm frowned and pulled out a cheroot, offering it to the sheriff, who declined, then lighting up himself. Longarm sighed. "I was on my way to supper when I ran into Dinky. Care to join me?"

"Thanks. Another time maybe."

Longarm nodded and said his good-byes, then made his way along to the cafe.

His mood, though, was not so easy as it had been when he'd left the courthouse a little while earlier. Norm Wold was in jail accused of serious crime. And now the town pet was lying dead for no good reason. There was too much here that made no sense, no sense whatsoever.

Longarm's belly rumbled with hunger, and he lengthened his stride. He hoped Dottie had more of that soon-to-be-famous dried apple pie tonight.

# Chapter 15

Longarm took a final look around the saloon, but there still was no sign of the court clerk coming around to collect on Longarm's promise of a free beer. Longarm felt he kind of owed the fat man for all the help he'd been, but it wasn't the sort of debt a man had to worry about overmuch. Schooner would come by one of these evenings or he wouldn't, his choice.

With no reason to remain any longer and the hour growing late, Longarm dragged his stake into a pile and scooped the coins into a pocket without bothering to count them. He knew he was up a little, probably less than a dollar. It wasn't exactly enough to get excited over. He excused himself, getting no argument from the other gents at the table. They looked like they were commencing to wear down too, and Longarm suspected the game would break up soon. "G'night, all," he said as he stood.

"Same time tomorrow?" a man named Kyle suggested.

"More'n likely," Longarm agreed without exactly committing himself to be there. In his line of work a fellow couldn't always count on what tomorrow would bring.

A blond whore with tits like big pink pillows intercepted him before he could reach the front door. She would have looked a lot nicer, he thought, if she washed her face and neck from time to time. Lines of charcoal-colored grime collected in her wrinkles, showing dark against the rice powder that whitened her skin like soot caught in the wind-ripples of a newfallen snow. Longarm found the effect to be more than a little off-putting. Not that he would have been much interested in the aging bawd even without that relatively minor imperfection, but with a woman like this one he couldn't help but think in terms of little bitty, itchy-crawly things. He couldn't even see one without his pubic hair and balls beginning to itch.

"Just a dollar, honey," she whispered by way of sweet talk. Longarm thought it over, and decided it was an offer he could manage to resist.

"Thanks, but not tonight."

"I'm awful good, honey. You try me and you'll see. Anybody here can tell you that. I'm worth it."

Longarm grinned and gave her a wink while he readjusted the set of his Stetson. "I'd bet you're worth a whole lot more'n that even," he said.

The whore seemed pleased. She smiled and simpered and rubbed her tits over his arm. Longarm hoped she didn't have anything that was too contagious.

"You're a fine-looking woman," he lied, "but I'm awful tired tonight."

She gave him a look of instant concern. "Of course you are, honey. I shoulda thought about that."

Longarm smiled at her again and tried to step away into the night, to a place where there would be clean fresh air instead of the stink of cheap toilet water that surrounded the hooker. She stopped him by grabbing his coat at the elbow. "Wait a minute, hear?"

"Look, ma'am, I already told you—"

"No, I . . . it isn't that. It's . . . I don't know just how to say this."

Longarm shrugged. And waited.

"We ain't such a much here, I don't suppose, especially not to a fine, handsome, big-city lawman like yourself. But we got our pride. You know what I mean?"

He didn't, but he did not think this was the time to discuss it. He continued to wait, giving the old whore time enough to say whatever it was that was on her mind.

"Everybody knows what happened to you this afternoon, and we're all embarrassed by it. Real upset too because we all of us like that boy Dinky. He was a swell kid. You know?"

Now that was something that Longarm for damn sure did not know. The one sure fact he had about Dinky Dinklemann was that the boy had tried to kill him. In Longarm's estimation, that was not much of a recommendation for upstanding character.

"Everybody's been talking tonight and . . . well, what we kinda think is that somebody in town here made Dinky try and do that today. We don't like that. You see what I mean?"

Maybe. He was beginning to think perhaps he was beginning to understand now.

"Anyway, I guess what I'm trying to say, Marshal, is we don't want anything more bad to happen in our town. We don't want you hurt nor anybody else. So . . . well . . . you just be careful when you go home tonight. All right?"

Longarm smiled again, truly meaning it this time, and leaned down to plant a very brief and gentle kiss on the old bawd's forehead. She meant him well. He couldn't object to that, could he? "Thanks."

Feeling if anything more puzzled than ever by the people of Crow's Point, Kansas, Longarm stepped out into the night.

No one shot at him on his way back to Norm's house. No one seemed to pay any attention to his passage whatsoever.

But somewhere in this town there was a person who—for reasons Longarm could not begin to comprehend—wanted him dead.

That was an annoying thought to say the least, and one he could have done without. Still, he'd been hunted before this. A man would have to be quick, accurate, and almighty lucky if he expected to put lead into Custis Long and walk away from the encounter.

He let himself into the house. This time there was no one waiting for him in the dark. It occurred to him that he would not have minded if Norm's lady friend Eleanor Fitzpatrick had been waiting for him again this evening.

He felt a little guilty when he realized where that train of thought could take him.

But only a little.

# Chapter 16

Longarm slapped the ledger shut with a disgusted snort. Nothing. Two and a half days of effort and he had absolutely nothing to show for it. Not so much as a sniff of a hint of a suspicion of an idea.

But dammit, a whole hell of a lot of lawing was like that. You busted your butt just to find out there was nothing up an alley worth learning. So then you turned around and found another alley to look into.

That, he supposed, was what he would have to do this time too. For sure he was not inclined to give up.

Longarm glanced up at the big Regulator clock on the wall. It was still short of noon. No point in looking for the next step to take quite yet. He stood, stretched, and told Schooner, "I'm gonna go up and visit with Norm for a spell, then go get lunch. See you back here later."

The fat clerk nodded absently. He was elbow deep in a stack of paperwork.

Longarm got his Stetson from the rack and headed out for the staircase, where he found Jonas Brown's young deputy coming down from the top floor.

"Marshal," the youngster greeted him with a nod.

"Hello, Jeremy."

"I'm on my way to fetch lunch back for the sheriff

and Marshal Wold. Can I bring something for you too?''

Longarm considered the offer and liked it. ''You bet.'' He dug into his pocket and pulled out a quarter that he contributed to the lunch. ''Bring me whatever looks good.''

''Sandwich be okay? That's what the others are having.''

''Fine.'' Jeremy continued down the stairs, and Longarm went on up. He found Norm and Sheriff Brown sitting on opposite sides of a chessboard laid out on top of the sheriff's desk. The door to Norm's cell was standing wide open.

''Be a helluva time for a jailbreak,'' Longarm said with a grin as he helped himself to a seat where he could watch the game in progress.

''Huh,'' the sheriff complained. ''If this man doesn't quit beating up on me, I may have to throw him out, never mind what the judge wants. I'm getting tired of this.''

''Now, Jonas, I keep telling you, if you had as much time as I do to study on these things, maybe you could keep up with me,'' Wold said. He seemed in a good humor. But then he ought to. The sheriff's queen, one of his rooks, and three of his pawns were sitting off the board, compared with only a lonesome pair of pawns that Brown had captured in return.

''Something we can do for you, Longarm?'' Brown asked.

''Don't let me interrupt you.''

''Frankly, I'm hoping like hell you will interrupt. Give me a chance to change my luck here.''

Norm chuckled. ''It would take more than a little interruption to do that, Jonas.''

''Hush up, prisoner, or I'll put you on bread and water for the next week.''

Norm laughed, not seeming to be particularly awed by the sheriff's threat.

"Oh, wait," Brown said. "There's something I want you to look at. You too, Norm. See if it means anything to either of you. It sure didn't to me."

Longarm lifted an eyebrow, but there was no point in asking questions right now. The sheriff stood and crossed the room to a filing cabinet. He pulled open the top drawer and extracted a piece of brown wrapping paper.

"Fancy stationery the county's buying you these days, Jonas," Norm offered.

"It's called having respect for the taxpayers' pocketbooks. Actually, what it is, Mr. Outlaw, is the list Cy Cantwell made up of all the people he can remember who've bought .44-rimfire ammunition in the past couple years or so. I saw Cy on his way to work this morning. He gave it to me then. I would've shown it to you earlier, Norm, but Jeremy had taken you down to the crapper, and by the time you got back upstairs I forgot. Anyway, for whatever it's worth, you should both look it over and see what you think." The sheriff handed the list to Longarm first, but it took Longarm only a few seconds to glance at the names listed on the sheet.

There were seven names on the list, but the only one Longarm recognized was that of Norm Wold himself. The others were complete strangers to him. By name anyway, although he supposed it was possible he could have run into one or more of them in town the past couple days without knowing it. Longarm shook his head and handed the paper on to Norm.

Norm studied the names for some time, then shook his head. "I know them all, sure, but I can't say that any of this means anything to me. Nothing suspicious about any of them. Certainly no reason I could think of why any of these men would want Dinky to shoot Longarm. For that matter, I can't think of anyone else who would want him dead either."

The sheriff shrugged. "It was worth a try," he said. "Keep rooting. There's always a chance you'll turn up an acorn if you dig through enough dirt,'' Norm encouraged him.

''I see your name on there, Norm,'' Longarm said. ''You aren't still shooting a Henry rifle, are you?''

''Nope. Used to. Back when the Henry was the modern, up-to-date ticket. Traded that old gun in, oh, '67? '68? Sometime along about then.''

''Why would you need the rimfires if you don't have a Henry?'' Longarm asked.

''Got me an old cap-and-ball revolver that I had a fellow in Dodge City convert for me back when I used to work as night marshal there. This was just after the Eastern Unpleasantness, right after Dodge City was formed as a town.'' He smiled. ''Some town too. A man needed a gun on the streets at night whether he was a lawman or not. And that old loose-powder revolver was a pretty fair gun too. Outmoded now, of course. Has been for years. But I got some memories attached to the old thing. And hell, it isn't worth anything. Wouldn't bring two bits if I was to try and sell it, I suppose. So I've kept it laying around. I bought those shells off Cy, let me think, a couple years ago it's been, I'd say. Ran across the old gun and wondered if it still shot as true as it used to, so I got me a couple boxes of rimfires from Cy and took it out one day to play with. Had a pretty good time too, busting clods of dirt out of the air and rolling stones along the ground. It still shot true. I don't suppose I've touched the old gun again since, though. Cleaned it up and put it away and the shells with it. Do you want it for anything, Longarm? Evidence or whatever?''

''Hell, no, Norm, I was just curious. It didn't seem likely to me that you'd still be carrying anything that out of date.''

''Not me, but don't make any assumptions about Jonas here. I'm not sure he knows yet that those old guns are out of date,'' Norm said with a laugh.

"You're just feeling cocky as hell today, aren't you?" the sheriff said.

"You would be too if you were up three games to none." Norm grinned.

Their banter was interrupted a moment later by the sound of Jeremy's boots on the stairs.

"Lunch is served, gentlemen," the young deputy called out as he entered the jail bearing a basket that had some mighty tantalizing odors seeping out of it.

There were the expected sandwiches, true, but Dottie had also slipped in a small crock of beans baked with molasses and the best part of a steaming hot peach cobbler. Of the two, Longarm couldn't make up his mind which smelled the better. And a few minutes later, he had equal difficulty trying to decide which tasted better. That Dottie could cook with the best of them. That much he could state without equivocation.

# Chapter 17

Longarm belched. His belly was full, and there was a nice warm feeling flowing through his whole being from the meal. If it hadn't been for his friend Norm's predicament, locked away upstairs inside a damn jail cell, Longarm would have counted himself pretty contented right now.

As it was, he came down and poked his head into the clerk's office. Schooner was gone, presumably to lunch, and the big room was depressingly empty. Longarm didn't know which records to look at next with Schooner not there for guidance. And anyway, the whole truth of it was that he just plain didn't feel like spending the rest of the day cooped up with a bunch of musty, soot-stained record books. He'd had more than enough of that lately. Another long and boring afternoon of it sounded more like a sentence of punishment than an opportunity to learn something new.

Longarm told himself he might do better by going out into the town and poking around for opinions about why Dinky Dinklemann had wanted him dead.

It wasn't that Longarm didn't trust Jonas Brown's or Jeremy's investigative abilities. It was just that no one else could do as good a job as Custis Long could. Not on something as personally involving as an attempt on his own life, they couldn't.

That was more than enough of an excuse for Longarm to continue right on down the steps and out the courthouse door.

He started across the street at the hardware, and asked his questions on down the block, at one store after another.

The fifth place he came to was a millinery. There was a familiar face behind the counter.

"Ma'am," Longarm said, taking his Stetson off and holding it in both hands.

"Good afternoon, Marshal," Eleanor Fitzpatrick said. Then she smiled, the effect of it lighting up the interior of the store in much the same way a sparkling summertime sunrise could light up the mountains. Lordy, but this was one fine, handsome figure of a woman.

Longarm glanced around. The shop was empty save for the two of them.

Mrs. Fitzpatrick followed his gaze and nodded. "It is all right. We are alone. You can speak freely."

"Actually," Longarm said, "there's nothing I wanted to ask you that I couldn't talk about in front of strangers. It's about the Dinklemann boy."

She frowned. "Oh, yes. I heard what you did. What Dinky tried to do, that is. I know you had no choice but to defend yourself. Still, it was a terrible shock. Everyone in town knew him. I daresay we all loved him. Such a nice boy." She shook her head. "I could hardly believe he would do such a thing."

"You knew him too then?" Longarm asked.

"Certainly. We all did. He did odd jobs for just about everyone in Crow's Point."

"You too?"

"Yes, of course. He would come in two or three afternoons a week to help out. I would go to the door to close the shop, you know, to lock my door and pull the shade down so I could close up and go upstairs—I have a small office up there—and Dinky would be standing there with that sweet, gentle smile. Not coming right out and asking if there was work for him, but being there, offering himself if I needed anything. Naturally I would let him in whether I really needed help or not. He would sweep the floor for me, doing any lifting or straightening that needed done. Take the trash out back to burn. Things like that."

"You paid him, I suppose," Longarm said.

"Yes, but not much actual cash. Most of us, I think, preferred to make sure he had food to eat and a place to stay. He had little use for money. Once in a while I would give him a few dimes or a quarter. Seldom anything more. Others gave him odd bits of clothing when whatever he was wearing became torn. I myself washed his things now and then. Whenever I would be about to wash something of my own, you see, it would be no trouble to throw something of his into the basin along with my own laundry."

"You do your own laundry?"

"Does that surprise you, Marshal?"

"Yes, ma'am, I guess it does. A lady like you . . ." His voice tailed away. He wasn't quite sure how to finish that train of thought.

Mrs. Fitzpatrick tilted her head back—damn, she did have a soft and pretty neck, white and tender and, well, a perfect place to put a kiss was the way Longarm was thinking of it—and laughed loud and long. "Thank you, Marshal. I believe I should take that as a compliment, don't you?"

"I reckon you could at that," he agreed.

"Good. I shall do so." Her body still jiggled some with her amusement. "Do you think me that prim and proper, then, that I should ask others to do my menial tasks for me?"

Longarm thought about that for a moment, then said,

"Not so much as you'd demand it, ma'am, as that others would want to offer it. An' do I think you're a powerful handsome an' high-class lady? Well, yeah. I expect I'd have to say exactly that."

"La, sir. I do thank you. You've made my whole day, I assure you."

"Then I'm extra glad I happened in," Longarm said gallantly, stepping back to give the lady a half-bow and a wide, low sweep of the Stetson to emphasize it.

Mrs. Fitzpatrick laughed again. There were other responses Longarm might have enjoyed even more than that one. But amusement would do nicely enough, he supposed. Anything that pleased her.

Trying to get back to business, Longarm asked a few more questions, but like all the other business people in town, Eleanor Fitzpatrick could offer no reasonable explanations as to why the Dinklemann boy would have wanted to shoot Longarm. Or more to the point, who would have—or could have—talked Dinky into an action that was so desperately out of character for the town's soft-witted pet.

Longarm might have gone on making excuses to stand there talking with the woman, but a customer came into the shop to browse, and soon after her, another pair wandered in. Being trapped in the midst of a hen party wasn't Longarm's idea of a splendid afternoon, so he quickly made his apologies and went to make his way through the remainder of Crow's Point's business district.

At one store after another, though, he found only the same answers to his oft-repeated questions. Yes, everyone knew Dinky. Certainly everyone was shocked by what the boy had done. But no, no one had any idea whatsoever who or what could have prompted such outrageous behavior.

Longarm kept at the questions doggedly but without any expectation, and at the end of the day was grateful for an excuse to quit and go get some supper.

# Chapter 18

Longarm stood outside the saloon listening to the thin, brittle sounds of the piano. There was gaiety inside. Bright lamps, bonded whiskey, unmarked cards, and a better than merely fair free-lunch spread.

He just didn't damn well want to go in and enjoy any of that.

It wasn't like him to be in such a sour mood, but the truth was that right at that moment he felt mean and grumpy and would have welcomed any excuse to lash out at somebody—anybody would do—to vent his ill humor physically.

But what the hell did he have to be mad about?

It was frustration, he finally decided. He was just plain frustrated.

And why the hell shouldn't he be? This whole thing with Norm wasn't adding up. Or anyway, none of it was playing out in a predictable manner.

Generally speaking, when Longarm conducted an investigation, he could count on facing and having to overcome evasiveness, misdirection, surliness, and downright lies. Witnesses and suspects alike hated to have anyone, particularly someone with a badge, poking into their private lives. Longarm understood that. He and every other peace officer dealt with it every day of their lives.

So what was he finding in Crow's Point? Why, friendliness, that was what. And cooperation. Smiles and a healthy, hearty helpfulness.

Everybody he talked to was the same, from the county officials right on down to the folks he passed on the street.

"G'day, Marshal; hope you're doing all right, Marshal; how can I help you, Marshal?"

So why the hell wasn't he *getting* anywhere? A body would think that with that attitude surrounding him, he would already know every secret in town. Instead, dammit, he was finding nothing. Not one damn thing worth knowing.

Everyone liked Norm Wold, and hoped he would be proven innocent despite the evidence against him.

Everyone liked John "Dinky" Dinkelmann, and found it impossible to understand why the boy had done such a terrible thing. But everyone expressed deep sympathy and understanding about it too.

Of course the marshal had had to shoot the boy; he hadn't had any choice about that. Oh, it was such a terrible thing that Dinky had tried to kill him, and how awful it was that he'd had to kill Dinky in order to defend himself, but thank goodness Longarm was all right. And is there any way we can help? Any records you want? See for yourself; feel free; go anywhere you want; ask anything you wish; the people of this community are behind you foursquare and all the way, Marshal.

Longarm should have been delighted. He knew that. Instead he wanted to puke.

Hell, he almost wished someone else would step out and try to shoot him. At least that would be something Longarm could understand, something he could deal with.

Yeah, he thought sourly, it was frustration that was

fouling his mood. And he didn't really know what to do about it.

One thing he was sure of. He didn't want to spend the evening drinking whiskey that he didn't want and poring over cards that he wasn't interested in.

He took the last few puffs off his after-dinner cheroot and flicked the wet, chewed-up butt into the street, then headed for Norm's little house on the edge of town.

And every step of the way he was hoping someone would try, just try, dammit, to lay an ambush for him or jump out of an alley with a cudgel or . . . or something. Something, anything, that he could face down and do something about.

Longarm's bad luck was that right at this moment nobody seemed all that interested in killing him.

"What a shitty turn of events," Longarm grumbled to himself as he made his way through the darkened streets of Crow's Point.

# Chapter 19

Longarm wasn't halfway through the doorway before he heard Mrs. Fitzpatrick's soft voice in the darkness. "Don't be worried. It's just me."

He closed the door behind him and glanced around to make sure the blinds were drawn before he felt his way slowly into the parlor. At least he was beginning to know his way around the place well enough that he didn't make a fool of himself by tripping or knocking something over. Then he struck a match.

Eleanor—Mrs. Fitzpatrick—was seated in Norm's reading chair, as she had been before. She was dressed as she had been in the shop earlier, in a tailored dress of some slightly shiny dark material. Longarm didn't much care what the garment was made of. What interested him was how it emphasized the lady's figure. She had—he took a deep breath and reminded himself sternly that this was his old friend Norm's woman.

"Nice to see you again," he said noncommittally, dropping his hat onto an end table and taking a seat on the spindly-looking loveseat that was tucked away to one side of the room like a just-for-company afterthought. The only man-sized piece of furniture in the place was already occupied. Of course it looked like it might accommodate two. But Longarm suspected that that might be pushing things just a bit much. He settled for the loveseat, which at least had a fine view of the room's major attraction, Mrs. Fitzpatrick.

"Can I offer you a brandy?" the lady suggested, adopting the role of hostess in the house.

"No, thanks."

"Would you be offended if I had one alone?"

Longarm felt a rush of heat into his cheeks. He was acting boorish, wasn't he? Shit, he didn't know who was supposed to do what in a situation like this. The place didn't belong to either one of them. And Longarm was the one staying here. But Eleanor—Mrs. Fitzpatrick, dammit—was the one who more or less could claim squatter's rights as lady friend of the owner. But on the other hand . . .

Longarm gave up worrying about it. He bounced quickly to his feet and said, "Allow me," heading for the brandy decanter and glasses, even though they were beside the big chair where Mrs. Fitzpatrick was sitting, all the way across the room from Longarm. But then, hell, it wasn't all that big a room.

Mrs. Fitzpatrick sat upright and proper where she was, and allowed him to pour for her. She smiled—and her fingers lightly brushed against his—as she accepted the small crystal snifter from him.

The lady bent her face delicately close to the rim of the glass and inhaled softly, then dipped the tip of her tongue into the amber liquid. Longarm almost got the shivers, watching her. There was something about the moist, pink tip of her tongue that . . .

"Is there something wrong?" she asked, her head still low but her eyes now peering up at him from beneath an overhang of hair on her forehead. The effect of that particular view was intense. Damn, but this was an almighty fine-looking female.

Longarm realized he was staring. Well dammit, he

couldn't help it and wasn't fixing to apologize. Nor explain either. He was sure Mrs. Fitzpatrick received her fair share of admiring looks and then some. "No, ma'am," he said, and retreated to the loveseat once again.

Mrs. Fitzpatrick sipped at her brandy slowly, seeming in no hurry to explain her presence. Well, Longarm wasn't in any hurry either. He wouldn't mind if she chose to sit there in silence the rest of the evening.

Or at least, he wouldn't mind looking at her a spell longer. He wasn't so sure about that a moment later, though, when he noticed a gap in the front of her dress.

There was a button loose. Maybe two of them. If a woman undid a couple buttons at her throat, Longarm would figure that that was deliberate and react accordingly. But this was obviously by mischance. The buttons that were undone were at her belly, not her throat. And the plain truth was that Eleanor Fitzpatrick probably was able to see her own belly only when she was naked and pulled those magnificent tits apart so she could look down beneath them. With clothes on, there was no way she could see the upper part of her own stomach, not without a mirror, like the fat man who didn't have any idea what his own pecker looked like after not seeing it for years and years.

The loose or missing buttons in this case wouldn't have been very distracting, except for the way the cloth of the dress gapped open so that Longarm could see the soft, pale skin of the lady's belly.

There was something vulnerable and sensual and just plain arousing about this secretive look where a man oughtn't to see.

Arousing? Longarm damn well thought so. And duly aroused, he responded with a hard-on that threatened the integrity of the buttons at his fly. He quickly shifted position on the loveseat so he was slewed kind of sideways. To make extra sure his embarrassment didn't reveal itself, he crossed one leg over the other to make double damn sure the bulge in his britches couldn't be spotted from the chair where Mrs. Fitzpatrick was innocently enjoying her brandy.

Longarm found himself wishing the damned woman would drink up and leave so he could . . . no, that wouldn't work either. If she rose to leave, he would have to stand up too. And what the hell would he do then? Grin and shrug? Tell Norm's woman he was sorry to bother her but would she mind helping him get rid of this little problem he seemed to be having? Her leaving would be worse than her sitting there with her skin exposed.

What he needed was to think about something else. Sure. Just look elsewhere. In a minute or two the hard-on would die a natural death, and he could stand up and move around again. Go get his traveling bottle out of the bedroom, maybe, and help himself to a shot of good rye whiskey. He hadn't wanted a drink earlier, but now he thought a stout shot would be a helluva good idea. In fact, now he kind of thought he needed one. Who would have thought that two lousy buttons would put so much skin on display.

Pretty skin too. Pink and pale and perfect. A tiny wrinkle or two when she leaned forward. Then flat and smooth again whenever she sat upright.

Damn, he wished the woman would quit moving around so much. Why couldn't she sit still while she drank her damn brandy!

Longarm was overheating. Starting to sweat. He could feel it beading up on his forehead and trickling down his cheek onto his neck. He wished . . . he wished he could tear his eyes away from Mrs. Fitzpatrick's stomach, that was what he wished. That and certain other things too. He wished. . . .

"I suppose you are wondering why I sneaked in again

this evening,'' the lady said as she finally emptied the brandy snifter.

Longarm tried to speak. The sound that came out more closely resembled a croak than any identifiable word. He coughed, cleared his throat, and tried again. ''Yes, of course.''

''After you left my store this afternoon, Longarm, I happened to think of something. I don't know if it will do you any good. Probably not, I suppose. That is, I am sure it was entirely innocent. But, well, I happened to observe something, something involving young Dinky, that was, shall we say, unusual.''

''Yes, ma'am?'' Longarm still had his hard-on. But it wasn't quite so insistent now. Horniness was important, but an attempt on his life was one of the few things of even greater importance to him. His attention was successfully diverted back onto business now, and the tent pole that had been straining his buttons began now to subside back to the size and consistency of a loosely cased sausage. Better. Much better. If he had to stand up now, he could probably do so without suffering terminal mortification in front of Norm's woman.

''Like I say, it is probably nothing at all,'' she said. ''But you did tell me I should speak with you if I remembered anything, did you not?''

He couldn't exactly recall right now if he'd said any such thing to her, but it was the sort of thing one normally said, so he supposed that was accurate enough. He nodded and waited for her to go on, noting as he did so that after she'd returned her empty glass to the tray, she'd turned in the chair a little, and now the dress was not gaping open quite so much. Longarm wasn't sure if he should be glad about that or not. He supposed that, in fairness to Norm, he ought to be pleased. More or less.

Mrs. Fitzpatrick frowned, and her eyes focused somewhere off in the distance in deep thought. ''This would have been, oh, yesterday afternoon sometime? Yesterday evening? I can't be sure of the exact time. Is that important?''

"I can't say if it is or isn't,'' Longarm told her, not bothering to add that he hadn't yet the least idea of what she was talking about, so of course he couldn't know if any of it was significant or not.

"No, I suppose not,'' Mrs. Fitzpatrick agreed. "At any rate, it was some time yesterday, definitely after lunch. I always close my shop between the hours of noon and two P.M. I am certain it was after I re-opened in the afternoon.''

"Yes, ma'am,'' Longarm said patiently.

"I stepped out back. To take something out to the trash, you see. And I noticed Dinky down the alley. He was talking with someone there. They were nearly a block away, but I think it might have been Luke Baldwin he was talking with. There is nothing unusual about that, of course. Dinky talks—I mean to say talked—with everyone. What I remember noticing, though, is that the person Dinky was speaking with handed him a package. Which is not unusual either. I believe I already told you practically everyone in town has given Dinky castoffs and hand-me-downs of one sort or another. I've done that myself many times. But what struck me this afternoon when I got to thinking about yesterday is that this package Dinky received was about the size and shape of a pistol. Except it was wrapped in cloth, of course. I mean, I could not actually see what was in the bundle, if you see what I mean. I certainly could not swear to what the object was. I mean . . . oh dear.'' She paused and gave him a wide-eyed look. "Am I making a fool of myself, Marshal?''

"No, ma'am, you are not.''

"Good. Because I certainly do not mean to cast any suspicions on Mr. Baldwin. He seems ever so nice a man. It is just, well, you did say I should pass along anything that occurred to me. I thought it might be best if I simply told you and let you decide if it means anything or not.''

''You did the right thing, Mrs. Fitzpatrick,'' Longarm assured her.

She smiled and said, ''Eleanor. Please call me Eleanor, Marshal.''

''Yes, ma'am.'' He noted, rather unhappily, that she'd turned in the chair just a little and now the damned buttons were gaping open again. He could feel a rising interest once more somewhere a little south of his gut.

Mrs. Fitzpatrick's—Eleanor's—smile brightened. She leaned forward to retrieve her glass and asked, ''Could I have another very small one before I have to go, please?''

Longarm groaned softly under his breath. Just how in hell was he supposed to stand up and walk over there in front of her in this embarrassing state?

# Chapter 20

Longarm stood and brushed the crumbs off his vest and britches. He tossed his napkin down and added a coin to pay for the meal. "I've enjoyed talking with you this morning, gents, but I'd best be on my way now. Been daylight out there long enough without me getting anything done." He'd been having breakfast with the mayor and several of Crow's Point's leading businessmen. As was usual, the tone of the conversation had been that of helpful concern. If there was anything they could do, anything at all . . .

"Remember now," Mayor Chesman admonished.

"Yes, sir, I know. I can count on you and the rest of the folks hereabouts. Believe me, I appreciate it," Longarm said. And indeed he did. He fingered his chin absently, as if only then discovering the beard stubble there, although he'd deliberately neglected to shave when he arose this morning. "One thing you gents could do for me," he said.

"Name it," a smith named Jones offered.

"You could point me to where I might find a shave and a trim." His hair could have gone a week longer before it needed cutting, but what the hell.

"That's an easy decision. Only one barber in town,"

Jones said. "His name is Baldwin. Luke Baldwin. Nice fella too, you'll like him."

Longarm nodded. He wasn't convinced that he was going to like their Mr. Baldwin, but Longarm was certainly eager to make the gentleman's acquaintance after what Eleanor Fitzpatrick had said last night.

One of the other gents at the breakfast table gave Longarm directions to the barbershop. Longarm thanked them all again, and reclaimed his Stetson off the rack by the door on his way out into the bright morning sunshine.

He felt pretty good, everything considered. Although, after the way he'd been worked up for a while there last night, it was a pure wonder he hadn't soiled his drawers by squirting off in a wet dream. That Eleanor was a handful. And considerably more than a mouthful. And one of the things that made her so damned desirable was that she didn't seem to have the least idea that she was so almighty sexy and desirable. That was a rare quality in a handsome woman. Most of them knew it and traded on it, although some were less obvious about it than others.

Longarm just plain liked Eleanor Fitzpatrick's style. He surely did. He stood on the sidewalk for a moment to light a cheroot and get his bearings, then headed down the street toward where they'd said he could find Luke Baldwin's barbershop.

There were several customers ahead of him, so Longarm deposited his hat on a rack, selected a recent copy of the *Hirt County Courier* from a pile of reading matter, and settled in to wait his turn in the chair. He was in no hurry at all, and in fact was pleased with an opportunity to bury his nose in the folds of the newspaper while he quite shamelessly eavesdropped on the chatter between the barber and the man he was shaving.

The talk touched briefly on the subject of poor Dinky Dinklemann—neither Baldwin nor the customer could fathom that one—then turned onto subjects of greater importance. Like the amount of moisture in the fields after the recent hot spell and whether the corn crop would fill out this year. Longarm couldn't claim to be much interested in that, so he returned his full attention to the newspaper.

The *Courier,* it seemed, was published in Jasonville, the farm town that was soon to become county seat. Longarm gathered that either Crow's Point had no newspaper of its own, or that the *Courier* used to be based in Crow's Point, but had already moved along to the new county seat. It was a shame, a town declining like this one was, but that sort of thing happened all the time. And in the mining country, unlike out here on the plains, whole towns could up and disappear practically in the blink of an eye. Crow's Point had made its run. It really didn't have all that much to bitch about now.

"You're next, mister."

Longarm looked up. The men who'd been ahead of him were all gone, and there were a couple of later arrivals waiting for Baldwin to finish with Longarm. Longarm had been wool-gathering for a bit there. About Eleanor Fitzpatrick, actually. He knew better than that. But he'd done it aplenty last night while he was trying to get to sleep and now found himself doing it again. Damned if he didn't, kind of envy his old friend Norm. Except for that one small fact about Norm being locked up in the jail, of course. But as for his relationship with Eleanor, well, that was something to make a man puff out his chest and count himself among the downright lucky ones.

"Step along, friend," Baldwin urged. "There's others waiting behind you."

"Right with you." Longarm laid the newspaper aside. There was nothing in the news of particular interest, but its editorial page offered a small tribute to Norm Wold's past services to the people of Hirt

County and hoped the Crow's Point marshal would be found innocent of the charges now pending against him. Longarm removed his coat to hang on the rack under his hat. Then he took his place in the comfort of the barber chair. "Shave and a trim, please. Someone said your name is Baldwin?"

"That's right." The barber draped a clean cloth over Longarm and tucked it tight around his neck, then said, "I know who you are, of course. Everybody in town does, I suppose."

"Notorious, am I?"

Baldwin smiled and shook his head. "Nothing like that. We're all wishing you well. Which reminds me, I hope you don't think the whole town is against you. We all feel real bad about what that crazy boy Dinky tried to do." He selected a razor from among an ivory-handled line of them laid neatly on a fresh towel, then began stropping it, his hand moving with the deft swiftness of long practice.

"I felt bad about it my own self," Longarm said. "Got any idea why he might've done that?"

"Not me," Baldwin said.

"You knew him, of course."

"Sure. In a town like this everybody knows everybody. But I didn't like him much. I expect I'm about the only man around who would say that, but I can't see any reason to think the boy's death is a big loss just because he's gone now. I didn't like him much when he was alive, and like him even less now that he went and tried to kill someone."

"I thought everybody here liked him."

"Not everybody," Baldwin said.

"Any particular reason?"

The barber grunted, decided his razor was sharp enough, and began whipping a fresh lather onto the soap in its mug. "You never know what a half-wit is gonna do, Marshal. Can't be trusted is what I've always felt.

Besides, somebody soft in the head like that''—he shuddered—''gives me the creeps. Not natural, being off in the mind like he was. Not healthy. You know?''

''Dinky wasn't a friend of yours then?''

''No, sir, I wouldn't claim that he was.''

''He didn't do odd jobs for you or come to you for handouts like he did everybody else?''

''Not me. He learned a long time ago it wouldn't do him any good to come begging to me for anything. It don't take me but a minute to sweep this place out come night. I never needed him nor anybody else to do that for me, and I wasn't about to encourage him to hang around here. I wouldn't have stood for that the way some did. No, that boy gave me the willies sure enough. I didn't like having him around. He never came to me for anything. Hadn't come around me for years. He was loony, see, but he was able to learn that much after a while. Whatever he asked for, I always told him to go away, that I wasn't no charity and he wasn't getting nothing here. Once he got it through his head that I wasn't giving in like the others, he never come around any more.''

''So you didn't know him all that well,'' Longarm said.

''Nope. Didn't want to neither. I got troubles enough without taking in crazy people.''

''You didn't give him food or presents or anything?''

''I thought I said that already,'' Luke Baldwin declared in a testy tone of voice, sounding more than a little peeved at having to repeat his denial.

''Sorry,'' Longarm said.

Baldwin spread lather over Longarm's face, the smell of it pleasant, and leaned down to use a thumb to smooth away the soap and stretch Longarm's cheek taut for the razor.

The man had a feather touch with the blade, Longarm could say that for him. Longarm was quiet throughout the rest of the shave. It didn't do to piss off a man who already had a razor edge at one's throat.

## Chapter 21

"Luke Baldwin? Of course I know him. Luke's been giving me my shaves ever since I came to Crow's Point," Norm said from the other side of the bars. Norm looked comfortable enough. He had a rocking chair in the cell with him, and was sitting in it now with his feet—in socks and a ratty old pair of carpet slippers; he had no need for boots at this particular moment—propped up on the edge of his bunk. "What do you want to know about Luke?"

"How friendly was he with Dinky Dinklemann?" Longarm asked.

Norm's gaze drifted up toward the ceiling while he thought that over. After a few moments he shrugged. "About the same as everybody else, I'd guess. Why?"

Longarm didn't answer immediately. Instead he tried to prod Norm's memory again. "Did you see Dinky in the barbershop often?"

"Hell, Longarm, I don't know. I mean, who pays attention. You know? And how much does it take to make something often?"

"Okay then, Norm, let me put it this way. Did you ever see Dinky Dinkelmann in the barbershop? Doing odd jobs there or getting a haircut or for any reason? Any reason at all?''

This time Norm cocked his head to one side and gave Longarm a speculative look before he answered. ''This is going someplace in particular, isn't it? Do you have a scent to follow about Luke and Dinky?''

''I don't know yet, Norm, but I need to find out.''

''Then let me make sure I answer you as best I can,'' Norm said. ''I can't honestly recall any particular time I've noticed Dinky in Luke's shop. But then like I said before, it isn't the sort of thing that anyone in this town would notice. You know? Dinky was just kind of . . . everywhere. He'd show up all the time, with anybody, and no one ever thought a thing about it. So, no, I guess I couldn't go under oath and testify that I ever saw Dinky getting his hair cut. But then there's probably two hundred men in Hirt County that I've never watched get their hair cut.''

''Ever see Dinky sweep up for Luke Baldwin? Anything like that?'' Longarm persisted.

Norm pondered the question for a moment, then shrugged again and shook his head. ''Not that I especially recall. Which doesn't mean it didn't happen. Hell, I generally only went to Luke's shop myself on Wednesday afternoons. I might have stopped in at other times or on other days once in a while over the years, but usually my schedule was for a trim after lunch on Wednesdays. For all I know Dinky could have worked for Luke every Monday evening and every Friday morning since he was big enough to push a broom. I just wouldn't know.''

''Let's try it this way. Did you ever pay particular note about Dinky *not* hanging around the barbershop?'' The question sounded stupid even to him, and Longarm regretted asking it practically before the words slipped off his tongue.

Norm laughed. ''That's like asking me do I find anything strange about walking into a room and not finding

Ulysses S. Grant there. Of course not. A man pays attention to what he does see, not usually to something that he doesn't. Unless there is some special reason, that is. I mean, I might look for the general if I was at a reunion of the GAR or something. But I wouldn't expect to see him at the bank in town here, and wouldn't think anything odd about not finding him there if I can ever walk in there again. I wouldn't expect, or not expect, to see Dinky anyplace in particular either."

"But you might reasonably expect to see him anywhere," Longarm said.

Norm held his hands palm up and hiked his shoulders. "What is this about, Longarm? Can you tell me?"

"I just . . . it's possible that Luke Baldwin could be the man who aimed Dinky at me."

Norm frowned. "Why?"

"I was hoping you could tell me."

"Lordy, I wish I could." He shook his head. "For the life of me, Longarm, I can't think of any reason why Luke would want harm done to you."

"But would he have anything against you, Norm? Is it possible he doesn't want me finding evidence that would clear you of the charges against you? Any reason why he would want you behind bars?"

The aging town marshal thought about that for a considerable piece of time before he finally answered. "If there is a reason, Longarm, my friend, I don't know what it might be. Luke and I have always got along just fine. Never been close particularly, but we've never had hard words. Never fought or gambled or anything like that. Hell, he's shaved me time to time. And taken a razor to the back of my neck every week for years. The man has never been in any kind of trouble with the law, not that I know of."

"Could he have been the one who set the courthouse fires?" Longarm asked.

"Anybody in the county might have done that, I suppose, but I can't think of any reason why Luke would want those records burned. Certainly there's no reason to put him higher on a list of suspects than anybody else. And plenty of reason to think of others ahead of him as suspects, like anyone in tax trouble or . . . I don't know. No, no reason that I know of why Luke would want Dinky to kill you, and none that makes me think Luke would have started the fires."

"This morning Luke told me he didn't like Dinky and never let him come around," Longarm confided.

"He could've been telling you the truth, Longarm. There's no reason I would have noticed that in particular."

"But do you know of anything to confirm that claim?"

Norm reflected on the question briefly, then shook his head. "No. Sorry. I've never heard any comment aye or nay about that. Not from Luke or Dinky or anybody else for that matter. If Luke didn't care for the boy, he never made any big thing of it. But then, it isn't likely that he would have, considering the way most folks regarded Dinky like a household pet or something. Anyone who didn't like the boy might have kept quiet about it so as not to upset everyone else. Dinky wasn't smart, Longarm, but he was plenty popular in his own way."

Longarm sighed. He felt exasperated. And of course Norm was right. Luke Baldwin might have been lying through his teeth this morning in order to cover up complicity in the attempt on Longarm's life . . . or he could in complete innocence have been telling the plain truth. "I was hoping you'd know something that would clear this up for me," Longarm said. "Getting it from anybody else might not be easy."

"Are people trying to keep things from you?" Norm asked.

Longarm snorted. "That's one of the things that's driving me crazy, Norm. Closed mouths is something I always expect. Hell, you know how it is trying to get folks to open up and tell secrets to a stranger. Or just trying to get them to tell perfectly ordinary things. Most men, once they know it's a lawman they're talking to, they turn secretive. Don't want their own sins exposed, and hope their neighbors will be as closemouthed as they are when the time comes to talk."

"Oh, indeed I do know," Norm commiserated.

"Well, here, dammit, all I get is smiles and cheery assistance. Or so they're claiming. The thing is, can I believe all this cooperation, or are they just trying to blow smoke up my ass and hope I'll go away soon?"

"They're good people here," Norm said, "and that's a fact."

"All of them?" Longarm challenged.

Norm gave him a small, sly grin. "Real close to it, but maybe not precisely all," he said.

"Yeah," Longarm grumbled, "but how do I shake out the not-precisely crowd from the rest of the herd?"

Norm Wold barked out a very slightly bitter laugh and responded with the old-time frontier lawman's time-honored credo: "Kill 'em all, Longarm, and let God sort 'em out."

"I'll keep that in mind," Longarm said with mock seriousness. He stood, the cartilage in his knees popping, and said, "Get you anything before I leave? Coffee? Anything at all?"

"I'm fine, Longarm, really. Jeremy takes good care of me." He laughed again. "And Jonas is a soft touch at the chessboard. He never has learned how to defend an attack by my knights. Confuses him every time, thank goodness, although if he ever works that out he might give me some trouble. Will you come back and have lunch with us later?"

Longarm nodded. "Sure, Norm. I'd like that. You'll be here when I get back, will you?"

"If I'm not, just have a seat and wait. I won't be long.

Just run down to Mexico and pick up a few things, you know?''

Longarm chuckled, and went to retrieve his Stetson from the rack on his way downstairs.

He still didn't know what the hell to think about Luke Baldwin. Was the man trying to cover something up? Or had he honestly not remembered encountering Dinky in the alley where Eleanor had seen them the other day? She herself had admitted she was not certain about what Baldwin handed to the boy that day. It was conceivable that the exchange was as innocent as Baldwin noticing that Dinky had dropped something and returning it to him. That sort of thing could well go unremarked and unremembered by a man who had nothing to hide. And yet . . . Eleanor had said she thought the bundle had had the approximate size and shape of a revolver.

Longarm's question now was whether he should return to his dreary examination of undamaged and reconstructed records downstairs in the clerk's office, or whether he should concentrate, at least for the moment, on learning more about the Crow's Point barber and any reason the man might have for wanting either Custis Long dead or— A slightly different way of looking at it struck Longarm like a bolt of lightning.

What if it wasn't Custis Long whose death was wanted? By Luke Baldwin or by some other unknown party?

What if it was Dinky Dinklemann who was a threat to someone? *What if it was Dinky they wanted dead?*

If the unknown party was clever enough, dammit, they could have aimed the half-wit boy at an infinitely superior target and, in effect, *used Longarm as their murder weapon* to eliminate Dinky as a threat.

Now wasn't that a downright intriguing possibility, Longarm mused as he made his way all the way down the stairs and out onto the street, leaving the courthouse, and the musty records, behind for the time being.

## Chapter 22

Longarm remained suspicious of Luke Baldwin. After all, the man had claimed a disinterest in Dinky Dinklemann that was quite out of character for most residents of Crow's Point. And he had been observed by Eleanor Fitzpatrick handing an unknown object to Dinky shortly before the boy had tried to murder a federal peace officer.

But Longarm did not intend to reveal his interest for everyone—for Baldwin in particular—to know and to wonder about. Better, he thought, to keep an eye on the town barber without being obvious about it, and hope some clues would arise from the man's behavior.

In the meantime, though, it would arouse no suspicions among the townspeople if Longarm were to inquire even deeper into the beliefs, the habits, and the person of Dinky Dinklemann.

No one needed to know if Longarm's primary focus was not on the murder attempt but on Dinky himself. Could the half-wit youngster have known something that made him a danger to Luke Baldwin? Or to someone else?

Longarm could not put aside the idea that perhaps it was not his murder that was intended the other day, but Dinky's instead.

It would take a clever son of a bitch to work that one out. But then unfortunately, not all criminals were stupid. Most were, it was true, but not entirely all.

Longarm chuckled a little, thinking about the stupidity of the average outlaw. There was, for instance, the one who'd held up a bank in Aurora, just outside Denver. The lone bandit had shoved a note, prepared in advance, at the bank teller demanding all the cash in the drawer. He'd written the note on the back of an envelope he'd gotten a few days earlier with a letter from his mother. The envelope had carried the robber's name and current address written in his mother's own flowery hand.

Then there was the stagecoach bandit in New Mexico who came riding out of the malpais near Folsom to hold up a coach making the run from Raton to Clayton. He fired a warning shot to force the driver to stop. It worked. But he accidentally shot his horse between the ears with the warning shot, and dropped the animal square in the middle of the road, forcing the stage to come to a halt. When the inept outlaw tried to escape on foot, he fell into a crevasse in the volcanic malpais and broke a leg. That was in addition to the cuts and bruises he'd gotten from falling eight or ten feet onto the jagged black pumice of the malpais. Capturing him afterward was more a matter of rescuing the poor bastard than taking him into custody.

Longarm could think of those and a dozen more equally stupid or worse. The simple truth was that most criminals were less than the brightest creatures around, a fact for which most peace officers were permanently, if quietly, grateful.

This gent in Crow's Point, though, seemed to be one of those few who had something more inside his hat than the filler needed to keep his ears apart.

Hell, Longarm still didn't know if Dinky had been aimed at him for reasons having to do with Norm Wold, to cover up an unrelated past crime that a federal deputy might be expected to know about, or for another reason entirely.

There were, dammit, no facts, clues, or even hints available to build on. Just one very dead boy who the whole town swore loved everyone and everything and couldn't have hurt a soul, Deputy Marshal Custis Long being the one tiny exception to prove that rule.

Longarm sighed, lit himself another smoke, and ambled on down the street.

He wanted, needed, to learn an awful lot more about John Dinky Dinklemann. That was first on his list of things to do today. And if he could find out a little more about Luke Baldwin while he was at it, well, so much the better.

Longarm lengthened his stride and headed purposefully toward the livery at the far end of town where the mayor earned his living.

# Chapter 23

"I've already told you just about everything I know about Dinky," the mayor said, leaning on the pitchfork he'd been using to muck out a stall.

"Yes, sir, and I appreciate it," Longarm told him. "What I was hoping for, see, was the sort of thing a man knows but doesn't particularly think about. I mean, I know you already gave me all the important stuff. You, everyone in this whole town has been wonderful. Forthcoming, helpful. I couldn't ask for better cooperation than I've gotten here. What I'm asking about now are, well, little things. What the boy liked. How'd he live? For that matter, *where* did he live? Did he have a room somewhere?"

Mayor Chesman brushed the back of his wrist across a sweaty forehead—the morning was already hot, and there was little air movement inside the barn—and looked just the least bit exasperated with Longarm's persistence. "I thought you already knew that Dinky slept one place, then another. He didn't have a regular home. One or another of us would just sort of take him in. Then after a few days he'd go stay someplace else for a while."

"Did he ever stay here in your barn?"

"Sometimes, sure. I told him more than once he was welcome to sleep here any time he wanted. I don't stay around at night, so I couldn't tell you how often Dinky took me up on that, but I'd say he was here every now and then."

That certainly sounded right. Longarm already knew the place was left untended overnight—which certainly said much about the general state of honesty in the vicinity—because he'd ended up sleeping in the mayor's straw pile himself his first night in town.

"You'd see him here occasionally?" Longarm asked.

"Oh, once in a great while I might find the boy still here when I'd come to work in the mornings. Other times I wouldn't actually see him, but I might find the dipper in my water bucket there instead of hanging on the nail where I generally keep it, or I'd see the straw mussed up and scattered just a bit like as if somebody'd come in and slept there without me knowing. I can't swear that it was always Dinky that did those things, but I assumed it was him. I didn't mind really, whether it was Dinky or somebody else. I'm not so hard up that I'd deny a man a soft place to lay down if he's on his uppers."

"That's good of you, Mayor."

Chesman shrugged. "I'm deacon in the Methodist church," he said. "It's a poor Christian who'll pray on Sundays and grab the rest of the week."

"Yes, sir," Longarm said. "Tell me, sir, d'you happen to recall if Dinky owned more than one shirt at a time?"

The mayor blinked. "I don't follow you on that one."

"I mean, when you saw him from one day to the next, was he always wearing the same color shirt, for instance. Or might he wear a red one today—like he had on the other day when he came at me—or maybe a blue one tomorrow, then back to the red one the next day. I mean, sir, did he seem to have changes of clothes available every now and then?"

Chesman wiped his forehead again and laid the pitchfork aside, leaning the implement against the stall railing and reaching into his pocket for the makings of a cigarette. "Mind if we step outside a minute? If I'm not going to be getting any work done, I may as well have a smoke and enjoy myself while I'm being lazy." He smiled when he said it.

"Sure." They walked out through the narrow alley separating the twin rows of stalls inside the livery stable, out onto the feedlot at the back of the place where a handful of mules and heavy horses were standing hipshot in the sunshine. Chesman carefully latched the gate behind them, then leaned against the barn wall while he first offered his pouch to Longarm, then began to build a smoke for himself.

"That's the sort of thing I never thought of before," he said.

"No, sir, there's no reason why you would. But I'd like for you to think about it for a second if you wouldn't mind. See if you can call to mind images of what Dinky would've been wearing when you'd see him on the streets or wherever."

The mayor grunted and snapped a match afire, dipping his head to bring the tip of the cigarette down to the flame rather than lifting the match to the cigarette. He inhaled deeply and with obvious pleasure, then slowly allowed smoke to trickle from his nostrils while he thought about what Longarm asked. "I think," he began slowly, "I think maybe the boy did change clothes now and then. I seem to remember seeing him with different pants occasionally. I think . . . sure, of course he did. He had this really awful-looking pair of old canvas trousers. You've seen them. Those ugly, baggy things cavalry troopers are issued for stable duty."

Longarm nodded. He did indeed know what the mayor meant.

"Sometimes when Dinky would come around to hit me up for work . . . which I gave him now and then, of course. Come to think of it I could use him this morning if he hadn't done what he did. Anyway, he'd be wearing those old army britches when he'd come looking for work cleaning my stalls or putting hay up for me.'' Chesman took another deep drag on his cigarette and aimed a stream of smoke toward the sky. ''He seemed to keep an eye on my loft—on my hay supply, that is. I never had to look for him when I'd buy a load of hay.

''About the time the wagon would pull up ready to unload, Dinky would always manage to be around ready to go to work on it. I always let him help with that. Glad to get the labor, actually. He worked cheap and he was always cheerful, always smiling, no matter how hard the work was or how hot the day. Anyway, what I started to tell you, whenever he'd know he was going to be working in the stable, he'd have on those old canvas fatigue pants. Other times he'd be wearing regular jeans or maybe corduroy pants, whatever. But when he was loading hay for me or cleaning out my stalls, he generally was wearing those fatigues.'' Chesman cocked his head to the side to let the smoke from his cigarette drift clear and not sting his eyes. ''Why in the world would you ask something like that?''

Longarm smiled. And told him. ''Because if he kept changes of clothes, sir, that meant he had a place. Maybe not a place to sleep in, necessarily, maybe not a house or a room or anything like you and me would think of as home, but he had a place that he thought of as a sort of home, a place he could leave his stuff and come back to.''

''I'll be damned,'' the mayor said in an admiring tone. ''I never would've thought of that.''

''Sure you would have,'' Longarm told him. ''If you'd been in my line of work for as long as I been. It just isn't the sort of thing an honest man would generally have come to mind, that's all. But a peace officer, or a crook who's used to being on the run, we'd think about it kinda natural like.''

''Live and learn,'' Chesman marveled aloud.

''I don't suppose you have any idea where Dinky's hidey-hole might be?'' Longarm asked.

The mayor shook his head. ''Nope, I sure don't. Sorry.''

''If you do happen to think of anything . . .''

''I'll find you and tell you, of course. Count on it.''

''Mr. Mayor, I do count on your help and that of the other good folks in this town. I can't usually say a thing like that and mean it, but you people in Crow's Point have been mighty fine.''

Chesman smiled. ''With one or two small exceptions, that is.''

Longarm laughed. ''Yes, sir. Except for a small detail here and there.''

''I'll think about it, Longarm. I can promise you that. I'll ask around for you too if you don't mind. If any of us can come up with anything, you'll know about it right away.''

''Thank you, sir. Thanks a lot.''

Chesman grinned. ''You wouldn't want some exercise this morning, would you? Not only good for your health, I'd pay you two bits on top of the benefit of the workout.''

Longarm laughed again. ''Thanks again, but I reckon there's other things I'd better do right now.''

''Yeah, well, it was worth asking,'' the mayor said pleasantly. ''Damn that boy for trying to commit murder, though. Now that I need him . . .''

''I'll see you later, sir,'' Longarm said.

''Join us for lunch if you like, Longarm. We'll ask all the boys at the table and see if any of them can think of where Dinky might've kept his possibles.''

''Thank you, sir. I'll do that if I get the chance.'' Longarm had pretty much developed the habit of taking his lunches in the jail now so he could visit with Norm at least once during the day. But he knew the mayor's offer was sincere, and he appreciated it. "Good day now."

Longarm left the mayor to enjoy the rest of his cigarette with just the few horses and mules for company.

# Chapter 24

Longarm leaned against the side wall of a mercantile across the street from the barbershop. His eyelids felt heavy with the lazy somnolence that comes from having too heavy a meal. He should have known better really. But it had tasted so damn good.

Besides, he'd eaten his supper early today, and that change in timing seemed to throw his digestion off a mite also. He'd wanted to finish the meal early, though, so as to be here on the street in plenty of time.

Across the way he saw Baldwin come to the door of his shop, and through the glass front watched the barber push a bolt closed and turn the dangling OPEN sign around to the other side to read CLOSED. Longarm grunted. The front door was bolted shut. That meant Baldwin would be leaving his place by the back door. That was all right too. Longarm had chosen this spot so he could watch the front of the shop, but at the same time look into the narrow alley the back door of the barber shop opened onto.

Longarm tipped his Stetson back and dropped a half-smoked cheroot onto the ground. He wasn't sleepy now. Not the least bit.

He saw Luke Baldwin step into the alley, turn, and use

a key to carefully lock his back door. Then the man went off through the much wider service alley behind the other stores in Baldwin's block.

It wasn't dark yet, and there were no shadows to keep to, so Longarm stayed well back of the barber as he followed the man. He had no trouble keeping Baldwin in sight, though, and was sure the barber had no idea he was being tailed.

Luke Baldwin lived, apparently alone, in a small, rather tidy house in the same residential block as Norm Wold. From the outside the house seemed identical to Norm's, and might well have been built by the same man. If so, the interior layout would probably be the same also. Not a bad thing to keep in mind if Longarm ever needed to go in after the man with a gun in his hand.

It was close enough to dusk that Baldwin lit a lamp in the kitchen to work by, conveniently letting Longarm know where he was and what he was doing. Not that the information was helpful. Sure wasn't exciting either. Lurking in the bushes watching a bachelor fry potatoes—or whatever the hell he was doing in there—was not Longarm's idea of a good time. Still, the vast majority of a lawman's work was a matter of standing around waiting for something to happen. It was far from exciting. On the other hand, the rare moments of excitement that did occur were more than enough to get the pulse to pounding. The juices did tend to flow hot and heavy when there were bullets sizzling past a fellow's ears. Longarm yawned. This was not exactly one of those moments.

Baldwin took his time with supper, then came out back to draw a bucket of water from the pump in his yard. He carried the bucket inside, and for the next little while Longarm could see him through the kitchen window as he washed the things he'd dirtied for his meal. He dried them carefully and put everything away, then blew out the kitchen lamp.

It was full dark by that time, but no more lights showed inside the house. Longarm was about to decide Baldwin was a really early sleeper when he heard the sound of a door closing at the front of Baldwin's place. Apparently Luke intended to step out for the evening. Good. Maybe Longarm would have a chance to learn a little more about him.

It was easier to follow Baldwin now that it was dark. Especially easy because the barber still had no idea he was being watched. He walked back toward the heart of town, Longarm hanging a block or so behind him, and past the rows of saloons without so much as a sideways glance.

Longarm felt a trifle disappointed. If Baldwin had gone into one of the saloons, Longarm would have been forced to go in and buy a drink too so he could keep an eye on his quarry. As it was, he couldn't take the time. But a short swallow of rye whiskey would have tasted mighty good about then.

Baldwin, however, marched straight on. He passed the darkened front of the Methodist church and, half a block beyond it, an equally silent and empty Pentecostal church. Longarm figured this must be the side of town devoted to clean living, unlike the part they'd just gone through.

The barber's destination proved to be a house somewhat larger than those over on Norm Wold's side of the community. It was a two-story affair, with porches on the front and one side and a young fruit tree of some sort struggling for survival inside a yard that was surrounded by a startlingly white picket fence. The whole downstairs of the place was ablaze with lamplight, and through a side window Longarm could see the sparkle from a fancy chandelier. He could also see there were a good many people gathered in the side room.

Longarm found a bush to stand beside, large enough and far enough off the street that it should help conceal him from any casual passersby. He only stood beside the shrub, though, not in it. That way, if anyone did happen to notice him, he could act innocent as a newborn. Hiding? Not him. He just happened to be standing there looking at the stars.

Baldwin was not the last of the group to arrive. While Longarm watched, a young lady hurried past, through the gate, and into the house without knocking. Then a pair of young and exceptionally pretty girls—where the hell had Crow's Point been hiding these belles, Longarm wondered—followed.

It occurred to Longarm that virtually all the guests he'd seen through that side window looked to be female. Was this some sort of high-class whorehouse maybe? The few girls Longarm had seen enter so far were mighty fine-looking fillies, a hell of a lot prettier than anything he'd seen back in the saloons. Was this where the really good stuff was? Did Barber Baldwin have something to hide here? He was. . . .

Longarm's train of thought was interrupted by a peal of music. Piano. Loud. Ah, they were getting down to it now, he bet. Of course. Longarm wondered if the line of duty would require him to go look further into this place of, um, business. Strictly of necessity, of course, and only for the benefit of his old pal Norm.

Before the answer came to him—perhaps fortunately—Longarm recognized the tune that was being played.

"Amazing Grace." There was no mistaking it.

And moments later a dozen voices or more were raised in sweet song.

Choir practice. Luke Baldwin and all these young lovelies were gathered for a mid-week choir practice.

Longarm decided he wasn't going to gather much dirt on Barber Baldwin tonight.

He lit a cheroot—there was no point in worrying about

drawing attention to himself with the flare of a match now—and wandered back the way he'd just come, leaving Luke Baldwin to his singing.

Longarm's belly rumbled. What the hell, he thought. He'd stop in for a drink on his way by. But tonight he was in no mood to play cards. He thought he'd have just one or two drinks then go back to Norm's place and get to bed early for a change. Dammit.

## Chapter 25

One drink. Two. Longarm was not drunk. Hell, no, he wasn't. Man in his line of work couldn't let down far enough to go and get drunk. Not never. Not even in a town as friendly as good old . . . Crow's Point. That was what this place was called. Good old Crow's Point. Damn right.

He stumbled a mite on the top step, leaned against the doorjamb, and fumbled in his pocket for the key. Took him a second or two to remember that the door wasn't locked. No need to lock up. Not in good old Crow's Point. Hell, no.

The tip of Longarm's nose was missing. Felt like it was anyhow. And his cheeks were numb too. Felt funny as hell when he tried to talk. Which he had tried back there at the saloon. Not now, of course. Nobody here to talk to. Felt funny just the same. He worked his mouth silently, forming a couple letters of the alphabet, just to make sure. Still felt funny, all right. He laughed a little, found the doorknob—damn thing wasn't all that easy to locate in the dark—and gave the door a shove. Maybe a little harder than he'd intended. The door slammed against the wall and rebounded, whomping him in the face as he tried to go inside. That seemed kinda funny, and he stood there laughing about it for a bit, then stepped the rest of the way indoors and spent some time getting the door shut behind him and setting the latch. No need to bolt it, though. No need to lock up. Not here in good old . . . Crow's Point. That was it. Good old Crow's Point.

Wasn't drunk, by God. Wasn't, Longarm told himself, then repeated it a couple times more just to emphasize the point. Only had a couple. Not but . . . hell, he hadn't been counting. Not but a couple anyway. He was sure about that.

He grinned. Paid for a helluva lot, though.

It was that Schooner's fault. All his doing. Man showed up to collect on those beers Longarm'd been promising. One thing kinda led to another. Then some of the other boys joined in. Longarm'd buy a round. Somebody else'd buy. Longarm'd buy. Somebody else. Damn if he could recall how many he'd bought. Or for who.

Nice folks, though, all of them. Everybody in good old Crow's Point was nice. Damn right. Good fellas. Knew how to have a nice time. Friendly. They could sing too. Just damn near everybody, it seemed like. That barber fellow singing. Then Schooner and the other boys at the saloon. Seems near about everybody in good old Crow's Point could sing.

Why, even Longarm could sing. Funny, he'd never fully appreciated until tonight what a fine singing voice he did have.

He leaned against the door—latched but not bolted, thank you—in good old Norm's house in good old Crow's Point, and gave himself a small demonstration of superior tonal quality by way of the opening bars to "John Brown's Body." Stupid sonuvabitch song, that one. Morbid too. Longarm decided he didn't like the damn thing. Sang a little bit of "Buffalo Gal" to make up for it. That was better. Happier. Helluva good voice too, if he did say so.

He heard somebody laughing. Not him. He was pretty sure about that. "What th' hell 're you laughin' at?" he demanded. Loud. Sharp. His good humor evaporated and he was on the prod. Ready to take on . . . who-the-hell-ever.

"You, silly."

"Oh. Well, that's all right then." It was too. Now that he knew. "What the fuck 're you doin' here, Ellie?"

"Ellie. My God, no one has called me that since I was twelve years old."

"How old 're you now?"

"Really, sir. A gentleman does not ask that question of a lady."

"Yeah. I know. How old 're you?"

She laughed again. "Can I give you a hand? I think you need one."

"Shit, I'm fine."

"I'm sure you are, but let me help you in before you trip over something in the dark and hurt yourself."

" 'M not drunk, y'know."

"I know you aren't. Here now. Give me your hand. There. Now put your arm over my shoulder. Like that. Fine. Now we go this way . . . noooooo, not there, this way. That's better. You aren't going to throw up, are you? Warn me if you feel it coming up so I can get out of the way. You're doing fine. Oh, sorry. Did that hurt? Good. Now this way. Turn around now. You can sit down. The bed is right behind you. Don't worry. I won't let you fall. I've got you. Now let me help you out of your shirt. Longarm. Please! I have to get your trousers off. Don't be silly now. I've done this before and more than once."

"Haven't neither," he said stubbornly. "Never been with you b'fore . . ."

"I didn't mean you, dear. And just never you mind who I was thinking about when I said that. Now do what you're told, please, and . . . be *still,* will you? If you keep moving around like that I'm apt to rip a button off. Then where would you be."

A couple things came to mind, actually. He thought about mentioning a few, but was distracted by the warm softness of Ellie's tit pressing against his shoulder as she leaned down to do something with his britches.

Longarm gave the tit a hearty squeeze. Damn, but that big, soft old thing was nice. Nice as anything he'd come across here in good old Crow's Point.

"Longarm!" She was laughing when she yelped, though, so he did too. He gave the tit another honk. "Stop that."

"Yes, ma'am." He gave her his very best contrite look. He could look just contrite as all billy-hell when he wanted to. Damn shame it was so dark in the bedroom so she couldn't see how nice and contrite he looked. He used both hands and gave each of those beauties a squeeze.

"Longarm! Really. Please stop."

Remorse rushed through him, bringing a stinging heat into his cheeks and a deep sadness into his chest. "I'm awful sorry, Ellie," he moaned.

"All right. I forgive you. Now cooperate with me a little here, will you, please? Can you lean back so I can get to this top button? That's better. Now lift your butt. I can't pull your pants off with you sitting on them. There that's . . . oh, darn. I forgot your boots. Hold still. No, don't fall. Please don't fall. You can lean on me. It's all right. Let me get . . . there. Now the other one. Good. Now the pants. All right. Feel better? Of course you do. Now lie down . . . no, dear, don't close your eyes. The room will get all swimmy and start to spin. Keep one eye open. And one foot on the floor. Can you do that for me?"

For some reason—he couldn't quite figure out why—she was laughing again.

Wasn't important why anyway, he decided after giving

it some thought. He was in the bed. That was the main thing. It was all right now. Everything was just fine. He'd lie here for a few minutes and then he'd feel his own self again, chipper and ready for anything, and then he could sit up and behave like a proper host for old Ellie.

That was what he'd do, all right.

Just rest. A couple minutes. That's all he needed.

Then he'd see what his pal Norm's woman was doing here in the middle of the damn night.

But not right now. . . . a few minutes. That was all he needed.

From somewhere in the distance Longarm heard a low rattle that he rather dimly recognized as a snore. He had no idea who was making the sound, and after a few seconds more he didn't care.

# Chapter 26

His mouth tasted like goose shit, hammers kept striking his forehead while a vise cranked tighter and tighter on his temples, and there was hair growing on his tongue. Apart from those few small details, Longarm felt just fine.

It was, he guessed, still some hours before daylight. He determined that on the basis of how bad he had to piss. He was hurting, but not yet to the point of rupture. After a night of beer-and-rye shooters, he would either have to get up before dawn or piss the bed. The choice would've been clear. So it was maybe three, four o'clock, he guessed with a yawn that rattled his teeth and made his head ache all the worse.

He went to pull the sheet back so he could stand up . . . and ran into a long, lumpy obstruction that had gone previously unnoticed.

Longarm was, it seemed, not entirely alone.

Closer inspection disclosed that his companion for the night was—was he still drunk and seeing things, or was this somehow true?—Mrs. Eleanor Fitzpatrick, sometime lady friend and nocturnal playmate of his old buddy Norm.

This was not . . . not exactly what he'd expected.

Longarm blinked. The question now was what the hell to do about it.

Later.

But first he had to get up and find the thunder mug, and be mighty damn quick about it lest he wake the lady by bathing her backside—she was sleeping soundly on one side, her back to him—in warm urine.

Longarm figured that could be considered an impolite way to reward the concern she'd shown him thus far, and crawled carefully backward off the foot of the bed so as not to jostle the sleeping woman.

He was still wondering just what in hell she was doing there when he finished with what was necessary and stood stark naked in the middle of the moonlit bedroom trying to work out why Eleanor might be there and what he should do next.

She was, dammit, Norm's woman. Was she trying to be nice to him for Norm's sake? Take care of him? He supposed she might have remained close by out of some sense of concern for his well-being, might have been afraid he was sick or something. She could have been sitting on the side of the bed keeping watch over him, say, and fallen asleep kinda by accident.

Longarm considered that possibility. But only until he noticed that the foot he could see sticking out from under the sheet on this side was bare. A woman didn't generally take her shoes and stockings off if she was keeping a nursing watch over a casual friend.

But if it wasn't something as innocent as that, then . . .

Longarm eased a little closer, gently picked up the edge of the sheet, and lifted.

Eleanor was as bare as a hard-boiled egg. And considerably more interesting to look at.

Longarm pulled the sheet the rest of the way back and spent a few moments admiring the scenery.

Eleanor was even better looking naked than she was with clothes on. And not just every woman could make a claim like that, although few enough of them seemed to realize it.

Those huge knockers were more than big; they were also firm and shapely, with unusually long nipples set atop rather large pink circles of areolae. Her waist was naturally small, at least in comparison with the rest of her overlarge frame. If she used a corset, it was a matter of fashion and not necessity.

Her upper belly was flat and firm, the lower stomach only slightly rounded before it disappeared into a soft thatch of dark brown curls.

Her hair had been unpinned and let down for the night. Brushed out too, he guessed from the appearance, although that would imply that she'd taken some time to prepare herself for bed. The hair lay in soft waves spread across her pillow. Had she been standing, he figured it would fall all the way to her waist, or close enough to it that the difference wouldn't matter.

Her thighs were somewhat on the heavy side, but again, that was mostly in proportion to the overall size of her. This was a very large female person in pretty much every respect that he could see.

Her eyes were. . . .

Longarm blinked. And looked again.

Her eyes were wide open, that was what they were.

Eleanor realized she'd been caught looking—her own attention seemed to be focused pretty much on the territory south of Longarm's belly button—and commenced to smile.

"You look like a cat that's got the canary cage open," he said.

"Meow," she told him.

"Should I ask why you're here?"

"Do you need to?"

"I got to admit to wondering," he confessed.

"I wasn't going to stay. Then when I undressed you . . ." Very deliberately, she looked at the cock that was dangling there for all the world to admire. "What did you do, rob a horse to get something that size?"

"Just a pony."

Eleanor kept her eyes on it and slowly, boldly, licked her lips. "Lucky me," she said.

The woman had an effect on him, no doubt about it. He could have denied it, of course. But he didn't think she would much believe him. Not when the evidence was growing and growing and then some.

"Come here," Eleanor instructed, her voice low and husky.

"Say please." He didn't know why he was all of a sudden feeling perverse. But he kinda was.

"Yes, sir," she said contritely. "Please." She lifted her eyes for a moment to meet his, smiled, and then looked back at his cock, which by now was standing to rigid attention with a parade-ground posture. "Please come give me a taste of that beautiful thing."

"Since you ask so nice," he said. And stepped half a pace closer.

# Chapter 27

Longarm arched his back, driving his hips upward. He didn't mean to. Didn't want to. He just couldn't help himself. It felt so damn good, what Eleanor was doing to him.

She had him deep in her mouth. No, that wasn't exactly right really. Where he was was deep into her throat. All the way in. He could feel her lips wrapped hard and tight at the base of his balls, her nose nuzzling the hair on his balls—the thought came to him that that probably tickled like crazy—while at the same time she used the fingertips of one hand to lightly stroke his scrotum, and with the other hand, her arm wrapped around and under his butt, she was gently dragging a fingernail across his asshole.

The combined sensations were damn near more than he could stand. Although, with great fortitude, he did manage to put up with it all.

Eleanor sucked hard and pulled slowly, deliberately away. Longarm wasn't sure, but he thought he just might go out of his mind.

''Damn,'' he muttered. ''That is almighty good, lady.''

She disengaged for a moment and turned to give him a grin. Her lips were soft and wet, and she seemed quite pleased with herself. That was fine by Longarm. He was well pleased with her too.

"You like that?" she asked.

"Give me a couple hours more of it so's I can make my mind up proper."

She laughed. "I'm glad you approve."

"Kinda special, that is."

"It really isn't that difficult," Eleanor said. She grinned again. "Have you ever been to a circus?"

"Of course."

"Ever seen a sword swallower in a sideshow?"

"Sure, who hasn't."

"I used to have a girlfriend who worked the sideshows. She told me about how they do that. It's all a matter of learning to ignore the place way at the back of the mouth, right at the top of the throat, where a person gags when something tries to go through there. You know what I mean?"

"Sure," he said. "Like when you want to throw up, you stick a finger down your throat."

"Exactly. Except if you try real hard and learn to relax instead of tightening up, you can learn to let something slide past that spot without you puking. Well, that's what those sword swallowers do. The fella my friend worked for explained it to her. And she, bless her heart, figured out if a man could do that with a sword, then surely a girl could do it with a cock. And it works. She learned how to do it, and she taught me. It isn't anything at all once you know how."

"And you damn sure know how," Longarm commented.

"Would you like a little more?" Eleanor offered.

"Maybe later. Right now there's something else I want to do." He reached for her, and Eleanor came into his arms. She kissed him, her tongue hot and busy, and his hands wandered over her tits and belly, and he fingered the soft wetness he found behind the curls of her pubic hair.

"Wet," he said.

"Ready," she told him.

"Not yet."

Eleanor writhed and squirmed under his touch. Her breath came quick and eager, but he would not relent. He wanted to take his time about this.

Longarm sucked and nibbled her left breast while she stroked him. He probed deep inside her with the fingers of his left hand, and squeezed the cheeks of her ass with the other. Eleanor began to moan and pump her hips.

He kept at it, stroking with his fingers, caressing her sensitive clitoris with the ball of his thumb while with two fingers he explored deep inside her. After a scant few minutes Eleanor tensed, her body growing rigid and her back and butt arching high off the bed. She cried out aloud, a sharp, high-pitched squeak, and he felt the muscles at the entrance to her pussy clench tight around his fingers as she spasmed into a climax.

Longarm gave her a moment to rest and recuperate, then once more began to stroke and lick her. Her nipples were rigid, as hard and erect as his cock, although on a miniature scale.

"God," she whispered, and quickly came again, her body trembling and quivering under the assault of pleasure he was giving her.

Longarm let the woman enjoy the moment, then placed a hand behind her neck, the spill of her hair cool and heavy on the back of his hand. He pulled, rolling her on top of him and pushing her face onto his cock.

"Yes. Give me a drink, baby. Let me," she murmured, then slid down and forward, impaling herself on his shaft and taking him again deep into her throat until the full length of him filled her there.

Once more Longarm tried to hold himself motionless, tried to let her orchestrate the sensations. But as before, the feeling was simply too intense. He could not remain still, not with all that going on.

In all too short a time he felt the rising, swelling excitement, felt the gathering force and then the ultimate release that gushed in a hot, electric flow, pulsing and spewing into the woman's throat.

Longarm groaned and let himself go limp. Eleanor continued to hold him inside her mouth for long moments, then slowly withdrew, smiling.

She dipped her head low to plant a soft kiss on the tip of his cock.

And then, no more willing to let him rest than he himself had been with her a little earlier, she ran her tongue up onto his belly, took one tiny nipple between her lips, and once more began to suck on Longarm's sensitive flesh.

He'd thought he was so thoroughly sated by the first explosion that he would not be able to rise for a repeat performance. Not for hours.

He'd been wrong about that.

Under Eleanor's expert ministrations, it turned out that he was more ready than he'd thought possible, and it was with pleasure that he allowed the woman to straddle him, taking his cock into her body. The flesh that engulfed him was burning hot, the feeling enhanced by his recent first climax, and she was already drenched in slick, slippery juices to ease his way inside.

This, Longarm decided without a hell of a lot of difficulty, was most definitely a fine way to wake up.

Hell, he didn't even have a hangover.

Maybe he'd gone and discovered the cure mankind had been looking for all these years. Great. But how was he gonna patent it?

Longarm chuckled at the thought, causing Eleanor to pause in what she was so busily doing and raise an eyebrow.

''Don't let me stop you,'' he said. ''I was just kinda enjoying myself.''

''So am I, dear. Now be quiet please and let me concentrate on feeling this lovely thing inside me, will you? It isn't every day a girl finds something this nice to play with.''

There wasn't much Longarm could say in response to that, so he did as the lady asked and quieted down. Eleanor closed her eyes and tipped her head back and returned to what she'd been so nicely doing.

Longarm did not mind that. Not even a little bit.

# Chapter 28

The tangy and entirely delectable scent of frying bacon brought him awake. Bright, full daylight showed around the edges of the blinds in Norm's bedroom. It was hours after Longarm normally woke. But then last night hadn't exactly been normal, what with one thing and another.

He sat upright, teeth chattering in the restrained impulse to yawn. There was a hollowness in his balls and a slight soreness in his pecker, but all in all he felt considerably better than he had any right to after a wet night out. It was the moist night in—in Eleanor, that is—that probably accounted for that. Damn, but she was a fine, accomplished filly. She could turn a man inside out, drain him purely dry, and still keep him coming back for more. Longarm could attest to that, but hoped he wouldn't have to.

It did occur to him, fleetingly, that spending a night screwing Norm's woman had *not* been written on his list of things to do in Crow's Point. He supposed he should feel pretty shitty about bedding his buddy's play-pretty.

Still, dammit, Eleanor was a big girl. And the call had been hers. Longarm might've felt worse about this if he'd been the one to make the first move. But he hadn't. The choice was most definitely hers.

And it would have taken a strong man—to say nothing of a stupid one—to kick Eleanor Fitzpatrick out of bed.

Well, he thought with a wry grin, he might kick her out himself. But only because there was more room to thrash around on the floor.

Longarm stood and wrapped the rumpled, stained, and more than just a little bit sweaty sheet around his middle, then threw the trailing end over one shoulder to keep from tripping over it.

The clothing he'd been wearing last night was tossed in a jumble beside the tiny bedside table—the lady was talented, but apparently she wasn't tidy—with the last things off at the top of the pile. Longarm dug down to the bottom and found his coat. He extracted a cheroot, then rooted through the mess again long enough to unearth his vest. He found a match, struck it, and lit that first tasty smoke of the day, then ambled out into the kitchen to check on the progress of the bacon. The smell of it had his mouth watering and his belly growling.

"Good morning." He planted a kiss behind Eleanor's ear, and got her butt pushed backward into his crotch by way of a response.

"You look like a Roman senator," she told him, "toga and all."

"An' you look like one of those Greek statues. Except you got all your arms."

She laughed. Eleanor was still bare-ass naked. Longarm decided he approved of her costume. On the other hand . . . "Isn't that kinda dangerous? I mean, if the bacon splatters or something?"

"If anything gets burned, will you kiss it and make it well?"

"Woman, I reckon I got to take that for a challenge. We'll see if I'm up to it. But I'm warning you. I bet you're the one walking funny when you leave outa here."

"I'll take the chance, baby."

Longarm spotted a coffeepot bubbling behind the skillet where bacon was frying. There was something in the oven too, although he couldn't tell what. Biscuits, he hoped. Biscuits, bacon, and bacon gravy. That sounded like just the ticket to get him set for another wrestling match with the big girl from . . . wherever. They hadn't yet gotten around to having any personal discussions. No time for inconsequentials like that. Longarm found a mug and helped himself to coffee, then poured another for Eleanor.

"Why don't you set the table for me, dear? This will be ready in a few minutes."

Longarm grunted and laid out places for two, then settled down comfortable and sassy, to enjoy the coffee and the rest of his smoke while admiring Eleanor naked in full daylight. Lordy, but she did have a round, plump, almighty pretty ass. He definitely liked what he saw.

Liked the way she acted afterward too. Eleanor was not a lady to squander time, nor was she sidetracked by unimportant details like clearing the table or washing dishes. Her thoughts were fixed on one thing, and they both hadn't much more than swallowed their last bites of food, nor drained off those last swallows of coffee, before she was reaching under the bedsheet toga in search of a pecker to play with.

Damned if she didn't find one too. Longarm didn't mind a little bit when she gave it a tug and pulled him back into the bedroom with it.

Didn't mind it either when, several hours later, Eleanor rolled over and said, "I hope you won't mind if I have to spend the day here."

"Mmm?"

"I overslept this morning, dear. But gracious, I can't be seen leaving this house. The whole town would know about it in ten minutes. Less, probably. I'll just have to stay here until after dark. Is that all right?"

Longarm grinned. "Does that mean you'll still be here

to cook me some supper?" The grin got wider. "And maybe grease my skids for dessert?"

"Don't tell me you can still be thinking about sex that quick again?"

"That quick?" he returned. "Hell, lady, I'm thinking about it again right *now,* never mind what might could happen tonight."

"Longarm, dear, I do like the way you think. Is it all right if I stay here then?"

"Yeah, I reckon so."

"Norman wouldn't mind." She giggled. "I've had to do it before a few times. When we've gotten carried away and . . . you know."

"Sure. I know."

She made a face. "I shouldn't have brought that up, should I?"

"I didn't say anything."

"No, but I can see it in your face. You disapprove of me."

"No, Eleanor. If I disapprove of anybody it's me, not you. But what's done is done. An' I expect I wouldn't take it back even if I could. I like you. You're straightforward." He softened his expression with a smile. "An' you're a damn fine fuck too if I do say so. No, I wouldn't change it now. But the man's my friend. I can't help feeling that I did him wrong here."

"Norman is my friend too, dear. I love him. No, don't look at me like that, I really do. Enjoying this time with you doesn't take anything away from that. And after all, what I have with Norman is love. What you and I have is sex. Delightful sex. Great sex. But that's all it is, Longarm, dear, is sex. I hope you understand the difference."

"That sounds like something the man oughta say."

"If you disapprove of me, dear, I can get dressed and march right on out of here. The town can say whatever they damn please. Just tell me if that is what you want."

He looked at her, and decided that damned if Eleanor

didn't actually mean that. It surprised him.

He answered her by wrapping her up in a bear hug that would have broken a smaller woman's ribs. He planted a kiss on her that was intended to curl her toes—and very likely did—then gave her right tit a squeeze for good measure. "All right?" he asked.

Eleanor laughed. "All right. But dear."

"Yes?"

"Before you go off to chase villains or whatever it is you deputy marshals do, I want to make out a grocery list. There are some things I want you to pick up while you're out. For supper. I can cook as good as I fuck." She showed him a dimple. "Maybe better."

"Nobody could cook that good," he swore. "But I'll give you a chance to prove your point this evening. Make out your list while I get dressed." He smiled. "But make sure you're still bare naked when I get back here this afternoon."

"It's a promise," she told him.

Eleanor went off in search of paper and a pencil for her list, while Longarm sorted out the mess she'd made of his clothing and dressed himself ready to face the day at—he dragged the Ingersoll out of his vest pocket and checked the time—at 11:23 A.M. precisely.

It was, he thought, one hell of a time to be starting one's day.

# Chapter 29

It was fairly early to be quitting for the day, not yet quite five, but what the hell. It hadn't been much of a day anyway. He'd found half a dozen folks who agreed with the mayor that Dinky Dinklemann kept changes of clothes someplace. None of them had the least idea where Dinky's hole-up might have been. It wasn't the sort of question anyone bothered to wonder about, not right up until the moment when Longarm asked them about it. No one even bothered to take a guess. Dinky's private place could have been anywhere, several said, indoors or out. Anywhere within a couple miles of town even, for the boy walked incessantly.

Unproductive as the day had been, though, Longarm had higher hopes for the evening. He stopped at the butcher's and got the couple pounds of lean pork chops Eleanor asked for on her list, then went by the greengrocer's for the few other items she'd written down. He was careful to remember that he shouldn't show either of the merchants the actual list he was buying from. After all, they might well recognize the handwriting, and that would give Eleanor away for—as he was sure the small-town folks here would think it—a wanton woman. It was the least he could do to repay the pleasures she'd already given him . . . and the additional ones he had every intention of collecting after supper.

He carried the groceries into Norm's little house, and let out a soft whistle to let Eleanor know he was back. She appeared seconds later, a broad smile lighting up her features, at the kitchen door.

And just as he'd requested, the smile was the only thing she was wearing.

"What a helluva sight to come home to," he said with a grin.

"Is that a complaint?"

"Not hardly." He wrapped her up in his arms and did his best to lick her tonsils. Eleanor began to wriggle, rubbing her belly hard against the erection that immediately swelled inside his drawers.

"No," she allowed, "I guess maybe it wasn't a complaint after all. Not with a reaction like that." She bent down and planted a brief kiss over the bulge at his crotch, then relieved him of the sack of food. "Did Ezra have lean chops like I asked for?"

"Romantic, ain't you," he said.

"Oh, don't worry. We'll get to that, I promise."

"He trimmed them to order," Longarm said. "They look fine to me."

"You do like pork, I hope."

"Damn right."

"Then make yourself comfortable in the parlor while I fix dinner. Will you have brandy or would you prefer coffee?"

"Coffee," he said, not bothering to explain his distaste for the sweet, prissy brandy.

"I'll bring it to you in a minute then. Go along now. And stay out of my way."

"Yes, ma'am," he said, mock seriously.

There wasn't much of anything in Norm's limited collection of old newspapers and magazines that Longarm found of interest, but he made do. From out in the kitchen he could hear thumping and banging so loud he had to sneak back there and take a peek. Eleanor, for reasons entirely unknown to Custis Long, had cut the bone away from the meat of the pork chops—damn shame, he thought; he liked to gnaw on a bone near as much as your average hound did—and was beating the hell out of it with a wooden mallet. That didn't make a hell of a lot of sense to him. But then Longarm never made any claims to superior talents in the kitchen. He tiptoed back to the parlor and settled down to read a copy of the *Police Gazette* that he'd first read at least two months ago. The articles hadn't gotten any better with age.

"It's on the table," Eleanor called after a considerable passage of time.

Now she was wearing an apron over her otherwise bare hide. Longarm was pleased to note that she removed it before she allowed him to hold her chair and seat her at Norm's kitchen table.

Longarm looked around, more than a little bit puzzled. "Where's the pork chops?"

"Here, of course." She pointed to a shallow dish that held some yellowish brown stuff that looked unpleasantly like watery baby shit. With lumps.

"What the . . . I mean, uh, what's that?" he asked just as polite and nice as he could while he tentatively sat and sniffed at the sharp, vinegary aroma that came off the dish.

"Medallions of cochon en Bernaise."

It sure looked like something you'd find underneath a coach, all right. He didn't say so. One of the things a man learned—or damn sure better learn—was that sometimes in order to have one's ashes hauled, one had to keep one's mouth closed. This, he reckoned, was one of those times.

Longarm forced a bright and cheerful smile and tucked his napkin into his shirt collar. "Give me lots of it, if you please."

• • •

"You didn't eat much. Are you feeling all right?" Eleanor asked.

"Fine. I was just feelin' in a hurry to get your pretty ass off that chair and onto the bed."

She smiled. And opened her arms and legs wide for him.

Longarm obliged, mounting her with eager pleasure. This, he decided, was worth waiting for. Even though she'd taken some perfectly good pork chops and ruined them. This, though, was all right.

An hour or so later, Longarm crumpled a pillow into an untidy wad and propped up on it against the headboard. Eleanor peed, used a damp cloth to clean herself, and then thoughtfully fetched a cheroot, match, and rusting jar lid he could use as an ashtray. "I haven't asked about your day yet, dear. Are you getting anywhere?"

"With what exactly?"

She trimmed the twist off the end of the cheroot and handed it to him, then struck the match and held that for him too. The woman wasn't just good in bed; she was useful in other ways too. But he didn't tell her that. He was old enough to know better.

"You know. Clearing Norman's name. Finding out about Dinky. Everything."

Longarm shrugged. "I feel like all I'm finding so far is dead ends." He told her his theory about Dinky, that perhaps it was the boy whose death was wanted by someone as yet unknown, and about his search for Dinky's private place, whatever and wherever that might have been.

"That's only a what-if, though," he said.

"A what-if? I don't understand the term."

"Unfortunately a whole lotta law work is just that. You don't have any damn idea what's happened, so you make up some ideas about what if this happened, or what if that person wanted that, or . . . anything. A lot of the time what you gotta do is look under all the rocks you can find an' depend on plain luck to turn up a worm or two.''

''Will you keep looking into Dinky and his doings?''

''Some, I suppose. I don't exactly have anything better to do at the moment. Except go back to the courthouse an' go through some more records.''

''I thought you already did that,'' she said.

''Yeah, I finished with the county records. I suppose I should look at the town records too. I mean, some of them were in that same cabinet. Maybe I'll get some ideas outa those.'' He made a face. ''Sure as hell is boring work, though. Sometimes I think it'd be better to take a whipping than have to sit the whole day bent over a desk looking at stuff that I don't understand to begin with.''

Eleanor was sympathetic. But no more helpful than she'd already been. ''That thing I told you about Mr. Baldwin didn't help?'' she asked.

''Not so far. I really don't expect it to. He doesn't seem the type.''

''Oh, dear. And I was so hoping I could be a help to you,'' she said, her expression a comic exaggeration of sadness.

He kissed her and said, ''Believe me, lady, you're a help.''

''I was hoping for something a little more constructive than a good fuck or two.''

''A good fuck or two?'' he asked. ''Which times weren't good?''

Eleanor laughed. ''I can't say yet, dear. I still need a few more to compare them with.''

''Yes, I reckon you do at that,'' Longarm admitted. ''Whyn't we do something to get to work on that?'' He reached for her.

Along about one o'clock in the morning, when both of them were so sated they were sore, Eleanor licked the limp, shriveled thing that used to be a tall, proud cock. "Good-bye, pretty thing," she whispered.

"Where're you off to?" he asked sleepily.

"Home, that's where. I can't allow myself to fall asleep here tonight. I have a business to run, you know, and I never even opened my doors yesterday. What will people think?"

"Ah, they'll think you're on the rag. They could think that two days in a row, you know."

"Don't tempt me, dear." She smiled. "But seriously, I do have to go home now. I can't hide in here forever. Although now that I think about it, there could be worse things than that."

She left the bed and began dressing. She looked fine with clothes on too. But best without them. Eleanor liked it when he told her so. "Now where are you going?" she asked as Longarm too crawled off the sheets and began pulling clothes on.

"It's the middle of the night. I'll walk you home."

"You don't have to do that."

"No, I expect I don't. But I want to. I'll feel bad about it if I don't."

"All right then." She gave him a kiss—not too many women could do that without having to go up onto their toes—and picked up her handbag. "We'll go out the back. It isn't far."

It turned out that Eleanor lived not more than a hundred yards away, in the same block as Norm's house, but facing the street behind his. Convenient, Longarm thought, and wondered which had come first, the choice of houses or the affair. Not that it was any of his business.

He walked with her to her back door, and waited outside until she was safely indoors and he heard the bolt drawn shut against intruders, then ambled back the way they'd come, across weedy backyards that enabled Eleanor to come and go without ever having to go out onto the road. She had to cross the alley that ran through the middle of the residential block, but otherwise was able to stay mostly among sheds and tall shrubbery that would keep her nighttime travels from being obvious to the people who lived nearby.

Longarm found the back of Norm's property, and turned beside the tumbledown shed that he assumed was the one Norm had spoken of where the incriminating evidence was found. It occurred to Longarm that he hadn't yet investigated the site. Not that there was any real likelihood he would find anything there. Sheriff Jonas Brown had already found too much there for Norm's good. Still, it might be something to look into one of these days. God knows he wasn't accomplishing anything doing what he'd been doing so far here.

Longarm yawned. Not tonight, though. It was dark and he was tired, and tomorrow would be along a little too soon for comfort.

He wasted no time stripping and collapsing onto the bed. The sheets still smelled strongly of Eleanor and of sex.

Longarm slept almighty well that night.

# Chapter 30

Son of a bitch oughta buy a better grade of cigar than that, Longarm thought. Any man that was going to smoke at least ought to learn how to tell the difference between a good cigar and a piece of used rope. This thing damn sure smelled like rope, all right. Or worse. It . . .

It brought him upright in the bed.

Smoke? Why the hell should he be smelling smoke when he was alone in the house. And he himself hadn't been smoking anything for hours. It . . .

It was smoke he was smelling, all right.

Lots of it. It . . .

It was all around him, dammit.

The whole bedroom was filled with smoke. He could hardly breathe.

Longarm rolled off the bed, grabbing for his britches and gunbelt without thought as he did so.

Not only was the bedroom filled with thick, curiously dark smoke, he could now see fire at the window—high flames already fully developed and beginning to crackle and spread inside the house.

Longarm stabbed his feet into his boots without bothering with such niceties as socks, scooped his carpetbag and Winchester into his arms, and threw them out through the window, taking out frame and all, scattering shattered glass into the fire-bright night out on Norm's lawn.

Longarm thought about jumping through the same window, but the flames were roaring now, the broken window feeding oxygen to the fire and adding to its fury.

He turned and headed toward the kitchen, only to be met there by another wall of flame, this one already fully engulfing the kitchen and back stoop. Heat drove him staggering backward toward the only remaining refuge, the parlor and foyer at the front of the small house.

There too he saw fire. The whole place was ablaze, flames licking at every window in sight.

Longarm bent down and snatched the rag rug off the floor close to the front door. The side wall of the parlor was burning furiously now. Norm's easy chair and reading nook were ablaze, and Longarm could see a sheet of flame licking at the front door as well.

It occurred to him that a fire as sudden and all-encompassing as this one was had to have been deliberately set.

The dark tendrils of smoke coming from the back of the house and a faint but unmistakable stink of coal oil added to that certainty.

This was the work of an arsonist. It could not be mere happenstance, not and be so quick and thorough.

It occurred to Longarm further that standing inside the fucking fire and thinking about shit like that was not going to do much to get him out of it.

And he had damn-all little time to act now. With fire in every direction, and growing by leaps and bounds, it would be but a matter of moments before the interior of Norm's little place became an oven, scorching his lungs and killing him from lack of air to breathe before the flames had time to attack his body.

Longarm had seen it more often than he liked to remember, house fires in which people lay unaware in their beds and died without ever knowing they were dead, their bodies consumed by flame afterward and sometimes not at all. Either way, dead was dead for eternity. It wasn't something Longarm was ready to try out just yet.

He wrapped the gritty, mud-smeared rug tight around his head as a protection against the flames, then pointed himself at the front door and made a blind, bull-like charge.

Longarm's shoulder smashed into wood. He heard glass break, and felt heat wash across his bare shoulders and his upraised arms.

Something, the remnants of the door he supposed, held him back for a moment. He drove forward with his legs, forcing his weight through the obstruction.

Trying not to breathe, above all not to inhale the deadly flames, Longarm bulled his way outdoors.

He fell, losing his footing as his headlong dash drove him across the porch and off it.

Pain shot through his left shoulder as, twisting, he landed on the flagstones laid as a walkway at the front of Norm's place.

He could smell scorched grass and overheated earth . . . and fresh, clean, mercifully smoke-free air.

Behind him the fire roared, taking on a life of its own as it continued to intensify, continued to consume every flammable scrap of the house.

But that was behind him. Cool, sweet air surrounded Longarm now. He crawled forward, ignoring the pain in his shoulder, breathing deep of the untainted air, trying to pay no mind to the heat that baked through the cloth of his trousers from the fire so close behind him.

He threw the rug aside and staggered to his feet.

Several blocks away, from the direction of the business district, Longarm could hear the strident clang of alarm bells and, almost immediately afterward, the higher-pitched small bells of the fire company's hand-pulled pump and wheeled barrels of water.

Someone had seen. The community was coming to fight the pestilence that could destroy an entire town in one greedy gulp if allowed to go unchecked.

Longarm looked at the flames rising twenty, thirty feet above the level of Norm's roof. Experience told him that the fire company need not hurry. Not so far as Norm's place was concerned. When they arrived their emphasis would properly be placed on drenching the roofs and facing walls of nearby structures to save them and keep the fire from spreading any further.

It had been . . . Longarm could not be certain. Only a scant few minutes, he thought, from the first whiff of smoke to this gigantic conflagration that now engulfed virtually everything Norm Wold owned in this imperfect world.

Only minutes, perhaps not more than moments. Someone, damn them, had done one hell of an efficient job of starting this blaze.

They'd set fires on all sides of the house, concentrating on the window openings and back door.

If there was any one area less affected, Longarm saw, it was at the front.

Thank goodness. It was that slightly less intense area that had permitted him to escape through the lone gap in what was otherwise a solid ring of fire.

Was that a result of the arsonist's fear of being observed? Longarm suspected so. The murderous son of a bitch—assuming he knew Longarm was sleeping inside—had been able to take his time at the back and sides, but must have been in much more of a hurry to splash and run when setting his fires at the front.

Longarm considered how the job likely was done. First splash the coal oil, and perhaps add some flammable material like straw, then prepare a torch. Race around the house touching off the oil-soaked piles of ready straw or other kindling.

And then quickly away into the night before anyone could see who the fucker was.

Longarm had no doubt that the job had gone unobserved by the neighbors.

He would ask. Of course he would. But he had little hope that he would turn up any witnesses. The arsonist had. . . .

Had done this before? Longarm wondered. Norm was in jail now on a charge of arson. Would this help convince the local justice of the peace that Norm was innocent of the accusations? Perhaps there was a bright side to this after all. Perhaps it would help get Norm out of that jail and on the street where he could help with his own defense.

The volunteer firefighters began to arrive. Longarm recognized a surprising number of them, including the mayor and Pete Hankins, and there was Luke Baldwin too, puffing and wheezing from the effort of running full out while he and three other men dragged a hand pump behind them.

The first folks on the scene brought buckets with them, some having had the presence of mind to fill their buckets before charging off into the night. Those few futilely tossed water onto one side of the charred skeleton of what minutes earlier had been a tidy little home. Others hurried to haul a hand-pulled water trailer into place at the side of the road and hook a pumper hose to it. Within minutes a thin stream of water, sparkling in the light of the flames, spewed from the pump into the heart of the fire.

"Let it go," Longarm advised the mayor, who seemed to be more or less in charge. "The house is finished. All you can do now is make sure the fire don't spread."

Chesman reluctantly, grumpily nodded. "I hate this, Long. We've never lost a house before. Couple barns and outbuildings, but never a whole house."

"I bet you don't hate it half as bad as Norm will when

he's told,'' Longarm said, reaching for a cheroot only to realize that his coat and vest—and his smokes along with them—were still inside the inferno that used to be a house.

All in all, he was just as glad he hadn't stayed any longer trying to gather up stuff that was replaceable.

Possessions seemed mighty unimportant to him right now, he decided.

Longarm felt someone at his elbow. It was Sheriff Jonas Brown. ''Want to tell me about this, Long?''

Longarm grunted. ''I'll be glad to tell you everything I know. I just wish that was a helluva lot more'n it turns out to be.''

Somehow, Longarm suspected he was done sleeping for this night.

He sure did still want a smoke, though, in spite of all of it that he'd accidentally inhaled. That wasn't quite the same thing.

''Reckon this is gonna turn into a criminal investigation, Sheriff, so if you like, I can write this down in a proper report for you.''

''Give me the quick version first if you don't mind. I'll get you to make out a formal statement when we open up come morning.''

Longarm nodded. ''All right, Jonas. To begin with, I was inside there, sound asleep an' minding my own business when . . .''

# Chapter 31

Norm Wold looked like he'd just been kicked in the teeth. Well, he kinda had been, Longarm conceded. It wasn't an easy thing for a man to learn he'd just been wiped out. And through no fault of his own at that.

"I'm sorry," Longarm said, the words sounding as lame and empty to him as he knew they would. But what the hell else could a man say? Weak as it was, sorry was all you had when something terrible happened to a friend. "If I coulda done something . . ."

"I know, Longarm, I know."

"If there is anything . . ."

Norm shook his head. He sighed and turned, finding the jail cell cot and dropping onto it with a thump. He looked suddenly old. Old and haggard and deflated. It was bad enough he was in jail charged by his friends with a crime. Now he was ruined completely.

"It's my damn fault," Longarm said. "If I'd been sleeping someplace else . . ."

Norm looked at him. "Sure. If you had been sleeping someplace else, it would have been the boardinghouse that burned down. Or the mayor's livery would be ashes now, or wherever. Doesn't sound like much of an improvement to me."

"Not when you put it that way, I suppose. But if I'd gotten awake quicker, or . . . or something. I dunno."

"You can't blame yourself, Longarm. Hell, I'm just pleased you were able to get out alive." Norm looked at Longarm and managed a smile. "You look like hell, actually. Couldn't you at least have grabbed a shirt on your way out? Or is this really an excuse to show off your chest for the local ladies?"

"I threw my bag out the window. Dunno what happened to it, but I should still have a shirt in there. Socks too. I'll go back later on and see what I can recover. In the meantime, I guess I'll have to do some shopping to replace what I lost."

"Do you have money?" Norm asked. "Do you need a loan?"

Longarm hadn't given thought to that yet. He patted his pants pockets, then breathed easier. "I got most of the cash I was carrying here in my britches," he said. It pleased him even more to recall that when he'd gotten undressed last night—well, this morning if one wanted to be picky about it—he'd taken his watch, chain, and derringer and dropped them into his carpetbag. If that had survived intact, the trusted old key-wound Ingersoll would have too.

"Let me know if you need anything," Norm said.

"Wouldn't that be a fine thing. You're the one been wiped out."

"Oh, the house is gone and all my things. But I would have left most of it behind when I moved on anyway. And I'm not strapped for cash. I've saved up a tidy sum over the years. You know. Getting ready for my retirement." Norm's laugh was short and perhaps just a wee bit bitter. "Not that I expected the day to come quite so soon, you understand."

"Thanks, but I'm all right."

"Do you have any idea who might have done this?" Norm asked. "Or why?"

Longarm had to shake his head no to each question. "I wish I did." He grimaced. "Dammit, Norm, I don't know what to think here. At first I thought somebody wanted Dinklemann on me to get me out of the way. Then I thought instead of that, maybe somebody wanted Dinklemann outa the way. Now I'm thinking again that it must be me that's the target here, because this morning it was for damn sure me they were trying to kill."

"Do you know anything worth killing you for?"

Longarm had to confess that he did not. "I wish to hell I did, Norm, but I'm coming up blank with this thing every which way I turn. I mean, none of it makes any sense to me. You know how that is?"

"Unfortunately, I do know. I've been there more than a few times my own self when I've tried to figure out the criminal mind. You really don't know why anyone would want you dead?"

"No idea at all. It isn't like I've learned anything that'd be dangerous to anybody. I can't honestly say that I know much more today than I did the first time you and me talked."

Norm grunted. He got up and began pacing back and forth across the small cell. "If nothing else," he said, "maybe this will convince the court to let me out on a surety bond. Surely Jonas will see that I can't have torched my own house last night." He smiled, the expression genuine and unforced this time. "I have a pretty good alibi for my whereabouts during this fire, don't you think?"

"I already asked the sheriff about that," Longarm admitted. "He's inclined to oppose any request for bail. Says now there's really nothing to keep you tied to Crow's Point an' you're likely to slope off in the night if he was to turn you loose."

"Don't tell me he thinks there can be two arsonists in a town this small?"

Longarm didn't answer that one. There wasn't any

need to. Because of course there could be two. Or ten, for that matter, once the first one had passed along the idea for others to copy. Norm knew that. Or would if he thought about it for a second and a half. Any lawman would.

"What can I do for you, Norm?"

"Find the son of a bitch that burned me out. That would be nice. And while you're at it, find out who it was that burned the courthouse records. I'd like you to do that too."

"Easy as pie," Longarm told his old friend. He frowned and rubbed his stomach, which was beginning to rumble in protest at having gone so late in the morning without breakfast. "Speaking of which, I expect I'd best go find me a shirt to put on and make myself decent enough to show up in a public restaurant." He paused before turning to go. "Norm."

"Mmm?"

"I want you to know I'm not quitting on you. I'll keep on digging. Might not be getting anywhere, but I'll damn sure keep on looking."

"I know you will, Longarm. That's one thing I've always known about you. Once you start off on a trail, you won't leave it no matter how cold it gets."

"Yeah, well . . . I'll be back to see you again later, Norm. Might not have time again today, but you know I won't be far."

"I know that, Longarm. I surely do."

Longarm couldn't help but notice that his old friend did not sound especially encouraged by that knowledge. If anything, Norm sounded more down in the dumps than ever.

Longarm made his good-byes and headed back to the smoky, stinking heap of still-hot ash and charcoal that was about all that remained of Norm's little house.

# Chapter 32

Longarm had seen sights that were more depressing than this one. Of course he had. He just couldn't remember where or when those things might've been. Norm's house was . . . gone. Smoke still lifted off the black smelly embers, and even from a distance of several yards away Longarm could feel the heat that radiated from the mess. But if one hadn't already known that this was what was left of a house, it would have been almighty difficult to tell.

The burned-out slag heap was still much too hot to walk around in, but from the yard Longarm could identify damn few items for what they used to be. And none of those few items were salvageable.

He could see a blackened, twisted mass of pipe and rods that he knew from the location would have been the brass headboard of Norm's bed.

The kitchen range was obvious. It lay on its side, its oven door fallen open like the mouth of a dead and decaying animal, next to some more or less flat slabs of metal that probably were what remained of the copper sink.

Toward the street side, in what would have been the parlor, he could see scraps of wire and metal representing lamps and part of the interior frame from Norm's big easy chair.

Crazily, there was a two-by-four-foot section of paneling lying atop a stone pier, one of the porch supports, that still had wallpaper that was unburned and hardly even discolored. Longarm could not imagine the chain of coincidences that must have occurred to allow the entire floor to burn away, yet leave those scraps of glue and paper virtually untouched by all the surrounding chaos.

Shaking his head, he walked around to the side of the place where the bedroom had been. It was somewhere in the side yard that his carpetbag and Winchester would have landed. He hadn't seen either of them since he escaped from the fire. But then he'd been a mite busy up until now.

The innate honesty of the Crow's Point townsfolk was underscored for him. Both the bag and rifle had been discovered by the firefighters this morning. Someone among them had bothered to pick up his things and place them safely aside, the carpetbag fastened shut—he was sure it had been gaping open when he grabbed it up and flung it through the window this morning—and the Winchester wiped free of dirt and grass.

Just about anyplace else Longarm could think of, both bag and rifle would have quietly disappeared during all the excitement. Not here. He breathed a silent thank-you to whoever was so considerate and honest as to do this for a stranger.

He was especially relieved to see that his Ingersoll railroad watch was there inside the bag. And on a more immediately practical note, he was delighted as well to drag out one of his two spare shirts—the only spare left, actually, as of the new accounting—and put it on. Even on a warm day, the air on his chest felt sort of unnatural. He did miss his vest, though, and decided to buy a replacement as soon as possible. He stuffed his watch and derringer into a pants pocket, and rearranged the angle of his holster just a little to accommodate the bulge they made there. Longarm was commencing to feel as heavily laden as a pack mule, and would be a whole lot more comfortable when he could get things back to normal.

That could be done pretty quickly, he decided. But meanwhile, he had to find a place to hole up and to stash his gear. The folks hereabouts might be more honest than a day is long, but a man would have to be pretty much of a damnfool to count on absolutely all of them refraining in the face of constant temptation. Leaving a perfectly good Winchester lying unattended in plain view was asking a bit much of people.

The shed at the back of Norm's property had escaped the fire. Longarm frankly couldn't recall if the night breeze had been blowing in another direction or if the shed's survival was simple luck. In either case, the place was handy. He could leave his things there, and come to think of it, likely sleep there as well. No one would mind, and he didn't particularly want to lug everything all the way to the other side of town and move into the hospitality of the mayor's livery stable. Besides, the inside of an unused shed would likely smell somewhat better than the barn, and have fewer rodents to provide a man with overnight companionship. Longarm gathered up his things and circled around what was left of Norm's house.

He wrinkled his nose as he did so. He surely did hope the wind tonight would be carrying the stink of the fire away from the shed, not toward it. Otherwise it might be worth the trouble to move in on the mayor after all.

# Chapter 33

Norm's shed was pretty much what one would expect. It was divided in two, the left side an open bay that was just large enough to shelter a small buggy, and the right side closed off to form a stall where one animal could be contained. At the back of the now-empty buggy side there was a wooden feed bin suitable for storing grain. Someone had taken the time to flatten tin cans and tack them over all the right angles on the feed bin to keep rats from gnawing their way inside, and Longarm could see where a hasp and latch might once have hung. Now only the misshapen screw holes remained.

There was no provision for inside storage of hay, so Longarm guessed that would have been stacked outside, perhaps against one of the side walls.

The place looked and smelled like it had been a very long time since any animal larger than a mouse had dwelled in it.

Still, it should be plenty good enough for Longarm's purposes. He could put his bag and rifle in the grain bin, where they would be out of sight if not exactly under lock and key, and the horse stall would be more than big enough for him to spread out a blanket and make a bed for himself. The side and front rails would even offer some measure of privacy in case any of the neighbors wandered along the alley.

Longarm peered into the stall. Remnants of ancient hay cluttered the floor, and he could see from a smoothed-over depression at the back of the stall that someone else must have taken up short-term residence here from time to time—vagrants or the like, he supposed. Whoever it was had already determined where the roof was least likely to leak, so Longarm accepted that as good advice and put his own blanket where that passing someone's had been before him.

He took his carpetbag and Winchester back into the open side of the shed, and lifted the lid of the grain bin.

There was no moldy grain inside to worry about, although a bundle of rags was wadded at one end of the bin. Longarm wondered if this was where they'd found the arsonist's materials that led to the charges against Norm. Longarm figured he would ask Sheriff Brown the next time he saw the man. Not that it would make any difference really, but you never knew which piece of information would prove to be of interest. Ask a whole lot, Longarm figured, and hope to learn a little.

Longarm dropped his carpetbag into the bin, and reached down to rearrange the discarded cloth already there. The rags would provide a soft spot to lay the Winchester where it wouldn't get scratched or banged around. Not that he could count on the sights right now as it was, seeing as how he'd pitched the rifle out a window a matter of mere hours ago. But old habits died hard, and it didn't do to discourage the good ones. Better to go on taking proper care of his weapons, even if he hadn't yet had a chance to sight the Winchester in for accuracy.

He fluffed the rags and spread them a little wider.

And then frowned, trying to think back to something somebody told him recently. It was. . . .

It was Mayor Chesman. And he'd been talking about John Dinklemann and the boy's habit of wearing an old pair of cavalry stable fatigues when he came to work at the livery.

This here, Longarm saw now, was—or used to be—a pair of canvas britches.

He set the Winchester aside and pulled the wad of "rags" out to where he could examine them better.

There was the pair of fatigue pants, all right. And a faded wool shirt that might once have been army blue. And a tattered kerchief. And a canvas belt. And some socks that were badly in need of darning. And some odd bits and pieces of other shit as well.

Longarm had gone and found Dinky Dinklemann's sometime home and hiding place.

How the hell about that, Longarm thought. Dinky must've. . . .

It took him that long before the obvious reached up and whacked him between the eyes.

This shed was where the arsonist hid his things.

And this shed was where Dinky kept his stuff.

Kinda followed, one thing chasing the tail of the other, that Dinky could've been the arsonist who'd torched the courthouse records.

Longarm scowled. That made sense, all right.

But why?

Whyever would a soft-in-the-head town pet like Dinky go to burn the courthouse down?

That made just about as much sense on the face of it as the question of why Dinky Dinklemann would suddenly come up with a gun and try to kill himself a United States deputy marshal.

And dammit, Dinky Dinklemann sure as hell was not the party or parties unknown who'd burned down Norm Wold's house in the wee hours this morning. Dinky had been cold meat on a slab well before that event took place.

Dinky was dead and Norm was in jail, and who the

hell did that leave to be running around setting fires? And above all, *why*?

Longarm had no illusions that he was the most brilliant son of a bitch on the face of this earth. But he knew he wasn't exactly butt-dumb either. And none of this was making the least lick of sense to him.

Somebody other than Norm and other than poor dumb Dinky had to be back of this whole mess.

But Longarm couldn't see any hint as to who it would be or why.

The only thing he knew for sure was that every tiny detail of it made absolutely perfect sense to the person who did it.

That was one thing he could count on. Often the oddest, craziest, most purely insane ideas were completely sensible to the person who was carrying them out, no matter how twisted and irrational they might seem to the world at large. To that person, if only to that person, these odd and disjointed events would be more than rational; they would be necessary.

Longarm grunted and reached for a cheroot, remembering too late that all his smokes had already turned to smoke and then to ash. They'd burned up along with Norm's house. One more thing he had to do today, along with too many others, dammit. Oh, well.

If he could just determine the motive for all this, Longarm thought, maybe the rest of it would start to fall into place too.

Was the arsonist trying to protect himself? Or someone else? Was the motive money? Or survival? Either one of those could be powerful incentives to go against the law.

Did someone have a hard-on for lawmen in general, and so target first Norm and then Longarm? Or did one or both of the lawmen somehow threaten the sonuvabitch?

And the question remained, assuming Dinky was the one who'd torched the courthouse, had he later been aimed at Longarm to get rid of Longarm? Or to eliminate Dinky as a possible witness against the instigator of the crimes?

There was just too damn much Longarm did not know here, and not knowing such things could drive a man crazy.

Even more annoying was the thought that not knowing could also lead to a man—himself in particular—winding up dead if he stood back and let someone keep on making attempts on his life.

Why, a thing like that would wreck a fellow's whole day.

Longarm stopped himself from reaching again for the cheroot he so badly wanted, then realized he was pissing time away standing here like this.

He dropped Dinky's spare clothes back into the grain bin, laid the Winchester on top of them, and headed for the town's business district. He still had a world of shit to get done today, including some shopping and getting some food into his belly.

After that he figured he needed to have himself a sit-down visit with Sheriff Jonas Brown and with Marshal—if he still was one—Norman Wold.

Then, well, Longarm would see how things shook out after those little details were taken care of.

# Chapter 34

Longarm ran into the sheriff on his way to town, and one thing led to another. The next thing he knew he was sitting in the sheriff's office, belly still grumbling over his insistence on ignoring it, telling Sheriff Brown, Norm, and a wide-eyed Jeremy what he'd discovered in the aftermath of the fire.

Brown took it all in silently, paying close attention to what Longarm was telling them. After a bit the sheriff leaned back in his chair to stare toward the ceiling in deep thought. He grunted, nodded to himself, and turned to his deputy. "Jeremy, I want you to go find the mayor and bring him up here. You can tell him what's going on, but don't go into any detail about it. You understand me, son?"

"Yes, sir, of course."

"Get on now." The young deputy hurried out, the sound of his footsteps loud on the staircase leading to the street level three floors down. Brown turned to Longarm and said, "I hope you don't mind."

"Not at all," Longarm assured him. "I always admire a thoughtful man."

Brown nodded, satisfied, and the three men passed the time in inconsequential pleasantries while they waited for the mayor to join them. Norm sat with them in an ordinary chair, his jail cell door standing open at the back of the room.

In fifteen or twenty minutes they heard Jeremy and the mayor puffing their way up the stairs. Well, Chesman was doing some puffing anyway. At his age Jeremy probably wouldn't have recognized what a lack of breath meant. Longarm could remember being that vigorous. A while back.

"Thanks for joining us, Mr. Mayor," Brown said, welcoming Chesman. "Did Jeremy tell you what we wanted to talk to you about?"

"Not really. He did say Longarm has some interesting news for us."

Without explaining any of that, the sheriff asked, "Do you recall a conversation you had with our friend Longarm about that boy Dinky?"

"Certainly do," the mayor said, reaching into a pocket for a stubby, rather dark cigar. Longarm sat there wishing the mayor would offer some smokes around to the others, like himself for starters, but the man either did not have enough to go around, or simply didn't think about passing the stogies out. In any event, he lited up alone, while Longarm sat there sniffing the aroma and wishing for this to get over with so he could go buy himself some cheroots. Damn but he did want a smoke right now, despite the fact that he'd had more than enough of the stuff in his lungs not too many hours back. "What is it you want to know, Jonas?" Chesman asked once his cigar was burning nicely and his head was wreathed in circles of pale smoke.

"I believe you had a conversation with our friend about Dinky's clothing?"

"That's right," the mayor confirmed. "He got me to remembering some things I hadn't rightly paid mind to at the time. Like Dinky's spare pants. Old horse-soldier stable fatigues, they were. You know them. Plain, unbleached canvas, ugly as sin and tough as iron. These pants Dinky had were so old they'd started to take on some color just from all the stains piled one on top of another, but you could still see what they'd been to start with.''

The sheriff looked at Norm Wold and nodded, then grinned. ''That sounds mighty good, Norman,'' he said.

''Was what I just told you important, Jonas?'' the mayor asked.

''More than you know,'' Brown told him. ''Longarm found those fatigue pants this morning.''

''He found the place Dinky kept his personal things? I'm sure that is all very fine, but what makes it so important?'' Chesman asked.

''Dinky's clothes were in the same place where we found the things that were used to set the courthouse fire. We'd seen them there at the time, of course, but nobody connected them with Dinky. We just thought they were some cast-off rags being used to cover over the other stuff.''

''Are you telling me you think now that Dinky Dinklemann set that fire, Jonas?''

''That's exactly what I'm telling you. Norman here is as innocent as the ugly old sonuvabitch said he was. And I will confess to you right here and now that I'm downright glad to be able to say that. It hasn't pleased me, not the least little bit, to have a friend sitting in my jail. This one in particular.''

Chesman grinned and got up, stepping over to grab Norm Wold's hand and pump it enthusiastically. ''By God, Norm, that's wonderful. Now you can go home . . . oh.'' For a moment he looked embarrassed. ''I guess you can't go home at that. Lord, I'm sorry about your loss. Pretty much everything you owned was in that fire, wasn't it?''

''That's what they tell me. Still, it will feel pretty good to get out of here soon.''

Chesman looked at the sheriff. "Can we all go to lunch to celebrate this turn of events?"

"Not yet, Marvin. Technically speaking I can't turn Norman loose until a judge says so. I need a writ before I can release him. Which reminds me. Jeremy?"

"Yes, sir?"

"I want you to go over to the livery and take one of the mayor's driving rigs." He turned to Chesman and added, "This will be at the county's expense, of course. You can bill us at your regular rate."

"Bill you nothing. For this the buggy and horse are on me. And I'm damn glad to do it too." Chesman was still grinning.

"Be that as it may, Marvin, we'll worry about the details later." He turned back to Jeremy. "Right now what I want you to do, son, is take a rig and go over to Jasonville. I believe court is in session there this week. I want you to find Judge Meyers or Justice of the Peace Cumberland, whichever of them has the time available. But you're to get one or the other of them even if you have to grab them by the coattails and drag them away, you hear?"

Jeremy grinned and nodded. Longarm hoped the boy knew better than to take his boss seriously about that little instruction. But then surely he did. Of course he did. Didn't he?

"You're to explain what we need here and have one or the other of them come back with you. It's . . . let me see." The sheriff checked his watch. "It's almost noon now. I expect by the time you hitch up a rig and drive over to Jasonville, it should be fairly late tonight before you can nab one of the judges and have them back here." The sheriff turned to the others. "Let's plan to handle this first thing tomorrow morning. Is that all right with you?"

The mayor nodded, so did Longarm.

"Fine," Brown said. "Norman, I hope you don't mind

staying over as my guest for one more night.''

''Hell, Jonas, I don't have any better place to sleep tonight.''

''That, unfortunately, is true enough,'' the sheriff agreed. ''Anyway, we'll all convene here again first thing tomorrow. I'll stop in this afternoon and ask Mrs. Bertrand to come act as our amanuensis. We'll need depositions from you, Longarm, and another from you, Mr. Mayor. I can have a writ prepared this afternoon. Then, as soon as your depositions as to the facts are duly taken and sworn to, we will ask his honor the judge, whichever of the old farts shows up, to sign the writ.'' Brown grinned. ''And Norman, you old son of a bitch, you'll be a free man again.''

Longarm felt pretty good when he heard that. It was, after all, what he'd come to Kansas to do.

He only wished he had finished the job while he was at it.

Sure, he was convinced now that Dinky was the arsonist who'd actually set the fire downstairs.

But knowing that did nothing to explain who in town had put the half-wit boy up to that crime, or to the attempt he'd made on Longarm's life afterward. Nor did it explain away the arson at Norm's house this morning. Poor, dumb, dead Dinky hadn't set *that* fire, that was for certain sure.

There were an awful lot of loose ends still lying around for folks to trip over. And if nothing else, it just graveled Longarm's gut to know that somewhere there was an arsonist and would-be murderer walking around loose.

Still, that was something Norm Wold and Jonas Brown could look into—and he was sure they would—at their leisure. They would still be here, both of them entirely capable and competent. Longarm's presence was not exactly required. The proper thing . . . no, not just the proper thing, the *only* thing . . . for him to do now was to get his scrawny pale ass back to Denver where he belonged.

But that would be tomorrow, when all the i's were dotted and all the t's crossed and Norm was free to walk downstairs into the sunshine and fresh air again. Longarm wasn't going to worry about any of it until then.

Except, that is, for getting something to eat and doing the shopping that needed done. Here it was lunchtime already, and he hadn't yet had a chance to surround a breakfast. He stood, stretched, and stomped the sit-too-long out of his legs. "Gents, if you would excuse me, I have some things to do."

"First thing tomorrow," the sheriff reminded him.

"Longarm . . . ," Norm began, then stopped, quite obviously at a loss for words. Longarm had rushed to his defense, dropped everything and come all the way from Denver. And now Norm would be a free man once again thanks to their long-standing friendship.

Longarm grinned at him. "Just promise me you won't get no uglier. You already hurt my feelings every time I have to look at you."

"Only because it reminds you that ugly as I am, I'm better looking than you," Norm returned with a huge grin.

Longarm waved brusquely. Hell, if he hung around here any longer, things were gonna turn maudlin. He could as good as see it coming.

He turned and got out of there, his boots clattering loudly on his way down the stairs.

# Chapter 35

Longarm treated himself to an easy afternoon. With a cheroot clamped between his teeth and a good meal spreading warmth through his belly—pork chops, eggs, and greasy fried potatoes, one of his favorites—Longarm felt pretty damn good.

On a whim he ambled over to Luke Baldwin's shop for a hot-towel shave and a trim.

Longarm still wasn't sure where Baldwin fit into this thing. If the man fit in at all. Far as Longarm could determine, the town barber had no reason to hold anything against Norm or Dinky, no motive for burning official records. If anything, he seemed unusually clean and civic-minded. Yet he'd lied about not having any kind of relationship with Dinky, hadn't he? Mmm, maybe he had and maybe he hadn't, actually. There could be some rational, reasonable explanation why Baldwin denied talking with Dinky even though Eleanor saw them together, saw Baldwin hand the boy a bundle that might, or might not, have been shaped like a pistol would be.

Shit, it was all so tenuous. Longarm wasn't sure what to think.

He sat there in the barber chair while Baldwin ran a razor edge up and down on his cheeks and throat. Baldwin's hand never trembled. Longarm would have sworn to that. If the man had anything to hide, he was almighty good at it.

Like if he was the one who crept near in the night, just hours back, and set fire to an entire house just in the hope of killing a man.

It seemed fairly hard to believe Baldwin could have done that under the cover of night and now be able to shave his intended victim without the least tremor of uneasiness making itself felt in the feather-delicate touch of his razor.

Longarm told himself it wasn't his to worry about any longer. He'd done his job here. He'd come in and shown the folks that mattered that his old friend Norm was innocent of arson. Now Longarm could go home with a clear conscience and leave Crow's Point's problems to the people of Crow's Point and Hirt County.

Norm and Jonas Brown could handle it just as well as Longarm could.

Well, so maybe nobody could handle things quite *that* well, Longarm told himself inside the privacy of his own thoughts Wouldn't Billy Vail get a guffaw out of hearing a brag like that? Or Norm or Jonas too, for that matter? Longarm damn sure knew better than to boast out loud. It was his experience that once a man started patting his own back, he was setting himself up to take some hard licks.

Better to admit that he'd done all he really needed to do here and let it go at that. Tonight he would get a good night's sleep; tomorrow morning he would swear out his deposition, and by evening, depending on the stage schedule, he should be on the road for Denver and the dressing-down Billy was sure to give him once he got there.

As for this afternoon, well, the rest of today he figured to loaf, eat, maybe have a few drinks. He would consider himself on vacation the rest of his time here.

# Chapter 36

Longarm came awake with a start, his hand reaching for the comforting presence of the .44 Colt before he could consciously think about the reaction.

He'd heard something disturb his sleep—he did not recall exactly what—and did not intend to take any chances.

After all, he'd twice been the target of attempts on his life here. And by two different people, at that.

There were times when he had the uncharitable notion that maybe this was not really the friendliest town in Kansas as it sometimes seemed.

And if two attempts had been made, he had to conclude that it was not altogether impossible for some asshole to make a third.

The sound that had wakened him was repeated, and Longarm felt taut muscles relax.

Someone was walking through the alley that ran behind the shed where, since his things were already there anyhow, he'd bedded down for his last night in Crow's Point.

Whoever it was, they weren't sneaking along, weren't tiptoeing around, didn't seem to be making any particular attempt to hide their passage.

Longarm returned the revolver to the holster laid close beside his head. As far as he knew it wasn't a shooting offense for someone to walk through a public alleyway after dark, so he reckoned he'd best calm down and quit being so jumpy.

Hell, he was done here, right? Wrap things up first thing in the morning and he could be on his way and never have to think about Crow's Point again. Or about whoever it was that had tried to kill him just about twenty-four hours back.

That part didn't sit well in his belly. But he could ask Norm to be sure and let him know what they turned up when Norm and the sheriff dug their way down to the bottom of the multiple arsons.

The person whose footsteps had wakened him walked on past the open mouth of the shed. Longarm didn't bother trying to peer out between the rails of the stall wall to see who it might be. It wasn't any of his business.

His attention did perk up again, though, when he heard whoever it was turn off the gravel of the alley into the thick weeds at the side of the shed.

Someone stopping in the shadows to take a leak? Probably, Longarm told himself.

But the party kept moving. Longarm could hear him plain enough. He left the alley, walked by the side of the shed, and seemed to be approaching the back of what used to be Norm's house.

Longarm wondered what the hell someone would want there in the middle of the night. The fire was completely gone now, so they weren't checking on that. There wasn't even any smoke rising off the wreckage now, although the smell of ash and charcoal remained unpleasantly strong, to the point that Longarm was hoping there wouldn't be a shift of wind direction during the night. As it was, the light evening breeze was carrying the stink in someone else's direction. He would be just as pleased if things stayed like that.

He sat up, yawned, and gave in to his curiosity, sliding over against the back wall of the shed, the wall facing toward the ruins of the house. He found a gap between two of the age-warped laths that formed the wall, and peered out between them.

Someone was there, all right. He could see a formless, shadowy figure moving, faint and pale against the hard black of the burned-out house foundation. The moon had already set for the night, and there was not enough starlight for him to make out much beyond the fact that someone was there. Longarm could not see what the figure was doing.

He heard a dull clatter as something, a board probably, was dislodged. The person was entering the ruins? What the hell for? Longarm wondered.

He grunted. Some son of a bitch picking through in search of valuables, he guessed. Bastard. This place was shot all to hell and gone, but it was still Norm's damned place. Whatever was still in that junk still belonged to Longarm's friend. Longarm did not particularly appreciate any asshole who would come along and try to steal from a man who'd already lost just about everything he owned. That wasn't exactly a decent way to act.

Longarm pulled his trousers on, stepped into his boots, and strapped the gunbelt snug around his waist. It might be considered un-neighborly in Crow's Point to shoot folks in the night. But he expected no one would mind all that much if he scared the shit out of somebody.

Some damned kid, more than likely, he thought as he light-footed out of the shed and followed along the way the intruder had just gone.

Longarm figured to put the fear into some inconsiderate soul this night.

He ducked low so as to avoid being spotted before he was ready to make himself known, then crept silently toward what once had been the back of a nice little house.

• • •

"My God, Longarm, you frightened me half to death."

"Eleanor? Is that you?" Damn, he expected it was. And he believed her. She sounded like she'd been scared out of ten years growth.

Well, she was a big girl. She didn't need any more growing. Still and all . . . "What the hell are you doing here?"

"I was going to ask you the same thing, dear."

"Yeah, but I asked first."

"Longarm, dear!" she gently chided.

"All right. I was sleeping in the shed over there. Didn't have any place better to go tonight."

Eleanor snickered. "You could have come to my back door, you know."

"Yeah, I bet your neighbors would've enjoyed that. It would've given them something to talk about the rest of this whole year."

Eleanor made a face. He could barely see her in the darkness even though he was close to her now. She grimaced. "You are right, of course. Thank you for thinking about my reputation."

"You haven't told me why you're here prowling around in the middle of the night."

"I can't exactly be seen doing it in daylight, can I?"

"Doing what?" he asked.

"If you must know, dear, Norman and I have exchanged some . . . how shall I put this . . . some rather indelicate notes. It became something of a game between us, one trying to shock the other, you see. I know Norman kept them in a metal box. And I was afraid if . . . oh, little boys or who knows who else might root through all this debris . . . I was afraid those notes may have survived the fire. If anyone found them, dear, I would be ruined in this town. And not only for the remainder of the year either. I might as well brand myself with a scarlet A on my forehead and take the first available transportation elsewhere. Certainly I wouldn't have a friend left here. Norman might get away with it. After all, everyone expects men to act like little boys. Women are held to a rather more exacting standard.''

Longarm had to admit that that much was true enough. ''Look,'' he said, ''you aren't gonna find anything in the dark like this. I doubt you could lay hands on the box even if you knew exactly where it was. Which, by the way, do you? I mean, I might could help you find it if you tell me where to look. But underneath the surface those ashes are still too hot to touch. If you go poking around through that shit, you're gonna end up burned and not accomplish anything in exchange for it. Do you know where to look?''

''No, I'm sorry,'' she admitted.

''Well, don't worry about it. By the time the ashes cool off enough for anyone to sift through them, Norm will be home.''

''He will? Why didn't you *tell* me, dear?''

''You didn't know?'' Longarm had naturally assumed that in a town the size of Crow's Point, everyone would know by now that the marshal was innocent and would be released from the jail come tomorrow. Longarm went through the whole story for Eleanor's benefit.

She listened with rapt attention while he explained it all. Then she said, ''Why, I needn't worry at all then, right? Norman will be here tomorrow. He will know where to find his lockbox. And of course it will be perfectly proper for him to go through and see what he can recover out of all this.'' She was smiling.

''Right,'' Longarm agreed.

''So I needn't worry myself about it tonight,'' Eleanor said.

''Right,'' Longarm repeated.

Her smile got bigger. ''So I have some unexpected time on my hands this evening.''

''Well, uh, I'd have to say that that's right too.''

Eleanor was positively beaming with pleasure now. "Longarm, dear."

"Mmm?"

"You know how I feel about Norman."

He grunted. The truth was that in fact he didn't know how Eleanor felt about Norman. She sure was willing to pin horns on the man's head. Longarm felt more than a little bad about that already, dammit. Funny too how it hadn't seemed quite so awful when Norm was still in jail. But now that his friend was about to be released . . .

"Longarm, dear . . ." Eleanor stepped forward, standing close in front of Longarm. Despite the smell of the fire, he was very much aware of the woman-scent that emanated from her. He could practically feel her presence, a sense of her crossing the short distance that separated them. She was large and lusty, and Longarm couldn't help but be aroused by her nearness.

"Longarm," she repeated in a throaty whisper.

"Mmm." He might have said more. Except Eleanor's mouth was covering his, wet and warm and softer than down. Her tongue dipped impishly into his mouth and out again, and she pressed her belly to his crotch, then withdrew her kiss so she could laugh. "That big, beautiful thing of yours, dear . . . may I have it one more time, please? Norman is a dear, dear man and I love him to pieces. But, well, he doesn't have anything to compare with this, dear." She reached down and gave him a sharp squeeze, just in case he was in some doubt about the focus of her interest.

Eleanor kissed him again. "Please?" she whispered.

Longarm felt like the worst kind of son of a bitch.

On the other hand, it wasn't as if it would be for the first time. And an egg once broken couldn't exactly be put back together again.

"Mmm," he grunted, his cock beginning to throb with

newfound interest as Eleanor groped and grabbed and practically knocked him over backward in her hurry to lead him away from the house and into the dark privacy of the shed.

# Chapter 37

"God, there's nothing finer than a big cock. Did you know that, dear? Do you have any idea the effect you have on a poor, innocent girl like me?" Eleanor laughed. As well she might. Longarm had no idea if she was rich or poor. But innocent was not exactly a description he would have applied to her. Not hardly.

She'd led him into the shed and wasted no time at all getting out of her clothes and urging him to hurry the hell up and get out of his.

All Longarm was wearing, for crying out loud, were pants, boots, and drawers. Yet Eleanor was stripped and ready quicker than he was. She was a marvel, this one was.

Lucky Norm.

Longarm gave himself a stern warning to quit thinking about damned Norm, at least for the rest of this night.

Not that Eleanor intended to give him a chance to think about much of anything except her and what she was so very busy doing.

She dropped to her knees to quicken his interest—as if he hadn't been near ready to burst already—then took him by the hand and led him over to the grain bin.

"Here," she said. "This looks like just the exact height."

"For what?"

Eleanor laughed again. And showed him what she wanted.

She was right. The top of the grain bin was just right.

She dropped onto it on her back, her butt and dripping wet pussy pointed toward the front of the shed. It occurred to Longarm to hope there weren't any late passersby wandering past, but Eleanor never seemed to give that a moment's worry.

She positioned herself with her shoulders jammed against the back wall of the shed and her legs pointing toward the roof.

"Come here, dear. Bring that big, beautiful thing to me."

Longarm stepped forward and discovered that Eleanor was downright perfectly placed, so he slid into her slick as could be, without having to bend or hardly hunch over.

Eleanor whimpered a little and wriggled her hips as Longarm's cock filled her. "That's what I need, baby. So big. So hard. Fuck me now, baby. And don't hold back. Don't hold anything back. I want you to hammer my ass. You hear me, baby? I want you to drive my butt right through the lid of this thing. Fuck me as hard as you know how, baby."

Longarm reared back and gave her a few tentative strokes.

"Damn you, baby, harder. Faster. Make me feel it, honey. Hurt me with it. Break me in two, damn you. Give it all to me."

Well, dammit, if that was what she really wanted . . .

He hesitated only a moment longer. She was clutching at his flesh, her hands digging into his sides as she tried to urge him harder and deeper into her body. Eleanor was a big girl, all right. Every part of her. And if she could take it, well, who was he to hold back from what the lady wanted?

Longarm withdrew until only the tip of his flagpole lightly tickled the wet, greedy entrance to her body.

Then, throwing all his weight behind it, Longarm rammed it home. Hard.

"Green River," he grunted, using the age-old term that meant shoving a knife in to the hilt. Or more accurately, to the British foundry mark GR found on the blades of Hudson's Bay trade knives, a mark that the old-timers used to misinterpret as Green River rather than the George Rex it actually stood for.

Eleanor squealed, quite unmindful of the noise she was making, and urged, "That's it, baby. Harder now. Give me more."

Longarm did his very best to comply.

And, funny thing, he didn't think about his old friend Norm even once in the next little while.

# Chapter 38

Longarm was feeling pretty damn good. No, better than merely good. He was feeling sharp as a whole handful of carpet tacks and ready for anything. He had a fresh shave, a full belly, and empty balls, all those little things that added up to put a man on top of the world. And the day hadn't hardly started yet.

He started up the stairs in the courthouse two at a time, grinning the whole way, his boots loud on the bare, hardwood steps.

"Longarm. I was hoping to see you this morning." It was Schooner, the genial clerk of county court, standing in the doorway to his office on the second-floor landing. "Can you come inside for a minute?"

Longarm thought about the others waiting upstairs for him. Jeremy had already told him the amanuensis was there. But hell, Longarm had just left the mayor still enjoying breakfast with his crowd of regulars at the cafe. It wouldn't hurt to stop here for a minute or two. He smiled and followed Schooner into the office.

"I thought you told me the other evening that you'd be by soon to start looking through those town records, Longarm," Schooner complained.

"I did, my friend, but I'm sure you heard what happened. Norm will be getting out of jail in another hour or two.'' Longarm laughed. ''He can come wade through his own damn records. Me, I've had enough of all that for one lifetime. I just want to wrap things up and get on home now.''

Schooner gave him a worried look, which seemed more than a little odd. ''I heard about that, of course. But there's something I want to show you.''

The clerk sounded plenty serious. Longarm nodded. ''Sure thing.''

''When you said you would be looking into the town's records, you see, I had a little time on my hands so I thought I would lay them out for you. Over here on the desk you were using. See?''

''Yes, I see them.''

''Right, well, while I was at it, I leafed through a few of the books that weren't too badly burned. Like you were doing with the county records before.''

''Uh-huh.''

''I . . . this isn't properly my business, you understand. I mean, I work for the county, not the town. And I don't want to cause anyone trouble. But . . . I think you should take a look at something here, Longarm. I could be wrong about this. But I don't think I am. I . . . want to see what you think.''

Frowning more in response to Schooner's tone of voice than to his words, Longarm followed the friendly fat man across the big room to the all-too-familiar desk where several very badly charred ledger books were stacked, each of them feathered with slips of bright, unburned paper that had been laid into them as bookmarks.

''Here,'' Schooner said, opening the topmost ledger.

''Aren't you going the wrong way?'' Mayor Chesman asked when he encountered Longarm at the bottom of the stairs. Chesman was on his way up to join the sheriff, Norm, and the stenographer for the formal depositions.

"I saw the judge this morning. He said he will be along in a few more minutes. Shouldn't we be getting started?"

"I'll be with you, uh, give me ten minutes, five, there's something I got to do. Tell them I'll be right up, will you, please?"

The mayor shrugged and went upstairs while Longarm bolted out the courthouse door.

"Did you forget something, Marshal?" Luke Baldwin smiled. "I know you aren't here for professional services. I just finished shaving you, what? Forty-five minutes ago?"

"I do need your services, Mr. Baldwin, but not your barbering skills. You act as undertaker hereabouts, don't you?"

Baldwin nodded. "It isn't one of my happier duties, but yes, I do."

Longarm had expected that answer. Most towns too small to justify having a regular undertaker relied on their local barber for that. And barbers often doubled—tripled, one might say—as physicians as well. Part of their training required that they study a certain amount of medicine. Those few who went to actual barbering schools were issued certificates proclaiming them to be barber-surgeons, in fact.

"I'd like to see John Dinklemann's body if you don't mind."

Baldwin frowned and laid his scissors aside, patting the gentleman in his chair on the shoulder as if to assure the customer that he was not being forgotten. "I don't know the law on this subject, Marshal, but you might need a court order if you need to do that."

"You mean you won't let me walk into your back room an' take a look at the body?"

"Oh, good gracious, you are entirely welcome to look at anything of mine that you like. It is just that we buried Dinky yesterday. Under the, um, circumstances I thought it best to make as little of it as possible. Herb Wainwright and I took him out and planted him in a pauper's grave. Herb liked the boy. He donated the coffin, and Sheriff Brown had already told me I could pick out a spot in the county cemetery, seeing as how Dinky was something of a town pet. But now that he is already in the ground, I really don't know about the propriety of digging him up again."

It was Longarm's turn to frown. "I didn't know that. But, well, maybe you can answer a question for me. I mean, you did look the body over when you were doing whatever it is that you do with them, didn't you?"

"Yes, of course. The boy was not embalmed. There was no one to pay for that service, and the county does not require it. But I did wash him and lay him out as nicely as I could."

"There's something I got to ask, Mr. Baldwin," Longarm said.

"All right."

Longarm hemmed and hawed for a moment, then said, "There ain't any delicate way to put this. Did Dinky Dinklemann have a big cock?"

"I beg your pardon?" Baldwin blurted out.

The man in the chair—Longarm couldn't see who he was because he had a warm towel draped over the lower part of his face—came wide awake at that one, his eyes popping open and cutting swiftly to Longarm.

"Look, I got a reason to ask. Believe me."

"I should hope so," Baldwin said.

"Well?" Longarm insisted. "Was Dinky hung like a horse or wasn't he?"

"If you must know, Marshal, I would have to say . . . how can I put this . . . it is probably a very good thing that the boy was too soft in the head to know anything about sex, because a club like he carried would surely have frightened even hardened prostitutes away." Baldwin blushed and quickly added, "Not that we have fallen women in Crow's Point, of course. I was, uh, speaking theoretically."

"Of course," Longarm said, amused. Baldwin was so quick to claim there weren't any whores here that the choir member almost certainly knew a helluva lot more about the local vices than he wanted to let on.

"Is that all?" Baldwin asked, puzzled.

"Yeah, I think that's everything I need to know," Longarm told him. "Thanks." He bowed and tipped his hat in the direction of the gent in the barber chair, then turned and hurried off toward the courthouse.

"Well, Norman. I think that takes care of everything," Sheriff Brown announced. "The charges of arson are officially withdrawn. You are a free man again."

Norm grinned and reached for the gunbelt and badge Jeremy had gotten out of a cabinet for him.

"Sheriff," Longarm said.

"Yes?"

"I hate to be the one to say this. What I mean is that I don't mind that it has to be done, because it damn sure does, but I wish it was someone else that had to do it. Anyway, I'm afraid you're gonna have to put Norm in cuffs again."

"But you yourself proved he did not start that fire, Longarm. Surely you are not trying to say now that—"

"The charge ain't arson this time, Sheriff. It's theft. Properly speaking, it'd be embezzlement, I suppose."

"God!" Norm groaned.

"I'd as soon you didn't pick that gun up, Norm. We've been friends a long time, but you know I'd do what has to be done regardless of that."

Norm nodded and, shattered stepped carefully back from the desk where his gun and badge had been laid.

"Would you please explain yourself, Longarm?" the sheriff demanded.

"Yes, please do," the mayor added.

"That arson downstairs," Longarm said. "It had nothing to do with county politics or moving the county seat over to Jasonville. It wasn't the county's records they wanted burned. It was the town's."

"You said 'they'? I don't understand."

"Norm and his partner. I suppose you'd call it a partnership. Norm and the reason he did what he did." Longarm looked at his old friend, who all of a sudden could no longer meet his gaze. "That's right, isn't it, Norm? You needed the money for your partner an' that's why you stole?"

Shaken, Town Marshal Norman Wold nodded. He looked about as thoroughly miserable as Longarm had ever seen any man be.

"I don't understand any of this," Brown said.

"Schooner has the proof downstairs, Sheriff. About the embezzlement, that is. Turns out Norm would make arrests an' collect fines from people, but he wouldn't record what he collected. He'd slip it into his own pocket. What he forgot was that the men who paid those fines had to have receipts issued. Otherwise they would've known right away that something was wrong. One of the receipt books Norm used to write out those slips got misplaced, got put into the town records by mistake. That's why they wanted to destroy those records. To cover Norm's ass and keep the money coming."

Longarm gave his old friend a look that was more sad than accusing. "You fucked up yesterday, Norm, when you mentioned you had money put away. I know you better than to think you coulda done that on a town marshal's pay. Do you want to know something, though? Your partner was gonna give you the shit end of the stick even after all this. I cottoned on to that just a little while ago. But last night I found her trying to locate your money stash in the ashes at your house, quick before you got out of jail an' could get it your own self."

Norm's eyes snapped around to meet Longarm's. He

looked disbelieving. The others looked even more confused. "You said 'her'?" Jonas asked.

Longarm nodded. "Mrs. Fitzpatrick. Her and Norm have been lovers. I'd guess he was stealing so he could keep her in style. Is that right, Norm?"

Norm wasn't saying much.

"Something else I'd bet on without having to be told. You kept your money in gold, right? She knew that. That's why she was poking through that shit last night. Currency might've burned up, but she knew the gold would still be there in the box where you hid it. Good thing you never told her where you kept that box, or she'd've had it and been gone by now. She wasn't as loyal to you as you seem to've been to her, Norm. I'm sorry to tell you that, but it's the truth."

Longarm had no intention of explaining the rest of his reasoning for accusing Eleanor Fitzpatrick. This morning, though, it had come together. Including how even in pitch darkness she'd gone straight to the grain bin last night. And knew it was a perfect height for her favorite form of fucking.

"I'm sure you can find some charges to place against the lady, Sheriff," Longarm said. "Conspiracy, intent to defraud, some shit like that. Let the county attorney offer her a deal and I bet she'll open right up. After all, no jury is gonna go hard on a woman that handsome. But she won't know that. Charge her with some small shit an' put a scare in her. She'll open up if she thinks she might have to spend some serious time behind bars. When you do that, I think you'll find she's the one that made that poor kid Dinky set the courthouse fire an' then come after me with a gun she gave him."

Longarm shrugged. "With Dinky already dead, there's not much hope of laying any charges about either of those things. But don't tell that to Miz Fitzpatrick. Give her some juice to stew in and there's no telling what else you might get out of her." Longarm looked at his old friend again. Although, funny, Longarm no longer felt particularly close to this man who had been damn near a father to him once upon a time. "Norm?"

"I . . . I won't give you any trouble. None of you. I'm . . . sorry."

"Yeah. Sure."

"I mean it. God, you don't know how sorry I am." The former Crow's Point town marshal looked at Longarm and gave him a lopsided little smile. "Thanks for getting me off on the arson charge."

Longarm felt something twist inside his gut. He wished things could have been different. He wished . . . fuck what he wished. "Sure, Norm. Glad to help."

Norm Wold sighed and walked slowly, woodenly, back into the jail cell that had been his residence of late. And would continue to be for some time to come.

Watch for

**LONGARM AND THE DEVIL'S SISTER**

244th novel in the exciting LONGARM series from Jove

*Coming in April!*

## *ARE YOU RUNNING SCARED?*

Neurotic people essentially go through life frustrated. They are afraid of risks, uncertainties, and dangers of the world. They are afraid of pain, ridicule, loneliness, frustration, helplessness, illness, etc. Since the fear and terror are always great, they seek relief and security, through many defenses and strategies: they avoid, deny, hide, distort, rationalize. Just how neurotic people do all this, what it does to their lives, and how they can change for the better, is the subject of this remarkable book of psychological insight and guidance.

# NEUROSIS IS A PAINFUL STYLE OF LIVING

SAMUEL I. GREENBERG, M.D., is a noted psychiatrist with wide experience. He received his M.D. from the University of Chicago and his psychiatric training at New York University Bellevue Medical Center. He is certified by the American Board of Psychiatry and Neurology and, in psychoanalysis, by the Karen Horney Psychoanalytic Institute. He is currently Clinical Associate Professor in the Department of Psychiatry, University of Miami Medical School. Dr. Greenberg is a Fellow of the American Psychiatric Association, a Fellow of the American Academy of Psychoanalysis, and past president of the South Florida Psychiatric Society. The author currently lives, teaches, and practices in Miami.

# NEUROSIS IS A PAINFUL STYLE OF LIVING

by
Samuel I. Greenberg, M.D.
Clinical Associate Professor,
Department of Psychiatry,
University of Miami School of Medicine
Fellow, American Psychiatric Association

*with a Foreword by*
*Helen Harris Perlman, A.C.S.W.*

REVISED EDITION

A SIGNET BOOK
NEW AMERICAN LIBRARY
TIMES MIRROR

NAL BOOKS ARE ALSO AVAILABLE AT DISCOUNTS IN BULK QUANTITY FOR INDUSTRIAL OR SALES-PROMOTIONAL USE. FOR DETAILS, WRITE TO PREMIUM MARKETING DIVISION, NEW AMERICAN LIBRARY, INC., 1301 AVENUE OF THE AMERICAS, NEW YORK, NEW YORK, 10019.



SIGNET TRADEMARK REG. U.S. PAT. OFF. AND FOREIGN COUNTRIES
REGISTERED TRADEMARK—MARCA REGISTRADA
HECHO EN CHICAGO, U.S.A.

SIGNET, SIGNET CLASSICS, MENTOR, PLUME AND MERIDIAN BOOKS
*are published by The New American Library, Inc.,*
*1301 Avenue of the Americas, New York, New York 10019*

FIRST SIGNET PRINTING, OCTOBER, 1971
FOURTH SIGNET PRINTING (REVISED EDITION), JANUARY, 1978

4 5 6 7 8 9 10 11 12

PRINTED IN THE UNITED STATES OF AMERICA

# Acknowledgments

It seems that I have been learning and teaching all my life. Almost everyone with whom I have come in contact has taught me. My patients not only paid me but also taught me. I am indebted to the faculty of the American Institute for Psychoanalysis in New York which was founded by Karen Horney; especially to Bella S. Van Bark and the late Nathan Freeman.

Without Sidney Kramer's encouragement, I doubt that the manuscript would have been completed or published. To Jean B. Read, one of the editors at the New American Library, I am indebted for a superb job of editing. Colleagues in the Miami area made very helpful suggestions, and I especially wish to thank Doctors B. Alspach, R. Greenbaum, E. Katz, and M. Notarius.

Most of all, I learned from my experiences in living as a member of a family; from my parents; my children—Debbie, Ben, and Jenny—and especially from my wife, Rose, to whom this book is lovingly dedicated.

The only thing we have to fear, is fear itself.
—FRANKLIN D. ROOSEVELT

Like one, that on a lonesome road
Doth walk in fear and dread,
And having once turned round walks on,
And turns no more his head;
Because he knows, a frightful fiend
Doth close behind him tread.
—SAMUEL TAYLOR COLERIDGE

Patient: "Before I start anything, I'm so anxious. Once I get started, it's all right. It happens over and over again. I can't seem to learn."

Doctor: "Then you are frightened, not by a realistic danger, but by your attitude to yourself."

# Foreword

You do not need to be a neurotic to enjoy and benefit from reading this book. You need only be an average, normal human being beset, in greater or lesser degree, with the many kinds of stresses and problems which daily living holds. You need only be aware that sometimes those problems feel too much and too many, and that while sometimes one is able to cope, there are times when the worry or sense of anxiety is overwhelming. You need, in short, only to have experienced, for brief or extended periods, in small or large degree, such emotions as may paralyze a person or push him to behave in ways that are more self-destructive than useful, more problem-complicating than problem-solving.

When such behavior is characteristic and entrenched, it is said that the person "is a neurotic" or "has a neurosis." When it is occasional, as happens to most of us, it is said that we are reacting neurotically. That is to say we are reacting with some lack of clarity about what the reality is or calls for; we are pushed by some feelings or perceptions that are inappropriate to the actual present situation. No one is altogether free from such skewed reactions; we all have our Achilles' heels. This is why this small book holds interest for a wide range of people.

What Dr. Greenberg sets out to do is help people see the typical kinds of feeling reactions and consequent behaviors that tend to be neurotic—that are driven or shaped by dynamisms within themselves that blind them to the here-and-now necessities. He then tries to help people consider some methods for defusing those forces and for practicing other and more effective modes of response.

The reader will find himself/herself in easy communication with a seasoned psychiatrist who is humanly understanding and compassionate, one who not only knows the complexities of his special subject matter but—more unusual—one who knows how to write about that subject matter in plain language. Moreover, Dr. Greenberg draws not only from his considerable clinical experience of doctor and patient closeted to deal with the sickness or pain of particular mental and emotional distress, but also upon his experiences as a husband, father, son, student, friend, out-in-the-everyday-world person; and it is his awareness and examination of these usual interpersonal experiences that contribute to the sound common sense that permeates the book.

The book does not pretend to offer a do-it-yourself recipe for instant joy or radiant mental health. It holds up a mirror in which the reader will repeatedly recognize himself—and many of the people with whom he has daily transactions. It describes the possible ways by which what you see may be clarified, may become less distorted, by which you may come to see yourself as a person less afraid, more self-regarding, more steady. This is modest promise—one that may be realized. Certainly it is one worth attentive persuit.

HELEN HARRIS PERLMAN, A.C.S.W.

SAMUEL DEUTSCH Distinguished
Service Professor Emeritus

The School of Social Service
Administration
University of Chicago

# Preface

"The mass of men lead lives of quiet desperation." This is as true today as when Thoreau wrote it a hundred years ago. Only now we would call it neurosis. The lives of approximately 80 percent of Americans are, to a lesser or greater extent, impaired by neurosis. Except for a small percentage, these neuroses will go undiagnosed and untreated. Most people will avoid facing their neurotic difficulties for as long as they can. When they finally do face them, they may seek help by discussing them with friends and relatives, by attending lectures, and by reading. Many worthwhile articles and books have been written on the subject, but the subject is so important that it deserves to be presented again and again and from different points of view. My overall approach follows very closely the work of Karen Horney, one of the great pioneers in the psychoanalytic movement.

This is a practical book, written as simply as possible, with a minimum of theoretical and technical terms. Theories never help anyone until they are applied. Technical terms may impress your friends, but unless they add to understanding, they are a distraction. Problems don't change because you give them a different label. You are no less jealous of your brother because you call it "sibling rivalry." Readers may get so involved with symbols and symbolism that they fail to see the reality underlying the symbols.

This book is intended to be of practical help in understanding the process of neurosis and its consequences. Neurosis itself is a household word; it is used all the time by people who don't fully appreciate its significance. It is applied rather loosely as a derogatory epithet. It is a label applied to the frantic, unhappy housewife and to the overly ambitious businessman with ulcers, etc. In order to understand it, let us start with the general statement that neurosis is a painful style of living. The neurotic essentially goes through life frightened; he "runs scared." He is afraid of the risks, uncertainties, and dangers in the world. He is afraid of pain, ridicule, loneliness, frustration, helplessness, illness, etc. Since his fear and terror are great, he seeks relief and security. He uses many defenses and strategies to obtain relief; he avoids, denies, hides, distorts, and rationalizes. How the neurotic does this and what it does to him is the subject matter of this book. These defense measures produce distortion in the way the neurotic sees the world and himself. They disturb his relations with others and with himself. They interfere with the fullest and healthy development of his talents and resources, on which his real security rests. The paradox of neurosis is that the devices used to provide security do just the opposite in the long run. The measures used to relieve anxiety produce more anxiety. As in Greek tragedy, the thing the neurotic most wants to avoid is the thing he brings crashing down on his own head.

The central processes in neurosis are fear and the defenses against fear. The neurotic does not consciously know what he is afraid of. He is too frightened to be able to look at the danger accurately and realistically. It is like a man driving along in a car when he hears loud noises coming from the engine. The sensible thing would be to stop the car, lift up the hood, and look. However, a frightened person finds it hard to act in a sensible way. Let us say that the driver is afraid that he will be late or afraid that the car will require costly repairs. So he continues to drive along, worried but hoping that nothing is seriously wrong and that he can get to his destination on time. This is similar to the way neurotic people deal with their problems. They go through life not knowing what their real problems are but worrying and hoping that they will get to their destination on time. It is not an efficient way to live. To continue with the analogy of the car, we would say that breakdowns occur at the most inconvenient places; important appointments are missed and repairs are costly.

The neurotic is too frightened to face what he is really afraid of. He doesn't ask the right questions because he is afraid of the answers he might get. The woman who is terrified of divorce cannot look at her marriage or her husband realistically. She demands that her husband change, even if he cannot, because she cannot bear to look at the alternative. The hypochondriac stubbornly insists that he has heart trouble even though several competent cardiologists have assured him that this is not so. It will be of little value to consult more cardiologists. As long as we worry about the wrong things, we can't do anything constructive about them. People continually worry about things that are only remote possibilities, that have very little chance of happening.

It is a mistake to believe that the world is orderly, consistent, and fair. There is evidence all around us to the contrary. The world is what it is and not what it should be. It is a serious mistake to assume that people are essentially sensible and logical. This is not so.

More important than what we think is how we feel. We act according to how we feel, how we experience ourselves, and how we see the world. People don't really know themselves. It is a rare gift to be able to "see ourselves as others see us." The capacity for self-deception is enormous. We get angry at the wrong people, say things we don't mean, and act in ways that we can't explain. We work hard at convincing ourselves that we are what we would like to believe we are. Great anxiety can occur in those brief "moments of truth" when we see that our goals are not obtainable, that our standards are unrealistic, and that our self-image is false.

Obviously, reading a book cannot take the place of competent professional help in the treatment of mental disorders. This book does, however, try to help people develop a healthier style of living by understanding their inner fears and the neurotic processes that develop from their attempts to cope with them. Its aim is to provide ideas and suggestions that may be helpful in dealing with the problems of living. Before you can get the right answers, you need to ask the right questions. In almost twenty years of experience and practice, I have found that some questions are more helpful than others. "Why?" is the question that furnishes the least useful information. It is usually answered by rationalizations. "When?" "What?" and "How?" are much better questions. So are: "What do I really want?" and "What are the alternatives?"

Some parts of this book need to be read slowly. Do not expect to grasp all of it at once.

As one patient said to me: "You have started me thinking about myself." That is the aim of this book.

—*Samuel I. Greenberg, M.D.*

*In order to preserve the anonymity of patients, the case material in this book is a composite that reflects the experience of the author.*

# Contents

ACKNOWLEDGMENTS v

FOREWORD *by Helen Harris Perlman* vii

PREFACE ix

**Part I. The Neurotic Process** 17

1. Fear and Anxiety 19
2. Patterns of Neurosis 28
3. The Creation of an Image 39
4. Neurotic Strategies 45
5. Consequences of Neurosis 56
6. Mental Health 64

**Part II. Interpersonal Relations** 71

7. Neurotic Interaction 73
8. Marriage, Love, and Sex 85
9. Parents and Children 99

**Part III. Toward a Healthier Style of Living** 113

10. Self-Discovery and Self-Help 115
11. The Helping Professions 126

APPENDIX: *Recommended for Further Reading* 144

# Part I

# *The Neurotic Process*

# Chapter 1

## *Fear and Anxiety*

Anxiety is a warning signal, a signal of danger to the equilibrium of our mental apparatus. It is sometimes experienced as dizziness, lightheadedness, or a fear of falling. It means that our patterns of living, our methods of coping with stress, our outlook and hobbies are proving inadequate. It means that a conflict we'd rather not face is emerging. It means that in some respects we are not what we are supposed to be. It means that we are making impossible demands on ourselves. It is a most unpleasant sensation and brings us to the realization that something is wrong with us emotionally.

Fear and anxiety are both emotional reactions to danger. The symptoms are familiar to us all: the pounding heart, rapid breathing, sweating, pallor, feeling of faintness, trembling, "jitteriness," diarrhea, etc. The difference is that with fear the danger is obvious, but in anxiety it is not. Fear is universal but anxiety is highly individual. We are all afraid of disease, storms, fire, acts of war, reckless drivers, etc.: it is no disgrace to be frightened in these circumstances. People readily recognize these as real dangers and are sympathetic to someone who has to face them. Since they are clearly seen, it is possible to be frightened and yet meet them adequately and with a degree of courage.

It is quite different with neurotic anxiety, where the individual is frightened of such things as flying, elevators, subways, heights, crowds, open places, etc. These are not universal dangers but highly individual ones. Most people are not afraid of such things or situations and they are somewhat contemptuous of one who is. The individual in the grip of anxiety does not know why he is afraid. It is not logical. He cannot understand it, nor can he control his reaction to it, and therefore he feels helpless. He feels ashamed and inferior. He cannot explain why he is acting as he is. People like to feel that they are in control of their own lives, but the anxious person recognizes that he is not.

There is no limit to the number of things and situations that may trigger anxiety. Patterns of anxiety vary as widely as people's personalities. The anxiety may be general, not tied to any one thing, and therefore called free-floating anxiety; or it may be set off by a specific object or class of objects—such as dogs, heights, tunnels, etc.—in which case it would be called a phobia. It is rare to find a person with only a single phobia. Closer examination into his life will usually uncover either other fears, or a long series of phobias down through the years.

Anxiety may be added onto a realistic fear and, for a long time, go undetected. Thus, a mother who is very upset by trivial illness or when her teen-ager is a few minutes late getting home with the family car can rationalize that her fears are realistic. However, in time it may become clear that her fears are out of all proportion to the actual risks involved. The full significance of anxiety can only be understood when the person who has it is understood. It does not depend on the inherent danger in the situation, it depends on how the person experiences it. The person with a phobia of dogs will be as terrified by a miniature poodle as by a Great Dane. To the person with a phobia of flying, a trip on a regularly scheduled airline is experienced as being as hazardous as flight to the moon. In some people, the slightest change in their routine greatly increases anxiety. For them, shopping in a department store or eating out in a restaurant may increase anxiety to intolerable proportions.

Anxiety stems from a neurotic pattern of living, from the pursuit of impossible or contradictory goals, from an unrealistic view of the world we live in, and from a distorted picture of ourselves. These are the conditions which permit the development of anxiety, and only when these basic conditions are changed will the anxiety stop. It is not a localized illness like a foreign body or tumor which can be removed surgically with little upset to the whole organism. Nor is it, despite so many books and movies, the memory of some painful event in childhood that has been repressed and needs only to be recalled into consciousness to produce a dramatic cure. There are few quick cures. A period of anxiety may be relieved by reassurance from an authority or from someone you trust. It may be relieved by drugs, alcohol, vacations, hobbies, etc. It may also be relieved by rationalizing, by trying to convince yourself that it results from unusual stress, overwork, or some temporary condition that will not occur again. While such factors do have a role in precipitating anxiety, they are not the major factors in its development. Only when the individual can express his emotional needs appropriately, when he can handle his problems in a mature way, when he has achieved a good understanding of his real self and sees the world in a realistic way do anxieties stop. I believe it would be helpful to illustrate some of these points with a case history.

A 28-year-old salesman who feared flying had recently been promoted to a job that required frequent plane trips. In the two weeks before he came to see me, he made several attempts to fly. He would go to the airport several hours before the scheduled flight, hoping that he could overcome his anxiety. He watched other planes coming and going, saw the people getting on and off, and finally boarded the plane. As the time for departure drew near he became more and more apprehensive. His heart pounded, he sweated profusely, he felt dizzy and faint. Just as the door was about to be closed, he would jump out of his seat, shouting to the stewardess that he was ill, and dash out of the plane, conscious that everyone was staring at him. He was embarrassed and humiliated. After several such attempts he tried to conduct his business by car and train but found that this was not possible. Then he came to consult with me, pleading and demanding that I do something quickly, explaining that his career was in jeopardy, and that his suffering was great. Over the next few months the following story emerged.

He was born and raised in Philadelphia, the older of two children. He had a sister who was five years younger. His mother was a kind, gentle, and ineffectual person who allowed herself to be pushed around by the patient. His father was a tough, hard-working man, who was successful in many business ventures and had worked his way up from poverty to considerable wealth. He was not home often, but he dominated the family and was very strict with the patient. On several occasions he beat him severely. The patient remembers that as a young boy he was afraid of the dark. He didn't study much in school and got poor grades, but was popular with his classmates and enjoyed sports. He went to a succession of schools and felt that he was "a bad boy" because his parents were disappointed in his scholastic achievements. However, he felt that he had little cause for worry because his father was wealthy. When he was 13 his father died, and within a few years his mother had lost most of a considerable estate. She then developed arthritis and moved the family to Florida for her health. They now had to live on a very modest scale. He managed to get through high school and into college. In college he was more interested in social activities than in study. He was personable, dressed well, and was popular with his classmates of both sexes. He flunked out in the second year. For a while he drifted from job to job, but three years before he consulted me he became a salesman of men's clothing. He was good at this job, got several promotions, and earned a reasonable salary. Then he was promoted to chief of the firm's entire southern sales district, a job that required much flying. This brought him to consult with me. He always had trouble making decisions. He was forever starting things and then stopping. He wanted to save his money, invest it, and become wealthy. However, he couldn't save. On impulse he bought things which he couldn't afford. At one time he bought an expensive boat and then found he couldn't maintain the payments on it; he was forced to sell it at a loss. He had wealthy friends with whom he tried to keep pace and whom he wanted to impress, but he couldn't afford the things they could. He wanted to be a successful business executive but was lazy and not disciplined enough to work at it consistently. The success he did achieve was on the basis of an engaging personality and a flair for style in men's clothing. He was uneasy with his last promotion because he was not sure he could handle the responsibility. This was also true in his relationship with girls. Quite a few girls were interested in him, but he always shied away from marriage. Two years before he came to see me, after much soul-searching, he married an airline stewardess. She was a very attractive, kind, and dependable girl, and he felt that here was someone who was just what he needed. The first year of their marriage was a reasonably happy one. Then the patient began a series of extramarital affairs. In the course of these he met another woman and thought he was in love with her. He could not decide whether to divorce his wife or not. When his wife found out about it she left him. There were some attempts at reconciliation but nothing came of them. The patient was content with his separation. He was enjoying his freedom and imagined that if he really wanted to return to his wife she would take him back. He was, therefore, quite unhappy when, two months before he came in to see me, she got a divorce. After his divorce the other woman began to pressure him to marry her and he found himself in a difficult position.

The patient had been aware that for many years he was uncomfortable in large crowds, a feeling that had worsened in the past few years. If he went to a ball game or the theater he tried to get a seat near the exit, and would often leave before the very end so that he would not be jammed in by the crowd. He also noticed that he became more and more uncomfortable on the few occasions that he went on plane trips. If he sat near the window and could watch the movements of the clouds his anxiety was less. When he became too anxious, he would turn to another passenger and tell him how frightened he was. He was aware that he was acting like a little child seeking reassurance from a grown-up. However, he could not stop. Finally, he gave up traveling by plane because the anxiety became too great. His promotion to the new job that required flying was the final straw that impelled him to seek psychiatric help.

As our sessions progressed, it became apparent to the patient, and to me, that his fear of flying was only a small part of his difficulties in living. The stage for the development of his phobia of flying was set by his divorce—which meant that his wife had abandoned him, by the other woman pressuring him to marry her, and by his promotion to a job of greater responsibility. His difficulties in living were that he was afraid of responsibility and had difficulty making decisions. He was frightened of close and permanent ties with people and wanted contradictory things at the same time. He wanted to be married but also to live like a bachelor, to become wealthy without saving his money, to be successful in the business world without working hard, to be a respected member of the community yet to be cared for like a child. His ideas about himself and his goals were vague and contradictory; he had a poor sense of identity. In the course of our sessions it became apparent that his mother had been a gentle and indulgent person, while his father was quite tough and cruel. These parental attitudes had contributed to his immaturity; he felt like a child in a grown-up world, and he acted like a child. Yet, getting on a plane for a business trip was a man's job. It meant a destination and the discipline to stick to it for a period of time; once committed, you did not change your mind in mid-air. At this time the patient was not capable of this. It became apparent to him that it was going to take much effort and persistence before he would grow up and be able to deal with his problems, business and personal, in a mature way.

As this case illustrates, phobias and anxieties are intricately interwoven with the individual's total personality and all phases of his life. Each individual is unique, yet has many similarities to others. In the same way, phobias are unique to the person who has them, yet resemble phobias in other people. To the salesman in the case above, a plane trip meant being closed in, committed, trapped, and not being able to get out when he wanted to. To another person, fear of flying may be a fear of death. To still another, there may be so much anxiety in daily living that the added stress of the novelty of flying is too much. It may cause a complete breakdown, like the proverbial straw that broke the camel's back.

There is no limit to the number of things and situations that trigger anxiety. Some people avoid heights because they may be reacting to an unconscious impulse to jump, thereby putting an end to all their troubles. Others fear heights because they symbolize the heights of grandeur from which they fear to fall. Fear of blushing may be related to the fear of exposure. Similar to this is the anxiety of students concerning examinations; they fear failure and humiliation—that some inadequacy will be exposed that will be painful for them to face. Some people are so anxious that they are afraid to go to movies because they have no control over what they will see on the screen. Others are too anxious even to go to a restaurant because they have no control over who may walk in. Agoraphobia, the fear of open spaces, represents the fear of exposure with no one to lean on. The fear of falling may represent the fear of walking alone, or the fear that one cannot stand up to the responsibilities of living. Fear of dying may represent the fear of facing some problems in living, problems that appear to be insoluble. Fear of insanity may be provoked by "strange" or "crazy" thoughts and may represent fear of loss of control. Intense feelings of helplessness and anxiety are often provoked by feeling trapped, whether in traffic, in a subway train that doesn't move, or in an elevator. The freedom to move about relieves anxiety.

The common denominators of many anxieties are fear of exposure and fear of loss of control. Exposure may lead to embarrassment, shame, ridicule, and feeling inferior. We fear being confronted with the realization that we are not what we are supposed to be. We fear exposure of our limitations and our defects that we are not the perfect parent: that we are not the 100 percent loyal friend, or that we are not always the kind, gentle, sweet person that all our friends admire. We find it hard to recognize and accept that we, too, have traits and impulses that we detest. It is especially difficult to accept the fact that we have hostile impulses or to admit to various sexual impulses. In order to convince ourselves that we are what we are supposed to be, we suppress and repress certain things. Most often we repress sexual and aggressive impulses. It should be emphasized that repression is an automatic and unconscious process; we do not know what has been repressed. Since we are not aware of our repressed impulses, we cannot deal with them in a logical or reasonable manner. Thus, if we have repressed certain sexual feelings, we are not aware of their existence at all. However, we may become aware of anxiety in those situations which threaten to expose these feelings, although we do not know the reason for our anxiety.

In our society today, we probably have more problems with the expression of anger and hostility than with the expression of sex. When these emotions are not adequately expressed they build up and increase in intensity, outside of our awareness. What finally appears in consciousness is an uneasiness or a feeling of precariousness—anxiety. On occasion, a fleeting thought or fantasy of hurting or killing someone may also appear in consciousness. This is quite frightening to the person who has been unaware of the slow development and build-up of anger and resentment. To make it more complicated and harder to understand, the anger may not only be repressed but also projected onto someone else. In this case, the first thing we are aware of is the fear that someone is angry at us for no reason at all. We are then not only frightened but puzzled.

In many anxieties the fear of failure is a prominent feature. The healthy person who fails in some endeavor is not devastated by it; he tries to understand what went wrong, he tries to learn from it—and at least he gives himself credit for trying. To the neurotic, failure in almost anything can be a crushing experience, proving to himself that he is worthless; the thing that he fears most because he secretly believes it to be true. This is one reason why the neurotic procrastinates: he is afraid to fail and, therefore, afraid to try. And should he succeed, he often feels that he was just lucky that time, but the next time he may not be so lucky. The terror is only relieved for a brief period.

At the deepest level, according to Karen Horney, is the basic anxiety of being "isolated and helpless" in a potentially hostile world. It is the terror of being abandoned and powerless in a world full of dangers. It is the equivalent of feeling impotent, inadequate, inferior, unlovable. At its core is the feeling of being so worthless that people will have nothing to do with you. This basic anxiety is sometimes seen in almost pure form, as for instance in one patient, an adult, who was terrified if either his wife or mother did not stay with him. Beginning in childhood, underlying anxiety forces the child to build up a series of defenses and to develop in the distorted way which we call neurotic.

To summarize: Anxiety, like fear, is an emotional reaction to danger, but the danger is an internal one. It signals a danger to the equilibrium of our mental apparatus, which has become precarious. It means that our pattern of living and our values and goals are creating more stress than our powers of adaptation can cope with. It is a most unpleasant emotional state and often leads us to seek help. In order to understand anxiety, we have to understand the person who has it and the pattern of neurosis in which it developed.

# Chapter 2

## *Patterns of Neurosis*

Neurosis is a household word. It describes a wide range of mental disorders: anxiety, phobia, depression, compulsion, hysteria, etc. More important than the symptoms, however, are the disturbances it gives rise to in behavior at work or school and in personal and social relationships.

People are mixtures, in varying proportions, of health and neurosis. On the basis of the best information available today, neurosis is negligible in approximately 20 percent of the adult urban population in America. One out of five adults, then, is emotionally healthy. In another 60 percent of the population, neurosis is mild to moderate. These are people who manage to get along in their daily lives, personal and professional, but with some reduced efficiency, with greater stress, and with diminished zest for living. In the remaining 20 percent, neurosis is severe. These are people who function under great handicaps; at times, some of them become completely incapacitated.

The core of neurosis is the basic fear of being worthless, of being helpless and abandoned. This is too painful to live with and relief must be obtained—and quickly. There are three ways to deal with it. The first is to cling for help and protection to the most powerful person in the environment. For the infant, this is usually its mother. The second is to withdraw and build an emotional barrier between the world and oneself. The third is to fight against the environment and conquer all obstacles. The frightened child would like to use all three methods at once but can't. When he is finally able to move in any of these directions, and thus find some relief, he tends to freeze and cling to one method. Afraid to try something new, the neurotic child sticks to what has given him some relief and feeling of comfort. The method he has chosen predominates and shapes his whole personality. It develops into a neurotic character pattern or type. If he clings to people for help, he becomes compliant; if he withdraws, he becomes detached; and if he fights and rebels, he becomes aggressive. These are the three major neurotic character patterns. The particular pattern he assumes has profound influences on his goals, ideals, values, and behavior.

## Compliant Type

This child copes with anxiety by clinging to his mother for help and protection. He becomes a "good" child, easy to raise, cooperative, and obedient. He grows up to be ingratiating, endearing, sympathetic, and sensitive to the needs of others. He has an insatiable need for affection, love, approval, and acceptance. He tries to be kind and unselfish. He goes to great lengths to avoid criticism, rejection, and disapproval. He is fearful of hurting others, is conciliatory and appeasing. If he cannot be accepted and liked, at least he would like people to feel sorry for him. He lives up to the role that others expect of him, whether this be the good-natured, sweet guy or the clown. He is so self-effacing that people at times forget he is around. Because he would rather lose than antagonize people, he may become frightened when he realizes that he is winning. On the whole, he prefers to be a loser. He is quick to help everybody—relatives, friends, neighbors, casual acquaintances. He automatically says "yes" and rarely is able to say "no," even when he would like to. It is easy for others to take advantage of him as he finds it difficult to speak up for himself, or make demands. The compliant person is generous with others yet finds it hard to ask favors for himself. He has trouble giving orders; he makes a good subordinate, but a poor boss. He hates to send a waiter back when he brings the wrong order or to return things to a department store. He avoids fights, arguments, and friction. He doesn't get angry, rarely carries a grudge, and smiles most of the time. When someone is unkind to him he is quick to make excuses or rationalize that the other person didn't really mean it, or to say, "What's the use of getting upset about it?" He lives for others and is not likely to enjoy doing things alone. In fact, he does not feel complete without someone else around. This other person may be a wife, a friend, a business associate—even a child. He enjoys doing things to please them, the trouble being that he does too much and doesn't know when to stop. His ideals are goodness, kindness, and unselfishness. He dislikes aggressive, cruel, and ruthless people, yet he may secretly admire them because they can do the things he cannot. Most of the time, the compliant person depends on other people for initiative, guidance, protection.

The person who develops along this neurotic pattern of compliance distorts the true picture of himself and of others. He needs to see himself as a nice, sweet, kind, generous, and fair person. He is elated when he gains approval and acceptance or admiration. Except under special circumstances, he cannot permit himself to become mean or angry, because this would shake up the image he has of himself, which he has to maintain at all costs. Without it, he is a lost soul without an identity. Because the compliant character needs to be liked and accepted by others he must see them as good and kind people, not as they really are. He tries to like everybody and is quick to see the good in people. In turn, he hopes to be accepted, liked, and loved by the "good" people in the world.

This neurotic style of living will be partially successful and will work some of the time, especially with the right partner. However, it has serious flaws: the compliant person is not living his own life. Since he is living for approval from others, he has to do what will please others and ignore his own wishes and ambitions and yearnings. His energies and resources are not used to develop his own potential and to grow into a whole human being. It is inevitable in this world that we will meet with criticism, disapproval, and rejection. When the compliant person encounters rejection in spite of all his efforts, he has little to fall back on and can be crushed. When rejection comes, he feels inferior, guilty, and unworthy. And since much of his life is lived in the fear of rejection, he is often chronically apprehensive and depressed.

Another major drawback is that this type of neurotic lives in an intensively competitive society but cannot fight his own battles. He cannot allow himself to be aggressive or ruthless because, again, it would disturb the idealized image of the good, sweet person he tried to be. His anger is repressed to the point where he is not aware of it. Furthermore, he cannot recognize his competitors and his enemy. In his neurotic view, people are kind, benevolent, and good, ready to be his friends as soon as they learn what a nice person he is. He cannot fight well if he does not feel angry and doesn't know who his enemies are. To make matters worse, the compliant person is quickly recognized as one who cannot or will not fight and he is often victimized. He becomes a favorite target for exploiters because his manner and bearing reveal at once what he is.

This is a short and oversimplified picture of the compliant character type. Actually, there are no pure types, as all cases are mixed. Compliant characters differ in intelligence, interest, talent, body type, susceptibility to disease, etc. While not identical, they do have important similarities, and most of us can quickly recognize a friend or acquaintance who falls into this pattern.

## Detachment

The second major way of dealing with anxiety is to run away, to withdraw. It leads to the development of the character pattern we call detachment. Instead of actively solving his problems, the detached person tries to avoid them. Either he puts distance between himself and his difficulties or he constructs an emotional barrier against them. Seen from a great distance, his problems do not seem very large or, shielded behind a barrier, he need not see them at all. The overall effect of this approach is that the detached person becomes an onlooker, an observer of life, rather than a participant in active living. At the same time that he shuts out the world, he shuts himself in, and, within these confines, develops his talents and abilities. Horney calls this approach, "moving away from people." In popular terms, he would be called a "loner."

The person who uses this basic defense against anxiety may appear outwardly as an easygoing, calm, unhurried individual. To most people he will present a picture of unruffled poise, of being above the frantic pace of modern living. Many people will look upon him with admiration and envy and remark that nothing seems to bother him.

He neither conforms nor rebels. He seems uninterested in fighting for money, prestige, political office, or popularity. While he rarely asks for favors, he often accedes to requests from others as the quickest way to get rid of them. He wants peace and quiet; he values freedom, independence, and self-sufficiency. He is not easily disappointed in others because he does not expect much from them. He needs distance around him. He dislikes people who stand too close when they talk to him and those who touch or hold him. He can be with a group of people and yet not hear and see much of what is going on, for he has a highly developed mechanism of inattention. For instance, it is hard for him to remember names when introduced. He dislikes pressure, coercion, and restriction; in fact, his sensitivity to coercion may be so great that he hates to make decisions far in advance which may tie him down. This would include such things as getting theater tickets, making social arrangements, dates, etc. He would rather drop in at the last minute and hope he can get what he wants rather than make prior arrangements. A long-term contract, a lease, or getting married would be most difficult situations for him. His sensitivity to restriction is so great that it may extend to tight collars or tight clothing, an office without windows, a small room, elevators, or crowded places. It often contributes to claustrophobia. The loner is not comfortable in the pressure of large crowds, nor is he at ease in the ordinary give-and-take of living. He is the last person you would expect to see at a tenants' meeting or chatting in the neighborhood grocery store. His overall attitude is that he wants to be left alone and not bothered, that he is indifferent to many of the ideas and values of the mass of people.

When the detached person is intelligent and creative, this basic personality often works well. An example would be Thoreau, the great writer and naturalist of the nineteenth century who lived alone for two years in a small house which he built with his own hands at Walden Pond in Massachusetts. Thoreau advocated simplicity, self-reliance, and freedom. With few demands from others, he was free to observe the natural world around him and to write about his day-to-day experiences in a way that few writers have surpassed.

Another characteristic of the detached person is integrity. Because he does not compete for power, money, or prestige, he is not tempted to compromise his principles and is free to live by them. Others know this and can depend on him. Although he does not make promises often, those he does make he keeps. It is a radical solution to the problem of anxiety because it eliminates so many things which enrich life and give a zest to living, but it often works well.

As with all other patterns of neurotic character, this one, too, can be carried to extremes. Again and again, the detached person will recoil from involvement and entanglement, to his detriment. Another mistake he will make repeatedly is in not recognizing potential problems until they become so large that they cannot be ignored. By this time the cost of rectifying them is very great. He evades and procrastinates, with the result that he operates far below his efficiency and lives an impoverished life. Work that is well within his capacity to achieve is avoided because it involves too close contact with others. He functions best with a co-worker or partner who will do those things that he finds uncomfortable to do for himself. He will have difficulty demanding proper recognition for his work or asking for a raise. He will frequently rationalize that it is not important, when the truth is that he hates to get involved.

The following case history illustrates many of the characteristics of the detached personality.

> A 38-year-old research chemist reluctantly came to see me because his wife insisted on it. He felt that their marital problems were not too bad and that they were intelligent enough to work them out without help. He saw himself as a hard worker who provided well for his family and had no major vices. When his wife sought psychiatric help for "nervousness" and depression, however, he had no objection. Several months after she started treatment, quarrels between them became more frequent and more intense.
>
> The wife complained that he didn't talk to her and that he was not attentive enough to her or to the children. As she described it, he came home, mumbled "hello," and retired behind the newspaper until dinner. During the meal he took little part in the general conversation and often appeared not to be listening. After dinner he watched TV or read. On weekends, except for a few chores around the house,

he did nothing. He had no hobbies and no close friends. One of his wife's favorite comments was: "He doesn't need people." When they went visiting, his participation was minimal. If the family went to the beach, he brought along the portable TV to watch the ball game. These excursions were almost always at the suggestion of the wife.

Another favorite comment of his wife's was that he never showed emotion. When she nagged him, he became quieter, which only made her more angry. On very rare occasions he gave vent to angry outbursts —once smashing a typewriter against the floor. While he sent her cards and gifts on the usual holidays, such as birthdays and anniversaries, they were obviously last-minute actions: perfume or candy from a convenient store. Little thought or imagination had gone into picking something that would really please her. He was not very comforting or solicitous of her when she was ill; and sometimes he even showed annoyance because her illness caused him inconvenience.

He petted the dog often, but rarely caressed her. She complained that he appeared not to like her too close to him or even to touch him. If she put her head on his shoulder or lap, he found the position uncomfortable and soon moved away. When she would hug him spontaneously, he stiffened up. Sexual relations were infrequent and usually initiated by the wife.

It was as hard for this husband to become involved in treatment as it was for him to relate to his family. Often, he had nothing to say, his mind was "blank." "What shall we talk about today?" was a common way of starting many of our sessions.

He canceled some appointments or came late, always for reasons valid to him.

However, he persisted and in time became involved in the difficult task of understanding himself. As treatment went on he began to understand what his wife had complained about all those years. On the surface, he performed like a good family man, but it became painfully clear that he brought home little but his pay check. He made very little emotional contribution to his wife and children.

This had been the pattern of his life for many

years. He had had a bleak childhood with an uncommunicative father. His mother died when he was 6 and he had little recollection of her. They moved often and he was a lonely child. One bright spot was school, where he achieved recognition as a bright student. Relationships were always superficial, whether in college or in the army. Sexual relationships were always casual affairs. On occasion he had been attracted to a girl but, reluctant to commit himself to a permanent relationship, he did nothing. The decision to get married was a painful one and delayed until he was 28 years old. His wife was attractive and bright, but the real reason he married was that it was preferable to remaining a bachelor.

His work, also, suffered from his pattern of detachment. Essentially, he liked his work and the firm. He was respected as competent and reliable and he was comfortable there. However, more often than he cared to admit, he was annoyed that others advanced more rapidly because they were more aggressive and more adroit at getting recognition. He rarely showed his annoyance and frustration, and rationalized that it wasn't worth getting upset about. Detachment gave him a pleasant, calm facade but impoverished his personal and professional life.

As with all neurotic solutions, detachment may work fairly well for a long time—even for a person's entire life. However, it has severe limitations. Though his life may seem well ordered and serene, it is impoverished and this type of neurotic will sense how much more he could be doing and enjoying. The penalty for neurotic defense against anxiety is distortion in one's attitude toward the world and toward oneself. Once you distort reality, it is harder to act in a realistic way and the consequences are far-reaching. There is always the danger that, when this defense does not work, the individual will be overwhelmed by anxiety.

## *Aggressive Character*

The third major neurotic character pattern is aggression. Expressed in the simplest terms, fear is converted into anger. Like the famous French general, this type of neurotic believes that "offense is the best form of defense," and so he attacks, attempting to destroy all obstacles that stand in his way. He feels he will be safe from attack because others will be afraid of him or look up to him. Quite different from the compliant personality, who is quick to think of himself as a loser, the aggressive one thinks of himself as a winner. He looks upon the world as a jungle where it is dog-eat-dog and survival of the fittest. Everyone is hostile, or will be, given a chance. He feels superior, strong, realistic. He can assert himself and fight his own battles, whether to ask for a raise, a new job, fire an employee, or ask for a divorce. He plans well and carries out his plans efficiently and sometimes ruthlessly. He is proud of his drive and ability to work hard, and is extremely ambitious. Driven by the desire for power, prestige, money, success, and acclaim, he needs to take over, to be in control. He would much rather be the boss than an employee. He wants others to recognize his superiority and his great worth. He despises softness and weakness in others; nor does he like to recognize these qualities in himself. He glories in hard work, willpower, and ambition. If he is also well endowed with intelligence and talent, the aggressive person often achieves impressive successes. The world's outstanding leaders in politics and business often seem to belong to this pattern.

In our world, where money, power, and fame are considered so desirable, the aggressive person will often be looked up to and admired. Others are impressed and envious of his achievements. However, in his personal life he is not likely to be so successful. Too driven to be able to relax, he is unable to be spontaneous and to enjoy things. Feelings of warmth, tenderness, and affection are not well developed in this well-oiled, success-directed machine. He can respect the accomplishments of others but does not simply and naturally like people. Rather, he thinks in terms of how they can be used in his pursuit of success. His friends tend to be business associates or acquaintances whom he may drop as he ascends the socioeconomic ladder. He can be benevolent and helpful to others, but only to those who do not challenge his influence and superiority. It is hard for him to marry because of his lack of deep feelings. When he does, he usually picks a wife who has some outstanding desirable quality—great beauty, wealth, or prestige—rarely marrying for love. And his wife must play a difficult role; she must be desirable enough so that he can impress others with her, but yet not eclipse him in importance. She must accept the fact that his family life will be secondary to his ambition and to his self-aggrandizement.

Of course, there are variations in the aggressive, expansive character. Some are perfectionists. In the things that are important to them, they set up extremely high standards of performance and try very hard to live up to them. Because of their ability and drive, they can succeed in accomplishing a great deal for a long time, but the cost in anxiety is great. For instance, one of my patients, a physician in general practice, expected that whenever he was called on in a medical emergency he would, in every case, make a correct and complete diagnosis, calm the patient, reassure the family, get treatment started, arrange for hospitalization, etc. Furthermore, he had to do all of this rapidly, never be flustered or uncertain or ill at ease. His frantic efforts could not keep pace with his anxiety, and the day came when he could not function at all. He could not leave his house and needed constant reassurance from his wife. At this point he sought psychiatric help. With medication and intensive psychotherapy he recovered and went on to make excellent progress toward a healthy mode of living.

The perfectionist sets up unbelievably high standards and struggles very hard to achieve them. Whenever he senses that he may fail, great anxiety may then be triggered.

Another aspect of the aggressive character is vindictiveness. The aggressive character operates on the general assumption that he is superior to others and that if he really tries, he will get what he goes after. He feels that his own needs are important and to be respected; however, he is quick to disregard as unimportant the feelings and wishes of other people. It is easy, then, to imagine the violence of his feelings when his wishes are disregarded, when somebody achieves something that he does not, or when he senses defeat. His fury is often channeled into defeating the other person, frustrating them, or gaining revenge. The aggressive character makes a dangerous adversary. Great writers have recognized these qualities, and the character of Captain Ahab in *Moby Dick* is an outstanding example. When out of control, the violence of their hatred may lead to their own destruction as well as that of their victims. As with all neurotics, the aggressive person does not know when to stop and tries too hard for too much. When he senses that he may be defeated or humiliated, great anxiety is stirred up.

It is well to remember that these three neurotic character patterns are oversimplified, for in real life we rarely see a perfect example of any one of the three. In addition to their healthy traits, people usually have certain neurotic tendencies drawn from each pattern. And, of course, they differ in intelligence, imagination, talents, and physique. However, if we look for it in a person, we can usually recognize one predominating neurotic pattern and see in broad perspective the overall approach he has toward life.

# Chapter 3

## *The Creation of an Image*

Patients often make such statements as "I have no sense of direction," "I don't know what I want," "If I could only do just one thing well," "When I die I'd like to think that I had made some contribution to the community, however small."

These statements originate in the yearning of the neurotic for a purpose in living, out of a need to feel significant and worthwhile in order to offset his sense of worthlessness. In the previous chapter I described how the neurotic copes with these painful feelings by developing a certain character pattern or style of living. As this develops, it does relieve anxiety and furnishes him with a set of values and a mode of reacting to other people. However, that is not enough. He still feels vulnerable, insecure, and inferior. He needs self-esteem and an identity. He still needs an answer to the question, "Who am I?" The healthy person can give a pretty good answer to this question because he can be realistic about himself and look at himself honestly. The neurotic is too frightened to be able to look at himself realistically. He is afraid to see his limitations and shortcomings. Because he feels inferior to others, he needs to lift himself out of the mediocre, above the mass of men. By creating in his imagination a picture of himself that will impress others and that he can be proud of, he is able to ignore some of the reality of what he is. Like the photographer who retouches the wrinkles and by trick lighting makes an ordinary person look quite glamorous, by wishful thinking, by magnifying some traits and minimizing others, the neurotic creates an idealized and glorified picture of himself. This creation of an idealized image has the most far-reaching consequences for every aspect of his life. It is a crucial component in the neurotic process, as it becomes more important to live up to this image than to appreciate and recognize what his real needs are.

Each person creates a unique self-image. A compliant person wants to be so charming that everyone will love him; the aggressive person wants to be so outstanding that everyone will look up to him; the detached person wants to achieve the height of serenity and wisdom. The picture varies for each person because each has different abilities, because what is feasible for one is not for another. To a man, the image may largely center around the kind of work he does, his occupation or profession. In a woman, the picture may involve her role as housewife and mother, both of which are important in our society. Some images will include achievement in sports, others in the arts, still others in intellectual pursuits. Some are extremely ambitious and grandiose in what they try to achieve: to become President of the United States or to hold other high political office; to amass great wealth or prestige. Others have more modest goals. Such people, perhaps, would like to think that they belong to a useful organization or are doing something of value in their community. These goals, modest or grandiose alike, arise from the same sources: self-esteem that is too low and a desire to be more than what one is. Most people are not conscious of their spectacular and grandiose wishes, but in the course of their psychoanalysis these are regularly uncovered. These widespread yearnings to be a hero are well described in James Thurber's classic story of Walter Mitty.

The neurotic desperately clings to this idealized image as if his life depended on it; and, indeed, his whole style of living does depend on it. Without it he could not function. It has become more real to him than his actual self, which he has pushed away because he cannot face his limitations. Far worse than being a "man without a country" is to be a man without an identity. This self-image, this pseudo-identity, can only be given up when his real self has developed sufficiently to take over the direction of his life. Even then this is an occasion for a most difficult conflict in the emotional sphere, for the idealized image provides an identity which enables the neurotic to feel unique, superior, secure, and confident. It furnishes him with an apparent direction, with standards, goals, ideals, and values. It coordinates all the other neurotic mechanisms.

Valuable as is the idealized image, like all neurotic processes it is carried to an extreme. Since the standards must be set higher and higher, the neurotic is engaged in a hopeless and never-ending struggle to mold himself into this perfect being he feels he must be. More and more of his energies are channeled into these strivings to be infallible and invulnerable, the "darling of the gods." He must be superior to others in every regard. Nobody should do *anything* better than he can. The neurotic tells himself that nothing is impossible if only he tries hard enough and long enough. If he does everything he is supposed to, then he will never be rejected or humiliated or ignored. If he does everything right, he will never be late, his car will never develop engine failure, his home will never catch fire, and his stocks will always go up. By his intellect and willpower he should be able to achieve anything he sets his mind to. As a matter of course, once he has set his mind to it, his plans are as good as achievements. Blueprints are as good as an actual house; an idea for a book is as good as writing the book itself. Once he has decided how he will make his fortune he begins planning how to spend it. The healthy person lives in reality and respects it; the neurotic lives in his imagination where nothing is impossible. No wonder that Karen Horney compares the neurotic to a magician. Thoughts and intentions mean as much as actions. To know right from wrong is as good as acting in a moral and responsible way. To apologize for a mistake is enough, wiping it out as if it never happened. The neurotic is therefore annoyed when somebody reminds him of his actions. He must continually perform mental gymnastics to keep himself convinced that he is living up to his idealized image, that he is, indeed, a superior being. He must succeed quickly and in a grand manner in carrying out whatever he has planned or he will suddenly lose interest in the project and decide that it was not worthwhile. He must continually distort reality, rationalize, and make excuses when events demonstrate that he is not, in fact, a superior human being.

Whatever enhances and glorifies this image becomes desirable and important. On the other hand, those qualities and tendencies that diminish or detract from this image are undesirable, bad, to be ashamed of and avoided. In the process, then, of maintaining the idealized image, a comprehensive set of standards and values is developed. Things are good or bad, to be proud of or ashamed of, depending on whether they glorify his self-image or detract from it. To the extent that he is neurotic, the person does not consult his own feelings and wishes in making decisions. He does not ask himself what he wants to do; he asks what he is supposed to do. He does not do things in his own real interest; above all he must maintain this picture of himself as a glorious human being. His goals are not his own enjoyment and growth, but rather what enhances or diminishes his image. The more unhappy and neurotic the individual is, the more desperately does he seek self-esteem. It becomes a powerful, driving force, and the whole process has been called "the search for glory."

There is another important aspect to this—a negative one. Once the neurotic decides what is good and desirable, by the same token, he must determine what is bad and undesirable. The opposite of the idealized image is the despised image. Since the neurotic process goes to extremes, there is no middle ground. You are either one or the other. If you do not reach the top you will fall all the way down to the bottom. The neurotic experiences himself either as his idealized image or as his despised image—what has also been called a positive identity or a negative identity. It is one or the other—all or nothing.

We usually can recognize one of two patterns in neurotics: those who are actively striving to attain their idealized image and those who desperately try to avoid proving that they are their despised image. The latter are afraid of making even a single mistake. Every decision, no matter how trivial, becomes an agony, lest they prove what they have been afraid of, that they really are their despised image.

Some neurotics will try to avoid making any decision, or will postpone decisions as long as possible. When, finally, they do attempt something and fail, they are vehement and merciless in their self-condemnation. By the intensity of their self-reproach they try to prove how high their standards are, and therefore what really superior people they are. It is quite commonplace to see people berating themselves furiously for trivial matters, when it is apparent that they protest too much. To understand what is going on, we have to go beyond the relative unimportance of the events and examine their underlying significance for the individual. For him, the most trivial occasion may be the proving ground for his inherent superiority or worthlessness, an occasion that can generate great anxiety.

The search for self-esteem serves a vital function in the neurotic process. As long as it succeeds it gives him a feeling of well-being. However, like all neurotic processes, it is not perfect, for as it relieves some fears it generates others. While it gives structure to his life, on those occasions when the neurotic sees his limitations, and realizes that he is not the perfect person he needs to be, he can experience great pain and anxiety. These occasions are inevitable because the idealized image is an absolute, a creation of his imagination, a fantasy, and impossible to attain.

These things that we have been discussing in this chapter—the search for self-esteem and glory, the striving for perfection and for an idealized image—have been recognized by many of the great writers and philosophers for a long time. The Greek legend of Pygmalion deals with man's striving to create perfection. In the play *Death of a Salesman*, by Arthur Miller, we see a dramatic portrayal of the collapse of an individual when his idealized image is shattered. The salesman in this play had built up an image of himself as a supersalesman, indispensible to his firm, known and admired by everyone in his business. This self-image was his most treasured possession and into it he had channeled his most strenuous efforts over many years. When he is then fired from his job, he is shattered; there is not enough left in his personality that is healthy to survive this traumatic episode.

Also relevant to the topics that we have been talking about are the many variations of the Faust legend. In the best-known story of Faust, a learned doctor sells his soul to the Devil for youth, knowledge, and magical power. While these are great assets, it turns out to be a disastrous bargain. The Faustian theme parallels the development of an idealized image in the neurotic, which brings many advantages but in the long run is disastrous for the individual. The neurotic, having lost control of his own life, is driven to spend his greatest energy in the pursuit of glory and self-esteem according to this idealized image.

The Bible also has many things to say of profound

psychological importance on this very subject. In Proverbs we read, "Pride goeth before destruction and an haughty spirit before a fall." Here, I believe the reference is to the pride that is invested in the idealized image and that glorifies it, not to pride in the sense of dignity and self-respect, which is healthy. The Bible uses the word "pride" in the sense of the term "arrogance." In arrogance we have a distortion of reality where the individual arrogates to himself powers that he does not really possess.

More of the psychological wisdom of the Bible is contained in the New Testament: "Blessed are the meek for they shall inherit the earth." Here, I believe the term "meek" refers not to the timid or frightened but to the realistic people who do not have false illusions about themselves and the world. They do not feel immune from any of the dangers that exist. These are the realists—honest and objective. Because they do not deceive or confuse themselves, they can lead their lives free of the crushing burden of neuroses.

In summary, every person needs a picture of himself in order to function, to give direction and significance to his life. The healthy person has an accurate picture of himself based on a realistic evaluation of his personal assets and liabilities. The neurotic is not a realist; he is too frightened to see himself objectively. He is chasing a mirage, an illusion. In his mind he constructs a picture of himself, of what he needs to be in order to feel worthwhile, and then he tries to live up to this. In the process, he sacrifices his real interests and cannot develop his talents and his abilities. It becomes increasingly necessary for him to criticize himself severely for any minor shortcoming as proof of what superior standards he has. His self-image leads to distortions in his attitude not only toward himself but toward the world. It makes his life extremely difficult because he is constantly afraid of failure and the collapse of the entire neurotic structure he has built up with so much effort.

# Chapter 4

## *Neurotic Strategies*

In the previous chapters were described the basic processes in neurosis. However, this is not the whole picture. Many other things are going on. In the constant struggle to hold down anxiety, to keep conflicts from erupting, and to maintain the idealized image, important maneuvers are taking place. In this chapter, the more important of these strategic measures will be described.

### *Suppression and Repression*

These have been mentioned before, briefly, but they are important enough to discuss again. There is much confusion about them. The term "*suppression*" is used when an individual deliberately and consciously pushes some thought or impulse out of his mind because he does not want to face it. He is aware of what he is doing. If suppression is largely successful, he may think about it only on rare occasions. Such a person may say, "Oh, I rarely think about it anymore, so it can't be important to me." This may not be true at all; it means only that he had the ability to suppress that material.

Suppression is entirely different from "*repression*," an automatic control mechanism that operates completely outside of awareness. The individual does not know how or when it operates, or what has been repressed. This mechanism automatically forces out of consciousness those thoughts and feelings that are too difficult for the individual to face, either because anxiety would be too great or the possible conflict too intense. Whatever has been repressed is "lost" to that individual's conscious mind. He cannot recall it by an effort of will, nor does he even know that it exists. One might say, what we don't know *can* hurt us.

We do not know what exists in the unconscious state. We can only infer that certain material is buried there from the content of dreams (where that material appears in a disguised form), by slips in speech, inconsistencies in our behavior, inappropriate reactions, etc. In the course of psychoanalysis, material that has been repressed is rediscovered. Repression is the most important mechanism we have to defend our psychic equilibrium. Sometimes entire events are repressed, sometimes the event is not, but the accompanying feelings are, sometimes only the connection between several events is repressed. In general, we repress those thoughts and feelings which would not fit in with our idealized image. The perfect mother cannot feel great anger toward her child; the virtuous wife does not allow herself to feel strong sexual attraction for a man other than her husband. These feelings are repressed because they would cause too much anxiety for that individual. The "sweet" person does not feel vindictive rage; the aggressive person does not feel indecision or tenderness.

Constant effort is required to keep conflict-full material out of our awareness. From time to time, the repressed material may threaten to break through the forces of repression and into consciousness. At such times, anxiety is produced and even greater efforts are mobilized to keep the troublesome material unconscious. This mechanism of repression is universal; however, the healthier the individual, the less is he subject to unresolved conflicts and therefore the less must be repressed to maintain his psychic equilibrium.

## *Symptom Formation*

All neurotic symptoms serve to relieve anxiety in part. Symptoms result from a compromise between an unacceptable impulse and repressing forces. It would be too disruptive of the individual's life if he gave in to these impulses, but they are too strong to repress completely. A compromise solution, then, is the formation of a symptom that contains elements of both. The symptom is far less disturbing than if the impulse appeared in its original form. Let us take the example of a person who cannot express anger because he cannot run the risk of rejection or the guilt feelings that would be stirred up by it. In such a case, a splitting headache or diarrhea, uncomfortable as they are, is preferable to the open expression of anger. Or, take the case of a phobia; as long as the person avoids the object or experience he is afraid of, he can be reasonably comfortable. True, this may be very inconvenient, but at the time it is less disruptive than facing the conflict underlying it.

All neurotic symptoms—phobias, compulsions, hysteria, and the whole range of physical symptoms that we call psychosomatic illness—represent compromises that, at the time, are more tolerable to the individual and reduce anxiety. In addition, symptoms have another advantage. Whenever an individual suffers from an ailment, be it physical or mental, other people are more sympathetic to him and not only help him but often excuse him from his customary responsibilities. These are secondary gains which may be of considerable benefit to the individual. However, all neurotic symptoms cause suffering and disability, impair our efficiency, and interfere with some aspect of living. So, while neurotic symptoms may be of considerable benefit temporarily, they do not work all the time and, in the long run, are very costly.

## "Neurotic Claims"

All people harbor great expectations, illusions, and dreams of glory. However, the healthy individual is realistic enough to know that in this world one also encounters obstacles, reverses, disappointments, illnesses, etc. He prepares for these eventualities as best he can, and when they do occur he is not too dismayed. The neurotic is too frightened to be able to accept this view of the world. He would like guarantees that the unpleasant things that occur to all men will not happen to him. In his own mind he constructs a plan of defense that will protect him against these dangers. The neurotic assumes that if he does certain things and acts in certain ways he will always be safe from harm and get the things he wants. In his own mind he has worked out a "contract with life." He assumes that as long as he lives up to the provisions of this contract he is entitled to be safe, to be treated in a special way, and to get what is important to him.

The word "claim" is usually used in the legal sense of "demand"; a person asserts that he is legally entitled to something. Karen Horney calls these demands of the neurotic "neurotic claims" because they are neither valid nor realistic. The person who asserts the demands is not in any way entitled to have them met; he merely assumes that he is, and is therefore ill-prepared to face it when his claims are not met.

To illustrate: A man drives his car a little faster than the speed limit allows. He is stopped by a police officer and gets a ticket. He is indignant. He claims that the road was deserted, that he did not endanger anyone, that he is a careful driver, that many other drivers do far worse things and never get a ticket. All of these points are true, but irrelevant. The central fact is that he broke a regulation, was caught, and penalized. He does not have immunity from traffic violations. Actually, what hurt him most was that he was not treated as someone special. He was treated as any ordinary human being who breaks a traffic law.

Another illustration: A young woman finds out soon after marriage that her husband has very little interest in sex. Once in six to eight weeks suits him fine, but to his wife, who has a more active sex drive, the situation is intolerable. She frequently becomes angry and resentful of her husband. She says, "One of the reasons you get married is to have a good sex life. Couples of our age have intercourse usually two or three times a week. Now, I am perfectly willing to adjust and meet him even more than halfway. I could be happy with sex once a week, but this once in two months is intolerable." While her wishes and needs are perfectly understandable, the fact remains that her husband has an unusually low sex drive. This is the reality that is hard for her to accept. There is room for constructive measures in this situation, but instead of the wife's recognizing the basis of the difficulty, she only makes it worse with her neurotic claims.

Still another illustration: After a routine annual physical examination, a man is told by the doctor that he has high blood pressure. Medication is prescribed, a diet is given, and he is told to ease up on some of his activities. The patient's immediate reaction is disbelief. "It can't be.

There was never anything wrong with my blood pressure before." He finds it hard to accept the unpleasant reality that he has hypertension. A little thought would lead to the logical conclusion that there is no basis for him to expect to be immune from a rather common medical condition. It is a neurotic claim.

Neurotic claims are extremely widespread and appear in innumerable forms. It is quite understandable to yearn for many things that are important to us; to hope that our friends will not reject us, that our children will always remain close and loving, etc. However, these hopes and yearnings are distorted in an unrealistic way and asserted as claims. We can be logical and realistic when we are not in such great need. It is hard to recognize them in ourselves; much easier to recognize them in others. For example, the wife of a patient left him and took their children with her. In a sad voice he said, "All I want is my family back. Is that too much to ask?" And I had to answer, that on the basis of their many stormy years together, their frequent fighting, both verbal and physical, this was a grossly unrealistic request. Behind this pathetic plea was a most grandiose claim. Another patient had many long-standing emotional problems including fear of flying. One day he said, "Everyone seems to be going to Europe this summer. How I wish I could just get on a plane and fly over. Is that too much to ask?" Here again I had to answer that this was a great deal to ask, in view of his as-yet-unresolved, long-standing emotional problems.

Each person asserts claims only to the things that are important to him. The compliant person is more likely to make claims to being accepted, liked, and loved by everyone; the aggressive person, to having his own way; the detached person, to being left alone. The rationalizations behind these claims are numerous and varied. They will not be readily detected by the person who harbors similar claims. Thus, when a mother asserts a claim "because I am a mother," most mothers will agree with her. Similarly a claim asserted "because I am a taxpayer" stirs a sympathetic chord and agreement in most other taxpayers. There are numberless reasons put forward to justify claims: "because I worked hard all my life," "because I never hurt anybody," "because I always meant well," "because one of my ancestors signed the Declaration of Independence," "because my uncle is a judge," etc.

One patient said to me, "Can you imagine a wife acting

like that!" I said that since there are all kinds of wives, it is realistic to expect all kinds of actions from them. In our society, mothers, particularly, feel entitled to have their children pursue certain careers, marry the right kind of person, etc., because they have given them so much time and effort.

Essentially, neurotic claims are unrealistic, magical, and selfish in a childlike way. One patient said to me, "I believe that what I really want I will always get." Claims disregard the needs of others. The neurotic confuses a wish or hope with a right that is only valid in his own imagination. The neurotic has an idealized picture of himself; he considers himself a special, superior person, and asserts that, therefore, he is entitled to exceptional treatment. Everyone should love him, he should never be bothered with ordinary details, and he should get what he wants without effort. This last claim, if prominent, can lead to almost paralyzing inertia. It impairs the neurotic's ability to sustain effort; he cannot work hard enough at anything to develop his potential and talents. Instead of realistically taking responsibility for his own life, he demands that the world recognize his superiority and make things easy for him. When he is in a hurry, he should not encounter any red traffic lights; when he wants to play golf, it shouldn't rain; when he wants a date, the girl should be available and willing; etc. When the neurotic does encounter the delays, disappointments, and reverses that fall to us all, he is poorly prepared for them and becomes resentful and vindictive. There is a chronic discontent and envy of those who seem luckier. He is quick to feel abused; minor disappointments become catastrophes. Whenever you hear, "I am entitled to . . ." or "The world is unfair," be on the lookout that here neurotic claims are being asserted.

## The Dictatorship Within

Stated in its simplest form, the neurotic expects too much of himself. He does not accept himself as he is; he *should* be better. He sets impossible standards and continually coerces himself to live up to them. There is a never-ending stream of orders to himself: "I should have done better"; "I shouldn't have let that happen"; "I should have known." These are dictatorial commands for him to perform in a certain way without regard for his feelings or the conditions that may exist at the time. The clue to what is going on is the word "should." Horney calls it the "tyranny of the Shoulds."

The neurotic can be sympathetic and understanding toward the shortcomings of other people, but not toward his own. Another person can have an accident, fail a course, do poorly in business, etc., and receive his sympathy. But when he makes the same mistake, he is merciless in his self-criticism. His best is not good enough if it is not perfect. When he does something well, he takes it for granted: "That's my job"; "That's what I get paid for"; "That's the way I always do it"; etc. But when he fails, he is furious. He ignores his successes and is constantly on the alert for his failures. With this attitude, he cannot win, he can only postpone failure. And so he lives under a dictatorship of his own making.

These inner dictates make no allowance for the conditions that exist at the time; the same standards must be maintained at all times. In fact, he must conform to these standards not only in his actions but even in his thoughts and feelings. Most of the time we have pretty good control over our own behavior, but not over our thoughts and feelings. It is not possible to force ourselves to think and to feel in a rigid and arbitrary manner. Furthermore, these dictatorial commands may be contradictory. For instance, it is not possible for a working mother to be perfect at her job as well as in the home. Nor can a man be the perfect father, husband, and friend simultaneously. You cannot be in more than one place at a time.

These neurotic "shoulds" are often confused with genuine ideals and high moral standards. People are often impressed with someone who expresses such sentiments, and for a long time the difference may not be discovered. However, the neurotic does not sincerely believe in these standards. He is driven to perform according to them at all times to prove to himself and to others that he is a worthwhile person. When the direction of his neurotic drive changes, he may abandon them all. An observer may be shocked at what looks like the abandonment of such high ideals and principles. Actually, they were never these, merely a set of neurotic compulsions.

Other neurotics who cannot rebel against these standards may become listless and appear to be lazy. Their feeling is: "What's the use? I can't do it right, so I might just as well not do it at all!"

The "shoulds" are many and varied: "I should be able to do anything, because I am so intelligent." Actually, intelligence is not that important in many things; sensitivity, flexibility, manual dexterity, persistence, motivation may be more important in many of our activities. The healthy person looks at the task before him objectively, tries his best, and accepts the fact that he did his best. For the neurotic, his best is never good enough. In judging himself he can make no allowance for how he feels or for the conditions that prevail.

An important consequence of this constant inner pressure is that these individuals overreact when further pressure is placed on them by others. At this point, their situation becomes intolerable. One of my patients, who was an excellent legal secretary and enjoyed the high regard of the people in her field, quit her job because her employer dared to criticize some work she did. As she said, "He has no right to criticize me; I am ten times more critical of my mistakes than he is." Such people will often volunteer to do things for others, but they themselves must take the initiative; otherwise, the work is experienced as extra pressure and is resented. The constant strain of inner dictates often makes them tired, tense, and irritable. Like all neurotic processes, it impairs spontaneity and the zest for living.

## *Externalization*

In its simplest form, externalization consists of blaming someone else for our own faults. For example, we provoke an argument and blame it on the other person's hostility and do not recognize that our own anger had anything to do with it. By shifting the blame to someone else it is much easier for us to maintain the illusions we have about ourselves. It spares us from facing many painful facts. As long as we need to see ourselves in an idealized way we have to minimize our own faults, and no way is more effective than putting the blame on someone else. A very common maneuver is to blame our current difficulties in living on events in childhood: Because certain things happened to us in our early experience we really can't be blamed for a lack of achievement today.

While it is certainly true that the events of childhood have an important influence, the neurotic ignores his own faults and his own contributions to the *present* difficulties. It is much more comfortable to blame it on his parents. This mechanism of externalization is commonly called "projection." To state it simply, something that occurs within us is felt as happening in the outside world. And since it is outside of ourselves, we have no responsibility for it. Instead of feeling angry at or disappointed with ourselves for some action, we feel angry at someone else. Or, instead of recognizing our own anger, we feel that others are angry with us. This can be a very important device in the production of anxiety.

Sometimes a painful conflict can be externalized. For example, a woman who was married to a younger man continually worried that he would meet and fall in love with a younger woman. It took many months of treatment before she began to recognize that she was dissatisfied with some aspects of this marriage and was not sure that she wanted to continue it. However, her strong feelings of obligation to her husband and children made this a most difficult dilemma and it was consequently repressed. As long as she saw the problem in terms of her husband's possible attraction for another woman, it was her husband's problem and not one that she could do anything about directly.

Because we can externalize all inner processes, the system provides a most useful safety valve. Probably the most useful aspect of this mechanism is that it enables us to channel much of our self-hate and self-contempt to other targets and so reduce their emotional intensity. It is an important emotional safety valve to be able to hate other people. In our society it is quite common to express anger toward people at a great distance—the governor of a state, a congressman, the President, foreign diplomats, etc.; these are culturally accepted targets for the expression of anger. This principle also operates in racial strife, where there is externalization of prejudice and anger toward an "inferior" group.

Valuable as is the process of externalization, like all neurotic processes it can be carried to extremes. Almost all feelings can be externalized until the individual can feel almost nothing for himself. He becomes an empty shell, living only for his job, for his wife, for his children. His opinions count for nothing; the opinions of others are all-important. He will do things for others but not for himself. The extreme externalizer needs other people around constantly to reflect back all feeling; he needs them to act as his "emotional Seeing Eye dog." He is sad when others are sad; he can enjoy something only if he sees another person enjoying it. In a restaurant, he waits for someone else to order first—he doesn't know what he feels like eating. He is not a complete individual unless someone else is there. Because his own life is too impoverished in feelings, in initiative, in spontaneity, all these must come from someone else. He sees things only when others call his attention to them; alone, he doesn't know what to think or what he wants.

## Rule by Intellect

There are many intelligent people who try to solve their problems by logic and reason. While these are valuable qualities, they have limitations. People who try to live by intellect alone tend to distrust emotion; they suppress and try to ignore feelings; they are more comfortable thinking than feeling; and they try to approach all problems intellectually. Before making decisions, they consult all the authorities and read all the books on the subject. Every decision they make is bolstered by an impressive array of facts and statistics. They buy things because they are on sale, not because they want them—"It was too good a buy to miss." In a restaurant, they order according to calories or price, rather than what they feel like eating. Usually, they are not sure how they feel. They tell themselves that they should be happy, because their life is so well planned and thought out. However, it may not be happy, for they have left out the most "alive" and spontaneous part of themselves: their feelings. Guided by intellect alone, some decisions are painfully difficult. In many instances, feelings are a far better guide and lead to better, happier decisions.

In addition to these important neurotic mechanisms, brief mention should be made of two more: *compartmentalization* and *rationalization*. Both are common terms. As the name indicates, the compartmentalized individual disconnects parts of his life and carries them about as if they were in entirely separate compartments. Thus, a married man may have a girl friend with whom he spends a lot of time, but balances the relationship by spending every weekend with his wife and family. Or, a very religious man may obey all the commandments of his religion in his private life but be dishonest in business. He justifies this lapse by calling it necessary business tactics similar to those his competitors use. As long as these remain separated there is no conflict and the individual apparently can have it both ways. However, he will often feel divided and uneasy because he is not wholeheartedly involved in anything he does. At times, the conflict that must be faced before the individual can resolve it may subject one to very great strain. Most of us are much more complicated than we seem on the surface and are often pulled in opposite directions. We have within us certain polarities: as for instance between being honest-dishonest, idealistic-opportunistic, timid-brave, humble-ambitious, etc. Great writers have often sensed that this dualism exists in people; that in one body there may be several personalities. Probably no writer has described this more dramatically than Robert Louis Stevenson in the novel *Dr. Jekyll and Mr. Hyde.*

Rationalization may be defined as devising a plausible excuse or explanation when these are not our real motives. Because we find it hard to see ourselves as we really are, we use this method of deceiving ourselves, and others as well, about our behavior. A young patient once defined rationalization as "the lies we tell ourselves." The human capacity for self-deception is enormous.

All the measures we have described in this chapter relieve anxiety and provide a degree of harmony for the individual. However, like all neurotic mechanisms, they do not work all the time and continually need to be reinforced and adjusted. Each defense has a limitation; one defense must be piled on top of another until a cumbersome system is built up that is often in a precarious balance. This is a costly process which interferes with healthy living, as we shall see in the next chapter.

# Chapter 5

## *Consequences of Neurosis*

For all its precarious stability, the neurotic structure may work fairly well for a long time. The compliant person makes friends and is liked by them, the aggressive person competes and wins many times, and the detached person is left alone. Whenever their style of existence runs into difficulty they repress, rationalize, externalize, etc., to minimize the pain and anxiety that is caused, and to restore balance. In some people a working balance may be maintained all their lives; others may gradually outgrow their neurosis. Each person is a mixture of health and neurosis, and his life will reflect both. In time, in some, healthy capacity becomes strengthened. These people learn from their experiences in living, they use their abilities and talents, do useful work, and obtain a good measure of satisfaction and self-esteem. If they are fortunate in their relations with a spouse, teacher, friend, neighbor, etc., healthy interaction and growth occur. However, many others are not so fortunate; the neurotic processes continue to escalate and have greater and greater influence on their lives. In this chapter we turn our attention to the consequences that follow from the worsening of the neurosis.

As the underlying neurotic processes increase in severity, life becomes more difficult. The neurotic finds it more difficult to carry out his work, to function at home and in social relationships. Things he could always manage to do are now impossible. He may no longer be able to work or to enjoy his favorite hobby. He is no longer able to cope; as a patient said to me, "I have run out of cope." Anxiety, phobias, and other neurotic symptoms become worse until the life of the person is severely restricted. In time, he may be unable to leave his home at all; or even to be left alone. Any new situation or extra stress may be so intolerable that it may precipitate a complete breakdown and the need for hospitalization. As the symptoms of the neurotic increase and his life becomes more restricted, he also suffers more. Incidentally, the great majority of neurotics do not exaggerate their suffering. While a few do dramatize their symptoms, the great majority try to hide them and their suffering. Furthermore, the neurotic person is not in good contact with his own feelings and does not truly appreciate the extent of his own suffering.

## *Underachievement*

When we look carefully at the lives of neurotics we see, quite regularly, a great waste of energy. We see that they are indecisive, drift without direction, or scatter their energies in too many directions. They cannot concentrate on the important things or they pursue goals that may be mutually contradictory. The neurotic doesn't live his own life; he lets others live it for him and they do it badly. According to advice from others or because of external events he starts and stops, and often changes direction in the course of his life. He fluctuates between inertia and frantic activity that he cannot sustain.

Neurotics, adults as well as children, are underachievers. I am sure all of you have seen youngsters of great ability and talent for whom everyone predicted great things. Instead, they leave school and go on to obscurity, their great promise unfulfilled. This lack of achievement is often blamed on bad luck, external circumstances, etc. However, the most common cause, in the majority of cases, is neurosis.

## *Repetition of Mistakes*

Another characteristic of the neurotic is his tendency to repeat the same mistakes over and over again. He can't seem to learn from experience. One person is repeatedly exploited because he can't say "no"; he always wants to be the good guy. Some are accident-prone.

Some girls have a habit of getting involved with unsuitable men. While they appear anxious to get married, they pick men who are unable or unwilling to sustain a permanent relationship. For instance, one of my patients, a 28-year-old secretary, told me that she had been trying to get married for the last six years, but had just had "no luck." When her college boy friend went into the service she still had hopes their relationship would eventually lead to marriage, in spite of his lukewarm and infrequent letters in which he was kind, but very careful to promise her nothing. Upon his return from service he took a job in a distant city and in time stopped answering her letters. The next boy friend was attractive and eligible in many ways, but not sexually attracted to her. In time, my patient found out that he was a transvestite. Only after much time, and repeated consultations with psychiatrists, did she give up the idea of "curing" him and turning him into a suitable husband. Her next involvement was with a man who had everything she wanted, but was, unfortunately, already married.

In the course of therapy, this woman came to see that she had not really been ready for marriage. Only then was she able to work through her difficulties to the point where she could be more realistic in her choice of men, and begin to accept the fact that she would have to make difficult compromises if she were to marry at all.

The aggressive person fights with too many people. He doesn't know when to stop. It is not unusual to hear of a man who builds up an extremely successful business, becomes overly ambitious, and loses everything only to repeat the same process over and over again. Such behavior is well recognized in the business world. Try to get a credit card from American Express if you have once been bankrupt. They know very well that history repeats itself, that the person who once has failed in business has a far greater chance of repeating the experience than one who never has failed. The pattern is not really surprising. Behavior is based on the character makeup of the individual, and until this is changed by the very slow process of growth and self-understanding, the neurotic will repeat the same actions. The philosopher Santayana once said that he who doesn't learn from history is doomed to repeat it. The psychiatrist calls this the "repetition compulsion." It is also seen in the endless repetition of antisocial acts by certain criminals, to the despair of the police, the courts, and the social agencies.

## *Extremism and Poor Judgment*

The neurotic does not develop his talents and abilities in an orderly manner that would give his life stability. Instead, he develops unevenly, swinging wildly between his idealized image and his despised image. There is no middle ground; he is either perfect or worthless, he can't be simply a good, kind person; he must be a saint. He can't compete in a healthy way for the things he really wants; he must beat everybody at everything. Excellent work is not enough, it must be the absolute best. He demands perfection not only from himself, but from all others close to him: his wife, children, friends, business associates. Often, there is no pleasing him. He is insatiable. If he can't get what he wants he may suddenly quit, whether this be a job, a friendship, or a marriage. Childlike, he cannot put reasonable limits on his appetites, whether for food, sex, or alcohol. He eats not only when he's hungry but also when he is anxious, unhappy, or bored. And when his weight becomes excessive, it leads to other problems, more unhappiness, and more eating. This same vicious cycle may operate with sex or alcohol, or both. Much sexual behavior is based not on sexual drive, but on the need to relieve anxiety, to express self-contempt, or to humiliate one's partner. Alcohol has been relieving anxiety in all parts of the world for many centuries. It preceded modern tranquilizers and, in moderation, can be very effective. In excess it leads to a host of medical, personal, and financial problems.

These wide swings and excesses impair the judgment and the discrimination of the neurotic. The formerly shrewd businessman begins making bad decisions, much to the dismay of his partners; or he may make equally bad decisions in his personal life. Often the first sign that something is seriously wrong with the emotional balance of a person is a display of poor judgment. He gets bogged down in trivial details, he cannot separate the important from the unimportant, nor can he stop before he has gone too far. The more mistakes he makes, the more his self-confidence is impaired, the harder he tries, and the more mistakes he makes.

## Depression

The most common reaction in neurosis is depression. More people consult physicians because of depression and its manifestations than for any other condition in the world. Plagued by unresolved conflicts and fears that he cannot understand, the neurotic becomes more and more dissatisfied with himself. He fels inadequate and inferior.

This depression may be covered up by a flippant or a cynical attitude. It may also be concealed by a hectic scrambling after thrills, excitement, and pleasure. For a while, this may appear to be the result of a true zest for living and the courage to live life fully. However, it is counterfeit, and in time the boredom, depression, and hopelessness become apparent.

It takes time before a depression can be seen clearly. It does not occur often in young people, who are generally full of high hopes and great expectations. The young have the illusion that they have all the time in the world, and the idea of ever growing old is very remote to them. They expect to have endless opportunities, any one of which may lead them to fame and fortune. They are quick to start many things with the illusion that they have at last discovered the most important thing in the world. This could be drugs, sex, a political cause, a new philosophy, a new religion, etc. Only with the passing of the years do they become more realistic, does their perspective change, and do they become more aware of obstacles and limitations. Dreams of glory fade slowly as they begin to realize that they cannot remain young forever. As the years pass, convincing evidence begins to accumulate. Hair turns gray, wrinkles appear, they gain weight and lose teeth. They lose some of their youthful vigor, endurance, and sexual drive. In women, the menopause is dramatic evidence of the changes that are taking place. For the woman who always wanted children but couldn't have them, this can be a particularly difficult moment of truth. In the middle years, men, as well as women, feel a great sense of loss. They realize that they will never get many of the things they yearn for. It is too late to go back to college, change jobs, or marry the girl they should have. There is a poignant awareness of wasted energy, wasted years, of missed opportunities that are now less likely to reoccur than ever. It is in the middle years that the individual finds it hard to avoid looking at the whole pattern of his life and seeing it for what it is, not for what he had hoped it would be. It is in these middle years that severe depression occurs with greatest frequency.

## Alienation from Self

The word "alien" means foreign or strange, and in the psychological process of alienation one becomes a stranger to one's real self. In the course of neurotic development, the person is led further and further away from his real self until he no longer recognizes himself or knows what he really wants. Children are spontaneous enough to feel deeply and to know what they want, but through brainwashing or because of repeated disappointment, they become afraid to want. To avoid hurt, they stop wanting, and in the process lose part of themselves. Neurotic processes distort reality; the reality of who and what the person is and the kind of world in which he lives.

We see dramatic samples of this identity crisis in cases of total amnesia where the person temporarily forgets his own identity, his name, address, age, etc.

Also severely alienated are those patients who don't like to look at themselves in the mirror; the reality of what they see upsets their mental picture. I had one patient who actually did not recognize himself in the mirror. At all times he avoided his own reflection; when he shaved he looked only at the exact spot he was shaving. During World War II he served with the navy. One evening he was sitting at a bar in Australia. This particular bar had full-length mirrors on all the walls. As my patient looked up, he saw across the room an American sailor who seemed friendly. Getting up, he started across the room to greet him and crashed into his own reflection.

Much more common are the cases where individuals only feel some degree of unreality or numbness about themselves. They ask such questions as "Who am I really?" "What do I want?" "Where am I going?" They carry out their duties and function in a mechanical way without much feeling; these people are "blanked out." They play the roles others expect of them or that are imposed on them by their neurosis. In a stereotyped manner, they go through the motions of being a loyal employee, a devoted mother, a dependable neighbor, the life of the party, etc. They are half alive. Some of them come alive only under special circumstances; at work, in their favorite sport or amusement, in sex, etc. Most of the time they move around as if anesthetized. Sometimes their lack of identity is covered up with forced gaiety or heartiness. However, from time to time the mask will slip to expose the emptiness and the impoverishment of their lives.

This loss of identity is brilliantly described by the French writer, Albert Camus, in his short novel appropriately entitled *The Stranger*. It is the story of an ordinary man, drifting through life without any deep feelings, without significance or dignity, until the final catastrophe, when he commits a senseless murder and is sentenced to death. Only in his last few days does he realize the futility of his life. The problem is so common that people speak of our society as the alienated society.

It is hard to describe the real self, but it manifests itself in deep and clear feelings. At times, all of us have felt something so deeply that we describe it as "feeling it in our bones." At such times we know that these are genuine wishes and thoughts. Unfortunately, we live in a world where material things are valued more than human feelings, where it is easy to become estranged from that unique, central inner force that is the most important part of ourselves. As the philosopher Kierkegaard said, "The greatest danger, that of losing one's own self, may pass off quietly, as if it were nothing; every other loss, that of an arm, a leg, five dollars, a wife, etc., is sure to be noticed."

## *Self-Hatred and Self-Destruction*

The ultimate despair of the neurotic occurs when he finally realizes that he can no longer attain his ideal life, and gives up the struggle. Realizing the futility of all his efforts, he turns the full force of his own contempt against the person that he actually is. It is a mistake to think that the neurotic loves himself, even if he pampers and indulges himself. Actually he hates himself for not being the wonderful person he would like to be. Patients are quick to say "I don't like myself," "I don't like what I am," "I hate myself." A patient's self-hatred comes out in a great many ways, sometimes quickly, sometimes over many years. It is revealed in many destructive acts: overeating, alcoholism, use of dangerous drugs, hazardous sports, reckless behavior of all kinds. In despair the neurotic punishes himself and jeopardizes his life in a great variety of ways. Sometimes the self-inflicted pain and suffering assuages his guilt, and for a time he can make constructive efforts on his own behalf or accept help from others. However, unless checked by healthy traits, the neurotic process continues to accelerate. It may end in a complete break with reality or in suicide. In the United States, 20,000 people every year are reported as suicides; the actual number is probably far higher. Suicide is the final act of fury and desperation, generated by the process of neurosis.

# Chapter 6

## *Mental Health*

Since neurosis affects, to a greater or lesser extent, over 80 percent of the population, what is average or typical behavior in our society is to a considerable degree neurotic. Thus, what the majority of people do is all too often not a good indicator of mental health. For reasons previously discussed, neurosis is not compatible with the full development of a person's talents and abilities. It produces an underachiever and a caricature of a healthy human being. Neurosis is a painful style of living and leads to an impoverished life. The opposite of neurotic development is healthy growth. I believe it would be of considerable value to describe the characteristics of an emotionally healthy person in contrast to the neurotic. This is one of those people who belongs to that fortunate minority in our society, those who have more or less fully developed their mental and physical faculties.

In the first place, the healthy person is basically courageous. Because he is not afraid, he is open and curious and can look calmly and carefully at the world around him. He is not afraid of new situations. He can tolerate risks and uncertainty; not everything has to be planned and organized beforehand. Above all, he is not afraid to try. If he fails, he usually has learned something from the experience which helps him to do better next time. He is not devastated by failure or embarrassment; his false pride is not great. He is confident of his own ability and resources and does not panic easily. He does not fear losing control of his emotions and is confident that he can express them in an appropriate manner. He respects dangers but doesn't magnify or escalate them, knowing that they do not automatically lead to disaster. He worries mostly about probabilities and not possibilities.

The healthy person is also a realist. There is little wishful thinking in his makeup. He sees things accurately and does not confuse what *is* with what *should be.* He doesn't expect something for nothing. He respects the limitations of time, energy, and money. Because he knows he can't do everything, he concentrates on what is important to him. His values are realistic ones. He does not waste time looking for perfect solutions where everything falls neatly into place and no one can possibly criticize him for anything. That is the stuff of myths and fairy tales. He looks at the alternatives and from among those things available to him he picks out a reasonable course of action. He does not seek the impossible; his best is good enough.

He accepts the existence of cause and effect relationships operating in this world: that he can't save money if he spends it; that if he wants to be on time he will have to start early; that if he wants to lose weight he will have to eat less, etc. Everybody "knows" these things, yet so few people live by them. The healthy person tries to improve what can be improved and realizes that with good effort and motivation many things can be accomplished. However, he also accepts his limitations and is not too uncomfortable with his shortcomings. He does not make a big thing about being a few inches too short, the shape of his nose, etc. He appreciates his own good qualities and assets as he does those of others. He is neither arrogant nor apologetic. As one patient said, "I'm not proud of some of those things I once did, but neither am I ashamed."

The healthy person is mature and disciplined. In the course of struggling to develop, he has worked out a set of values that are appropriate for him. He accepts conventional standards when they are convenient. Most of the time it is simpler and less complicated to do things in a conventional way; however, he modifies or rejects them when it is better for him to do so. He neither timidly accepts everything that has been imposed upon him by his parents and society, nor does he have to reject all of these standards to prove his independence. He retains what is valuable and modifies or rejects what is not, but they are now his values and he can live with them and accept responsibility for them. Discipline shows also in the ability to postpone gratification. He does not have to satisfy all impulses and needs immediately. He can wait, whether it be for food, sex, amusement, or whatever. He can put down something he is working on. He does not have to complete every single detail before he goes on to something else. He is oriented toward growth and does not allow himself to be diverted from his real goals by needs that clamor for immediate gratification. His main emphasis is on the development of his own skills, talents, and sensitivities, from which he gains his greatest satisfaction. The healthy person is in control of his own life, not driven by his neuroses. He listens to others, but makes up his own mind and takes responsibility for his actions. He does what he has to do, in a good spirit, with a minimum of whining and sulking. He can work as well as play. The neurotic has difficulty working and then feels guilty at play, doing well at neither. The healthy individual does well at both.

Good judgment is another quality of the healthy individual. He is discriminating and selective. Where the neurotic seems to make all problems very complicated and confusing, the healthy person seems to simplify them. He can get down to the essentials, to the heart of the matter. He does not get lost in unimportant details and trivial issues. Nor does he look for perfect solutions; he identifies the important thing and then looks for the best available solution. He usually avoids extremes and sets realistic limits. He can be courageous and not reckless; frugal and not stingy; flexible without being wishy-washy; dignified and not arrogant.

The healthy person has a good measure of self-respect and self-esteem. He feels all human beings are worthwhile and valuable, including himself. He treats himself with dignity; doesn't belittle, demean, or degrade himself. He does not constantly have to seek approval from others or continually to prove he is a worthwhile person. He is not ashamed of his origin and background, parents, religion, or color. He respects his own assets and abilities and his own efforts. He appreciates how hard he has worked to achieve some of the things he has done. Also, without being vindictive or hostile, he does not let himself be pushed around; he can speak up firmly to defend himself and what is important to him.

The healthy person is productive and creative. The major thrust of his life has been to develop his own abilities and resources. He has not scattered his energy in the pursuit of prestige or to impress others. Depending on his intelligence and talents, he does many things well. One of the great joys of living is to use our faculties, physical and mental, and to use them to their fullest extent. The healthy person experiences this often. It is a widespread and romantic notion that the world's greatest accomplishments are the works of geniuses who are neurotic. This is not true. Many geniuses are not neurotic—and those who are would produce more if they were healthy. For a limited time, it is true, a neurotic with talent may be driven by his neurosis to produce a great deal, but sooner or later, the neurotic processes interfere with his entire pattern of living, including his work. He cannot forever escape from the recognition that his goals are contradictory, that his neurotic needs are insatiable, and, when he is engulfed by the consequent despair or depression, he may not be able to function at all. The healthy person lives and grows and can maintain his productivity, barring unforeseen events, for many years.

The healthy person is in good contact with his own feelings and can express them. He feels strongly and deeply, whether it is sadness or joy, love, anger, frustration, hunger, or fatigue. He is not usually in doubt about how he feels. He is sensitive to himself and his own needs. He knows what he likes and wants, even if he cannot have it. He does not have to pretend that he is not disappointed when he is. He is a good observer of himself and has the ability to stand back and look clearly at what is going on. He can express feelings appropriately. If he is hurt he feels anger right away; he doesn't get an unexplained headache a day later. He knows when he is angry and reacts appropriately; he does not have to store it up unconsciously until one day he explodes over a trivial incident. He can respond simply and directly to what is going on at the present, whether it be with anger or with love.

The healthy individual has a good sense of self. He knows who he is, what he wants, and in what direction he is going. It is characteristic of him that he does not think in terms of "What am I supposed to do?" He knows what he would like to do and if circumstances permit he proceeds in that direction. He consults with himself and is very much involved in his own life. He is natural and spontaneous; he can "be himself." He does not have to impress other people, appease them, or fight with them.

Finally, his relations with other people are good. People are attracted by his warmth and spontaneity and zest for living. Very disturbed people repel us; they impress us as being strange or weird or hostile. Because healthy people live efficiently and are not preoccupied with their own problems, they can be generous and helpful to others. Mental health can be said to be the enjoyment of good relations with other people and with one's self. The healthy person feels lovable and capable of loving. Freud was once asked, "What is important in this world? What is it important that people be able to do?" His answer was, "Love and work." The healthy person is capable of both in full measure.

As a brief summary, the outstanding qualities of health versus neurosis are tabulated below:

| | *Healthy* | | *Neurotic* |
|---|---|---|---|
| 1. | courageous | 1. | fearful |
| 2. | realistic | 2. | given to wishful thinking |
| 3. | disciplined | 3. | can't wait, wants immediate gratification |
| 4. | good judgment | 4. | goes to extremes |
| 5. | fresh outlook, open-minded | 5. | prejudiced, closed-minded |
| 6. | spontaneous | 6. | driven, compulsive |
| 7. | flexible | 7. | rigid |
| 8. | assertive | 8. | hostile, vindictive |
| 9. | loving | 9. | clinging, dependent |
| 10. | zest for living | 10. | apathetic, impoverished |
| 11. | sincere | 11. | self-deceiving, fragmented |
| 12. | feels deeply | 12. | "numb," half alive |
| 13. | self-respect, dignity | 13. | vacillates between arrogance and self-contempt |
| 14. | orderly | 14. | inconsistently orderly |
| 15. | good relationships with people | 15. | exploits or is exploited |
| 16. | productive and creative | 16. | wasteful |

| | |
|---|---|
| 17. oriented toward growth | 17. oriented toward fame prestige |
| 18. good sense of identity | 18. alienated, "a stranger to himself" |

# Part II

# *Interpersonal Relations*

# Chapter 7

## *Neurotic Interaction*

All neurotic processes impair good relationships between people. Into his dealings with other people the neurotic brings his anxiety, his "neurotic claims," impossible standards, unresolved conflicts, and a painfully low self-esteem. He is so preoccupied with these that he cannot genuinely be interested in the problems of others.

In a previous chapter we have referred to the standards of the neurotic as the "tyranny of the shoulds." Not only does he coerce himself, but he externalizes these standards and demands that others live up to them, too. When such claims are not met, he becomes resentful and frustrated. It becomes even more complicated when these standards are experienced as coming from others. The neurotic then feels that others expect him to live up to the impossible, unconscious of the fact that he himself imposed these standards on himself in the first place.

Deep down inside himself, the neurotic feels that he is really unworthy and unlovable. One patient told me, "I am nothing." The neurotic hopes that maybe he is wrong and that others will see something good in him, but at the same time he is apprehensive that they may not. He constantly needs help from others to maintain his shaky self-esteem and relieve his anxiety. Depending on his needs, he sees others in a distorted way. When he feels weak and helpless, he tends to see others as powerful figures who can help him. If he needs other people for victims—as does the aggressive person—he tends to see them as inferiors who deserve nothing better than to be defeated by him. Needless to say, these views are inaccurate, as he may eventually find out to his surprise and dismay. Of course, the picture of neurotic interaction is complicated by the fact that not only are neurotic processes operating, but healthy ones as well.

As we have seen, the relationship between two people can be quite complicated; when more than two people are involved the complexities increase in geometric progression.

## *The Compliant Person*

Since the compliant person constantly needs approval from others, he tends to see people as good and kind. He will, therefore, trust too many people too readily—and be taken advantage of by some. He may rationalize that he loves people and that he is quick to see the good in everybody. The compliant person tends to use the word "love" very freely. One could even say that he loves everybody. However, this is not love in a mature sense but a neurotic need for affection and approval. When other people show that they like him he is relieved from anxiety and receives a measure of security. But, like all neurotics, he is insatiable, needing more and more people to demonstrate their approval of him. Because he tries very hard to please everybody, he cannot be very discriminating. As a result, compliant people often develop great sensitivity to what others expect of them. As one patient said, "I can be whatever people want me to be." Her goal was to please others.

The compliant person is not in control of his own life because he is unable to determine what it is that he really wants for himself. He continually underestimates himself; his good qualities he takes for granted, but he magnifies his faults. For fear of antagonizing other people he is afraid to be too aggressive and competitive. He cannot disagree or argue because he is afraid of losing friends.

A healthy degree of friction between people leads to better communication, better understanding, and mutual respect. However, the compliant person cannot risk it. This same trait often hinders him at work, because he is afraid to succeed and, thus, antagonize someone else. He waits for others to give him permission before he will do many things. Needing the goodwill of everyone, he prefers to lose out rather than create hostilities. This leads to passivity that can be very incapacitating.

The compliant person is also in a dilemma when he simultaneously tries to please several people with varying opinions and different values. He finds it much easier to deal with only one person at a time when he can find out what the other wants and act accordingly. In his attempt to please several people, who hold different views, he must frantically search for a compromise that will be acceptable to everyone. In the process he will see merit in everyone's opinion and tend to agree with the last person to speak. His vacillation may be painful and his efforts to please everyone sometimes end in pleasing no one. Other people see his inconsistencies and his inability to stand up for his convictions.

The compliant person likes people who are warm and quick to demonstrate that they approve of and accept him. He is more uncomfortable with people who are cold and detached, as they do not meet his need for comfort and reassurance. Also, in his heightened sensitivity to rejection, he is quick to misinterpret detachment as rejection when actually it is not. In addition, because he is not a good fighter, and is easily intimidated, he is careful not to provoke aggressive and hostile people. When attacked by others, he prefers to placate or surrender. He may readily accept the role of follower or protégé of some strong person, but, because of these defensive maneuvers, he cannot enter relationships with others in a spontaneous, direct, and sincere manner.

## *The Aggressive Person*

The predominantly aggressive person finds reassurance by defeating others. It proves his mastery and his superiority. He has a sense of well-being when he moves from one triumph to another. He carries this to extremes and fights too many battles for things he doesn't really want. His battles, however successful, do not lead to significant achievements or real growth as a person; they merely allay anxiety. Like the compliant person, he, too, sees people in terms of his own needs, as competitors and rivals, not as individuals. He does not trust people. Fearing to be attacked, he attacks first—including many who had no intention of attacking him. Such incessant competitiveness and exaggeration of his achievements may win him some admirers, but they also drive other people away. The aggressive person usually leads a lonely personal life. While he is a good fighter, he fights too much and at times will encounter a superior competitor. As it says on a tombstone out West, "He kept asking for it until he got it." Once defeated, the aggressive person overreacts with rage, frustration, and humiliation. It is a severe blow to his idealized image.

## The Detached Person

The predominantly detached person has difficulty with those who make demands or cling to him. He is much more comfortable with people who respect his privacy and do not move toward him too quickly. Unless he can proceed at a very cautious and slow pace, he will usually not be able to establish good relationships with people. His life will be lonely, with too few people to share his experiences. Detachment, like all other neurotic trends, can be carried too far and result in an impoverished life.

## Role Playing

A disturbing element in human relations is the influence of the idealized image. As an actor who has played a certain character role so often can begin to identify with that role, so the neurotic identifies with a dominant aspect of his idealized image. It becomes his trademark, one that gives him a measure of distinction and identifies him from all other men. Everyone recognizes this and encourages him to continue playing it. Commonly encountered are such roles as: "The Nice Guy," "The Martyr," "The Perfect Mother," "The Fearless Fighter," etc. While most roles fall into several broad categories, there are numerous variations. We can easily recognize other roles: "The Life of the Party," "The Supersalesman," "The Invalid," "The Worrier," "The Do-Gooder," "The Politician," "The Uncomplaining Wife," etc. Once established, the individual clings rigidly to his role and carries it to the point where it disturbs and distorts relationships with others and holds back healthy growth and spontaneity.

For example, in order to play "The Perfect Mother," you need a dependent child. The more the child needs you, the better the role. When the child grows up, the mother may not be ready to give up her role. There is little else in her impoverished life that is significant to her. Unconsciously, she will foster dependence and helplessness in the child to maintain her role. Take the child with a history of illness—rheumatic fever, asthma, etc.—who has fully recovered and is eager to take part in all the activities of his peers. However, the mother cannot permit this and continues to foster an attitude of invalidism in the child. She needs to be needed. Based on her own needs, she sees the child as immature and weak, the one who cannot stand on his own feet.

Another common role, seen with many variations, is that of "The Martyr." One variation is the long-suffering wife of the alcoholic, illustrated in the following case history:

> A 30-year-old woman came to the out-patient department of the hospital where I was working. She was poorly dressed and looked older than her years—mainly because she had neglected her teeth. Some of the highlights of her history were that she married at 17, primarily to get away from intolerable conditions at home. Her father was an alcoholic. Soon after her marriage, it became apparent that her husband was also a problem drinker. He was an industrious and capable electrician when sober. However, quite regularly, once a month, he went on a drinking spree that usually lasted from several days up to a week. During these periods he abused her physically (once she required hospitalization) and terrorized the children. They had financial difficulties because a considerable part of his income went for alcohol; their situation was further complicated by the unwillingness of some employers to hire him. When he sobered up, he was remorseful and penitent, pleading for forgiveness and promising that he would never drink again. He would stay sober for a number of weeks and then the pattern would repeat itself. This went on for many years, during which time the wife struggled to keep the home going and to meet the needs of their children. She spent only a bare minimum on herself, sometimes even denying herself necessary medical

and dental care. To the neighbors she was a sweet and pretty woman, a saint, and they marveled at her patience and willingness to sacrifice so much to keep the family together. They often wondered why she didn't leave him, and even why she had married him in the first place. She never complained about him. To close friends she confided that she loved him and prayed that he would one day give up drinking.

One day her husband did stop drinking and began to attend AA regularly. This day that had been so eagerly awaited for many years only proved that solutions to problems bring other problems. My patient was now married to a reformed alcoholic. Previously, he had been either drunk and abusive or sobering up and penitent. Now he was a different person, clear-eyed and firm. He began to notice things that he hadn't seen before. He saw that his wife was an indifferent cook and a poor manager of the household money. He didn't like the way she dressed, or took care of the house or of the children. He wanted sex more often, to his wife's dismay. The focus now was on her deficiencies and not on his. Some of his drinking had been a reaction to an unattractive home life. Evidently, his wife was better at being a "martyr" and nursing an alcoholic husband than at living with a mature and responsible man. His drinking had spared her from looking at her own problems. In time, with help from me, she was able to face them, as they were, and learn to deal with them.

Another role often seen is that of "The Invalid." In many families there is often the "sickly one," whom, because of a physical or mental disorder, the other members of the family try to protect. The invalid is often all that holds many families together. When the invalid becomes well, husband and wife may realize that his care was the only thing they had in common. Bickering and quarreling become more frequent; many such marriages end in divorce.

For the invalid himself, there are some advantages to being ill: the help and attention from others, and the relief from many of the responsibilities that other people face. After a number of years of being chronically ill, it is hard to give up this role and go back to facing the problems of everyday living.

One of my patients suffered from epilepsy for many years. Although a college graduate, he could not keep a job because his seizures were frightening to onlookers. His employers also feared liability in the event that he was injured while at work. Many doctors had been consulted but all therapeutic measures were ineffective. For over ten years he lived the isolated life of an invalid, supported by a sympathetic family. Then a new drug was introduced which, for the first time, successfully controlled his seizures. This happy development was short-lived; his freedom from seizures brought new problems. His family now pressured him to get a job and become self-supporting. He made some efforts to do this, but found it very difficult, for the world had changed a great deal in ten years. After all these years of invalidism he could not become an independent, self-sufficient person. As a result, he suffered a severe emotional breakdown that required hospitalization.

Once established, roles are held rigidly. After years in prison, a convict may find it hard to adjust to the freedom outside the prison walls he hated. There are many similar instances where people are not able to adapt when they lose their accustomed roles. One of my patients, an extremely compulsive man, was proud of the fact that he never missed a day of work. He once said, "At least I can still work." My answer was, "At most you can work. You are not doing anything else." Only when this patient improved, was he able to miss an occasional day at the office without feeling guilty.

## The Victim and the Oppressor

On occasion, we come across a strange relationship between two people, in which one suffers great abuse and torment at the hands of the other. People observing such a relationship will often ask, "Why in heaven's name does she put up with him?" It seems incredible.

One of my patients was married to a man who degraded and ridiculed her constantly, beat her on occasion, bragged to her about his exploits with other women, made continual and extravagant demands on her time and energy, etc. In spite of all this, she continued to be a devoted wife and rarely complained. When her indignant friends and relatives asked why she allowed this to go on, her only answer was that she loved her husband. This unusual relationship has been called a morbid dependency or a sadomasochistic relationship.

A masochist is a person who derives some perverse pleasure from suffering. However, this is a much too simple explanation of the motivation in a complicated relationship. I don't think people enjoy suffering: they may *need* to suffer. Such a person is extremely compliant and almost always becomes involved with a very aggressive individual. In our culture, the compliant person is more often a woman who sees fulfillment in love for the right man. She has so little self-esteem that she is convinced that her only chance for happiness is to live for someone who is worthy. With him she will find the protection and support she needs to live in this difficult world. By losing herself in this relationship, she will become a whole person. And the more she gives to this relationship, the more she suffers in the name of love, and the more she becomes a worthwhile person.

She will be especially attracted to the man who rejects her or is indifferent to her at first. This proves he is a superior person. The man who immediately shows her that he likes her does not appeal to her. Since she does not think highly of herself, anyone who does cannot be a really worthwhile person. An arrogant person who insults or ignores her impresses her with his strength. Her need to surrender makes it necessary for her to idealize her lover. She is ready to give up everything and abdicate the responsibility of living her own life for this wonderful man. She is prepared to sacrifice lifelong interests, old friends, or a career that was important to her. Nothing matters except that she please the man she loves.

In time, she becomes isolated; all she has is this relationship to her man. Their relationship may be fairly well-balanced for a time, she surrendering and he taking. However, like all neurotic behavior, it goes to extremes. While the compliant woman is prepared to give up everything for love, in time it becomes apparent that her partner cannot return her love. The aggressive person is afraid of closeness, warmth, and tenderness, which he feels as weaknesses. Also, he is repelled by her clinging and possessiveness, which he feels as coercion. His wife may become aware that her husband is not returning her love, but clings to the hope that one day he will. It is very hard for her to relinquish a goal in which she has invested so much of herself. Eventually, she is forced to recognize that her lover cannot ever be the person she hoped for. At this time, her self-contempt and self-hatred may become so overwhelming that they lead to destructive behavior against her partner or herself. Suicide in such instances is not unusual. If the compliant person has enough healthy traits in her makeup, she may at long last recognize the great danger she is in and begin the painful struggle to extricate herself from the situation and to achieve a healthier life with some measure of self-respect. Great writers have recognized the stormy relationship between the extremely compliant person compelled to sacrifice all for love and the aggressive person who is driven to victimize others. Somerset Maugham has given a brilliant description of this neurotic interaction in his novel aptly entitled *Of Human Bondage*.

## Neurotic "Games"

In dealing with other people, the neurotic wants it both ways. He wants to have his own way and yet avoid criticism or loss of self-esteem. He wants someone else to take the blame if his own actions fail. This often involves a series of actions that involve deception of one's self and deception of others. It does not bring out the best in people, but rather resentment and guilt. For example, one patient told me she wanted to decorate and furnish her new home. Actually, she was quite fearful of making mistakes that would be costly and hard for her to live with. However, she could not face her doubts, but suppressed them and tried to act with assurance. As a result, she went about this task with interminable delays, consulting numerous decorators and department stores, and with frequent changes of mind. Her husband complained about the delay, especially about having to sleep on borrowed folding cots. Finally, in disgust, he went out and ordered a complete set of bedroom furniture. At this point, his wife got angry and protested that her husband never let her do anything, that he always got his own way in everything. The wife felt both abused and secretly relieved, while the husband felt guilty.

Also quite common are instances where a couple have a

stormy marriage with many arguments, threats, provocations, etc. In one case, the husband made his life more tolerable by drinking heavily, which infuriated his wife still more. Her method of getting back at him was to needle him with sarcasm and insults until she provoked him into hitting her. At this point she would rush to the phone to call the police and report that her husband beat her. The incident thus ended to the wife's satisfaction. The police would come and take her husband away and she could complain about his behavior to her friends and neighbors. In this way, she was able to put her husband in a bad light and herself in a relatively good one, that of the injured wife. Dr. Eric Berne in his book, *Games People Play,** describes in considerable detail the neurotic transactions people become involved in. He has given many of them such colorful names as: "If It Weren't for You," "Schlemiel," "Now I've Got You, You Son-of-a-Bitch." The essential point in these games is that those who play maintain their glorified image, prove their superiority, express hostility, and avoid a large measure of responsibility for their own actions.

For example, the game "If It Weren't for You" might proceed something like this: A wife toys with the idea that someday she will go back to college and get her degree. However, she is afraid that she may not be able to keep up with the courses after several years out of college and broaches the subject to her husband apologetically. He feels this would be inconvenient for him and senses that his wife isn't really that eager about it, so he refuses. The wife reacts to this with annoyance and, secretly, some relief. In her own mind and to her friends the story is that she sacrificed her ambitions for the sake of her husband.

These games or transactions involve self-deception and blurring of the real issues. They lead away from any real understanding of our motives and perpetuate neurotic interaction.

## *Self-Hatred, Prejudice, and Race Riots*

The most violent upheavals in interpersonal relations occur in riots, religious persecution, and wars. While there

* Grove Press, New York, 1964.

are historic, economic, and political reasons for all of these events, there are also important psychological factors. People obtain a measure of superiority by looking down at other races and nationalities as inferior. This is especially true for those who lead wretched lives themselves. They need a scapegoat and a target on which to vent their hatred. The person who has a great deal of self-contempt and self-hatred feels better if he can externalize some of it. The degree of self-hatred can be enormous if the person feels that he has failed to reach the standards that he hopes or needs to obtain. Those traits we despise in ourselves are the very ones we attack most fiercely in others. The Negro is accused of being lazy, inferior, shiftless, and amoral by those whites who experience themselves as lazy, inferior, shiftless, and amoral.

Self-contempt constitutes a prejudice against the person himself. All neurotics, to a greater or lesser extent, experience themselves as their despised image and perpetuate and magnify this by daily distortion of events. When the neurotic does something that is good, he attributes it to luck; when he does poorly at something, he accepts this as proof that he is worthless. He continually falsifies the evidence of his eyes and ears, and rigidly maintains the view he has of himself. Since we obtain some relief from painful self-contempt by striking out at someone else, we often externalize or project our prejudice against another group. Since it is too painful to accept our limitations and inadequacies, it relieves us when we can attack others whom we hold to blame for what is wrong with our own lives. For economic and political reasons, people in power have kept animosities alive between different nations, races, and religions. The frustrations and despair of the Germans after World War I were a major contribution to the rise to power of the Nazis. It was a great relief for the Germans to believe that they never were really defeated but had been tricked by Jews who were international bankers and Communists at the same time. It was very reassuring to be told that they really were men of a superior race. It helped them to channel this enormous self-contempt against a convenient scapegoat: in this case, the Jews.

The answer to racial strife, civil riot, and religious persecution is self-respect, dignity, and a feeling of worth. A self-respecting person who believes in the worth and dignity of the human being will not engage in brutality and atrocities against other human beings. In spite of enormous pressure, many self-respecting and prominent Germans did not follow Hitler. They chose to leave their fatherland or went to jail in preference to conforming to the barbaric decrees of Nazi Germany. A man who truly loves himself also loves his neighbor.

# Chapter 8

## *Marriage, Love, and Sex*

Marriage has come in for a lot of criticism in recent years. The incidence of divorce is steadily increasing, and many prominent people state that it is an out-moded institution and will disappear entirely before too long. Certainly much has changed in our society, and this is reflected in the patterns of marriage. Divorces are easier to obtain, carry much less social stigma, and do not present as much of a financial burden as before. The women's movement is now a potent influence. With greater career opportunities open to them, many women are choosing not to get married. In increasing numbers, some couples simply live together. And yet, with all of this, people still get married and two-thirds of all marriages endure.

To the extent that a person is neurotic, he expects everything; this is especially true of marriage. A man expects that his wife will be a paragon of all the virtues and a source of never-ending joy. She will be cheerful, comforting, uncomplaining, helpful, reassuring, admiring, capable, efficient, strong, dainty, amusing, unobtrusive, etc. She will have all the qualities that he likes and none that he dislikes. The neurotic woman is equally unrealistic about her husband; she expects that he will be handsome, loyal, devoted, and a hard worker who will achieve a good measure of distinction and wealth but will always have time for all her needs. Actually, marriage is a relationship that involves two human beings, and like all human relationships it involves friction, struggle, disappointment, and frustration. The personalities of the two people who get married do not undergo any sudden transformation: the unhappy bachelor becomes an unhappy husband; the immature and hysterical girl becomes an immature and hysterical wife.

Neurotic traits do not automatically disappear after marriage. On the contrary, the closeness of the relationship often magnifies neurotic traits. The realities of marriage prove so different from expectations that, in America, many of the couples decide to end their marriages by divorce. Many unhappy marriages do not end in divorce, but simply go on and on.

## *Choice of Mate*

Choosing a spouse is an important and difficult decision for everyone. It should, therefore, not be too surprising that the neurotic often picks an unsuitable person to marry. In fact, his choice is often remarkably bad. This is due in part to his bad judgment about people, but also because people act differently during the courtship than at any other time in their lives. There is an excitement during this period that mobilizes an extra amount of energy and spirit. Not only do people try harder to live up to their own idealized image of themselves but they try to impress the one they are courting. They frequently succeed in deceiving themselves and misleading the other person. Not all of it is deliberate or fully conscious. One of my patients was attracted to the man she later married because he seemed so carefree and happy-go-lucky and he was so much fun to be with. Soon after marriage it became obvious that he was just the opposite. He was gloomy, depressed, and always worrying about one thing or another. The virile suitor sometimes turns out, as a husband, to be not so interested in sex, and the girl who was so popular in college may turn out to be difficult and demanding.

Sometimes the neurotic may see a pattern of behavior clearly, but misinterpret its significance. For instance, one of my patients was engaged to a young attorney who had just started in practice. Invariably, he was either late for his dates or they had to be postponed because he was working on important cases. This happened again and again. At the time, my patient admired this young man's ambition and his devotion to his responsibility and was willing to put up with his work habits. However, after they were married the same behavior continued, to the detriment of their family and social life. My patient rarely saw her husband. Now she realized with dismay that this man would sacrifice everything to the demands of his practice.

The neurotic has little real freedom in choosing a mate, hampered as he is by fears and compulsions. The compliant person, to whom rejection is too painful, cannot seriously pursue anyone who might turn him down. He therefore avoids courting some of the more desirable girls he meets and restricts himself to the safe ones, that is, those who will not turn him down. He does defend himself against the pain of rejection but at the cost of limiting himself to what may be second best. The predominantly expansive person will often marry after a whirlwind courtship in which he is the active and aggressive suitor. He will be most attracted to a girl who presents a challenge or one who will bring him prestige. Because the detached person fears the intimacy of marriage and the loss of freedom, he is generally the most reluctant of all to get married. He usually marries late, after much urging and pressure from relatives and friends. When the time comes, he is likely to marry the first available girl who will take the initiative but not be so aggressive that she frightens him off. As opposed to the detached individual, the severely alienated person is not able to experience any deep feelings of love and affection. Since major decisions are best made by our feelings, he is under a great handicap regarding marriage, and likely to drift along without getting seriously involved with anyone. Lacking any close contact with his own feelings, he cannot be guided by them. He may finally marry the girl who knows what she wants even if he doesn't.

The above is a greatly simplified description of some of the patterns involved in choosing a mate. As has been pointed out before, we are all mixtures of neurotic and healthy traits. Since courtship involves two people, each of whom are both healthy and neurotic, the decision to marry is a complicated one. Timing is very important and even chance plays a role. It seems to me that there has been too much emphasis on *whom* to marry and not enough on *when* to marry. It is remarkable how quickly people marry when finally they are ready to; if one match doesn't work out, another one will. The person who is not ready to marry usually picks out faults in those possible mates who are available rather than face the fact that he is not prepared for the responsibility that marriage entails.

The decision to get married is essentially an emotional decision. Logic and reason play a minor part. For instance, it is quite common for a person to go through a painful and costly divorce only to marry someone very similar to the spouse he just shed. Sometimes they even remarry the same person. As the result of emotion, people often make what may seem to be strange choices. A bright, cultivated young man may marry an uneducated woman twenty years his senior. A young and pretty heiress may marry the chauffeur or gardener who is old enough to be her father. Grossly unsuitable marriages usually indicate serious mental disturbance. A well-known New York psychiatrist once said that he often learned as much about a patient by meeting his spouse as he could from a battery of psychological tests. It is readily apparent that many of these marriages express feelings of inferiority and unworthiness, or the need to seek a parent substitute rather than a mate.

It is striking how often one partner succeeds in establishing a family that is very much like the family he or she grew up in. Such patterns occur too often to be purely accidental. We are decisively influenced by the experiences we had as a young child and often are driven to reestablish a family similar to the one we grew up in. The motivation for this is not conscious. The daughter of an alcoholic who flees from an intolerable family situation will frequently marry a man who turns out to be an alcoholic. A girl will often marry a man who has some of the characteristics of her father or she may pick out someone who is the extreme opposite.

To marry because of social pressure, to prove that you are independent, or to defy your family are all poor reasons. So is marriage because of guilt feelings from premarital sex. The courtship should be long enough so that each can evaluate the personality of the other. Everything being equal, backgrounds and values that are similar make for more compatible and satisfactory marriages. "I'm in love" sounds exciting and romantic, but all too often these are fleeting and not genuine feelings. The word "love" is used carelessly. I once told a patient whose girl friend treated him very shabbily, "That's not love, that's neurosis."

## *Marital Conflicts*

Neurotic traits do not disappear with marriage. They persist and may be magnified by the closeness of the relationship. In earlier chapters, "neurotic claims" and the "shoulds" have been described as important components in the neurotic system. These operate with special intensity in marriage because there is an interaction and escalation of these traits between husband and wife. The neurotic husband makes extravagant claims on his wife. He feels very clearly that he is entitled to special treatment at home, that his wife should meet all his demands—or what is a wife for? The neurotic wife may feel that her job is to make her husband happy at all costs. There is a constant stream of "claims" and "shoulds" going on between neurotic husband and neurotic wife. When all these demands cannot be met, as is inevitable, it leads to anger, frustration, resentment, and guilt. Neither partner sees that these demands are impossible to fulfill, yet they go on trying, failing, and feeling guilty. Unless there is enough that is healthy to counteract the neurotic interaction, it continues and becomes more intense and painful.

Also characteristic of the neurotic is a great self-contempt and self-hatred. Because this can be easily projected onto the spouse, they are destructive influences in marriage. The neurotic husband feels that he is not worth much and neither is his wife, otherwise she would not have married him. With the possible exception of his children, he will treat her worse than any other person in the world. He is much more courteous to friends, casual acquaintances, or strangers than he is to his wife. He will listen respectfully to everyone else's opinion but not his wife's. She makes an easy and ever-present punching bag for his self-hatred. Since the married couple identify with each other, and think of themselves as a unit, they are especially vulnerable to each other's actions. A man may be quite tolerant when someone else's wife or girl friend says something stupid or wears a miniskirt that exposes too much of her thighs. However, let his wife say or do anything like that and he is furious because he feels it reflects unfavorably on him. Since he has more than enough self-contempt to begin with, his wife must never do anything to embarrass him.

## Points of Friction

We cannot have it both ways; if we want the advantages of a partnership we must put up with its drawbacks. Two people have differences in temperament, energy, taste, and values. If they are to live together in the close relationship of marriage, then there is bound to be a constant need to adjust and compromise, and there is bound to be friction. In my experience, the major battlegrounds of marriage concern money, sex, children, and relatives, although not necessarily in that order. I think it would be helpful to discuss some of these typical arguments in marriage.

### *Money*

Money, obviously, is very important, and most of the time two cannot live as cheaply as one. If there is real poverty, then the concern for money makes all other problems secondary. In the impoverished family, the overriding concern is how to get enough money for the necessities and some of the comforts of life. In most families, however, real poverty does not exist, but neither is there money for everything; choices have to be made, and friction develops over what the money should be spent for and by whom. For example, a wife will resent it if her husband keeps her on a tight budget while he regularly indulges himself in small luxuries. She has to account for every dollar but he will casually buy equipment for his hobbies without even consulting her. It is often not the actual amount of money available but the attitudes toward it that are important. In many affluent homes there are bitter fights about trivial expenses such as those resulting from forgetting to turn off the electric lights or wasting hot water, etc. The husband may be very touchy if he feels his wife does not fully appreciate how hard he works to earn the money he provides. He may nag his wife about wasting pennies on groceries, yet spend many thousands on costly fishing equipment, cameras, etc. Money matters provide a convenient area for the expression of hostility between a husband and wife: when the wife is angry she will waste her husband's money by buying luxuries; when the husband is angry he will provide less money for his wife or force her to ask for it in a way that degrades her. Control of the purse strings often enables a husband to pressure his wife and maintain a certain degree of control over her.

In our society the most important way for a man to be successful is in a financial way. It is hard for some men to accept the fact that they do not have the drive or the talent to amass a great deal of money, that they will never be able to afford many of the acquisitions which give a family status: a pretentious home, expensive clothes, luxury automobiles, prestige schools for their children, etc. These men are vulnerable to pressure from their wives who are unhappy that they have to do without these status symbols. Many otherwise happy marriages are spoiled by the overriding concern about making enough money to compete successfully with friends and relatives. Many women take for granted the good qualities of their husbands—sensitivity, kindness, loyalty, interest in the family, etc.—and overemphasize that he is not a good provider. It is also hard for men to gracefully accept the fact that their wives may be more successful in business. Both lead to needless discord.

In those few homes where there is money enough for everything, the battle between the spouses will shift to some other area: sex, children, or relatives.

### *Sex*

Sex means different things to different people. It involves biologic drives and rhythms, capacities for physical and emotional closeness, tenderness and love. All the experiences a person has had shape his attitudes toward sex. Sexual feelings and interests vary considerably from time to time in the same person. Sometimes it is predominantly a physical need. An old-fashioned word for this is lust. It is then primarily a physical act. At other times, it is an expression of tenderness and love, of giving and receiving pleasure. At such times the emotional and physical intimacy are the important components.

It is rare to find a couple whose sexual preferences and rhythms coincide. Compromise is almost always necessary. In a marriage of two mature and loving persons, the needs of both will be carefully considered and satisfactory adjustments worked out. If they like and enjoy each other, they will also enjoy sex. It is unusual to find a good marriage in which the sexual adjustment is poor. However, this does occur. The reverse—"a bad marriage" in which nothing is good but the sex—also occurs, but infrequently.

Neurotic couples bring out the worst in each other. Anxiety, guilt, hostility, and self-contempt will be carried over into their sexual relations. They may use sex to dominate or humiliate the partner. This may be done in subtle or not so subtle ways. Sometimes sex is withheld, to punish or frustrate a spouse. Sometimes one partner finds sexual pleasure only when inflicting pain on the other. The motivation for much of this is often unconscious, so the couple may not be aware of what is really going on.

Anxiety may increase sexual drive or decrease it. Sexual activity promotes relaxation and a feeling of well-being, and is thus an outlet for anxiety. In periods of stress, some people will seek more activity; for others, the reverse is true, and anxiety impairs sexual functioning and may lead to impotence, premature ejaculation, or frigidity. Anxiety about sexual performance is especially detrimental; sex should be fun, but it is often approached as an ordeal. With the emphasis on women's liberation, many women now express their sexual desires more freely. While this is stimulating at times, it may not always be welcome. Not many men are able to respond at all times. In the past, frigidity in women was the most common problem seen by clinicians, but today male impotence and premature ejaculation are more prominent. Sexual intercourse is a natural function and proceeds best when it is not forced but allowed to develop spontaneously. Today's widespread overemphasis on sexual gratification leads to impossible standards, frustration, and disappointment.

Sexual problems can usually be worked out if the partners can talk to each other without embarrassment or guilt. Sometimes physical closeness and being held, not intercourse, is all that is desired; but this may be misunderstood by the spouse. Many men are particularly sensitive to rejection by their wives. They assume that, in marriage, all their sexual needs (and even fantasies) will be fulfilled. This ideal is almost never attained. The situation can be compounded by wives who feel guilty if they are unwilling to perform their "marital duties" at all times and under all circumstances. Some men demand that their wives respond with an orgasm each time. I once saw in consultation a very disturbed man who would not let his wife out of bed until she had achieved orgasm, no matter how long it took. This was an impossible standard. This was "making war," not love. Essentially, each person is responsible for his or her orgasm. It is not a reflection on the ability or technique of the partner if this is not achieved. I should here mention the work of Masters and Johnson, who have made such great contributions to our understanding of sexual behavior.*

In recent years there has been a sexual revolution that has profoundly influenced all aspects of our lives. Books, magazines, theaters, movies, styles of dress, etc., all reflect the new freedom. Censorship is almost nonexistent. Some of this freedom is beneficial and will result in less ignorance and guilt about sexual matters. However, there are some unfortunate results too. Young people are pushed into sexual activity by peer pressure before they are ready to handle the emotional consequences. Unwanted pregnancies still occur in spite of all the methods of birth control, and venereal disease is widespread. There is confusion when old standards are discarded and people are left to work out their own guidelines. Many new things are advocated by a variety of "experts." These include trying every conceivable position, making use of all body orifices, using mechanical gadgets to enhance sensation, experiencing group sex, switching partners, etc.

There are too many authorities to listen to, and it is difficult to draw a line between healthy and unhealthy sexual practices, between what is normal and what is abnormal. I have some thoughts on the subject. A mature, self-respecting person will not permit himself (herself) to be intimidated or shamed into doing something that is not right for him (her). Some thought needs to be given to possible consequences. Acts that degrade or traumatize the partner are unhealthy. Freedom includes the right to say "no." There is certainly room for innovation and experimentation to achieve a rich and varied sex life, but this is not desirable if one of the people is hurt. In my clinical practice, I have found that switching partners is never good for all four participants. One person is usually hurt by it. Each couple must work out what is right for both of them, and it must be acceptable to

* *Human Sexual Response*, W. H. Masters and V. E. Johnson, Little, Brown and Company, Boston, 1966.

both or it is not good for either. In my opinion, sex is an intimate and meaningful act, best carried out in privacy by two responsible and caring individuals.

### *Children*

It is a rare family in which both parents want the same things for their children—and from them. Neurotic parents both want reflected glory from the accomplishments of their children but differ as to how the child will accomplish this. Since the values and goals of parents differ, they will push the child in different directions. It is unusual for both parents to see their children as they really are; the picture is distorted by their own needs and fears. One parent may grossly overestimate the child's abilities while the other underestimates them. One parent may not trust the child enough while the other one cannot see even his most glaring defects: lying, stealing, the use of drugs, etc.

The battling that occurs between husband and wife is often carried over into actions against their children. Children are a convenient target for the expression of hostility. They are small, dependent, and cannot fight back. It is safer to strike a child than a wife (or husband). A parent will scold a child because he does something he dislikes that reminds him of similar actions by his wife. He cannot punish his wife but he can punish the child. This message often gets across.

Where parents have been divorced and remarried, children of the former marriage may still provoke many unpleasant feelings: jealousy, memory of an unpleasant past episode, problems of support and custody, etc. In such cases, children are punished not for their actions but because of the things they represent to the parents. In stormy marriages, children are also used to transmit hostility from one spouse to the other.

### *In-laws*

The young couple who marry and think that now they have only themselves to think of soon find out that they have been unrealistic. There are the in-laws, and the many jokes about them is a good indication that these relationships can be troublesome. One of my patients referred to his in-laws as "out-laws." To any newlywed it is quite a strain to accept the fact that these strangers have played an important role in the life of his or her spouse for many years. It takes a lot of flexibility to act toward them in a cordial way and call them "dad" or "mother." Frequently, it is more than some young couples can manage. In an earlier generation, or in some other parts of the world even today, there is greater recognition that marriage involves families. In America we are less tolerant of this intrusion by others into our personal lives. But if there is a sound relationship between a husband and wife the difficulties concerning the in-laws can be resolved. The young bridegroom does not really have to suddenly love the mother-in-law he barely knows. If he recognizes that she has had an important role in the life of his wife over many years, out of consideration for his spouse, he can at least treat her respectfully and courteously. If, however, there is friction and hostility between husband and wife, it is often through the in-laws that they find the means to attack one another. It is easier for a husband to attack his mother-in-law than to express hostility directly toward his wife. Even though the mother-in-law provides a good excuse for hostile behavior, the wife may correctly sense that her husband's target is really herself. When he attacks her mother he is attacking her. She gets the message.

The above examples illustrate some of the common areas of disagreement and conflict in marriage. What is basic to a successful marriage is the attitude that two people have toward one another. If there is a sincere concern for the other person's welfare, then points of friction will be handled well and resolved. A certain amount of friction is healthy in any close relationship; it leads to better communication and, in the long run, to a smoother relationship because the rough spots have been polished down. Fighting can be constructive when it clarifies issues; it is also an important form of communication. Stick to the relevant issues; don't bring up things from the distant past to hurt or degrade your spouse. Stick to the pronoun "I" and not "you." "*I* don't like this" is better than "When are *you* ever going to learn?" Sometimes there is no greater hostility than *not* fighting. Loving couples are also fighting couples. Needless to say, there is also a time to stop fighting and a time to make up. A home in which there are never any arguments is "too good" and usually means that the participants are not enough involved with each other. A classic story in psychiatric circles is the one in which the husband comes home and finds a note from his wife that she has left him. The husband then says to his psychiatrist, "I don't understand it, we never had any fights," and the psychiatrist comments, "But you never had anything else either."

## *What Makes a Good Marriage*

As a contrast to the neurotic pattern in marriage, it may be helpful to describe some of the qualities that exist in a good marriage. A. de la Torre, a prominent psychiatrist in Miami, said, "There are no sick marriages, only sick people." I would paraphrase this and say, "Sick people make sick marriages, mature and self-respecting people make good marriages." Karen Horney described three important qualities that are present in a good marriage: acceptance, sincerity, and mutuality. The first involves a mature and disciplined effort to get along with a spouse as he or she is. It is unrealistic to expect that a person can change his basic character quickly, and any demand or threat that he do so will only create friction, frustration, and resentment. In a good marriage, the person may not like certain traits in his spouse but he accepts the fact that she cannot change quickly, and in the meantime, he tries to accept her as she is. Accepting reality, he does not make impossible demands.

The second element in a good marriage is sincerity. It is a common word—sincerity—that is all too often used loosely and casually. Very often it is an empty gesture. We sign our letters "sincerely yours" when we may not mean that at all. Sincere means wholehearted, honest, and without evasion or deceit. The sincere person is a whole person who gives the best that he has. He does not maneuver or exploit, wheel and deal, or try to bargain: I will do so much for you if you do so much for me. A sincere relationship is a completely honest relationship. In my opinion, one harmful effect of infidelity in marriage is that it leads to deceiving the other partner by evasion, half-truths, and outright lies. The unfaithful spouse cannot speak freely for fear that he will give himself away; he must always be on guard. As these restrictions persist, a barrier is built up that is not helpful to good communication. Infidelity is complicated and does not always mean the same thing to different people. To some it may be a transient or casual experience, one that may even be hard to avoid in certain circumstances: prolonged separation or illness, for example. However, the man or woman who regularly seeks extramarital affairs—who wants to have his cake and eat it too—does not enter into a marriage wholeheartedly. In this marriage there are always concealment, evasion, and feelings of guilt.

The third element in a good marriage is what Horney calls "mutuality." This is the quality in marriage wherein the husband and wife think in terms of "we" or "us." They think of themselves as a partnership, as members on the same team. Through mutual encouragement and help, they bring out the best in each other. They fully appreciate each other's good qualities. They do not store up things the other has said or done in order to hurl them at him or her the next time they argue. As one patient said to his wife; "Let's not escalate this argument. We've both had our say, now let's stop." They are quick to praise and slow to criticize. When they do criticize they do so gently and only when it is actually constructive. Complaining—that is, unconstructive criticism—is a means of attack, not communication. Good communication consists in telling your spouse how you feel and what you think, so he may understand. It does not consist in attacking. The wife who would like her husband to talk more to her asks questions to help him get started. She doesn't brusquely complain, "You never have anything to say to me." If the husband comes home late, she says, "I was worried," not, "Where the hell were you all this time?" The couple with a true sense of mutuality do not have a feeling that they live on a seesaw—when one is up the other is down, when one is dominant and the other is subservient. There is no feeling that one is the boss, the other the slave. They are a team, each doing what he can do best. If one partner excels in one area, that becomes his major responsibility. Such couples help each other to grow, and as the years go by, their relationship becomes richer as their understanding and respect for one another becomes greater. While not everyone should marry—some people are better off single, in my opinion—marriage is the best pattern that has been worked out for a long-term relationship between a man and a woman. It offers no magical shortcuts whereby two miserable individuals can become a happy couple, but it does offer an opportunity for two people to help each other to grow.

# Chapter 9

## *Parents and Children*

In recent years, we have grown very afraid of doing wrong by our children. In our present age of anxiety, one of the great fears of parents is that, by a single mistake or in a moment of carelessness, they may cause permanent harm to their children. Since parenthood involves an almost endless number of difficult decisions, parents may feel that they are constantly on the brink of disaster. Reinforcing this fear are numerous books and movies which dramatize the harmful effects of a single traumatic event on the life of an individual. It makes for exciting reading but it is a distortion of the truth. Single traumatic events are not nearly as important as the sum total of all that happens between parent and child. There is also a widespread misconception that everything that goes wrong with a child is the fault of the parent. This is a gross oversimplification. About ninety years ago, at the time that modern psychiatry began, all mental disturbance was blamed on heredity, with the idea that nothing could be done about it. Modern psychiatry did stress, and correctly so, the crucial role of childhood in the development of the personality and in mental disorders. However, it is carrying the idea much too far to blame everything that goes wrong on the parent. These misconceptions make the difficult job of being a parent still more difficult. One or two generations back, children had no rights. Now it is the parent who lacks them. Even two generations ago Freud called the job of being a parent "an impossible profession."

## *Avoiding Responsibility*

It is no wonder, then, that parents look around for relief from their crushing burden of responsibility. One way to escape is by saying "yes" to almost everything the child wants. The parent can rationalize that he is making the child happy, and, therefore, he is a good parent. The trouble with this is that the child lacks the maturity to assume so much responsibility for himself. Furthermore, the child does not really want everything he asks for. Often he is only testing the limits of how much the parent will allow. What he really wants is guidance.

Another common way to relieve oneself of the responsibility of parenthood is to rush to the "child experts" for advice. Then, if anything goes wrong, you can blame it on Dr. Spock, Dr. Gesell, or some other expert. Parents feel that they are not to blame because they have carried out the instructions of the expert. This method, too, has many drawbacks. Even the best of experts gives information and suggestions only about children in general and not specifically about your child. These theories are too broad to be applied to any one child. The expert has, in fact, never even seen your child. In addition, general advice and suggestions must be used with discrimination. The parent must know not only what to do but how and when to do it. Parents differ greatly: what one can do easily another cannot do at all. If a parent does not believe in what he is doing, or doesn't fully understand it, he will probably not carry it out well. In such a case, he would do better not to follow the expert at all.

## *Parental Attitudes*

More important than what a parent says or does is how he feels about his child. Children cannot be fooled all the time. Beneath the kind words and patient tone of voice, the child senses the anger, the disappointment, or the indifference of his parent. What the parent feels usually comes across to him. If the parent is disappointed in him, the child will sense it and feel unworthy. His self-esteem is diminished. Conversely, the child who sees that his parents are pleased with him will experience a sense of well-being and a sense of worth. One of the best things a parent can do for a child is to enjoy him.

There is no easy way to be a parent. No formula will work all the time. Advice is much easier to give than to follow, and it must be applied with discrimination. Parents often ask, "Shall I be strict or permissive?" The correct answer is "both." But the difficult part is to know when and how to be strict, and when and how to be permissive. Listen to the advice and suggestions of the experts, but develop your own ideas and methods. Do the best you can and, if you make a mistake, learn from the experience. Learn to trust your own feelings and instincts. Try to understand what your feelings are in relation to the child. Develop your own style of being a parent, a style that fits you.

We tend to see our children as we want them to be, rather than as they are. We tend to oversimplify. For example, no child does something just for attention. That is an inadequate explanation. Why does the child need attention at the time? And why does he choose this way to get attention? Try to understand what is going on in the child. Don't jump to conclusions; keep your impatience in check. Ask yourself, "What is he trying to communicate?" or "What is he trying to cover up?" Is he worried that he will be displaced by the new baby or is he having trouble at school, etc.?

It is easier to be a parent if you can see your child realistically and if you have a good idea of what you are trying to accomplish with him. Observe what you do and say to him and, above all, how you feel about him. This last will explain a great deal. For example, how do you feel when you refuse a request from the child, when you say "no" to him? Do you feel guilty or angry? Indecisive or sure of yourself? The child will usually sense some of these feelings and will react to them. He may sense when you mean "no" or when your "no" means "maybe." It explains why some children obey their parents and others enslave them.

Parents may love a child but not like him. Some children are easy for parents to like; others make it very difficult. As a rule, the ones who make it hard for you to like them are the very ones who need love and approval the most. Don't try to be the perfect parent. This can't be done and failure promotes guilt. It is quite human to dislike your offspring and be annoyed with him at times. If you can face these negative feelings honestly, you will be able to place them in proper perspective; later on, positive feelings will appear too. The mother who can never permit herself to feel anger and disappointment because a mother is not *supposed* to, will have to keep such a tight lid on her feelings that she will not be able to express any spontaneous and genuine feelings. Only the parent who can honestly face his own feelings can develop an honest relationship with his child.

Of all the difficult jobs in the world, few are entered into with so little preparation as parenthood. The physical act of conception usually is so easy that people often blunder into parenthood with little thought. Or, if they do think about it, they may believe that since they are prepared to love their children, that is all that is needed. However, love is not enough. Incidentally, that is the exact title of an excellent book about children—*Love Is Not Enough*, by Bruno Bettelheim.* Being a parent also takes hard work, much thought, patience, and maturity. Neurotic people may want children because it is "the thing to do," or to prop up a shaky marriage, for reflected glory, or for status. When the neurotic parent gives up his dreams of glory for himself he often transfers them to his children, hoping to attain these dreams through them. None of these reasons is good. Healthy people want children because they feel they will enjoy them.

## Overprotection

The first job of being a parent is to protect the child so that he may have the freedom to grow and develop his own talents. Each child is a unique human being, similar to all others, yet different. Whether good-looking or plain, bright or dull, gifted or retarded, he has the right to develop fully his own capacities and potential. The greatest expert cannot tell what this child is capable of, what he will be like at 10 years or 20 years of age. No other creature on earth is so helpless and needs care for such a long period of time in order to develop fully. It is, therefore, the first responsibility of parents to protect their

* The Free Press, Glencoe, Ill., 1950.

child from many dangers. They need to protect him from harmful chemicals, sharp instruments, traffic accidents, frightening TV programs, and a host of other physical and emotional dangers. Parents are thus confronted with a typical dilemma of parenthood: how to protect without overprotecting. Parents need to protect the child without robbing him of curiosity and initiative, without making him a timid and fearful child. It takes good judgment to know when to restrain him and when to let him explore. We can be guided by our knowledge of the child and by an educated guess as to whether he is ready for a particular new experience. But parents tend to transfer their anxieties to the child and confuse him. The timid parent restrains too much, while the aggressive parent tends to push too quickly. Both behaviors are harmful because they are based on the needs of the parent, not the child's needs. For example, a mother may be too frightened to let her son play football, although he has demonstrated that he is probably ready to do so. All too often, the mother will forbid him to play and will rationalize her decision by pointing out how dangerous the game is. The child may sense that his mother is magnifying the danger and he is confused. Honesty would be better. If his mother could say, "I am too nervous to let you play," then he would know who is afraid of what.

Another source of confusion is generated by parents when they disapprove of something the child wants but do not say so. When a child asks for something that is potentially dangerous or too expensive, they may say, "Oh, you don't want that." They tell him what he *should* want and think. This is brainwashing. In time, the child learns to want whatever his parents want him to. By conforming to their wishes he gets their approval. He must fit into a certain role, and if he doesn't, his parents will be disappointed in him and he will feel guilty. This interaction prevents the child from growing in freedom and developing his own potential. It is exactly like programming a computer. As he grows farther away from his own feelings he becomes alienated from his real self. In time, the child does not know what he really wants and this attitude may persist and influence his activities for many years. He becomes one of those adults who continually needs someone else to tell him what he is supposed to do and how he should think. It is not healthy growth.

## Teaching by Example

What can parents teach their children that will be of value to them in this changing world? Some parents say they only want to make their children happy. This is too vague a goal; you can't teach happiness. But parents can help children to learn that there is a lot of satisfaction in hard work, that there is joy in using the muscles and the mind, and all the faculties and senses. Parents, through their own attitudes, can help their children learn that there is fun in being alive; that there is pleasure and satisfaction in using one's talents fully. Children need to learn that, even with its deficiences, this is a good world.

The best way to teach is by example. It is good for children to see parents acting with enthusiasm and spontaneity. It is good for them to see their parents enjoy various things as well as being able to work. It is healthy for children to see their parents resolve differences in a constructive and dignified way. Deeds are better than words. One of my patients gave her children a much more generous allowance than she could afford because she wanted them to have fun. It was something she had never learned to do for herself. She said, "I don't want them to be like me." My answer was: "If you don't want them to be like you, try to change and set them a better example. Your children will be more impressed if they see you enjoying something yourself."

## Developing Self-Respect

It is hard to be a child. He is surrounded by people who are taller and stronger and who know more. A lot of the time he will feel inadequate and inferior to the people around him. He needs to develop self-respect and confidence in himself. In order to do this, he needs an enormous amount of sincere encouragement, approval, and recognition from his parents. He needs to be accepted and loved unconditionally, no matter what he does. His self-esteem will go up when his parents treat him kindly and courteously, and indicate that he is a worthwhile person in his own right. If they act this way consistently, he can become convinced of this and his actions will reflect it. Yet parents do not do this often enough. It is obvious that if a child is scolded, stormed at, cursed, or beaten, his self-esteem will go down. He will feel that he is no good, that his parents are disappointed in him. He will place more importance on their judgment of him than on his own. Parents become angry when a child does not come up to their expectations, whether these expectations are realistic or not. They are annoyed when a child interferes with their plans, but are oblivious of how often they interfere with his. As an experiment, I would suggest that parents keep a record of how many times they scold and criticize a child in the course of a single day. It may be very illuminating. I would suggest that they be quick to praise and slow to criticize. A little criticism goes a long way. One angry outburst by a parent, one "You rotten kid," will wipe out the effect of dozens of expressions of affection. If the parents do not respect themselves, they cannot respect their children; their self-contempt will be expressed (externalized) against them. A good guide to dealing in a respectful way with children is to observe how we treat our neighbors' children. How polite we are to the boy who lives next door. We greet him courteously, rarely scold him, and it would be unthinkable to hit him. When he becomes absolutely obnoxious, we quietly but firmly tell him that it is time he went home. This is an excellent model for dealing with our own children.

You will notice that the words "self-respect," "self-esteem," "self-confidence" are all hyphenated words that include the word "self." The child needs to develop a sense of self, a sense of his own identity. He needs to know who he is, what he can do, what are his assets and talents, what is important to him, what his feelings are, what he wants, etc. Dr. Donald J. Holmes* defines identity as "the feeling of being separate and particular, composed of all that a person consciously knows and unconsciously senses about himself." A child is robbed of his real self if he gets the idea that his parents will not love him unless he acts in a certain way. He will try to measure up to the performance expected of him, to fit into this role. In doing this, he will be getting away from his real self, even if he begins to believe that he really wants what his parents

* The author of *The Adolescent in Psychotherapy*, Little, Brown & Co., Boston, 1964.

want. Parents want it both ways, too. They want to give their children freedom to make their own decisions, but decisions that will please them, and impress the neighbors.

## *Encouraging Your Child*

Parents need to help a child understand himself. Listen to him, ask questions, and help clarify his own feelings. Don't brainwash him by telling him what he is *supposed* to think and feel. Don't rush in with explanations and pronouncements when you don't know what the problem is. No person can be sure of what is disturbing another. The best a parent can do is to help the child discover what is troubling him, to help him think his problems out for himself.

Another important point is for the parent to try to avoid making the child feel guilty. A healthy sense of responsibility is fine, but so many of us walk around with an enormous burden of guilt. It is cruel to tell children that they make you sick, give you ulcers, or that they will drive you to an early grave. These are not true, but children take such statements literally and feel guilty. Young children react to the death or desertion of a parent with feelings of guilt; a child will conclude that it happened because he, the child, was bad. Another cruel maneuver is to punish the child and then blame him for your action. Parents sometimes say, "Don't make me hit you." Now, no child "makes" a parent hit him; he does not control the parent's muscles. If you punish him, take responsibility for your own actions. You may say, "If you do so-and-so, then I will do thus-and-so." This is an honest statement with the issues clear. In this way, the child has to take responsibility for his actions, and you for yours. Of course, parents can foster guilt in more subtle ways: by gestures and facial expressions which indicate what a great burden the child is to them.

A little criticism goes a long way. How well do you take criticism from a boss or a spouse? If you want fine children, tell them and show them that you think they are fine and worthwhile. They can be convinced of this, if you are. When criticism is necessary, make it clear that you disapprove of the behavior or action, and not of the child himself. "That was not a smart thing to do" is a much better comment than "How could you be so stupid?"

Parents expect too much of themselves and too much of their children. When children do not come up to these unrealistic expectations, parents show disappointment in one way or another and make them feel guilty. A good rule for parents is not to be "too good" to their children nor to expect too much in return.

In our overly competitive society, there is too much emphasis on performance and achievement, and not enough on growth. In school, there is too much emphasis on grades; in the business world, on money and prestige. Children become afraid of giving a poor account of themselves, of not performing well. They are afraid of ridicule, humiliation, and failure. It may block them from trying and, therefore, from learning. Children often operate on a principle of "nothing ventured, nothing lost." Parents can be of enormous help if they can teach the child to try; then, if he does not succeed, at least he has learned from the experience. Because we learn most from our own mistakes, if a child can be genuinely convinced to try his best and to accept the outcome without guilt or alibi, he has acquired a most valuable attitude. It will stand him in good stead the rest of his life.

## *Adolescence*

Adolescence is a particularly trying time for parents. The young child who is cute, tiny, and helpless has now grown into a strong, bright, adolescent boy who may be taller than his father. Or, in the case of a girl, she may be more sexually attractive than her mother. These developments are often very disturbing to the parent who has some unresolved problems in regard to aggression and sex. Furthermore, the adolescent is not so easily intimidated. Parents who have relied too heavily on threats and intimidation to control the youngsters may now become frantic about their loss of control. They fear their children will do something that may disgrace them; and children are very good at sensing when and how to disgrace their parents. They know the vulnerable spots in their parents' makeup. In addition, parents may feel rejected because their adolescent children will listen to their peers rather than their parents. Don't take this personally. It may help parents if they realize that the first business of the adolescent is to "make it" with his peer group, as John L.

Schimel points out in his book *The Parent's Handbook on Adolescence.** It is not really disloyalty or rejection of the parent, but the sensitivity of the parent regarding rejection can complicate the issue.

## Sex Education

There is much emphasis on sex education for children today. In my opinion, more important than the facts about anatomy and physiology are certain attitudes. If the child has learned to think of himself as a worthwhile human being his self-respect will not permit him to act in a sexually degrading and destructive way. Sex is a desirable and pleasurable activity of human beings. The important questions are *when* and *how* to express these feelings. In a mature sense, sex is the expression of affection between two people. If a person's relationships with other people are good, then, most likely, his sexual relationships will be good, too.

Parents can help by trying to answer their children's questions honestly. The child will sense when a parent is embarrassed by certain questions. It is probably better for parents to admit this to themselves than to try to hide it. We are not all emotionally equipped to teach our children in this area, and in such cases referral to a family doctor or to a suitable book is probably best.

The other thing that parents can do is to prevent too early and excessive sexual stimulation of their children. From my experience, the most damaging type of stimulation comes from the seductive behavior of parents, much of which is unconscious. Warmth and affection are desirable, but sometimes caresses go beyond this and become a form of sex play which frightens at the same time that it stimulates the child. This is true of the mother who parades around scantily clad in front of her sons who have reached puberty or are even older. There is a time and place for modesty in the home. When it comes to sexual stimulation from the mass media, in my opinion, sexy and pornographic movies or books are not nearly as harmful as those that present acts of violence, sadism, and perversion.

You can help your child by discouraging too young

* World Publishing Company, New York, 1969.

dating, especially with older or sexually advanced partners. A reasonable curfew is in order; a teen-ager may rebel against it yet be relieved that it has been imposed.

It is wise to encourage your children to wait for some gratifications, to learn to tolerate some frustrations, to have something to look forward to. The mature person can wait. This seems most desirable, whether it is driving a car or having sexual relations.

## Parental Guidance

What can parents do when it looks as if their child is about to make a very bad decision? If the bright child is about to drop out of college? If another is seriously considering marriage to some totally unsuitable person? In the first place, try not to panic. That makes it worse. Your fears are communicated to your child as a lack of confidence in him. Secondly, stick to the issues involved and do not make it a tug-of-war between parent and child. He may then have to defy you to prove his independence, which is the last thing you want. The real issue is whether dropping out of college is a wise decision or whether the contemplated marriage is a good one. Encourage the child to make his own decision and help him. Suggest that the decision and the responsibility are his and you hope he makes a good choice. Sometimes a delay permits a more thorough appraisal of the situation and leads to a better decision. It may be useful to say to a child about to rush into a major decision something like, "Is it urgent?" or "Can you wait?" Not all mistakes can be prevented; some children cannot learn any other way. Some children are too old to be spanked either physically or verbally. There may be nothing the parent can do in some circumstances, except pray and wait.

One of the most important functions of a parent is to set a good example for his child. You are the first adult he gets to observe at close range for a long time, and he will start off with the belief that all people in the world are more or less like his parents. A good attitude at home will lead to a good attitude toward other people. If there is a good relationship between you and your child, he will tend to imitate you, *if he is not forced to*. However, the neurotic parent has difficulty setting a good example. He is anxious, frustrated, inconsistent, and filled with self-contempt. The easiest target on which the unhappy parent can take out his frustrations is the child. He may rationalize his nagging or intimidating behavior toward the child as discipline and say that it is for his own good. Discipline, however, means to teach, to set limits. Hitting a child only demonstrates that the 150-pound father is stronger than a 60-pound child. It would take an extraordinary parent to always control his impulses, and hitting a child cannot always be avoided. Sometimes, it may even do some good for the parent to let off steam and more quickly come back to normal. But it rarely helps the child. If you are trying to teach him to solve his problems by logic, patience, and understanding, and then attack him physically, you have set him a poor example. It impairs your own dignity and hurts your child's self-esteem. It is the last way to teach him self-respect and independence. With effort and imagination, most parents can find better methods.

## *The Neurotic Parent*

The Bible tells us that "the sins of the fathers are visited on the sons." I would change the word "sin" to "neurosis." The neuroses of the parent interfere with their seeing their child objectively and dealing with him in a just and realistic way. The compliant parent is so anxious to please his child that he has great difficulty in saying "no." This child will get his way too often and, since he lacks judgment and experience, he will make many mistakes. Instead of learning from his mistakes, he is more likely to feel guilty; his self-confidence suffers. A healthier parent would provide more guidance and leadership, even at the risk of not being so popular with the child. The compliant parent has abdicated too much of the responsibility of parenthood. The aggressive parent trends to make the opposite mistake. He is arrogant and thinks he knows what is best for everybody and so he pushes the child, ready or not, toward a goal he has picked out for him. He does not let the child try enough things on his own. The child of such a parent may become a timid, frightened person, or go to the opposite extreme and become extremely rebellious and discard everything his parent values. The detached parent wants to be left alone and finds it difficult to get involved with his children. He withdraws from them and refuses to see problems, his own or theirs, until they can no longer be avoided. The child will often take this to mean that his parents are not interested in him, or that he is not worthy of their time and attention. His self-esteem suffers and he feels inferior.

I would suggest that it is wise for parents to approach each child with humility. Each one is unique and the greatest expert in the world cannot tell you what effect your action will have on this child ten years from now. The story is told of the mother who was pushing her new baby in the carriage and met a famous psychoanalyst. When she asked him for advice as to how she could prevent the baby from becoming neurotic, he said, "I can't answer that question, but come back in a few years and I will tell you what went wrong."

Not all married couples should have children. Being a parent requires hard work, endurance, patience, understanding, imagination, and resourcefulness. The amount of time spent with the child is only one factor in his healthy development. Many working wives and widows make excellent mothers because they use their limited time wisely. Most of us enter this job, parenthood, with too little preparation for its enormous physical and emotional demands. The best parent is not the one who has read all the books, but the one who is a whole human being, self-respecting, who has good relations with the important people in his life, and does work that is useful and from which he derives satisfaction. Such a parent is best equipped to help the child grow and develop, to help him learn from his mistakes, and to help him think his problems through.

# Part III

## *Toward A Healthier Style of Living*

# Chapter 10

## *Self-Discovery and Self-Help*

How can a person help himself to work out a healthier pattern of dealing with his problems? What can a person do to be more productive, have less anxiety, and lead a more satisfying life? I believe that, with much hard work and persistence, he can do a great deal. The motivation must be good; he must want to help himself. He can learn by becoming a better observer of others and himself, as well as by reading about the experiences of others. It is a long, hard process and will take years, but the rewards will be great. People can accomplish many difficult tasks by sustained efforts—including the difficult one of learning about themselves.

### *Discovering Ourselves*

It is very hard to see ourselves as we really are. People are quick to say, "Oh, I know myself," or "I don't fool myself." These statements are not entirely true: there is much we don't know about ourselves. We are a much more complicated mixture than we realize and our capacity for self-deception is enormous. Certain traits are so deeply buried that they rarely come to the surface; and when they do we don't want to recognize them as belonging to us. Sometime or other most persons say, "I never knew I had it in me," or "I never knew I was capable of saying or doing something like that." We all have thoughts, feelings, or impulses of which we are ashamed or frightened. People expect too much of themselves; they believe that even in their thoughts and fantasies they should not have certain feelings or impulses. This is too much to ask of human beings. Our thoughts are not deeds and we can try to understand the significance of certain thoughts if we don't panic, try to push them away, or refuse to acknowledge their existence. We must learn to suspend judgment and hold off preconceived ideas of what we should be if we are to see ourselves accurately. Most people underestimate themselves: they are prejudiced against themselves. They are quick to see their faults but not their good points. They compare their weak points with other people's strong points, and suffer by comparison. To be realistic and objective, we need to see the whole picture.

The first step in self-discovery is to take a fresh look at yourself, to become a better observer of yourself. Try to become aware of your patterns of behavior, of the way you usually do and say things. Forget the theories that you may have read about and don't really understand. They are only theories and they may not apply to you. Like an artist who from time to time steps back from the painting he is working on, try to develop a habit of occasionally stepping back and watching what you have just said or done. Listen to the words you use and the way you express yourself. Did you really mean what you said; if not, why didn't you say what was on your mind? Listen to your words—especially the word "should," which means coercion and compulsion, and the word "entitled," which usually expresses a claim that may not be valid or realistic. Become more observant of your tone of voice, the way you dress, your characteristic manners of walking, standing, sitting, etc. Try to observe your basic pattern: are you mainly compliant, aggressive, or detached? At what times do you act out of character? Use your own words to describe yourself and avoid theoretical terms which serve only to impress others and have little real value for you.

Try to develop better contact with your own feelings: become more sensitive to your feelings. Before you rush into explaining or rationalizing, stop and consult with yourself. "How do I feel about it?" "What do I really want?" These are difficult questions to answer, yet they lead to real self-understanding. We have to do this again and again; it takes a lot of practice before we can develop good contact with our feelings. It is surprising how many people do not know what they feel. They do not recognize when they are angry or sad or tired or hungry. They only become aware of feelings when they become very intense. All too often, people feel what they are supposed to feel, or guide themselves by the feelings of others. Many people go to lunch because twelve o'clock is time for lunch, not because they are hungry. Once in the restaurant they ask the waitress, "What's good today?" because they are not sure what they feel like eating. There is a humorous story about a famous mathematician who stopped to talk with a friend on a university campus. After a while, as they were about to part, the famous man asked his friend, "When I met you, what direction was I coming from?" When this was pointed out to him he said, "Oh, then I've already had lunch."

Many people only recognize that they have a confusing mixture of feelings. Others can only identify a feeling of numbness, which often means that intense and alive feelings have been repressed. Many people cannot express emotions except under special circumstances. Many cannot express feelings toward the significant people in their lives, but can to strangers or casual acquaintances. Others can express feelings only in the movies or in the theater where they watch emotions that have been portrayed in an exaggerated form for dramatic purposes. They often guide themselves by the opinions of others. They don't feel anything about a movie, a play, or a painting until they read what the critics have to say. They are afraid to express their feelings: they need, in effect, "an emotional Seeing Eye dog" to lead them.

Another obstacle to self-understanding is the tendency to blame yourself. At the first sign that anything is going wrong, people are quick to heap blame and abuse on themselves. They are quick to say, "I should have known better." This is unreasonable: no one has the gift of prophecy; no one can predict the future. The best a person can do about some future event is to make an educated guess about it. The person who uses the expression "I should have known" is one who expects to fail, one who has a poor opinion of himself. He feels inferior and inadequate and expects that things will not turn out well for him. Also, he is so sensitive to criticism that he cannot bear to wait for anyone to criticize him—he will do it first. Instead of "I should have known," it is better to say "Apparently, at that time, I couldn't have done it any better," or "If I could have done better, I would have."

The only sure way to avoid failure is never to try. This road leads to inertia and inaction and an ineffectual style of living. Without being reckless, we do have to try and run the risk of failure. And when we fail, before rushing in with self-blame, the proper questions to ask are: "What happened?" "What went wrong?" and "How can I do it better next time?" Such questions may lead to answers that enable us to learn from our mistakes; and unless we learn from our mistakes, we are doomed to repeat them.

Also blocking the path of learning and growing is the tendency to blame others. While many are quick to blame themselves, some are quick to blame others. Let anything go wrong and the cry goes up: "Find the guilty party!" or "Who's to blame?" The loudest complainers are those who are most afraid to face the facts. Complaining releases frustration and anger and may intimidate others, but it blocks learning. "What's wrong?" is usually a better question than "Who's wrong?" Try to stop complaining if it doesn't change anything. It is more important to do something constructive, to get on with the job at hand, than simply to find someone to blame.

We can also learn a great deal by observing our dealings with others and by trying to understand them. What kind of people are we most comfortable with? Which traits in others do we like best? Which do we dislike? Once again, by answering such questions about others, we also uncover important aspects of our own makeup. We generally like people who contribute to our self-esteem and who do not stir up our inner conflicts. In general, the compliant person likes people who accept him, the aggressive person likes those who admire him, and the detached person likes those who do not crowd him. In general, we dislike people who have traits that we dislike in ourselves, especially if the others have them in an exaggerated form. The stingy person dislikes one who is even stingier, the loudmouth dislikes other loudmouths, and the "phony" dislikes other "phonies." It is easy to recognize certain traits and motives in others long before we can recognize them in ourselves. By learning about the character and motives of others, we may one day recognize these same traits in ourselves. We are more like other people than we care to admit.

We can also learn a great deal from reading about the ideas, thoughts, and experiences of others. There is an enormous volume of books, magazines, and newspaper articles that have been written about human relations. TV and radio pour out a constant stream of advice on all phases of psychiatry, psychology, child-rearing, sex education, drugs, etc. The soundness and the value of these offerings vary widely. Many of them have little of value to say, but they may say it in an amusing or glib way. You can't listen to all the experts, because their advice and suggestions are often contradictory. You will have to evaluate what they say, and if it seems reasonable to you, try it. If it doesn't work for you, try to learn what went wrong and how you can do it differently. There are many reasons for failure: the timing may be wrong; you didn't apply it well; the idea or suggestion may not be of value in your specific circumstances. As a guide to further reading, this book contains an appendix in which there is a list of works that I have found helpful. It is a very incomplete list and many good books have been omitted. However, these titles have often been helpful to my patients.

It is my opinion that more useful knowledge can be gotten from reading famous poems, novels, and plays than from books on psychology and psychiatry. Poets often express the feelings and hopes of people far better than any clinician. The world's great novelists and playwrights were excellent observers of people and described them with great sensitivity. The plays of Shakespeare, Shaw, Ibsen, O'Neill, and Arthur Miller contain masterful descriptions of the conflicts between human beings. The same is true of the novels of Dickens, Hawthorne, Dostoyevsky, and Camus, to name only a few. Aside from its religious aspect, the Bible certainly belongs among the masterpieces of world literature. And, finally, let me not slight that modern art form, the movie, which occasionally provides brilliant insights into human character and motivation.

## A Personal Five-Year Plan

People tend to drift along and become dulled to the passage of time. Year after year slips by, until some event forcefully reminds them that life is moving relentlessly on.

It may be a birthday—the twenty-fifth, the thirtieth, or the fortieth—a conspicuous achievement of a former classmate or neighbor, the death of someone significant to us. Just as nations or large corporations find it useful to plan some project over a five-year period, I find this a useful device in personal planning. I have found it helpful to say to some patients, "What would you like to see happen in the next five years?" "What would you like to accomplish in your work and personal life within the next five years?" These questions may lead to a rewarding appraisal of a person's values and goals, of his style of living. Five years is a useful span of time in thinking about one's life. It is long enough so that we can look beyond the immediate and daily pressures, and yet it is not so long that we feel we will never reach it. It confronts us with the reality that we cannot postpone forever. You cannot get that college degree if you never go back to college; you won't get that better job unless you acquire the necessary skills. Looking at their lives in the perspective of five years, some patients start actions that had been postponed, while others accept the fact that they have been paying only lip service to certain hopes and yearnings. It may be painful, but it is realistic to face the fact that you are not going to achieve some goals. In planning a realistic style of living, it is a great help to stop self-deception and to be honest with oneself.

Sometimes, phrasing the question differently, I say to patients, "Unless you work hard and change things, the next five years will probably be much like the last five years. How do you feel about that?" This often confronts the patient with a reality that he has been avoiding. There are only twenty-four hours in a day. If you want a successful career and a prominent place in the community, there will not be much time left for your family or for leisure. Some things must be given up. This is very hard for many to do, because people basically want everything. The more mature and realistic ones know that they must decide what things to leave out, that they can't have everything.

Necessary for a healthy style of living is a personal set of values. Each person must firmly decide for himself what is of most importance to him, what is not so important, and what is least important to him. Each person needs to ask himself, "What do I enjoy? What do I really want?" Good decisions start with knowing what you want.

The next step is to assess, realistically, the price you are willing to pay for it. Then you either proceed with it or you choose an alternative. If you can't attain your first goal then you try for the second one. There is an orderliness in such a life, an overall plan. Decisions are based on the knowledge an individual has of himself and the world he lives in. He doesn't flounder around uncertainly, drifting or waiting for something to happen. People who don't know what they want are likely not to get it. And if by luck they do get it, they can't appreciate it.

Many patients ask, "What is the purpose of living?" This is a most difficult question and involves religion and philosophy more than psychiatry. I think the function of a psychiatrist is to help the patient see clearly what he is doing and to help him work out a better style of living for himself. In my experience, the people who are most content with their lives are those who continue to grow and develop as long as they live. By struggling and hard work, people can grow in acquiring various skills, knowledge, sensitivity, understanding, courage, wisdom, and self-respect. The happiest people I know are those who, without being reckless, are not afraid to get involved and try new experiences. There is a widely known prayer that goes, "God, grant me serenity to accept the things I cannot change, courage to change the things I can, and wisdom to know the difference." To this I would say, "Amen."

## *Relief of Anxiety and Fear*

As a person comes into better contact with his own feelings and sees the world more realistically, he will work out a healthier plan of living for himself. Periods of great anxiety will become less frequent and less intense. However, there still will be periods of anxiety which are extremely painful. At such times, what can a person do for relief? From past experience, people learn that certain things give them relief or shorten the duration of their episodes of panic and fear. What helps one person may not help another. One person eats a lot, gorging himself when anxious, another may lose his appetite. One takes to bed and rests, another turns to strenuous activity. Allowing, then, for the great variations among individuals, we can discuss some of the measures that help people during the trying times of severe anxiety.

In the first place, people are comforted by food and drink. To be well-fed is symbolic of being cared for. Drinking, eating, and smoking all provide gratification and some measure of relief from anxiety. Depending on personal and cultural factors, some foods rate higher than others in their ability to bring comfort. To one, chicken soup is the best; to another, a plate of pasta. The English find comfort in a cup of tea. In America, the drink is more likely to be whiskey. Alcohol, in my opinion, is the original tranquilizer and almost every nation in the world has produced its own variety. All over the world millions of people have found comfort in bourbon, Scotch, vodka, or saki. Taken in moderation it helps to relieve the discomforts of living. Of course, the cure can be worse than the disease; by relying on liquor, to excess, the problem drinker only compounds his difficulties.

Tranquilizers have been on the market only for the last sixteen years, but they are now the most commonly prescribed drug. Miltown, Librium, and Thorazine are household words. Used carefully, they are valuable aids for the relief of emotional disturbances of all degrees of severity. Of course, tranquilizers do not solve the underlying problem, but they do furnish comfort and relief until other resources can be brought to bear to change the fundamental condition which produced the anxiety.

Other measures which usually relieve anxiety are rest and recreation of all kinds. A vacation, going on a trip, a change of scenery are all useful. Once again, these do not change any of the problems that the person carries around with him, but they provide a period of respite. At times, running away from a problem is the sensible thing to do: "He who runs away lives to fight another day." Compulsive and perfectionistic people feel that they have to respond immediately to every demand or challenge. Sometimes it is healthier to postpone such action. For instance, one of my patients, a competent physician, felt he had to respond immediately to every house-call or emergency, no matter how tired he felt at the time. As a result, he was often in a turmoil: How could he go on this emergency call when he felt so weary but, on the other hand, how could he refuse the call? In time, with psychotherapy, he learned to handle these problems in a flexible and efficient manner. When he got a call from a patient he evaluated it: "How urgent is the medical condition?" and "How do *I* feel?" Most of the time he made the call; on rare occasions he would get another physician to cover for him. Sometimes he would postpone his call, wait and rest, and, if he felt better, he would then go. This flexible approach made it possible for this extremely competent physician to stay in practice, and it will probably prolong his life. In the long run, I guess that his chances of ever getting a coronary are much reduced, to his own benefit and to the benefit of his patients whom he serves so well.

Some people find comfort in taking to bed when they are very anxious. They may sleep or rest, but for a period of time they shut out the world and its problems. It provides a "breather" by postponing facing some event that, at the time, seems overwhelming. Others do just the opposite: instead of resting, they find that activity is the best way to relieve anxiety. The range of their activities is enormous, varying from simple setting-up exercises to gymnastics or yoga. Or they may play tennis, handball, or golf, or take up gardening, etc. I. Breakstone, a well-known Miami psychiatrist, feels that square-dancing is a particularly suitable activity for tense people. Some prefer passive activities such as massage, sauna, or steam bath. The range of activities that will help a person, temporarily at least, to forget his difficulties is a very wide one.

Some people, of course, find relief in their customary work or business; the more anxious they are, the harder they work. And all the while, their friends and relatives worry that the extra pressure will get them into difficulty. However, this is putting the cart before the horse since they are having difficulties already. These people work hard because it relieves their anxiety: they can only slow down when they become less anxious.

Not too surprising, another activity that provides gratification and relief from anxiety is sex. Stressful periods in business or family affairs often increase the sexual drive. Sexual gratification is a good outlet. If not carried to excess, and when the person has some knowledge of his motivation, it does relieve anxiety and promote relaxation. In my experience, some people go on sexual binges the way others go on drinking or eating sprees. Some of these great lovers are really anxious people. It is not libido, it is really anxiety that drives them. This is especially true, in my experience, of men in their middle years. Just as a "nervous breakdown" may be ushered in by a period of drinking, sometimes it is ushered in by a period of sexual escapades. Thus, a respected university professor or bank president may become involved with a totally unsuitable woman and carry on an obvious affair that provides an open scandal for the community. One of my patients was a successful businessman who had been a devoted and faithful husband for twenty-five years. During a difficult period of business reverses, his emotional balance began to fall apart. For the first time in his life, he became involved in a series of sexual adventures with almost any available female. Before he recovered he had wrecked his business and had come close to wrecking his marriage. The affairs were meaningless except as a means of relieving anxiety.

Another important measure in controlling anxiety is the knowledge that problems do not go on forever. We can be overwhelmed when confronted by a problem that seems permanent or irrevocable. We need to remind ourselves that nothing goes on forever, that any problem is limited, and, with sufficient time, adjustments and compensations will take place. People can endure a great deal as long as they can see that it will end someday. One of my patients was a school principal who had a phobia that he would faint in an embarrassing and conspicuous manner. A particularly bad time for him was commencement exercises when he had to give out diplomas to a large graduating class in front of the entire faculty, the student body, and their families. On these occasions, it helped him get through this ordeal by counting the rows of graduates still waiting. He could estimate that in another forty to fifty minutes it would be over and he could resume his seat. Another patient would take a Librium and then make a mental note: "I'll wait for another hour and if I don't feel better I will phone the doctor." It is difficult to wait, but if we know that it is for a limited time, we can hang on. There is a story that a king once asked his wise men for something to say that would always be of comfort to others. They came up with the words, "And this too shall pass."

A great source of strength and solace in time of trouble is religion and prayer. Karl Menninger, the eminent psychiatrist, once said that religion has helped far more people than psychiatry. The traditional prayers and rituals of the religion we are raised in often give us comfort during times of death and disaster. They help us to put things in perspective and remind us that our fathers and grandfathers also went through trying times. In addition to ritual and dogma, the world's great religions contain profound insights and wisdom about human beings that help many people go through times of stress with dignity. According to one psychoanalyst, N. Freeman, prayer is an attempt to mobilize the resources of the individual in order to meet the crisis at hand.

The most effective way—and the hardest—of dealing with anxiety is to analyze it, to ask oneself, "What is the real extent of the danger? Am I magnifying it or not?" Not every difficulty leads inevitably to disaster; some lead only to discomfort or embarrassment. It is extremely helpful to see the danger in proper perspective and not exaggerate it. Great anxiety is generated when we finally face the hard reality that we have been avoiding for many years. For instance, the woman who finally faces the fact that her marriage is completely unsatisfactory but that she is too passive and frightened to obtain a divorce. Or the man who finally recognizes that he does not have the ability to succeed in a certain career. Great anxiety occurs when we realize that we have to face and accept our limitations; that, in spite of our best efforts, we can still be rejected or fail to attain an important goal. There are no guarantees. If we are not too frightened to look, we can ask ourselves, "What is happening? How did it happen? And why at this time?" If we can answer these questions, we may then be able to answer the most difficult question of all: "Why?"

Human beings do not function well in isolation; this is especially true during periods of anxiety. It is a great comfort to be able to talk to someone, even if that other person cannot provide any practical help. It is a comfort to have someone just listen. Airing our thoughts, feelings, fears, and angers relieves some of the intensity. When we "blow off steam" we feel better. Problems can be seen more clearly after we talk about them and get them out in the open. During periods of anxiety it is a help to talk to a spouse, relative, friend, neighbor, clergyman, family doctor, the bartender, the beautician, etc. It is even a help to talk over the phone. People help by listening and by indicating that they feel for you, that they would help if they could. Of course, it helps even more if the person we talk to is one whom we trust and who, by experience and training, has expertise in some of the problems that we face.

# Chapter 11

## *The Helping Professions*

Most readers of this book will not seek professional help for neurosis. However, for those who may, I should like to discuss briefly what is available. Workers in mental health include people who come from a great variety of backgrounds: nursing, the clergy, education, law, etc. However, the three established "helping professions" are psychiatry, psychology, and social work. From these disciplines come most of the trained people available for help with mental and emotional problems.

*Psychiatry* is the medical specialty that is concerned with the "study, diagnosis, treatments, and prevention of behavior disorders." Psychiatrists are physicians who, upon graduating from medical school go on to four years of specialized training in mental hospitals and clinics. Upon successful completion of their training and of a comprehensive examination, they are certified as specialists by the American Board of Psychiatry and Neurology. Like other physicians, their education is never complete and they continue to study and to attend courses and lectures in various aspects of psychiatry. Some obtain further training and are then certified in child psychiatry, others in psychoanalysis, etc.

Before World War I relatively little was heard about psychiatry. Its practice was mostly limited to large hospitals ("insane asylums") that were located in rather remote parts of each state. Here people were "put away" because they could not function in society or because they were dangerous or disturbing to others. Once committed to these institutions by legal authority, many were rarely heard from again. No effective treatment existed, and these hospitals provided only custodial care. Less severe forms of mental illness were largely ignored. In the past sixty years tremendous changes have come about. World Wars I and II brought to light the great prevalence of mental and emotional disturbances in our population. In World War II, the most common cause for rejection from military service was mental illness.

Early in this century the monumental discoveries of Sigmund Freud were becoming widely known. Psychoanalysis started as a treatment for neurosis and developed into a comprehensive theory of personality, and a research method as well. It has provided a great amount of information about human character and motivation and has had a profound effect on all phrases of psychiatry and psychology. Principles of psychoanalysis have been applied to many other forms of treatment: short-term psychotherapy, group therapy, family and marital therapy, psychodrama, etc. The theory and practice of psychoanalysis has been enriched by the findings of contributors too numerous to mention. It is now quite different in many respects from what it was in Freud's time.

In the 1930's, electroconvulsive treatment (also called electroshock) was introduced for severe depression. With modern equipment, it is quite safe and does not lead to brain damage or permanent memory impairment. It is often lifesaving.

In the past two decades, effective medication for anxiety and depression has become available. With the help of these newer medications, many patients who formerly had to be hospitalized can now be treated in doctors' offices and outpatient clinics. Tranquilizers and mood-elevating drugs are probably the most commonly prescribed drugs today. Within the last ten years another medication has come into prominence: Lithium. First used only for the manic phase of manic-depressive illness, it is now used for severe depressions and other conditions as well. When it does work, it often produces dramatic improvement in patients who previously failed to respond to any other medication. Like all potent medication, it requires careful supervision.

The effects of all these developments have been profound. While the old-style mental hospital still exists, the use of medication has made it possible for many patients to return home and resume normal lives. The population of these hospitals is steadily declining. In addition, psychiatric wards have been opened in many general hospitals. This makes it possible for patients to be treated within their own community and return to a productive life much sooner. Psychiatric facilities have become more varied and flexible. There are now "day hospitals" where several types of treatment are available and patients return home in the evening. There are also "halfway houses" for patients who are released from hospitals but are not yet entirely capable of managing all the responsibilities of daily living. There are residential treatment centers for a variety of problems: alcoholism, drug addiction, etc. Patients recover more quickly and more economically now because treatment programs are more flexible and adapted to their needs.

The specialty of psychiatry is a very large one, and there are many subspecialties within the field. Some psychiatrists do only administrative work, others teach, and still others are consultants for government agencies and the courts. Some do hospital work only, others practice exclusively from their offices. Some treat only adults, others children, and still others limit themselves to adolescents. There are some general psychiatrists who cover most of these areas and use many methods, but many restrict their practice to those areas and methods in which they have had the greatest experience and training. Some will use drugs and electroshock treatments predominantly; others, individual psychotherapy or psychoanalysis. Still others do group therapy, family therapy, psychodrama, etc. Finding the appropriate psychiatrist usually requires help from someone with a lot of knowledge of the field. Often the family physician can recommend an appropriate psychiatrist. Other sources of help may be the local Mental Health Association, the County Medical Society, or family service agencies in the community. The poorest way to find a psychiatrist is simply to look in the Yellow Pages of the telephone directory. If at all possible, I would recommend consulting the chief psychiatrist of the largest hospital, the chairman of the department of psychiatry of the medical school, or the most prominent psychiatrist in town. These people should be most able to refer you to someone suitable for your needs. Of course in many areas there will not be much of a choice—there may be only one psychiatrist, or none.

*Clinical psychologists* are becoming increasingly important in providing care for mental and emotional disturbances. Psychology may be defined as that branch of science that deals with behavior and mental processes. It, too, is a large field, and much that has been said about psychiatry also applies to psychology. However, since psychologists are not physicians, they cannot prescribe drugs. There are many different kinds of psychologists: experimental, industrial, educational, and clinical, to name some major groups. Some teach and do research in colleges and universities. Many work in the public school system; others are involved with personnel selection and guidance for industry. All psychologists administer a wide variety of psychological tests: to measure intelligence, personality development and functioning, special aptitudes, etc. An increasing proportion of psychologists are now in clinical practice and treat emotional disturbances in children and adults. Their training, after college, is obtained in the graduate schools of universities, where they receive Ph.D. degrees in clinical psychology. Admission to accredited programs is highly selective, and the training usually takes four to six years to complete. Most of the fifty states now certify psychologists for private practice. Psychologists have made outstanding contributions in child development and the behavioral sciences. Many are very competent clinicians and will continue to play an increasingly important role in the mental health needs of the community.

*Psychiatric social workers* constitute the third of the traditional helping professions. Upon graduation from college they go on for two further years of training in graduate schools of social work affiliated with universities and obtain a master's degree. Their training is rigorous and intensive. The well-established schools of social work are highly selective in their admissions and carefully screen applicants for maturity, motivation, and intelligence. After graduation, social workers gain further experience by working in mental hospitals and clinics, family service agencies, government agencies, etc. There are ever increasing opportunities for postgraduate study in clinical fields such as individual and group psychotherapy, marital and family therapy, etc. This has resulted in more experienced and highly competent clinical social workers. In time I believe that the basic professional in mental health will be the social worker.

## Psychotherapy

While drugs, electroshock treatments, and hospitalization are important in helping patients—and may even be lifesaving—the unique form of treatment in psychiatry is psychotherapy. This means treatment by psychological means. It consists, in general, of two main types: supportive psychotherapy and intensive psychotherapy. The emphasis in each one is quite different, although in the actual treatment of a patient, elements of both types are combined. This important subject deserves much more explanation.

## *Supportive Psychotherapy*

The purpose of this type of therapy is to help the patient quickly, to give him relief from symptoms, and to enable him to maintain or return to the usual adjustment that he formerly had worked out at home and at work. The doctor provides advice, suggestions, and reassurance. As quickly as he can, the doctor helps to sort out the patient's problems: which are the major ones, which the minor ones; which have to be tackled first, and which can be postponed for later. He uses all the means available to him for help. He may use medication where it is indicated; he will speak to the important relatives and friends of the patient; he advises him about all aspects of his daily living, recommending vacations, changes in jobs, hospitalization when needed, etc. He tries to get the patient to suppress those problems with which he cannot cope at the time. His rationale is that these problems may be handled more easily at a later period. The goal of this type of therapy is to support the patient emotionally until the current crisis passes and the situation becomes more favorable, or until the patient's resources can be more adequately mobilized. The object is not to change the patient but to restore him to his former level of adaptation. In some cases, supportive therapy is all that the patient is interested in or can use to maximum benefit. All physicians, as well as friends and relatives, use some of these techniques in order to help their fellow human beings in distress.

## *Intensive Psychotherapy and Psychoanalysis*

Intensive therapy is also called uncovering, dynamic, or analytically oriented psychotherapy. It differs from supportive therapy in that the emphasis is not mainly on relieving symptoms, but in understanding the conditions that lead to the development of the symptoms. It involves a careful, methodical, and thorough attempt to help the patient understand his thoughts, feelings, and actions in order, eventually, to modify his behavior. It attempts the difficult task of changing the personality structure of the individual and helping him work out a healthier style of living. Its object is to help the person grow in self-knowledge, insight, sensitivity, and judgment. Its purpose is to help him direct his energies into more productive channels and to enrich his life. It is an ambitious undertaking, and a large measure of the responsibility for the success of this treatment rests on the patient. The doctor helps the patient to help himself; he gives little direct advice but helps the patient learn to make good decisions for himself.

Modern-day intensive psychotherapy is derived from psychoanalysis and the monumental discovery of Sigmund Freud. These were further developed, extended, and modified by the many other workers in the field of psychoanalysis who followed him. While many of Freud's original guidelines are still valid, the theory and practice of psychoanalysis is quite different than it was in his time. There is less rigidity in the frequency of treatment, the use of the couch, the use of drugs, and the kinds of patients accepted for treatment. There are many people with serious problems who cannot be treated successfully unless treatment is intensive. Everything else being equal, it is obvious that much more can be accomplished by three visits per week than by one. However, I feel that success depends chiefly upon the individual patient and the individual doctor, and the relationship that develops between them. I have seen patients who came only once a week and managed to deal very well with long-standing problems. In my opinion, the distinction between psychoanalysis and intensive psychotherapy is not a sharp one. The remarks that follow apply largely to both.

## *What Happens in Psychotherapy?*

There is great curiosity and many misconceptions about what happens in the psychiatrist's office. Of course, it varies considerably, not only with the patient but also with the doctor. While the objectives of most therapists are the same, their theoretical viewpoints vary, as do their techniques and, of course, their personal characteristics. Even psychiatrists and psychoanalysts from the same theoretical school differ considerably. And yet, with all the variations, many things remain the same. The first few visits will largely be devoted to having the patient tell the story of his life and of his difficulties and what he seeks from the treatment. After that, either sitting up and facing the doctor or lying on the couch, the patient will be asked to say everything that comes into his mind. This includes thoughts, feelings, and sensations, without selection and with as much spontaneity as possible. Nothing is unimportant. This is the basic rule, and the process is called free association. Of course, from time to time the patient will come up against a blank period when nothing comes to mind. The doctor usually does not rush in to fill up the silence, but prefers to wait and give the patient a chance. If the silence is too long or too painful, the doctor will try to help the patient get started again. Most doctors will indicate that the number of words spoken is not that important, and that not every minute of the session must be used fully. This is how treatment begins. Some doctors are more active than others, but all of them will make comments and ask questions at appropriate times.

The atmosphere in the psychiatrist's office is quite different from that in any other physician's office. The doctor will see only one patient in each hour. At the beginning of treatment, the doctor and patient will agree on the time for the visits, and these hours will be adhered to with great regularity. The session will usually start on the hour and end precisely ten minutes before the next hour. This is the so-called fifty-minute hour. The sessions will start promptly; delays common in other doctors' or dentists' offices rarely occur here. There will usually be no interruptions during the session; most psychiatrists do not even answer their telephones. This schedule will be followed week after week, interrupted only for illness, vacation, or some important event. At one of the early sessions, the doctor will usually explain that the patient is responsible for his hour and that unless he gives forty-eight hours' notice of cancellation, he will be charged for it. If the patient "forgets" an hour, he will also be charged for it. These rules seem harsh but it is not possible to conduct intensive therapy in any other way. The doctor has set aside that hour for the particular patient, and it is a wasted hour, and often a missed opportunity, if the patient does not appear. Some of the most productive hours are those the patient wanted to miss. The doctor will also discourage the patient from telephoning him when he is upset or when he has something on his mind between sessions. He will encourage the patient to wait for his next appointment when the matter can be adequately discussed. This requires considerable strength and maturity on the part of the patient, but in the long run, treatment proceeds more rapidly because of it.

The doctor will also discourage the patient from talking about treatment with friends and relatives. If he talks about his problems to several others before he gets to his therapist, he may not describe these events with any spontaneity. He may even be bored, or tired of all the discussion. He may also report the opinions of the others with whom he has talked, rather than develop his own ideas and feelings, during the session with the doctor. There are, of course, exceptions to all rules, but in general, treatment proceeds better if these time-tested guidelines are followed.

With all patients, the question of fees comes up. There is a widespread idea that psychiatrists charge exorbitant fees. In my opinion, this is not true, and psychiatrists are usually among the least affluent of the medical specialists. Over the country, fees range from $40 to $70 per hour. It is true that the fees are a hardship on many patients who need treatments several times a week, especially since treatment may go on for months and years. However, the psychiatrist sees only one patient per hour, whereas other physicians can see several in that same period of time. Compared to the other expenses of living, the fees in psychiatry are not out of line. It is often a question of motivation. Some people who permit themselves many luxuries believe they cannot afford treatment, while others in rather modest circumstances somehow find a way to pay for treatment. In my opinion, psychiatric treatment may be more important than a college education for some. A neurosis is a painful and expensive condition to live with. As one patient told me: "Psychotherapy is the best investment I ever made. I will benefit from it as long as I live."

Most patients are anxious when they start therapy—frightened of what they may discover about themselves. They sense that certain things about themselves have been deeply buried because they are too painful to face. However, they are pushed by the desire to end their suffering and their difficulties in living, and by faith and hope. The authority and prestige of the doctor help the patient get started. As treatment continues, the way the therapist listens and the care and effort he makes to accurately understand the patient will make quite an impression.

The psychiatrist's reactions are different from those of anyone else the patient has encountered before. He doesn't criticize, lecture, or bully; he listens, tries to understand, and helps the patient to understand. As the patient comes to trust the doctor, he begins to speak more and more freely. The essence of free association is that the patient reveals himself with utter frankness to somebody he trusts with his confidences. He knows that what he says within the office remains there. Friends and relatives of the patient sometimes complain that the doctor will tell them so little about what is happening to the patient. If therapy is to succeed, the doctor must never betray his patient's confidence or even appear to do so. This rule is broken only for important and compelling reasons. What the patient tells the doctor will never be used against him, it will only be used for him. As he comes to trust the doctor more, he speaks more freely. This may be a good place to point out that the patient who comes to the psychiatrist only to please his relatives but intends to consciously avoid telling him what really bothers him, probably cannot be helped. The patient who deliberately lies to the psychiatrist effectively blocks therapy. The psychiatrist can only help patients who want to help themselves.

While the process of treatment is complicated, we can identify some of the things that go on. The first can be called ventilation: the patient talks about many of the things that bother him; usually, strong feelings accompany the words. He gives vent to his emotions, he gripes, expresses anger, feelings of depression, and in general "blows off steam." People generally feel better when they can discuss things and get them off their chests. While they feel better and many things are expressed openly, this by itself does not lead to any fundamental change in character or personality.

Another process in therapy is that the patient gains in self-knowledge, learning things about himself of which he was unaware. All patients will say such things as, "I never realized what a frightened person I am," or "I never realized what an angry person I really am." They begin to pay more attention to themselves, come in better contact with their own feelings. They face fears that they have avoided for many years, and once these fears are in the open, they can see them realistically and try to put them in perspective. They begin to understand what is threatening them; not every danger is a major catastrophe. Slowly, what was unconscious becomes conscious. After twenty years of marriage, one patient became so angry at her husband that for the first time in her life she slapped him. Her comment was: "That's not me." She could not accept that she was capable of such an action. Only after many months of therapy could she accept how great was her rage and disappointment both at her husband and at herself. When patients say, usually at the beginning of the treatment, "Oh, I know myself," they are only partially right. While they may recognize certain traits, they do not recognize the intensity and the extent of them. As one patient said: "I knew these things before, but now I am convinced of them." Until the patient gets the whole picture—and clearly—nothing effective can be done about it. We may know certain things in an intellectual way, but we don't change until we feel them deeply. At the beginning of treatment, a patient may say, "Sometimes I act like a child." Later in treatment, the patient may say, "I feel like a child" or "I am a child." Only now do certain childlike actions become fully understandable. We act in a way that is consistent with how we feel.

Slowly, the patient begins to become fully aware of the kind of person he is in actuality. He becomes aware of his feelings and is no longer able to fool himself. With the help of the therapist, he sees clearly what he does. Only as he becomes fully aware of this, can he begin to master it. You cannot fix a car with only a theoretical knowledge of how the gasoline engine works: you need to know the practical aspects in great detail. As the patient develops real insight, he comes to understand the relationships between feelings, symptoms, and events. He begins to see clearly cause-and-effect relationships; he sees what happens, when it happens, and how it happens. He sees how he contributes to what does happen: that some of the things that happen to him are, in part, his own doing. He is, in part, responsible for what happens to him. Knowledge alone is not enough: knowledge doesn't change anything until it is applied. Change comes about only by practice and hard work. The patient will probably continue to make mistakes, but each time with an ever-increasing understanding. And one day the patient will catch himself before he is about to repeat the same mistake. The hard work and the struggle then begin to pay off in very important dividends.

The most important process in therapy is the relationship with the doctor. The patient has never had a relationship that was quite like it. With all other people the roles and expectations are defined. With a friend, neighbor, employee, business associate, serviceman, clergyman, etc., certain things are expected and customary. You know what you expect from these people and they from you. The psychiatrist, however, keeps his personality, ideas, and preferences out of the relationship. It is desirable that the doctor chosen not be a friend or relative for this very reason. All the patient really knows about the doctor is his name, sex, reputation in the community, the way he dresses, and the way his office is furnished. The doctor does not lecture, scold, or criticize the patient or even defend himself against the accusations of the patient. Since he does not intrude his personal feelings, it becomes easier for the patient to see himself for what he really is. When the patient becomes angry, frustrated, or depressed, his feelings can then be analyzed with a minimum of distortion. In the course of treatment, the patient will transfer to the doctor certain feelings he held toward significant people in his earlier life. He will act toward the doctor as he acted toward the important people with whom he grew up. If he was eager to please his father, he will probably try to please the doctor. If he wanted to compete with and defeat a brother, he will try to do the same with the doctor. This process is called *transferrence*; analyzing the transferrence is a key method in intensive psychotherapy. Furthermore, the patient begins to model himself after, to imitate, the therapist. He sometimes describes an action and says, "You would have been proud of me." By his behavior, not by words, the doctor gets across to the patient certain of his characteristics: his respect for another human being, thoughtfulness, patience, reasonableness, and his desire to help. The doctor gets across to the patient his concern that the patient develop his own resources and live his own life in a responsible and a mature manner. When a good therapeutic relationship does develop, it is a most valuable emotional experience.

There are many misconceptions about psychotherapy and about those who seek it. People are quick to say, "I don't know why you are going, you don't need it." This is a statement that is based on an incomplete knowledge of the person who is seeking help. Often, the things that are most painful are the things that we conceal most deeply. A common misconception is that therapy is only for the very disturbed, the "crazy." Actually it is more helpful to the less disturbed person. Another common remark about therapy is, "It's only a crutch." Well, it is not a crutch. In fact its objectives are just the reverse: therapy aims at making the patient more independent and self-sufficient, enabling the person to stand on his own feet. In addition, there is nothing wrong with a crutch when it is necessary—it may be a most useful device. A crutch is only harmful when it is used for too long a period of time, when the person clings to it even though he is now able to walk on his own two feet.

Still another misconception that many people have is that going for therapy is an indulgence, that the person is pampering himself by devoting so much time and money on himself. This seems to me a strange accusation in an affluent society where people readily accept the cost of expensive cars, lavish homes, extensive travel, etc. It is not an indulgence any more than going to college is an indulgence. Therapy is a challenge, a time of difficult and painful soul-searching, and an opportunity for growth. Many of the detractors of psychiatry are really afraid of it—afraid to face those things they sense may be in themselves. They are afraid to seek help for themselves and they try to reinforce their fear by criticizing anyone else who does go for help. Some of the criticisms about psychotherapy are contradictory. For example, a person may criticize psychotherapy because it makes the patient too dependent on the therapist, and yet at the same time criticize the therapist for not doing more. But you can't have it both ways: a therapist who does little is waiting for the patient to develop initiative, to lead, and to become more independent. The eventual result of this is to make the patient less dependent on the psychiatrist, not more so.

Another point that has been magnified and exaggerated about psychiatry is that the patient falls madly in love with the therapist. As in any long-term relationship, the patient comes to have sincere feelings for the therapist. The doctor's thoughtfulness and knowledge impress the patient, who comes to respect and have feelings of affection for him. The same would be true of long-term relationships with a teacher, an athletic coach, or a helpful co-worker. The patient-doctor relationship may have an erotic tone, and dreams about the therapist may be sexual, but rarely does this cause any real difficulty. The doctor is able to handle his patient's feeling of love, as well as those of hate, and use them for the patient's benefit. They are often transferred feelings and can be handled by analyzing their origin in relation to the patient's current problem. Only rarely, and then usually with a very disturbed patient or an inept therapist, do the patient's feelings for his doctor cause serious difficulty. It is a dramatic event that has been magnified in the literature and in the gossip about psychiatry. In my opinion, patients are more likely to fall in love with their obstetrician than with their psychiatrist.

There is much discussion about the results of psychotherapy, and some prominent people today question whether it has any value. Psychoanalysis and its offshoot, analytic psychotherapy, have endured for ninety years against great opposition from those who are essentially afraid of it. In my experience, rarely does a patient not benefit at all. However, most complain that is has taken much longer than they had hoped or expected it would. Many patients start therapy when they are beginning to fall apart and it is too late for psychiatry to prevent it. If the correct state of affairs is not really known, it then appears that psychiatry actually made the patient worse. Few question what would have happened to this patient without any psychiatric help. Many poor results are incorrectly attributed to psychiatry. I would estimate that one-third of my patients are helped enormously by therapy. Some people have more talent for getting well than others, and sometimes intercurrent events, chance, or bad luck enter the picture to the detriment of the patient.

There is always much discussion about ending treatment. This is best worked out by collaboration between the patient and the doctor. Treatment is never 100 percent complete. It usually ends when the major objectives have been attained and the point of diminishing returns is reached. Sometimes the patient takes a vacation from treatment and see how he gets along; he may decide to come back for further treatment or not. Some patients may benefit considerably from even a few sessions; most require several years of treatment. There are some patients who have emotional problems that probably cannot be resolved, but the patient can learn to live with them. Some of these people need a continuing relationship with a psychiatrist, even if they see him at infrequent intervals. Acting like a rudder on a boat, the doctor helps these people steer their way through life's problems.

## Group Therapy

While I have described individual therapy in some detail, as it is the best established and time-tested, there are other methods of treatment that deserve to be mentioned. *Group therapy* differs from individual psychotherapy in that the doctor treats a group of four to ten people at one time. Sessions usually last one and a half to two hours and are held one to three times a week. While the prospect of talking about one's troubles before a group of strangers may startle or repel some, the method does help. The doctor will usually select patients who are well motivated and likely to benefit from treatment, and screen out those who are liable to be disruptive. Patients benefit from listening to other people talk about their problems and how they deal with them. Often a patient may feel that the other patients are closer to him and more understanding than the doctor. Patients help and encourage each other. The new patient may, at first, merely observe what the others say, but in time he will speak up and interact with the others in the group. The feelings a patient has toward other members, and their feelings for him, may lead to important insights about his relationships with people in his daily life. Recently some therapists have taken to recording the sessions on videotapes which are then played back for the group to see and hear. This may be a very valuable experience. There are distinct advantages to group therapy, and of course, since the doctor's fees are paid by several people, the cost is only a fraction of what it would be in individual therapy.

## *Family Therapy and Marital Therapy*

Another form of treatment is *family therapy*. Instead of a group of unrelated people, an entire family unit—mother, father, children, sometimes a grandparent or others—is treated together. By dealing with the whole family, doctors feel that they can favorably influence some problems more quickly and more economically than by individual therapy. It is rare that only one member of a family is disturbed and that all the others are well. The truth is more complicated: all members of a family are both sick and well in varying proportions and influence each other by a complex series of interactions. Family therapy does not permit one member to be made the scapegoat who then has the burden of "straightening himself out." The emphasis is on the whole family and seeing how they sometimes bring out the worst in each other. Family therapy attempts to help them work out more constructive attitudes toward each other. The healthier members, because they are mature and capable, are asked to make the greater contributions toward restructuring the family into a happier unit. It is a very worthwhile approach in many instances.

*Marital therapy,* or *couple therapy,* is similar to the above but involves only the couple. The focus is on the interaction between the husband and wife, what they do to each other, and especially what they expect from each other. It includes an evaluation of each person and his (her) degree of health and neurosis. The therapist needs to be aware of unconscious factors, even though he may not always be able to bring them into awareness. It may be combined with other methods such as individual psychotherapy as well as medication or even hospitalization of one of the partners where that is necessary. The scope of marital therapy therefore demands a very experienced clinician who can recognize the many factors involved. It is not superficial at all, and needs to be distinguished from the ordinary forms of marriage counseling. This latter is essentially a supportive approach toward periods of crisis in the course of a marriage. While often helpful, it does not have the depth of marital therapy.

## Other Forms of Therapy

*Transactional analysis* or TA became very popular with the publication in 1964 of Dr. Eric Berne's book *Games People Play.* In this approach, the emphasis is also on the relationships or transactions between people. It can be useful and very helpful, but in my opinion there is a danger of paying too little attention to the individual's inner conflicts.

The mental apparatus of a person from the TA standpoint consists of child–adult–parent aspects. Transactions between people proceed at any combination of these levels. TA has developed a vocabulary of its own, and the terms used are often simply stated and easily grasped. The fundamental concepts of transactional analysis are derived from the monumental work in interpersonal psychiatry of Dr. Harry Stack Sullivan and the many other contributors to this field.

*Behavior modification* or *behavior therapy* is quite different from anything we have discussed up to now. It does not focus on the whole personality, but is directed toward the removal of symptoms, especially phobias. Behavior therapy is based on learning theory. Symptoms are considered undesirable, persistent habits, which can be modified or eliminated through the application of the principles of learning. It uses some age-old principles of reward and punishment. Desirable behavior is rewarded (reinforced), and undesirable behavior is discouraged. An example of this would be the use of Antabuse in the treatment of alcoholism. The patient is placed upon medication and if he drinks any whisky he will become violently ill. This sometimes works very effectively with people who have problems with drinking.

Relaxation techniques and conditioning are some of the procedures used. When a procedure shows signs of diminishing the patient's anxiety in certain situations, it is applied in a systematic manner until the anxiety is diminished or eliminated. Some workers in this field have reported good results in dealing with certain symptoms, and the approach is a promising one.

*Biofeedback* is a new development that is directed toward the relief of certain symptoms: Tension headaches, high blood pressure, and others. The patient is attached to machines which record and measure brain waves, muscle tension, skin temperature, etc. The patient performs certain exercises and when he achieves the desired effects, the machine signals this by readings on a meter or an auditory signal. With training, some individuals can develop mastery over certain functions that were formerly thought to be impossible to control consciously. This method and the equipment used are still in their infancy, but results are promising.

*Hypnosis and hypnotherapy.* Patients often ask about a quick method to remove symptoms of any kind. Hypnosis is an induced state of altered consciousness in which the suggestibility of the individual become markedly heightened. In this state suggestions made by the hypnotist are usually carried out by the subject with great determination. It has therefore been used to break the individual of "bad habits" such as nail-biting, smoking, overeating, etc. It has also been effective in producing anesthesia, and on the stage performers have demonstrated dramatic effects with hypnosis. In my opinion, hypnosis is only rarely of any value. The symptoms removed may recur or may be replaced by a more damaging symptom. One man, who later became my patient, went to a hypnotist in order to stop smoking and stay on his diet to lose weight. The suggestions worked and the patient stopped smoking and lost weight simultaneously, only to promptly develop an ulcerative colitis that was so severe that it was life-threatening. The approach of hypnosis is based on the patient passively accepting the suggestions of the hypnotist and giving up symptoms. He does not understand nor work through the conflicts that produced them. Symptoms may be eliminated by hypnosis before the individual is ready to give them up. Psychotic reactions have occurred following hypnosis. Most of the time, in my opinion, other methods are preferable.

## The Consciousness–Human Potential Movement

In recent years, there has been an explosion of groups all over the country that claim to accomplish remarkable things for people. Literally millions of Americans have been exposed to a bewildering assortment of movements, the earliest ones were the postwar sensitivity and encounter groups, and these were followed by arica, bioenergetics, creative consciousness, est, gestalt therapy, guided fantasy, nude marathons, psychosynthesis, Rolfing, Silva Mind Control, transcendental meditation, etc. All these groups borrow considerably from each other and blend concepts of modern psychotherapy with philosophic and religious ideas from Zen Buddhism and other Eastern religions. There are many differences in organization and techniques, but their goals are essentially similar. These are to promote personal growth, expand consciousness, bring people into greater contact with their own feelings, liberate emotions, increase sensitivity in interpersonal relationships, help relaxation, and enrich people's life styles. Such groups are intended for "normal" people, as educational and experiential happenings. While not intended to restore sick people to health, some of the techniques are described as useful in relieving symptoms such as migraine headaches, hypertension, etc. The leaders of these groups, also called facilitators or trainers, include outstanding behavorial scientists, gurus, clever salesmen, and plain charlatans.

For years, the most prestigious leaders of the consciousness movements were at Esalen Institute in California. At Esalen a great variety of techniques were experimented with in a very permissive atmosphere. The activities were held outdoors as well as indoors, and included a wide variety of physical and mental exercises, games, dancing, art, psychodrama, nude marathons, massage, warm mineral or sulphur baths, encounter groups and group psychotherapy. Participants were encouraged to express their feelings—erotic as well as aggressive—to touch each other, wrestle, etc. Today Esalen appears to be declining in influence and importance.

Currently, the most prominent group is probably est, which stands for Erhard Seminars Training. It is quite different in setting and atmosphere from Esalen. The course is concentrated, lasts sixty hours, and is given on two consecutive weekends. A large crowd of people gather in a barren hotel ballroom for this training, which costs $250 for each person. Various methods are used, including inducing physical exhaustion, temporarily restricting food and drink, producing mental stress by frequent verbal harangues. Some trainees faint or get sick. Following this they are then shown various exercises to relieve their discomfort. Many people have criticized the authoritarian methods of est, even though they agree with the goals of greater self-acceptance and assuming greater individual responsibility.

Obviously it is beyond the scope of this book to do more than make some general comments about this important subject. The groups vary widely. Some may be helpful and achieve at least some of their stated goals. Others are cleverly merchandised moneymaking schemes for their founders. Still others may be dangerous in my opinion. Few of these groups do any thorough screening to recognize and eliminate those who are severely disturbed. Suicide, nervous breakdowns, divorces, and other personal disasters have apparently been precipitated directly by experiences in these groups. Not everyone can take the assault on the emotions, the "verbal karate," that may occur. To be suddenly and forcefully confronted with impulses and feelings that have been deeply buried may overwhelm the defenses that have been built up and provoke greater anxiety than the individual can bear. It is naive to think that "letting it all hang out" is always good; in fact it may be very bad.

Only time will tell what these groups can and cannot do, their benefits as well as their risks. Some are fads and will disappear after a brief existence. Others will be modified to retain what is valid and eliminate what is undesirable. Recent experience with acupuncture is an example: hailed with great enthusiasm a few years ago, it is now only used in a very limited manner. The great interest in these groups and in the whole consciousness movement deserves much careful thought. It indicates that many individuals feel isolated in our urban, impersonal, automated, and rapidly changing society. It reflects the ineffectiveness of the family, organized religion, and the community in providing opportunities for meaningful relationships for much of our population.

# Appendix

*Recommended for Further Reading*


*Our Inner Conflicts,* Karen Horney, M.D., W. W. Norton & Co., New York, 1945.

*Neurosis and Human Growth,* Karen Horney, M.D., W. W. Norton & Co., New York, 1950.

*Compassion and Self-Hate,* Theodore I. Rubin, M.D., David McKay Co., New York, 1975.

*Human Sexual Response,* W. H. Masters and V. E. Johnson, Little, Brown & Co., Boston, 1966.

*The Pleasure Bond,* W. H. Masters and V. E. Johnson, Little, Brown & Co., Boston, 1975.

*Dialogues with Mothers,* Bruno Bettelheim, The Free Press, Glencoe, Ill., 1962.

*How to Meditate,* Lawrence LeShan, Ph.D., Little, Brown and Co., Boston, 1974.

*The Relaxation Response,* Herbert Benson, M.D., Wm. Morrow, Inc., New York, 1975.

*Mental Health In the Metropolis,* L. Srole, *et al.,* McGraw-Hill Book Co., New York, 1962.

*I'm OK—You're OK,* T. A. Harris, M.D., Harper & Row, New York, 1967.

*The Parents Handbook on Adolescence,* John L. Schimel, M.D., World Publishing Co., New York, 1969.